FOUND IN
PIECES

A NOVEL

GEORGE ROLLIE ADAMS

BARN LOFT
PRESS

Library of Congress Control Number 2020908647

Publisher's Cataloging-In-Publication Data
(Prepared by The Donohue Group, Inc.)

Names: Adams, George Rollie, author.
Title: Found in pieces : a novel / George Rollie Adams.
Description: First Edition. | [Pittsford, New York] : Barn Loft Press, [2020]
Identifiers: ISBN 9781733366953 (Hardback) | ISBN 9781733366946 (Paperback) |
     ISBN 9781733366939 (eBook)
Subjects: LCSH: Interracial friendship—Arkansas—20th century—Fiction. |
     Journalists—Arkansas—20th century—Fiction. | Segregation—Arkansas—
     20th century—Fiction. | Missing persons—Investigation—Arkansas—20th
     century—Fiction. | Arkansas—Race relations—History—20th century—Fiction.
     | LCGFT: Historical fiction.
Classification: LCC PS3601.D3745 F68 2020 (print) | LCC PS3601.D3745 (ebook) |
     DDC 813/.6--dc23

🏠 BARN LOFT PRESS
Paperback ISBN: 978-1-7333669-4-6
Hardback ISBN: 978-1-7333669-5-3
eBook ISBN: 978-1-7333669-3-9

Cover Photograph by iStock Images/www.markborbely.com
Cover Design by Bruce Gore, Gore Studios, Inc.
Interior Design by Amit Dey
Author Photograph by Amanda Adams

Barn Loft Press and the "BLP" logo are trademarks of Barn Loft Press.
PRINTED IN THE UNITED STATES OF AMERICA

This book is dedicated to the ideal of truth, honesty, and integrity in journalism.

CHAPTER 1

Pearl Goodbar, new owner of the *Unionville Times*, slammed the door of her '51 Ford hard to make sure it closed all the way. Seven years removed from the showroom floor, the once-gleaming sedan now had more rust than shine. It still took her where she needed to go, though, and that was good enough, especially after the last twenty-four hours. She gathered the lapels of her coat against the early March wind and climbed her front steps, careful to avoid the loose plank at the top. In dim light from a single bulb on the wide porch, she fumbled in her purse for her housekey, while still trying to decide what more to tell her girls about their daddy. For the entire twenty miles home from the hospital she had tried to ignore the knot in her stomach and think how to begin.

She had taken the girls with her when she got the emergency call the day before, then let them stay through the night. Early this morning, after the head surgeon said Wendell would pull through, Pearl told them everything would be all right. Then she called Hazel Brantley, her only employee, and asked her to come up to El Dorado, a city of twenty-five thousand and the county seat, and get the girls so they could go to school. Nancy, a junior, and Alice, a freshman, did not argue. They needed to earn scholarships to help pay for college, and they knew as well as their

1

mother that their daddy would not want them to miss classes.

Wendell's doctors had kept him heavily sedated in a recovery room all day and let Pearl see him only briefly. When not pacing in hospital hallways, she sat in the visitors' lounge with his sister Jean, waiting anxiously for updates on his condition. In mid-afternoon, Jean went home for a nap and fresh clothes and returned prepared to stay through the evening. Eventually she and Wendell's nurses urged Pearl to go home herself and try to rest. Reluctantly, she agreed.

When she turned her key in the front door and pushed it open, the warmth of the house and smell of fresh coffee washed over her, and she heard the hall telephone ringing and Nancy and Alice rushing from the kitchen. She ignored the phone and hugged both girls long and hard. She doubted the hospital was calling, because Wendell had been stable when she left. And right now Nancy and Alice needed her holding them close. She needed it, too, and they clung to each other without speaking. After a few moments the ringing stopped. Then it started again, and she reached for the receiver.

"I know you probably just walked in and all," Hazel said on the other end of the line, "but there's been some Negro trouble up here at the café and I expect you'll want to talk to folks."

A woman of medium height in her early forties, Pearl pushed a strand of brown hair off gold-rimmed glasses and said, "Hold on a second." She put her hand over the mouthpiece and told her daughters, "This is Hazel. Let me see what she wants, but stay right here."

"Now, what was it you said happened?" Pearl asked, holding the receiver in one hand and trying to get out of her coat with the other.

"I'm not sure exactly," Hazel said, "but there's a bunch of folks out in front of Emmett's Café cussing and stomping around like they want to fight. I was scared to get too close, but I heard somebody say something about a colored boy giving the Trailways bus driver trouble. I didn't see any Negroes myself, but everybody's all stirred up, and even if there ain't no more trouble tonight, I expect there'll be talk about it all over town tomorrow. I thought you'd want to know." Hazel, who was in her sixties but was built sturdy and had more energy than most people half her age, did not talk like a newspaperwoman because, among other reasons, she had been one only a few weeks. But she was thinking like one.

The *Unionville Times* occupied a large one-story, board-and-batten building next to the café on the west side of Main Street, which doubled as a stretch of US 167, a major north-south travel route. It ran smack through the middle of Unionville, Arkansas, and Unionville, Louisiana, two towns sitting straddle of the state line, separated by geography and law but united by practicality and community feeling. Each side had about a thousand residents and its own mayor and town council. But except for a few formalities such as taxes and voting, everyone thought of Unionville as one place. Emmett's Café was its biggest eating establishment and also the bus station.

Hazel had seen and heard the ruckus when she went back to the office after supper to make sure she had locked up everything after a haggard day of answering the phone and dragging stuff out of the last owner's small apartment in the rear so they could use it for workspace.

Pearl thanked Hazel for letting her know, told her to call again if anything more happened, and said she would ask around about it tomorrow. Truth be told, Pearl was not sure

3

what she would be doing tomorrow, or on the days after. Right now she could not think past what had happened to her husband. Wendell was the head bookkeeper for a wholesale grocer in El Dorado. Yesterday morning he had walked out onto the company's loading dock to pick up some shipping receipts and had fallen between the platform and a produce truck backing in to unload. The fall fractured his skull and the rear truck tires crushed his legs. His doctors did not believe he had brain damage but they were not sure. They also did not know if he would be able to walk again.

Pearl and Wendell had gone deeply into debt so she could buy the newspaper, where she had worked for two previous owner-editors, and when she and Wendell signed all the papers, they had figured on having two incomes. Now, at least for a while, they would have only one. And even with insurance they would likely have huge medical bills.

Time was a problem too. Pearl was already short on it. Each of her former bosses put out the paper every week with only her and some kid to help out occasionally. She was a confident writer and editor and had learned a lot about printing by watching, but in addition to Hazel, she needed an experienced press man and had yet to find one. She also needed to get more subscribers and advertisers than her predecessors in order to cover her mortgage payments and higher operating costs, and that meant adding more news content. She had some ideas about how to do that but was still working out the details. Back in February, she had promised her financial supporters she would have the paper up and running by the end of March, but now, with Wendell to look after, that no longer seemed possible.

Elton Washington set his duffel bag on the porch of the two-story white house, stepped back, and looked around. The sun was long down, but the moon shone enough that he could look across the dirt road he had come on and take in the big, unpainted, barn-like building on the other side and the free-standing storage shed a little way from it. They stood at the far northeast corner of the black section of Unionville, the part white folks called "the quarters." Together with the house and several acres of land, the simple structures made up the con-siderable domain of Elton's mother Sadie Rose, whom he had not seen in more than ten years.

Sadie Rose Washington was a large, dark woman who always wore bright-colored muumuus. In her forty-plus years, she had outlasted three husbands—one legal and two she never let near a preacher or a judge—and come away with most of what little each of them owned. She poured that, herself, and everything else she could get her hands on into the tin-roofed structure that Elton was now looking at and remembering from when he helped out there as a kid. A hand-painted sign reading "Sadie Rose's Place" stretched partway above a long narrow porch and a set of double doors that opened into a general store, barbershop, pool hall, and juke joint all mixed together. Almost everyone, blacks and whites alike, called it simply "Sadie Rose's." She called it "the store."

On each side of the entrance, a jumble of colorful metal advertising signs announced Coca-Cola, Dr Pepper, Nehi, and Royal Crown soft drinks and a variety of tobacco products. None hyped Jax, Pabst, or any other beer because Unionville was in dry Anderson Township, but its citizens could get hard stuff if they knew where to look. Sadie Rose sold bootleg whis-key and sometimes moonshine openly to black people inside her place and secretly to white people back of the shed. She hauled in whiskey from where it was legal and made her own shine. Local and county authorities knew about the hauling but not the making, and they nearly always looked the other way until a fist fight or some other kind of dustup sent somebody to the hospital. When that happened, which was not often, sheriff's deputies issued a few fines and warnings then let things get back to normal. That was okay with most everybody in town except a few white church ladies who seemed to like fussing and gossiping about it almost as much as they hated the thought of such goings on in the community.

Elton, who was tall, slender, lighter than his mother, and sported a thin moustache, pulled himself up straight, turned, and rapped on the screen-door frame. A dog barked inside, a light came on above the door, and his mother drew back a window curtain to peer out at the man standing there in wrinkled gabardine slacks, suede bomber jacket, and a felt Fedora with the brim turned up all the way around. Instead of throwing open the wooden inner door in welcome, she cracked it, stuck the barrel of a .12-gauge pump through the opening, and asked, "Who are you and what do you want?"

"Momma, it's me, Elton," he said, stepping back.

For a moment the only sound was the dog barking. Sadie Rose hollered at it to stop and said, "Lordy, boy, what're you doing here?"

"I come to visit," he said, glancing at the shotgun, still pointed in his direction.

"I thought I'd seen the last of you when you run off up to Chicago after that no-good, high-tone daddy of yours," Sadie Rose said, still not moving. "You go off all that while, you don't ever write, and now you just show up out of the blue. What're you up to, boy?"

"I'm on my way somewhere, Momma, and I just thought it'd be good to stop in with you for a spell. Are you gon' let me in or not? It's cold out here."

"Yeah," she said, pulling the inner door the rest of the way open and leaving the screen for him to manage. "Come on in." She stood the shotgun against the doorjamb and watched him grab his bag and stroll in grinning like he owned the world, same as how he acted before he took off with his daddy at fourteen. Elton was her only child but she had never felt a lot for him. She was always too busy she guessed. Too interested in getting men, having a good time, and making money. His running off did not surprise her. For a while after he left, she sometimes wished she had paid him more attention, but the feeling never weighed on her.

"How'd you get down here?" she asked, hands on hips, staring, still almost not believing what she was seeing and hearing.

"Come on the bus, same way I get around up home," he said, dropping the bag onto a chair with a brightly colored quilt draped over the back and heading over to warm himself in front of the propane heater. "Except they made me sit in the back. That's part why I come. I'm on my way to Mississippi, or over to Alabama. I ain't decided which yet. Anyways, I'm gon' join up with the folks over there protesting and stuff."

"You liable to get your blamed head busted, or worse," Sadie Rose said, still standing. "I know things need changing, but you go over there and mouth off to some white man, you'll end up shot, like as not."

Elton did not say anything. He rubbed his hands together and waited for Sadie Rose to continue. "You go ahead on, if you got to," she said, "but I don't want you stirring up something around here first. I can't have it. I don't need white folks nosing around in my business."

Elton still did not say anything. He could see that his mother was not finished. "Did you come straight out here from town?" she asked.

"Yeah."

"Don't you say, 'yeah,' to me, boy. I'm still your momma."

"Yes, ma'am."

"Did you walk?"

"How else you think I got here?"

"You smart me one more time, and you can just walk right on back. You hear me?"

"Yes, ma'am."

"That's better," Sadie Rose said. "Did anybody much see you?"

"No, ma'am, you know it's prayer meeting night and most folks are at church. Ain't that why you ain't open out yonder? I remember you saying that closing on Wednesday nights helped keep the preachers from nagging at you. Anyways, why you want to know?" Elton did not want to tell her that a bunch of white men had heard the bus driver yelling at him when he got off, or that he had stopped back down the road a ways and watched a white man in a blue car drop off a pretty, light-skinned girl in front of her house, or that after she went inside, he, Elton, had stepped into the shadows to try to glimpse her through her windows and then had seen the white man come back around, driving slow and peering in himself from the road. Elton had already decided he would go back there sometime soon and have another look. His mother did not need to know about it.

"People are kinda skittish these days," Sadie Rose said, "what with all that trouble up in Little Rock last fall and that stuff over where you're going. It's best you stay away from uptown. I don't need nobody coming out here and asking me or my customers about some strange Negro hanging around."

Having said her piece, and hoping he would leave in a couple of days, she asked, "I bet you ain't had nothing to eat, have you?"

"No, ma'am."

"Come on," she said, heading to the kitchen, "I'll heat you up something."

CHAPTER 2

Following a restless night, Pearl Goodbar decided not to tell Nancy and Alice anything further about their daddy's injuries. She did not want them worrying more than they already were. It would not help them or Wendell, and she was worrying plenty for all of them. To help hide that, she put on one of her best shirtwaist dresses—a dark print with elbow-length sleeves—and prepared one of their favorite breakfasts—pancakes with sausage and ribbon-cane syrup. Despite her efforts to make the day feel routine, however, no one ate much.

After they did the dishes, Pearl called Hazel and said she would be back in touch later in the day. Then she drove Nancy and Alice to school and headed back to the hospital in El Dorado. Although she had seen Wendell briefly in recovery yesterday, when she walked into his private room today and saw him still motionless in a sea of white—bandages covering his skull, sheets over his torso, his legs in traction, and thick bindings hiding what she imagined were long lines of stitches—she had to reach for the bed railing to steady herself.

Wendell was not a big man or even an athletic one, but he had always been fit and active, dabbling in carpentry learned from his father and shooting hoops in the back yard with Nancy and Alice. The doctors told Pearl nothing had changed and said this was a good sign but he probably would not be able to talk for another day or two. All she could do now was sit and hold his hand, whisper a prayer, and try to put good thoughts before bad. But she kept thinking about who the blazes would fix the loose porch step now. She wondered how Wendell could have been so careless and put his family through all this. When she realized, after a while, that she had let go of his hand and was squeezing the bed rail and kicking one of the wheels, she leaned her head on her hands and cried.

Wendell's sister, who had sat with him all night, had gone to the cafeteria to grab some breakfast, and when she came back, she said she had been thinking since yesterday about what else she could do to help. A small woman with a sunny disposition, Jean Edmonds was older than her brother, had three grown children, and lived in Camden, thirty miles north. She worked part time in a clothing store, had flexible hours, and knew Pearl was trying to get the newspaper up and running. Jean said her own husband could fend for himself and she would be happy to spend afternoons and nights with Wendell for as long as he was in the hospital. Pearl hated to impose but had no other good option and gratefully accepted the offer.

Early in the afternoon, after Jean had gone home for a spell and returned, Pearl drove back to Unionville and went to the newspaper office. She needed time to think, so she told Hazel, who was bustling about in one of her flowered dresses she said put her in mind of spring all year round, that she could go home for the rest of the day. There was plenty for Hazel to do, but Pearl wanted quiet. Hazel was a talker and still trying to get used to the notion that newspaper work and non-stop gabbing did not go together. Pearl had hired her as a general office gofer but not for that alone. Long-retired from being a file clerk at Bowman Lumber Company, Hazel now lived on

Social Security, her late husband's pension, and rent from half of a duplex she owned. She did not need more income, but the notion of working for a newspaper sounded exciting and she eagerly accepted when Pearl offered the job. More important than her limited office skills, Hazel knew everybody in town and seemed to know almost as much about their private lives and various comings and goings as their family members did. Despite her well-earned reputation for gossip, however, she was big-hearted and never knowingly malicious. Pearl wanted to publish more social news than the previous owners and thought Hazel would be good at gathering it. Further, having taught English, Pearl believed she could help Hazel clean up her grammar and write well enough that fixing whatever mistakes she still made would be easy.

Before Hazel left, she put on a fresh pot of coffee, and when it was ready, Pearl filled a mug, hung a "Closed" sign on the front door, went to her desk, and looked out over the huge open room. For some reason she never understood, a low railing separated the workspace in the back two-thirds of the room from a large vacant area up front along the street. She had thought about trying to rent out that part of the building, but it offered no privacy and there were no likely tenants. She hoped to come up with a way to make money from it sometime down the road, but for now it was at least easy to keep clean.

Pearl's desk sat on the left side of the large rear section, behind the railing, with the front door and windows to her right and workbenches and open cabinets of printing type to her left. Beyond them a Linotype machine for typesetting and a casting machine for making printing plates for ads took up the remaining space on that side. Three printing presses—a large one for the newspaper and two smaller ones for job work like flyers and such—sat across from the Linotype machine. Hazel's desk and assorted worktables filled the rest of the room. The sharp smell of printer's ink and lubricating oil still hung in the air even though the machinery had been still for several months, and Pearl imagined it pinging and clanking now. As she tried to focus on what else was needed to set it in motion again, her thoughts kept going to what life would be like for Wendell if he could not walk and what would happen to the family if she were unable to earn enough to cover their growing expenses. Her hand shook when she reached for her coffee.

Pearl had never planned to work on a newspaper let alone own one. After growing up in Stephens, southwest of Camden, she went to Henderson State Teachers College in Arkadelphia to study education. There she met and married Wendell, who was studying accounting. During World War II, he served stateside as an Army disbursing specialist, and when he was discharged, they settled in his hometown, and Pearl landed a teaching position at Unionville High School. She liked writing more than teaching, though, and when a job opened up at the newspaper in 1954, she grabbed it.

Three months ago, after her boss ran afoul of the law and had to close the paper and put it up for sale, she thought about trying to buy it. But she did not see how she could, and soon set the thought aside. She was not the only one to imagine her running it, however. Over time, Neal O'Brien—who owned City Hardware and was president of the Arkansas-side town council—and several other community leaders began kicking around the same idea. They believed a good community newspaper was essential for commerce and civic pride, and they did not want another outsider coming in like the last owner and stirring up race trouble so he could pontificate about it and try to use the *Unionville Times* as a steppingstone to a bigger stage somewhere else. Pearl was the only person around who knew anything about newspaper work, and after a lot of back-and-forth, Neal and the others settled on her as the only easily accessible alternative, and certainly the only local one. They doubted she had the means to acquire the paper, though, so almost the entire council, along with Arkansas-side mayor Alan Poindexter, went to see her and asked if she would be interested in making an offer on it if they helped her get the necessary funding.

She was thrilled about the possibility but uncertain about the financial risk. She knew a fair amount about the paper's revenues and expenses, though, and Wendell was good with numbers. Together they examined them every way they could think of. Eventually, they decided that with enough help, they would take a chance even though they still owed money on their house and it needed repairs. The mayor and council members lined up more than a dozen local business owners who pledged a heavily inflated sum of money to buy a shared ad of congratulations in Pearl's first issue and a series of regularly priced individual ads in each issue after that for the next two years. With that in hand, the town leaders then approached Horace Bowman, president of Farmers State Bank, about lending Pearl the additional amount she would need to buy the paper, plus make some building improvements and have a little something left for operating capital.

It was not an easy sell. Bowman was an aging bachelor with a trainload of money and a well-earned reputation for tight-fisted crustiness. He had never heard of a woman newspaper editor and did not like the sound of it. He said he did not believe people would accept a woman in such a highly visible position in the community or, even if they did, that she could manage the business side of it. "It's just too complicated," he said. When the men kept pressing their argument, he agreed to think on it for a day or two but said, "You'd best not get your hopes up, 'cause I'm just not seeing it."

Even though the mayor and council members had, themselves, questioned turning to a woman to run the paper, they had eventually concluded that Bowman would likely agree with them simply to get the paper back up and running. As they waited while he ruminated on the idea, they landed on another point of persuasion that had not occurred to them before. The next time they met with him, they pointed out that Unionville already had four enterprises owned by women—a general merchandise store, a grocery, and a dry-cleaning shop, all in spitting distance of the bank, and a juke joint and catchall in the quarters—and they asked him how many of them he was doing business with. Not surprisingly, he acknowledged that all of those women had accounts at Farmers State Bank. After arguing for a long time that running a newspaper was much more involved and risky than owning a store or operating a dry-cleaning shop, Bowman reluctantly gave in. He caved again during his loan discussions with Pearl. She insisted right up front that the loan agreement include a provision blocking him from any operational or editorial input into the paper, and she kept on demanding it until he agreed. She had the same understanding with Wendell, though it was not in writing.

As Pearl thought back on all this and about what to do now, she longed to talk things over with her husband. The newspaper was in her name, but he had co-signed the loan, making them co-owners at least on paper. In any case, they shared responsibility for the family's well-being. If she were going to come anywhere close to the deadline she had promised for her first issue, there might not be time to wait for him to weigh in. There would be no legal penalty for putting things off, but doing so would delay revenues while expenses kept mounting and eating up the little cash they had. She could ask out of the entire arrangement, but then she and Wendell would have no way to pay back what she had already spent, to say nothing of the medical bills.

Almost as important in Pearl's thinking, she had never liked not meeting challenges. Her mother had often told her that she could be stubborn to a fault, and Wendell had said it more than a time or two himself when they disagreed about something or other. So, after a few hours of mulling things over, Pearl decided that whether Wendell could return to work or not, she had to try to make a go of the paper. There was no other choice. She would have to pour over the list of things that still needed doing, revise it to fit their new circumstances as best she could imagine them, push her timetable back at least two or three weeks, and figure out what to tell her backers and the advertisers she already had lined up.

She turned to look at the clock on the wall behind her and realized that Nancy and Alice were home by now. The Goodbars lived only a few blocks south of the school, which sprawled along Newton Chapel Road near the northwestern edge of town, and weather permitting, the girls usually walked there and back like dozens of other town kids. Pearl called Jean at the hospital, learned there was nothing new with Wendell, then phoned the girls to let them know she would be working late. She told them to make supper and eat without her and said if she got hungry she would go next door and get a hamburger at Emmett's Café.

Elton Washington could have had pancakes and ribbon-cane syrup for breakfast on Thursday morning, too, the same as Pearl and her daughters, if he had gotten up when his mother did. Sadie Rose did not much expect to see him for breakfast before she went across the road to open the store at seven o'clock, but she made enough food for both of them anyway. When he did not stir himself in time to eat with her, she threw his portion in the garbage. He stumbled down to the kitchen a little before noon, found some milk and the makings for a peanut butter and jelly sandwich, and was sitting with his feet propped up on the table when Sadie Rose came in to fix some dinner, which is what all Southerners, black and white, called the noon meal. Most noontimes she grabbed some bread and baloney or some cheese and crackers out at the store, but while she had not been happy to see Elton, his showing up had stirred at least a little something motherly in her. She was still wary, though, and getting dinner was also a good excuse to make sure he was not searching the house for something of value to take when he left.

"Boy, get your damned feet off my table!" Sadie Rose shouted, when she came swishing into the room wearing a green muu-muu with big yellow flowers on it. "This ain't no flophouse."

They glared at each other for minute or two, then he put his feet on the floor and surprised them both with, "I'm sorry, Momma. I wasn't thinking."

"You damn right, you wasn't," she said, then added, "I'm sorry I hollered." She got out a plate and a glass and made a sandwich for herself. They had not talked about anything much while he ate last night except his trip from Illinois and his daddy's failed efforts to make it as a blues man in the Windy City. Music was how Sadie Rose got mixed up with Trudell Washington in the first place. A harmonica player from somewhere over in the Mississippi Delta, he had come to town with a traveling band, a wad of dough from crap games, a lot of fast talk, and a fondness for full-figured women, and Sadie Rose had ended up pregnant and married. Trudell kept traveling and rolling dice, but he stopped back from time to time to shake off the dust and do a little matrimonial organ grinding. Each time he showed up with money, Sadie Rose took a hefty share, and for a long while she satisfied his appetites enough that he did not mind. Eventually, though, he tired of her and took off for good, with Elton tagging along. Her only regret was that she had not told Trudell to get lost before he thought of it himself.

"You never said what you been living on," Sadie Rose observed between bites of sandwich. "What've you been doing?" When Elton did not answer right away, she said, "I bet you ain't never finished school. Have you?"

"Nah. It wasn't helping me none so I quit. I been doing a bunch of things. Most of the time I paint for a man that has lots of rent houses." Elton did not say he had also been running numbers for the same fellow on Chicago's South Side, or that he had become as good at hustling pool as Trudell was at shooting craps.

"How come you decided to come down here and get mixed up with that stuff over in Mississippi and all? What good you think you gon' do?"

Elton pushed his plate away and sat back in his chair. "You ever hear of Emmett Till, Momma?"

"Yeah, sure," Sadie Rose said. "That's the boy them two white men killed and threw in the river over there around Greenwood someplace just because he talked to a white girl. They got off scot-free. It was all in the news."

"Well, I reckon what's why I come. Emmett Till was from Chicago, and his momma put on a big funeral for him up there and I went. Me and about fifty thousand other folks, according to what somebody said on TV. He was beat plum to a pulp and all rotted up from being in the water so long, but she kept the casket open. Said she wanted people to see what was done to him. It's been three years and I still got a picture of him in my head I can't get out. Anyway, there's a Negro newspaper up there called the *Chicago Defender*, and I've been sort of keeping up with things. You know, like the boycott Miss Parks started over in Alabama, and then the government saying we can sit anywhere we want to on buses and white folks can't keep us from voting, even though they keep on somehow."

"I know about the *Defender*," Sadie Rose said. "Some people down here get it and pass it around or leave it over at the store for other folks to read. Same with the *Pittsburgh Courier*. It's a Negro paper too." She was starting to believe maybe Elton might not be as shiftless as she had thought, and this set her to worrying some. "You didn't answer my question. What is it you think you gon' do?"

"Like I said last night, I don't know exactly. I just want to go to some place like Jackson or Montgomery and hook up with people that're trying to make things better and see if I can help somehow."

"What're you using for money?" she asked.

"I saved up some," he said, shifting in his chair. He did not tell her how little because he figured on getting by hustling pool, maybe starting across the road.

"When you think you gon' be leaving?"

"Monday or so, I guess. I want to visit a little first. Is that all right?" he asked, though he thought he might stay longer, depending on the pretty girl he had seen.

"Yeah, sure," she said, "but like I told you last night, you stay out of trouble. It ain't as bad here as it is some places. Fact is, I got things pretty good. I worked hard for it, and I ain't about to risk it with no protesting and stuff, not right now anyway. I don't think enough folks here abouts have the stomach for it. If they do, I ain't seen it. Looks like the schools are gon' be desegregated pretty soon, and we already can vote if we pay the poll tax. I know most of us ain't got money for it, but leastways us that do don't have to take no fool test like some places where white folks make up questions ain't nobody can answer, them included." She did not go on to tell Elton that for several years she had been slipping a handful of blacks whom she trusted to keep quiet about it the two dollars they needed to pay the tax.

"I don't know how you can talk like that, Momma. Damn white man's still holding us down, just like always. Don't you see that?"

"'Course I see what he's doing. And it makes me mad as hell just like it does you. I could tell you some stuff you ain't never heard of, and when I see something I can do about it that's gon' make a difference, I'll be all over it, but right now ain't the time, at least not for me. Like I told you, this ain't as bad as lots of places, 'specially since the white bastard that ran the newspaper last year and got a bunch of crackers all riled up for a while is gone. So, if all you gon' do, boy, is mess up what good we've got, you can just get on down the road. I ain't scared of no white folks, but I ain't gon' give up nothing to get at them till I know I can beat them."

"All right, Momma, all right. I get it. Don't worry," Elton said, and changed the subject. "I see you're still making quilts. You got them all over the place. You still making shine back there in the woods too?" Sadie Rose's daddy, dead going on fifteen years now, had made his living peddling vegetables to blacks and whites alike from a mule-drawn cart mounted on Model-A Ford wheels and occasionally selling moonshine he made in a still he cobbled together himself. Sadie Rose had grown up helping him with all of it.

"That's just the kind of thing I'm talking about," Sadie Rose said. "Yeah, I still got it. But you stay away from it and you keep your mouth shut about it. And yeah, I'm still making quilts, when I get the time. It's restful and I like having all the colors around."

"Yeah, I remember you always did, "Elton said. "Don't worry about the still. I ain't gon' bother it. Ain't got time anyway. I was just asking because I still got that Indian head penny Granddaddy gave me back there one day when I was little. He said I could keep it as long as I stayed away from there." Elton pulled a chain from under his shirt and held up the coin. "It's my good luck charm."

CHAPTER 3

Hunger hit Pearl Goodbar a little before eight o'clock. She had been at her desk all afternoon and believed she was making progress, but she was not ready to stop for the night. After jotting a few more lines in the Blue Horse notebook she always carried—a throw-back to her teaching days—she got her coat and purse and headed to Emmett's Café to get something to bring back to the office. She remembered telling Hazel she would ask around about what happened over there last evening, but now that she had decided to postpone her first issue, she did not want to take time for that tonight. She wanted to get back to her desk and finish her planning.

Pearl did not care much for the café. It always smelled of tobacco smoke and cooking grease, and while Emmett Ledbetter, a baggy-eyed man of middle age, always wore a white long-sleeve shirt with cuffs rolled up to his elbows, to Pearl's mind the grease-stained apron he also always wore did not suggest anything good about his kitchen. In the past, he advertised regularly in the newspaper, though, and she did not want to offend him. Maybe, she thought as she walked in, she ought to reconsider and eat on the premises. Even if Emmett was not working tonight, whoever was would likely tell him she stopped in.

She sat at a corner booth and looked around for him, thinking all the while about who his customers were, because many of them were her customers too. A counter ran across the back wall, booths lined the other three, and tables filled the middle of the floor. A door in the north wall led to another dining room with more tables. A jukebox and a pair of pinball machines sat near the front entrance. She had eaten here enough to know that Emmett's clientele differed according to the day and hour. Store owners, clerks, truck drivers, and sometimes farmers in town on errands came for breakfast and dinner on weekdays. Fish fries drew a regular supper crowd on Fridays, and after church on Sundays other regulars dropped in for roast beef and mashed potatoes. On Saturday mornings, loafers drinking coffee and talking sports filled the café, and after supper on Fridays and Saturdays, teenagers overran the place for cherry cokes, pinball, and rock and roll on the jukebox. Other times, the place belonged mostly to single adults and to disgruntled married ones who would rather be anywhere but home with their spouses.

A high school girl Pearl did not recognize took her order and told her that Emmett had stepped out and might not be back before closing. Pearl was beginning to wish she had gotten takeout, when Claude Satterfield came in for coffee, spotted her, and walked over to say hello and ask about Wendell. Before retiring a few months back, Satterfield, whom nearly everyone called "Mr. Claude," had been town marshal on the Arkansas-side for nearly forty years. Not long after leaving to spend more time gardening and sitting on his front porch reading, he had agreed to serve as night watchman on a strictly temporary basis while the town council, having fired the incumbent, looked for someone willing to do it long-term. Like almost everyone, Pearl was fond of Mr. Claude. Although he was past seventy, he still dressed and carried himself pretty much the way he always had. He stood a good five or six inches shy of six feet, but he was wiry and fearless and always wore a black felt hat, black suit coat, and khaki pants with a leather-covered blackjack stuck in his right hip pocket. These days, he carried a flashlight in the other. It was generally believed that he did not carry a gun because he thought it unnecessary, but he sometimes had one tucked under his coat. In any case, he had been known to bust a skull or two with his noggin-knocker, so few people dared mess with him. Pearl invited him to sit with her, told him what she could about Wendell, and asked him how his wife Irene was, how she felt about his working evenings, and how he liked it.

Mr. Claude said Irene did not mind, and he enjoyed walking around shaking doorknobs and making sure all the merchants locked up at night and no one was up to no good in the dark. Said it kept him young. He was used to getting a lot of exercise because until he retired as marshal, the town did not own a police car. That was because he did not know how to drive. In 1901, when Mr. Claude was in his teens, his daddy had sold their farm and moved the family into a house three blocks from the business district and gone to work in a mercantile store. From that point on, all the Satterfields walked to work, school, church, the grocery store, and the doctor. If they needed to go out of town, they took the bus or train or got a ride with friends, and they had plenty of them.

"You didn't say what you're doing in here this late, what with Wendell in the hospital and all," Mr. Claude said, after their orders came. Few in Unionville, including Hazel Brantley, knew more about what went on around town than Mr.

Claude, and no one knew better how to keep his mouth shut. So, with no one sitting close enough to hear, Pearl talked about some of the things troubling her and told him some of her ideas.

"Well," Mr. Claude said after a while, "I was thinking about you earlier this evening, and I'll get to why in a minute. The main thing, though, is you need to keep in mind that most everybody except a few hot-heads couldn't stand the low-down dirt bag that owned the paper last year, and they're gon' be rooting for you. And now here's the other thing. Because most of the merchants and other business owners didn't like the guy, they didn't advertise as much with him as they did with old man Trammell before him. I expect you know that already, but it's a good thing to focus on. Let me show you how I mean. And this is just from me making my rounds tonight."

Most of the town's businesses stood along the last two blocks of the highway before it left Arkansas and the first block after it entered Louisiana, and almost everyone on both sides of town thought of the last block on the Arkansas side as the town's commercial center. "Uptown," they called it despite its size. Every night Mr. Claude covered it several times. On occasion he ventured over to the Louisiana side because it did not have a marshal or a night watchman. The town officials over there welcomed his coming across to look out for things even though he had no legal standing for it.

"Just for the heck of it," he said, "while I was on my rounds, I got to thinking about my stops like they were ads in your paper and sort of picturing them that way. I don't go the same way every time, but tonight I started out over at First Street and walked down the east side of Main to State Line Road. Then I crossed the highway and came back up the west side.

Think about this for a minute. After the post office over there on the corner, you've got shoes and clothes at Gene's Dry Goods, everything from nuts and bolts to tools and plumbing stuff at City Hardware, checking and savings accounts at the bank, all kinds of house things at Vestal's Furniture Store, flowers at Bailey's Floral Shop, sugar and eggs and all at Watson's Grocery, and picture shows at Liberty Theater."

"I know all that, Mr. Claude."

"Wait, now. Let me finish. On this side, you've got gas and oil at the Sinclair station, magazines and haircuts at the barbershop and newsstand, a whole bunch of patent medicines and notions and stuff at Smith's Pharmacy, more shoes and clothes at Lawson's, car batteries and appliances at the Otasco store, more groceries at Perry's, about anything you can imagine at Unionville Variety Store and Shoe Repair, more groceries and all kinds of livestock stuff at Hadley's Food, Feed, and Seed, then more gas and oil at the Gulf station. And that doesn't include a bunch of other things like lumber at South Arkansas Oak Flooring, hamburgers and specials here at Emmett's, cars and trucks at the Ford place across the street there, dominoes and billiards at the pool hall, and baby chickens and gardening stuff at Unionville Feeds over on the Louisiana side."

"I know all that too," Pearl said. "I made up a list before I got into this, and a lot of those places have already committed to advertising. I have to say, though, that hearing you call them out that way makes me feel better. It also reminds me of all the selling I still have to do. What I need most right now, though, is to find a good press man, a sort of jack of all trades, someone who can run all the presses and also operate the Linotype when I'm too busy. I've looked everywhere I can think of for one. I even talked to folks at the *El Dorado Daily News* and the

Ruston Daily Leader down in Lincoln Parish to see if they know of anyone not already working for them."

"Did anybody up at El Dorado mention Grady Atwell to you?" Mr. Claude asked.

"No," Pearl said, cocking her head and squinting. "I know he works in the press room up there, but I've never met him. Anyway, I couldn't afford somebody from a big operation like that. How do you know him?"

"He's Irene's second cousin once removed, and I happen to know he's been thinking about retiring because he doesn't like some of the new-fangled equipment they're bringing in. I don't know all the particulars, but I know he's still only in his sixties, and I don't think he'll like sitting around doing nothing. He lives out on Plank Road, near about as close to here as to El Dorado, and I expect he'd like working with you. If you want, I'll call him up and feel him out for you."

"Oh, Mr. Claude, I'd really be grateful if you would," Pearl said. Most of her hamburger lay untouched on her plate but she was glad she had not ordered take out. After Mr. Claude finished and excused himself to check on the tin-clad warehouses that hunkered down in the dark behind the stores, she realized she had missed an opportunity to ask him what he knew about Tuesday night's dustup.

Elton Washington, now in jeans and a faded brown shirt, spent much of Thursday morning hanging out in his mother's store, letting the lingering smell of tobacco smoke, barber's tonic, and oiled sawdust used in sweeping the floors bring back memories as he watched customers come and go. What few there were. Most black people were at work during daytime hours—the men chiefly in the town's two lumber mills and the women chiefly in white people's kitchens or taking in white people's laundry. Elton helped his mother and an old woman who worked for her move boxes and clean shelves. Early in the afternoon, having seen no one he remembered nor having been introduced to anybody new by Sadie Rose, he slipped out back. He walked through a field where his mother's hired man grew turnips and corn for sale and for whiskey mash, then he cut through a stand of woods to the still. The contraption stood in a clearing carved out of a dense thicket next to a creek, but any authorities who wanted to find it would be able to easily enough. Seeing it again gave Elton new respect for his mother's moxie.

After supper, Elton lied to Sadie Rose and told her he wanted to walk over and see the New Bethel A.M.E. Church where Trudell used to take him sometimes to hear the music. He promised again to keep out of trouble. Then he set out early enough, he hoped, to get to the pretty girl's house in time to see the white man bring her home again. Elton assumed she probably worked for the man's family because, while it was not common, a few white folks both picked up their household help in the morning and brought them home at night. He recalled that most of those women made it home by late afternoon, but there was something about yesterday, though he did not know exactly what, that made him think this girl's return well after dark was normal for her.

The black section of Unionville extended along the entire eastern edge of town. Generally sitting four or five blocks back from US 167, it started about half a mile north of Sadie Rose's Place and ran southward to State Line Road and then beyond it for another a mile or two. Most of the houses on the south end were unpainted shotgun affairs packed shoulder to shoulder along dirt roads and were owned either by the Rock Island Railroad or by Bowman Lumber Company. Most houses toward the north were painted, had yards with flowers, and sat along streets with an occasional smattering of gravel. That weak effort at street improvement stopped short of Sadie Rose's Place, which lay some distance east of the regular town lots. The Rock Island tracks, running roughly parallel to the highway, cut through the entire north-south length of the black neighborhoods.

Only a couple of dogs noticed Elton as he walked to the girl's house in the dark, and no one came out to check on the racket they made. Because her house sat close to the railroad tracks, with only a poorly maintained alley between it and the rail line, he managed to find cover in some bushes and settled down to wait. After what seemed like an hour, when he had grown cold and almost given up, the same car as last night stopped in front of the house, and the girl got out. As the man pulled away, Elton watched her walk through the short yard and up the front steps under a porch light, her hips swaying and her hair bouncing on her shoulders. She wore a belted coat, and like last evening he admired her thin waist and ample breasts but most of all her face—as beautiful as an angel's he thought, but tired and sad.

She went inside but he stayed still. The car disappeared briefly up the alley then came circling back almost at a crawl, with the man turning and staring after the girl. Elton could see him better tonight and made him out as good-sized and fiftyish. When he drove on, Elton looked back at the house and saw a curtain move. The girl or someone else had been looking out.

Warmed by seeing her again, Elton tried to think how he could meet her. He could ask his mother about her, but he did not believe Sadie Rose would help him. Eventually, he decided that inasmuch as he did not have a lot of time, he would do the same thing he did when he saw a pretty girl in Chicago— turn on his Washington charm. He walked onto the porch and knocked on the doorjamb. When no one came, he knocked again, and when there was no answer still, he knocked a third time. Several minutes passed, then Elton heard locks turning, and an old man with white hair and whiskers opened the door a crack and asked, "What do you want?"

"Evening, sir," Elton said, standing tall and trying to look friendly and sincere at the same time. "My name is Elton Washington, and I have taken note of the young lady who lives here. She's so beautiful, I feel sure she must be an angel from the Lord, and I would like to meet her. I wonder if I might come in and make a proper introduction of myself?"

"Boy," the old man said. "You trying to get somebody killed or something? You get on away from here." And he closed the door.

CHAPTER 4

On Friday morning, Pearl arose hopeful, had breakfast with Nancy and Alice, saw them off to school, and headed for the hospital wearing her nicest shirtwaist dress, a royal blue number with white collar and cuffs. She found Wendell awake and improving but still too sedated to do much talking. She kissed him, and each of them said, "I love you" and "I'm fine." Then she sat beside his bed holding his hand while he drifted off to sleep again. When he did, she went looking for his surgeon, who, when found, said they might have a better idea about Wendell's legs in a few days.

With Wendell resting, Pearl told his nurses she would be back in a while. Then she drove across town to the *El Dorado Daily News*. She had already met with the editor, Derwood Isom, and renewed arrangements from earlier years to buy newsprint through his paper and have him make printing plates for her photographs along with papier mâché mats she could use to cast plates for local ads. She imagined Isom knew about the accident because the El Dorado paper had run a story about it, but she wanted to be sure he also knew that she intended to go ahead with her plans.

After seeing Isom, Pearl called on several potential El Dorado advertisers before swinging back to the hospital to stay with Wendell until Jean arrived. When she did, Pearl grabbed something to eat in the cafeteria and headed back to Unionville to see Neal O'Brien and Horace Bowman and reassure them.

She parked in front of the newspaper office, walked by Emmett's Café, crossed Main Street, and trekked past the post office and Gene's Dry Goods to City Hardware, thinking all the way about last night's conversation with Mr. Claude. She found Neal, a slim, studious-looking man with brown hair and glasses, mid-way back in the store standing on a rolling ladder hanging from tall shelves filled with electrical and plumbing supplies. All the wire and steel seemed at odds with the dress shirt and slacks Neal always wore because he felt they suited his role as Arkansas-side council president. A similar ladder hung along the opposite wall and, in between, appliances of all kinds competed for space with rakes, hoes, lawn mowers, fishing tackle, and locked cases containing shotguns and hunting rifles.

"Hello, Pearl, how's Wendell?" Neal called, climbing down from his perch, where he had been filling bins from a basket he set on the floor. Pearl told him, then described some of her plans, including rolling back her timetable. He said it all sounded fine to him.

"I'd appreciate it if you'd tell the other council members when you see them," she said, "and go with me to tell Mr. Bowman. He wasn't too keen on me before."

"I think that's a good idea," Neal said. "Let's go over there now and see if he has a minute. Gimme a second to tell them in back that I'm leaving."

Most of the stores along Main Street were brick buildings with cast-iron fronts, sidewalk sheds, and oiled wood floors, and the bank's classical front and well-appointed lobby made clear its importance among its neighbors. Pearl and Neal found their way to Bowman's partly glassed-in office in the back. His curtains were open, and when he saw his visitors, he frowned but waved them in and motioned them to low chairs in front of his polished desk. A short, stout man with a round face and thinning gray hair, he sat behind it in a raised chair that made clear his influence in the community to all who called on him. He was wearing a dark suit and tie with a starched white shirt. A stogie smoldered in an ashtray to one side of papers fanned out in front of him.

"Well, what is it?" he growled, skipping pleasantries. "I don't have all day."

"I assume you've heard about my husband's accident," Pearl said, looking up at him, "and I wanted to let you know he's gon' be all right and this will not affect the newspaper."

"It sure as hell better not," Bowman bellowed. "You owe me a bunch of money."

Heat filled Pearl's face but she kept it out of her voice. "I'm gon' have to put off my first issue for a week or two," she said, "but I'll make my payments on time."

"You better see that you do," he said, picking up a sheaf of papers to signal the end of the meeting. Then he added, "And I'm holding you responsible, too, O'Brien."

Neal did not reply, and when he and Pearl were outside, he said, "I guess my going along didn't help much, Pearl. I'm sorry he spoke to you that way, but he's like that with everybody. Anyway, he can't say you didn't keep him informed."

"It's okay," she said. "I just hope I can do what I promised."

⌒

On the way back to the newspaper office, Pearl decided to stop at the café and ask about the hullabaloo with the bus.

It would be old news before she could get out a paper, but she was curious, and Hazel was bound to bring it up again. There might not be anyone around who saw what happened, but if Emmett had not seen it, he would at least have heard people talking about it. He came out of the kitchen in his white shirt and stained apron right as she was taking a seat at the counter. Pearl was acquainted with Emmett only well enough to know that she did not like him. He was moody, did not keep up the house he lived in alone, drove around town in a beat-up pickup truck with a shotgun hanging behind the seat, and was known now and then to add a shot of bootleg whiskey to the coffee he served to some of the town's good ole boys. One of them, Waylon Hicks, a skinny ne'er-do-well everyone called "Crow" because of his hook nose and shrill voice, sat at the other end of the counter talking to another of them. Odell Grimes, a pale butterball of a man, owned the barbershop and newsstand along with his much smarter brother Lester. Odell was wearing his starched barber's jacket and Crow had on his usual faded bib overalls but not the pistol he had carried in a western-style holster for years. Mayor Poindexter had made him stop that when the town council took away his night watchman's badge for sleeping on the job.

Emmett came over, grunted a greeting, and asked Pearl what he could get for her. She ordered coffee, and when he returned with it, she said, "I understand there was some excitement with the bus Tuesday night. What happened?"

Emmett wiped his hands on his apron. "There was a nigger got on up at Little Rock and tried to sit up front, and the driver had a hard time getting him to move to the back. When they got to Fordyce, he tried to move up front again. I guess him and the driver were hollering at each other all the way to El

Dorado. Apparently he didn't do nothing when they stopped up there, but just when they was pulling in here, he set in to yelling again. Something or other about his rights. When the bus stopped, he disappeared real quick like—I guess he got scared—but the driver was already so mad he was hollering at anybody who'd listen. There was a few fellows here getting coffee before the White Citizens' Council meeting, and they did a lot of cussing, but that's about all there was to it."

"I thought the Citizens' Council met on first Thursdays out at Brother Spurlock's church," Pearl said. "What were they doing in town?"

Elmer Spurlock was a part-time house painter, a some-times farmer, and the self-taught pastor of the Mercy Baptist Mission about four miles west of town. He had grown up dirt poor over in Columbia County, and the only thing that had given his family an edge over their neighbors was skin color. He hated blacks and last year had organized the local Citizens' Council.

"They was meeting out there on Thursdays," Emmett said, "but they changed to first Tuesdays, and Mr. Kramer said they could meet at the high school this time. Thought they'd get a bigger turnout." Pearl started to say she did not care if Herbert Kramer was president of the school board, using school facilities that way was not appropriate. But she thought better of it, at least for now. "That boy's lucky there wasn't somebody with balls on the bus and the folks in here didn't see him get off," Emmett continued, "else somebody would've beat the crap out of him. I'd have helped them do it too."

Pearl did not like this kind of talk, but this was not the first time she had heard it. She did not shy away from saying so when she thought it would do any good, but most times she knew it would not. This was one of those. "Un huh," she said. "So that was all of it?"

"Yeah."

"Did anyone know the man?"

"No, not as far as I heard."

"What did he look like?"

"He was just a nigger, that's all," Emmett said, and headed back to the kitchen.

When Pearl turned to leave, Crow and Odell came over.

"We heard what you was asking," Crow said through broken teeth stained with chewing tobacco. "We reckon you're gon' write about this and put them coloreds in their place like Upshaw did, ain't you?"

Pearl had bought the newspaper from Preston Upshaw after working for him longer than she wanted. His deep hatred of blacks and his angry editorials against integration made her uncomfortable, but she had stayed on because she needed the job. She knew someone would ask her something like this sooner or later, and do it about the way Crow had. "Gentlemen," she said, "I have no intention of doing any such thing," and she walked out leaving them with mouths open and eyes squinting, wondering if they had heard right.

⌒

When Pearl got back to her office, Hazel, who was still cleaning and arranging stuff and answering the phone, was full of questions: "How's Wendell? Where'd you go after you got back? Did you find out what happened Tuesday night?" Pearl filled her in about Wendell, what she learned at the cafe, and Crow's remark.

"You know you're gon' hear a lot of what Crow Hicks said, don't you?" Hazel asked.

"Yes, but it doesn't matter," Pearl said, going to her desk. To avoid any misunderstanding, she had told Hazel before offering her the job that the paper's editorial stances would differ from Upshaw's, and she saw no need to repeat it now. "Let's go over that list of community events you've been putting together. I want to see what you've added. Then I've got another idea to run by you."

Hazel did not agree that comments like Crow's would not matter, but she said, "All right," took off her cleaning apron, and pulled up a chair.

"Have you been studying that grammar book I gave you?" Pearl asked.

"Yeah," Hazel said. "Some of it's kinda interesting, but some of it doesn't make any sense."

"I feel that way myself sometimes," Pearl said, "but there're usually good reasons for the rules. Just concentrate on the ones I marked. Like we talked about, you can use some of my old stories for examples of how to write up wedding announcements, obituaries, and the like, and I'll make up some samples for club meetings, people traveling, and relatives visiting from out of town. We're gon' put in as much of that as we have room for. People want to see their names in the paper and see what their neighbors are doing. This'll get us more subscribers, and more subscribers will get us more advertisers, and we need both. Start working on what you already have, and I'll go over it with you when you finish. I've told Neal O'Brien and Horace Bowman I'm rolling things back a couple of weeks, and that'll give you more time to practice."

"You got a date in mind yet?"

"Yes," Pearl said. "We're gon' print the paper on Fridays and put it in the mail and on sales racks on Saturday mornings. I'm aiming for April 5 if I can find a press man in time. In the meantime, I'm gon' see if we can get some more writing help, and that's the thing I wanted to talk to you about. I'm gon' ask Coach Roberts if he'll report on high school sports for us, and I want to find someone to do something on hunting and fishing and on cooking and sewing. I can buy some syndicated stuff for filler, but I think local stuff will be more popular."

"Well, nobody knows more about hunting and fishing than Boomer Jenkins," Hazel said. "But I doubt he'd do it, or could. And you don't want him anyway." Everyone called Jeremiah Jenkins "Boomer" because he was a big man with a loud voice and wore a wooden leg that made a lot of noise when he walked, and he liked the racket and the nickname. He had lost his left leg below the knee in World War II, and when he got home, he had thrown away the artificial leg the government gave him and carved one out of cypress wood. He kept it on with black leather straps wound around his knee and a wide belt buckled around his waist, and he had fitted up his Dodge pickup so he could drive with the thing. Boomer lived on a bayou over in Claiborne Parish and made his living partly by selling catfish and frog legs to restaurants in nearby towns. He hated blacks and cussed a blue streak, and most folks were afraid of him and the big skinning knife he always wore. No one knew the outdoors better, though.

"You're probably right on both counts," Pearl agreed, "but I bet if he'd do it, people would want to read it."

"Arlan Tucker is another one," Hazel said. "Anytime he's not embalming somebody or doing a funeral, he's off in the woods or out in a boat somewhere. He probably don't know as much as Boomer Jenkins, but he's more likely to write good enough."

"Maybe I could ask both of them," Pearl said. She resisted correcting Hazel's speech.

"Better you than me, hon," Hazel said. "I don't want nothing to do with Boomer Jenkins. Cooking and sewing are easier. You need Emma Lou MacDonald for that. She makes her own clothes, she's the best quilter around, and her and her husband Purvis are both good cooks. I hear a lot of men take up deer hunting just to get a taste of the camp grub he makes. And I hear Emma Lou subscribes to just about every good women's magazine there is—*Ladies' Home Journal*, *Good Housekeeping*, *Family Circle*, *McCall's*, you name it. Purvis is retired, their kids are grown and live out of town, and I'm pretty sure Emma Lou's got enough time. She's smart too. The question is whether she'd want to do it."

"I may ask them all," Pearl said, smiling. She was about to say they should knock off and go home, when the phone rang. Mr. Claude was on the other end and said he had spoken with his cousin-in-law Grady Atwell and he was interested in the job of press man and wondered if he could come down in the morning around nine o'clock and see the layout and the equipment and talk about it.

"Please tell him I'll be expecting him," Pearl said. "And thank you, again, Mr. Claude. You're a saint." Without giving Atwell's name, she explained briefly to Hazel, who was bursting to know what the call was about, and asked her not to tell anyone. Then she said, "Let's lock up. I'm anxious to see my girls and call the hospital."

Elton Washington spent most of Friday much the same way as the morning before, thinking about the pretty girl and how to meet her, and hanging around Sadie Rose's Place. This time he tried to help out a little more because Fridays trailed only Saturdays for business. He got in the way about as much as he helped, but Sadie Rose did not say anything. She was still trying to decide if she was glad he had come and wondering if he was up to more than he had told. She noticed he seemed more interested than she would have thought in whether some of the kids he went to school with were still around and what folks had moved to town or away from it since he left.

After supper, at what Elton guessed was about the right time, he headed off toward the pretty girl's house, keeping his head down and ducking folks coming toward him for an evening at Sadie Rose's Place. When he got close enough, he took up a position in the bushes like the night before and waited. Juke box music drifted through the night air, and he hoped Sadie Rose would not miss him and ask later why he had not stopped back in. Having not come up with any different plan for when the pretty girl got home, he decided to try the same thing again and not let the old man shoo him away this time with some made-up threat.

After a while, a dark late-model pickup stopped in front of the girl's house. She got out and hurried to the front door like before, but this time she glanced back toward the road before going inside. The driver of the truck was the same man who had dropped her off in a car the night before. Elton thought the man must have seen the girl look back, because he stopped the truck for several minutes before moving on around the corner. Like last night, Elton waited, and in a few minutes the truck came crawling back, but this time the man stopped in front of the house and sat staring at it for several more minutes before driving on.

Elton kept still as long as he could stand to then slipped out of his hiding place, went to the front door, and knocked, softly at first then hard, until his knuckles hurt. Finally, the old man with the white hair and whiskers turned the locks, cracked the door, and said, "Boy, don't you hear good? You don't know what you're getting into. You got to get on out of here. And don't you come back no more." He closed the door and Elton heard the locks clicking again on the other side. He stood rooted in place, trying to imagine what the old man meant and what was going on with him and the girl. Then he heard the locks again and the old man reappeared, not saying anything at first, only staring at his unwanted visitor with fear in his eyes. Seconds ticked by. Then a tear ran down the old man's face into his whiskers and he said almost in a whisper, "Get on, now," and shut the door and turned the locks.

CHAPTER 5

Pearl got up on Saturday morning so anxious to meet Grady Atwell that she was cross with Nancy and Alice, who were eager to know how soon her appointment would end and she could take them to see their daddy. "Look," she snapped after they asked for what seemed the tenth time, "I'm in a bind here, and there's a lot riding on this man being what I need and this job being something he wants. And it's important for you too. I will be home when I get home, and we will go to the hospital then. Meanwhile, you get your chores done."

She regretted saying it as soon as the words came out of her mouth, and she gathered Nancy and Alice in her arms and told them so. She was on edge in part because Wendell might be awake enough to talk today, and she had not told the girls how serious his injuries were. If she did not want to risk their finding out at his bedside, making a scene, and upsetting everyone, she would have to come up with something on the way to El Dorado.

When Pearl pulled up in front of the newspaper office at a quarter to nine, a man she assumed was Grady Atwell was standing with his eyes pressed to the front door glass, looking in. She could see he was of medium height and build, had shaggy white hair, and was wearing gray work pants, a denim jacket, and a brown hat of some kind. He turned around when she approached, and she saw he also had on a black bib work apron and the thing on his head was a newsboy cap, popular in England generally since Charles Dickens's *Oliver Twist* and particularly with American newsboys since the 1920s. Atwell did not know it, but the job was practically his right then.

"Mrs. Goodbar?" he asked, removing the cap and revealing a scalp that was mostly bald. "I'm Grady. Grady Atwell."

"I'm pleased to meet you, Grady," she said, unlocking the door. "Call me Pearl. I like your cap, by the way."

"Yes, ma'am. Can I see the presses first?" he asked, wasting neither time nor words.

Well, Pearl thought, if she hired him, it would be interesting to see how he and talkative Hazel got along. She switched on the lights, Grady put his cap back on, and they headed to the rear. "We have a hand-fed Babcock cylinder flatbed for the newspaper and two Chandler and Price letterpresses for job work," Pearl said. "The little one is pedal-operated and the big one has both a hand lever and an electric motor."

"Yes, ma'am," Grady said. He walked slowly around each machine, poking, prodding, turning parts, and listening for the sounds they made, like a doctor examining patients. Pearl saw now why he wore his printer's apron to the interview. "I reckon they'll do," he said, when he finished.

"The Linotype machine is over there," Pearl said, pointing and wondering what he was thinking.

"Yes, ma'am," Grady said, "I saw it." He went over and poked and prodded it. "You got spare parts for all this stuff?" he asked.

"Only what's on that shelf you passed," Pearl said.

"Figures. We'll likely need more," Grady said, as if he were already hired.

"But I haven't even told you about the job," Pearl said, both pleased and surprised. He had worn the same poker face since he arrived, and she had been unable to read it. "I haven't offered it either, for that matter," she said. "How do you know you want it?"

"It's printing, ma'am. It's what I do," Grady said. "What do you want to know about me?"

"Well, you couldn't have any better personal reference than Mr. Claude, and I know Derwood Isom. If you hadn't been doing a good job for him, you wouldn't have lasted this long at the paper up there. Mr. Claude told me why you decided to leave and I understand that. So, tell me how you got started in printing and why you want to keep working even though you're able to retire."

"Yes, ma'am. When I got drafted in World War I, they made me a mechanic because I was good with motors and stuff, and when General Pershing started the *Stars and Stripes* over in France, they put me to working on the presses because I was good at tinkering. I liked it, and when I came home, that's what I went to doing for a living. I want to keep on and this looks like a good place to."

"Are you always like this, short on talk I mean?" Pearl asked.

"Yes, ma'am."

"Don't you have any questions about how many people work here and what the paper's like?"

"No, ma'am. I know it's a weekly, like the *Stars and Stripes* was."

"If I hired you, could you just call me 'Pearl,' and leave off some of this 'ma'am' stuff?"

"Yes, ma'am."

44

"Don't you want to know what the salary is?"

"Yes, ma'am. I figured you'd tell me."

Almost unable to believe her good fortune, Pearl signed up Grady to start in two weeks and made a mental note to do something nice for Mr. Claude. Then she rushed home to pick up Nancy and Alice and go see Wendell.

After the usual argument about who would sit in the back, no one said anything for a long while after they set out for the hospital, driving under grey clouds that had rolled in on a cold front and brought a fine mist. Each seemed lost in her own thoughts. They were halfway to El Dorado before Pearl broke the silence. Might as well come right out with it, she decided.

"Girls," she began. "I don't want you to worry, now, but there's something I have to tell you about your daddy."

"He's gon' be all right, isn't he?" Nancy asked, turning in the front seat to face her mother.

"Yes, but...," Pearl started.

"But he might not be able to walk? Is that it?" Alice asked. She leaned forward and rested her arms on top of the back of the front seat.

"What makes you think that?" Pearl asked, glancing in the rear-view mirror at her youngest.

"Aw, Momma," Alice said, "You think we couldn't figure that out for ourselves? We have eyes and ears."

"Yeah, Momma," Nancy said. "We know you're worried about that, but don't be. We've already talked about it. If it turns out he can't walk, we'll be sad, but we can help take care of him. And we'll get extra jobs to pay for college, even if it takes longer to get through."

Pearl could not speak. She leaned over and squeezed Nancy's arm then reached behind and patted Alice's. As they drove on, Pearl thought about how quickly the girls were growing up. Nancy was tall and slender, had her daddy's dark eyes and black hair, and like him, was good at math, though she wanted to be a teacher like her mother had been. Alice was shorter and filling out early, had her mother's blue eyes and brown hair, and, also like her, loved English. They both liked boys but neither had gone crazy about one up to now. Restricting their outings to school functions, occasional movies at the Liberty Theater, and Emmett's Café drop-ins that were only long enough for milkshakes undoubtedly helped, but Pearl believed they just naturally had their heads screwed on straight.

When they got to El Dorado, they stopped for flowers, and at the hospital, they found Wendell awake, able to talk, and happy to see them. He did not remember much about what had happened, except that he had fallen. He still did not know the full extent of his injuries, but he knew he was in for a long recovery and kept saying he was sorry. They told him not to worry about anything except getting better. Wendell's sister Jean and three people from the grocery company had brought flowers, and several others, including Pearl's eighty-something-year-old Aunt Myrtle from over near Stephens, had sent arrangements, and they brightened his room, the day, and everyone's spirits. Aunt Myrtle's arrangement had come with a note saying that if Wendell did not "behave right around all the pretty nurses," she would personally come down to the hospital and "sit on" him. That produced the smiles and chuckles Aunt Myrtle intended, and they spent the rest of visiting hours talking idly, mostly about school and relatives. Wendell asked about the newspaper, and Pearl told him everything was going well. He did not press her for details.

Elton woke up wondering if the pretty girl worked on Saturdays and if she did, whether she worked all day or only part of it. It did not matter much, however, because he could not hide in the bushes and watch for her in the daytime, and he had other plans for tonight. He thought again about asking his mother about the girl, and again he decided not to. Do it and Sadie Rose would know he was thinking about staying around longer, and he did not want to raise that with her until he was sure. Besides, he needed to hustle some traveling money, and she was certain not to like that. He ate a bowl of corn flakes then went across the road to see how Saturday morning was shaping up at the store and take enough practice shots of pool to warm up for what he hoped would be more serious evening action. He offered to help out again and was relieved to find that Sadie Rose had extra help on Saturdays and there was little for him to do.

In the front half of Sadie Rose's Place, grocery staples and household sundries filled shelves and tables on the right, and a barber's chair and two pool tables sat in a railed-off area to the left. Toward the back, a snack bar ran along the right wall, a juke box and tables and chairs occupied the left side, and the middle was left open for dancing. A low platform for performers extended part way across the rear wall. To the left of it was another, smaller, more discreet railed-off area where men gathered to shoot craps. An upright piano, three wooden folding chairs, and two microphones on stands sat on the platform, and two speakers hung above them. Behind the snack bar, an attached shed housed a kitchen and storage room. Advertising signs and posters cluttered the walls, along with hand-lettered signs about menu items and Sadie Rose's rules. The largest one read, "No Knives, Guns, or Booze." The first two prohibitions were real, and Sadie Rose enforced them personally. The liquor reference was there for any authorities that might come around, in which case everyone knew to make whatever hard stuff was in sight disappear in a hurry.

Elton watched women buying things they did not want to go uptown for and men getting haircuts and cigarettes, swapping tall tales, and reading worn copies of the *Chicago Defender* and *Pittsburgh Courier*. A few folks remembered Elton from his childhood and asked what he had been doing with himself and if he had come home to stay, but he did not know any of them well enough for much conversation. Sadie Rose was busy and paid him little attention, and after a while he went over to the pool tables, which stood empty awaiting players. They looked in good shape except for broken coin-op mechanisms. He dropped a dime into a cup sitting on a makeshift wall shelf with a sign reading, "Ten Cents. You Play, You Pay! You Don't Pay, You Better Pray!" He studied the cue sticks, picked one, and rolled it on the table to make sure it was straight. Then he racked some balls and started shooting by himself, making sure to miss as many shots as he made, in case anyone might come over.

He did not, however, have to try to miss the shot he had lined up when he glimpsed the pretty girl coming into the store. He jerked the stick so hard he almost tore the felt table cover. She was wearing the same belted coat she had on when he saw her before, but she looked even more beautiful in the daylight. He wanted to walk over and speak to her, but he noticed she was avoiding other customers and getting what she came for in a hurry, and he remembered the words of the old man. When she left, he put down his cue stick and, keeping his distance, went outside and watched her heading toward home on foot. He reckoned he ought to chance asking his mother about her, but first he had to make some money.

Sadie Rose always tried to have live music on Saturday nights, and this night a blues singer named Big Sugar Smith from over northeast, near Crossett, had come to sing, play, and stir bodies and souls. By nine o'clock, with help from a couple of local men on guitar and drums, Big Sugar's steely voice and wailing harmonica had forty or fifty people clapping, stomping, and dancing. Some had driven in from outlying areas. Many had on clothes that were only a tad short of their Sunday-go-to-meeting best. Some of the men wore hats and ties, and most of the women sported colorful dresses with skirts that flapped and snapped in the air like fluttering butterfly wings as the dancers swung their hips and legs.

Elton was wearing shabby jeans, an old shirt, and a faded denim jacket he had brought along for occasions like this, when he did not want to look anything close to the sporty way he usually saw himself. For a long while he stood casually watching the pool tables and sizing up the shooters. When he thought enough time had passed, he took a cue stick off the rack on the wall, asked if he could play, and was told he could. The men were playing eight-ball and betting dimes, and after stealing a glance down the length of his stick to see how best to turn it to make up for any bend in it, Elton made enough shots to look like he was trying and missed enough to lose several games while winning only one. Then one of the men, a stocky fellow who was slicked up in a purple shirt and white shoes and had won a lot of games from Elton and others, suggested playing for twenty cents a game. Elton hesitated then said, "Okay," and split two with the man. All the while, the music was going and people were dancing, but more men were edging over to the pool tables. Elton suggested they play for fifty cents a game, and the fellow thought that was likely easy money and agreed. Elton beat him four games in a row. "Hey man," the fellow said, "you hustling me? You are, I'll kick your yellow ass."

"Nah," Elton said, putting his cue down and his hands up, "I just got lucky."

At that, a skinny fellow in a plaid shirt and dress pants, older than Elton and a head taller, said, "Hey, brother, you think you all slick and cool, how'd you like to play for two dollars a game? Bet you ain't got the balls for it."

"I don't know, man," Elton said. "That's a lot of bread."

"You little chickenshit," the man said. "You just won two bucks. Pick up that stick and let's play."

Elton did, and let the man win.

"Come on, play me again," the man said. "I'll give you double or nothing."

"Nah," Elton said. "I've had enough."

"Yeah, sure, you little cocksucker," the man said, getting loud. "You scared." More men and a few women drifted over. The man looked at them and nodded, smirking.

"Okay. Tell you what," Elton said. "Let's play for ten bucks."

"You crazy, man? That's too much."

"Who's chickenshit now, asshole?" Elton asked. "Get on away from me."

"Goddamn you, put your fricking money on the table," the man said, "and let's play."

They laid their bills on the lip of the table and took lag shots to see who could leave the cue ball closest to the end cushion and get to break the racked balls. Elton left the cue ball within a hair of the cushion and got first shot. He took his time re-chalking the end of his stick and lining up his shot to break the rack then proceeded calmly to pocket all of the stripes and the eight ball. His opponent never got a chance to shoot. Elton picked up the bills and stuffed them in his jeans without even looking at the fellow and was starting to walk away, when someone shouted, "He's got a knife!"

"You slimeball son of a bitch!" the man said. He was waving an open pearl-handled switchblade and walking slowly around the end of the table toward Elton as if the two of them were alone. "I'm gon' cut your nuts out!"

"Watch it!" another onlooker shouted, and Elton turned to his left and saw the man in the purple shirt climbing over the top of the table toward him. "And I'm gon' help you do it," the fellow said.

No fool when it came to fighting, Elton's first thought was to duck under the table and try to run away. Before he could, however, Sadie Rose came hurdling out of the crowd in a red blur of flapping muumuu and thrashing limbs, smashed the man with the knife against the table, and sent his switchblade flying. The man fell to the floor gasping for air and Sadie Rose landed on top of him and got him in a strangle hold.

This left Elton trapped in the path of the stocky man in the purple shirt, and he braced for a blow that never came. A pair of powerful arms snatched the attacker off the table. "Time for you to get some air and cool off, sonny," Leon Jackson said, twisting the man's right arm high behind his back and forcing him up on his toes. Leon, a tall, dark man with close-cropped hair and gold-rimmed glasses, owned a dry-cleaning shop uptown behind the bank and was wearing his usual white shirt, suspenders, and black pants and looked almost like a preacher. But he was muscular and an army veteran and even some whites were afraid of him. He had been over in the corner shooting dice, but when folks started edging up to the pool tables, he had joined them. He pushed his guy toward the front door, and Sadie Rose climbed off the other one, picked up the knife, lifted the man by his belt, and dragged him along behind Leon.

When they got outside, Sadie Rose said, "Y'all bring that shit back in here again, I'm gon' wipe the floor with you and feed your black asses to my hogs. Now, go on, get."

"Gimme back my knife," the tall man said. "It's got my initials on it."

"Nah, I think I'll just hold onto it," she said. "Now, get, or I'm gon' whop you upside the head again." The two turned and headed off toward the scramble of cars in the dusty parking area. Then the tall fellow looked back and said, "I'm gon' be back, and I'm gon' kill that bastard."

"Let it pass," Leon said to Sadie Rose. "They're not worth any more trouble." Then he said, "I didn't know you had hogs."

"Don't," she said. "They stink. Nobody wants to go juking around a hog pen." Turning to head back inside, she asked, "You know them two?"

"Yeah, happens I do. The tall one's Jewell Vines and the other one's Ossie Reddin. They're from over around Strong somewhere, or at least they used to be. I guess they came to hear Big Sugar. I played baseball against them several times."

Leon was the playing manager of the Unionville Black Tigers, an amateur baseball team that drew big crowds on Sundays in the summer. "They're not very bright, but they're mean as hell. They could've killed Elton, you know."

"Yeah, I know," Sadie Rose said. "What I don't know is what I'm gon' do about that boy. I feel like beating the crap out of him, but I guess I'm probably just gon' yell like hell at him. Funny thing, him coming back like this. I didn't expect it."

CHAPTER 6

Wendell was the faithful churchgoer in the Goodbar family and sang in the First Baptist Church choir. Pearl was not keen about Baptists, her husband excepted, of course. She had grown up a Methodist, believing that sprinkling sinners was as good as dunking them and backsliders would never get past St. Peter. But she thought she and Wendell ought to worship together, and eventually she joined his church. She did not like it as much as her own, though, and was not above skipping a Sunday here and there when she had an excuse, never mind if her Methodist friends might think she was starting to backslide. This Sunday she had two excuses, Wendell and work, but she also had plenty to be thankful for, so she went and took the girls.

Everyone asked about Wendell, and in her pew she silently thanked the Lord he was alive and prayed for his return to health. She did not hear much of the sermon because she was too busy thinking about him and the newspaper. Plus, although she liked the preacher because he told stories about how he found Jesus after sinning about every way he could, she was long tired of hearing the same revival-sounding message almost every Sunday. Today even the music was mostly lost on her.

Like most folks, Pearl and her daughters sat in the same pew every week, and from their spot in the back, she could see

Emma Lou MacDonald sitting down front with her long-time friend and quilting partner Almalee Jolly. Almalee liked being up close because her daughter Opal often sang solos with the choir, and she did again today. Pearl decided that after the preaching would be as good a time as any to bring up newspaper writing with Emma Lou, provided there was some way to get her away from Almalee, who had an even bigger reputation for gossip than Hazel Brantley. Pearl feared that if Almalee overheard them talking, she would blab it all over town before anything had been decided. When the last amen was said, Pearl whispered to Nancy and Alice that she needed to speak with Emma Lou privately, and she asked them to catch Almalee on her way out and tell her how much they loved Opal's singing. They did, which set Almalee to beaming and bragging and gave Pearl enough time to pull Emma Lou aside and persuade her to come by the office on Monday afternoon to talk further.

After a quick dinner at home, Pearl and the girls headed to the hospital to see Wendell. With the sun shining in a nearly cloudless sky, with Grady Atwell on board to run her presses and a conversation with Emma Lou all teed up, and with Nancy and Alice looking forward to seeing their daddy for the second day in a row, Pearl felt the tightness in her shoulders slacken. As the miles passed, her eyelids began to droop.

"Momma!" Nancy said, alarmed when the Ford veered onto the shoulder of the highway. "Are you all right?"

"Yes, honey, I'm fine," Pearl said. "Let's sing some songs."

～

Sadie Rose thought since she gave a lot of folks in and around Unionville plenty of opportunity to sin—depending upon how they regarded drinking, dancing, cussing, and gambling—she ought to show up at the Mt. Zion Baptist Church at least occasionally to let the preacher and the Lord know that although she did not necessarily agree that any of these things were wrong, she had nothing against those who thought they were. She also knew that she could always count on seeing friendly faces among some of the deacons, including Elton's rescuer Leon Jackson. She knew, too, that neither they nor Reverend Hosea Moseley would reject her generosity when the collection plates were passed. Some of the church ladies were less welcoming when she attended services, but others of them were grocery customers who at least spoke to her. In short, nothing about Sadie Rose ever kept the Holy Spirit from stirring the congregation. So, on this Sunday, she got up thinking that even if the Lord never moved her like He did the others, she did not mind letting Him take another shot at her.

Elton was asleep when she left the house in a green-and-gold muumuu and matching head wrap, and she did not wake him. She was still trying to sort out how she felt about his showing up out of nowhere the way he did. She did not need bad memories, guilt, or distraction, and he brought all of those. Yet he seemed more together than she would have imagined, and until he pulled the pool-hustling stunt, she had begun warming somewhat to the notion of having him around and worrying about what might happen to him in Mississippi or Alabama. If a little preaching, praying, singing, and shouting did not help with that, or otherwise clear her head this morning, at least it would not hurt anything but her pocketbook.

The Mt. Zion Baptist Church was a brown concrete-block building four blocks east of the highway, in walking distance of much of its congregation, including Sadie Rose. Nevertheless, she usually drove there in her black panel truck, the same one she used to haul bootleg liquor, to ensure she could get away from any after-preaching carrying on in a hurry. Even driving she arrived late, but it did not matter because she always sat in the back. Reverend Moseley, a thin brown man with short gray hair, was already giving the opening prayer. He had on a dark suit and bright tie and stood behind a pulpit made by the deacons and in front of a choir wearing red robes made by church ladies. Sadie Rose waited while he finished praying then found her seat and joined in singing familiar hymns. Two deacons took turns lining out the words for others to follow, and piano, electric guitar, and drums provided rousing accompaniment.

When all the preliminaries were over and the congregation was uplifted and ready for his sermon, Reverend Moseley returned to the pulpit and opened his King James Bible, the only version any Baptists in Unionville ever used. After drawing himself erect with a deep breath, he read from the New Testament, Ephesians: 1-3, "Children, obey your parents in the Lord: for this is right. Honour thy father and mother; which is the first commandment with promise; That it may be well with thee, and thou mayest live long on the earth." Then he turned to the Old Testament and read Proverbs 29:15 and 17, "The rod and reproof give wisdom, but a child left to himself bringeth his mother to shame," and "Correct thy son, and he shall give thee rest; yea, he shall give delight unto thy soul."

Sadie Rose's first thoughts were that Moseley must know Elton had come home, and if the old minister aimed to preach at her, she was not going to stand for it. If he did, she would not get up and walk out, but she would get even with him somehow, probably through the collection plate. Moseley went on to talk about parents and children and their responsibilities to each other in a general enough manner, however, that she did not feel singled out. When she greeted him after the service, she joked in a voice only he could hear, "Reverend Moseley, I thought for a while there you was gon' get onto that prodigal son story, and I was gon' have to tell you I ain't about to give my fatted calf to no son of Trudell Washington." Moseley chuckled, and Sadie Rose left the church wondering if she had let Elton get away with too much when he was little.

When Sadie Rose got home, she found Elton in the kitchen frying bacon and getting ready to scramble eggs. "I figured you'd gone to church," he said, and "I knew you wouldn't stay for potluck with all the ladies, so I thought I'd make us some dinner." He knew she was going to light into him about last night, and he hoped this would calm her at least a little bit. If it did, then maybe he could ask her about the pretty girl. The timing was not good, he knew, but he could not hold his curiosity any longer.

"You know I'm good and damned mad at you, don't you?" she asked, filling the kitchen door with hands on hips and fists clenched. "I told you I didn't want no trouble, and you ain't here but three days and you go hustling my customers and get yourself in a knife fight. You lucky you didn't get cut."

"I know, Momma," he said, looking up from the stove then quickly turning from her stare. "I'm sorry. I didn't mean to let things get out of hand, but that dickhead was so cocksure, I didn't have no choice but to take him down."

"Yeah, you sorry, all right. Just like your daddy," Sadie Rose said. She shook her head and came into the room and sat at the table. "And here I was starting to think you might have more sense than he does. Boy, what I'm gon' do with you? If you gon' keep this up, you gon' have to get on over to Mississippi."

Elton turned and looked at her. "If I promise to keep out of trouble, can I stay a while longer?"

Sadie Rose tried to read his face, but all she could see was how much he reminded her of Trudell. "How do I know I can trust you?"

"I can't do nothing but promise you," Elton said. "If I can't hustle pool, though, I need to find some other way to get some more traveling money." He knew if he did not try to get work somewhere, she would eventually run him off.

"They near about always need help in the woodyard over at South Arkansas Oak Flooring," Sadie Rose said. "I know somebody that can probably get you on for a while. I can ask if you want me to."

"I do," Elton said. "Thank you. And thank you for saving my ass last night too."

"Yeah, well, you better be sure there ain't no next time. If there is, what I'm gon' do with your ass is kick it to high heaven."

When the food was ready and they were eating, Elton asked, "Momma did you see that pretty girl in the brown coat that come to the store yesterday morning, grabbed up a bunch of stuff in a hurry, and left without talking to anybody much, like maybe she was scared or something?"

"Why you want to know?"

"I just think she's pretty, that's all, and I'd like to meet her. Maybe bring her over to the store to dance some night."

The muscles in Sadie Rose's face tightened, and she put down her fork and said, "Elton, that girl's dangerous. You stay away from her. You mess with her, and you gon' get worse than a knife fight."

"Why's that? I don't understand."

"You don't have to understand. You just have to do what I say. It's for your own good." As soon as the words came out, Sadie Rose knew they were not enough. Even though she had not seen Elton in ten years, she knew he had too much of her ownself in him to let go of the notion of a woman as appealing as Priscilla Nobles simply because his mother said she was dangerous. "All right," she said, after a deep breath. "I'm gon' tell you because I know you ain't likely to turn loose of this till I do, and I'm doing it more for her sake and for her folks than I am for you. And if you tell anyone about this, Elton, I swear I'm gon' beat the living crap out of you, and you better know I'll do it too.

"The girl's name is Priscilla Nobles. She lives with her grandmomma and granddaddy, Bessie Mae and Henry, and she works for a big-shot white man that's one mean son of a bitch. His name's Herbert Kramer. He's got a big dairy farm and a bunch of timber out there off Newton Chapel Road. Got a big old sign out front with his name on it and all. He's president of the school board and some kind of bigwig in the White Citizens' Council. But that ain't the half of it. He's also Priscilla's daddy."

Elton stopped eating and Sadie Rose kept on talking. "Don't nobody know that but him and Priscilla and her grandmomma and granddaddy and me, and Kramer wants to keep it that way. He probably don't know about me knowing it, 'cause he ain't never mentioned it to me. But he's threatened to kill Mr. and Mrs. Nobles if they tell anybody, and they stay near about scared to death because he's always watching them. He drives by their house random like, and if he sees anybody there, he comes back later and threatens all three of them. Bessie Mae's got all kinds of stuff wrong with her and can't hardly get around, and Henry ain't well neither. Kramer brings them stuff from his farm, and they need it, but he only does it 'cause it gives him another way to check on them and keep them quiet. He's beat up Henry a bunch of times, but there ain't nothing they can do about it. Ain't nobody they can complain to."

"So, is that why Priscilla works for him?"

"Yeah. He threatens them if she don't."

"How come you know all this, Momma?"

"Because Priscilla's momma Yulanda was my friend. She was a pretty thing, and smart too. She worked for Kramer's people back before the war, and he raped her more times than she could count. Beat her when she tried to stop him."

"Why didn't she quit? The job, I mean."

"Couldn't," Sadie Rose said sadly. "Her family needed the money and there wasn't no other job she could get. Anyway, Kramer got her pregnant, and I was there when Priscilla was born. Helped Yulanda pick out Priscilla's name. It's from the Bible. Book of Acts somewhere. I forget exactly. I think she was a missionary. Anyway, Yulanda liked the way it sounded. I found out later it means 'respected.' Too bad it ain't helped her get none."

"What happened to Yulanda?" Elton asked.

"She run off to get away from Kramer. Last I heard she was up in Ohio somewhere. I got a postcard from her. It just said, 'Don't be worrying about me. I'm okay.' It wasn't signed but I knew she wrote it."

"Ain't there something somebody could do for them?"

"I take them food and things Priscilla can't buy out at the store, and I go get things for them when they need me to,"

Sadie Rose said. "But, no. The law don't care nothing about stuff like this. Ain't nothing unusual for house help to get raped. Been going on forever. You know that. Don't do no good to report it. I've thought about killing the bastard myself, but I ain't done it because I know I'd never get away with it. Besides, that'd start holy hell for everybody over here."

"Yeah, I guess it would."

"So, you stay away from that girl. And you keep your mouth shut about this. You hear me?"

"That man ain't screwing his own daughter, is he?"

"I didn't say that."

"Yeah, but you as good as said it, 'cause you ain't saying he's not."

"Listen to me, boy, and you listen good! I'm done talking about this and you better be done with it too."

CHAPTER 7

On Monday morning, Pearl swung by a bookstore in El Dorado and bought some Zane Grey novels Wendell did not have, along with Boris Pasternak's *Doctor Zhivago* and Nevil Shute's *On the Beach*. At the hospital she found him uncomfortable and impatient to know more about what to expect with his legs. Fearing that giving him all the books at once would suggest he was going to be there for a much longer time, Pearl decided to give him only the Zane Grey novels. Except for moments when Wendell, still on pain killers, nodded off, they spent the morning waiting unsuccessfully to learn whether the doctors had any news for them. Around noon, a nurse came in and said Wendell could have a hamburger if Pearl wanted to go out for one. She drove to a nearby diner and brought back a burger and milkshake for each of them, chocolate for him, strawberry for her. When his sister Jean arrived for the afternoon shift, they said their goodbyes, and Pearl headed back to Unionville eager to talk with Emma Lou MacDonald.

"If you will agree to four weeks in a row, we'll give you a fifth one at half price," Hazel Brantley was saying to someone on the phone when Pearl got to the office. She had not told Hazel she could give discounts, but this sounded like it might be a new customer, and if so, Pearl liked that Hazel had thought to throw in something extra to get the account.

"I hope you don't mind," Hazel said, when she hung up the phone. "That was the manager of that new flower shop in El Dorado, and this is the third time I talked to her. She kept saying she needed more time to think about it, and I thought it might help to give her a little something for free."

"I don't mind at all," Pearl said, as she settled into her desk. "I'm glad you did it."

"Good," Hazel said. "I have a couple more follow-ups that discounts might help with, if it's okay with you."

Pearl nodded her approval. Then she told Hazel about finding a press man who could start in two weeks. Hazel wanted to know who it was, but Pearl explained that she could not tell until he had given notice to his present employer. She could see that Hazel did not much like waiting, but she shrugged her shoulders and went on with her work, and Pearl began making sales calls of her own.

Shortly after three o'clock, Emma Lou MacDonald came through the front door calling out, "Hey, ladies! How're y'all doing?" About the same age as Hazel but a little taller, Emma Lou had long enjoyed both her own cooking and that of her husband Purvis, and it showed. She was carrying a quilted handbag with a floral pattern that matched her burgundy dress, and Pearl thought she looked perfect for writing about food and sewing, and especially making quilts.

After they got coffee, Pearl explained how she planned to subscribe to a national news syndicate for tidbits about cooking and sewing but also wanted to print things connected directly to people in Unionville. She said she hoped she could include some of Emma Lou's favorite recipes, ask readers to send in some of theirs, and have Emma Lou write a few words about them, like how long they had been in someone's family and maybe tips for preparing them. Emma Lou liked the sound of all of that, except for the writing, but Pearl gave her the same reassurances about it that she had given Hazel. When they got around to talking about the sewing part and Pearl mentioned quilts in particular, Emma Lou was practically beside herself.

"Oh, hon," she said, "I love making quilts more than anything. Could we maybe print patterns like some of the magazines do? I mean show designs that women could follow?"

"Sure," Pearl said. "We can do that."

"Maybe we can have a show or something," Emma Lou said, looking at the vacant space in front of the railing, "and display people's quilts up front there, like they do up at the county fair. I could get Purvis to build some sort of frames to hang them on, that is if you don't mind. He's got plenty of time on his hands."

"Yes, maybe," Pearl said. "I don't have any other plans for it." This was going to be even better than she had imagined.

"Well, sign me up, hon," Emma Lou said. "I'm gon' like this."

Sadie Rose left the store on an errand Monday morning, and when she finished she went home, rousted Elton out of bed, and told him to get over to South Arkansas Oak Flooring and see Robert Swanson about a temporary job cleaning up around the saws. Someone had gotten hurt and they needed a replacement until the fellow could come back. Elton had not expected anything that hard or potentially dangerous but he knew he had better go. Swanson hired him and told him to come back at six o'clock the next morning, the early start making another thing he had not counted on.

Despite his reservations, Elton discovered that he liked the molasses-like smell of the rosin and the dance of men and machines moving together. The work he found dirty and tiring, but that and the whining roar of the saws kept his mind off Priscilla Nobles, except during evenings.

Wendell Goodbar spent the week frustrated and mad. His accident remained a blur, and the doctors still could not tell him anything concrete about what to expect with his legs. They said he was progressing, but he could not see it or feel it. Pearl continued to spend part of her mornings with him, as his sister Jean did for the afternoons. But at Wendell's urging, both cut back the length of their visits, and he plunged deeper into his books and magazines.

In the meantime, Pearl and Hazel continued to sell advertising. On each trip to El Dorado, Pearl called on prospects, while Hazel made follow-up phone calls and talked to businesspeople in Unionville. With all of that, plus working with Hazel on her writing, Pearl had not been paying much attention to things happening around the country. From the outset, however, she had planned to report and write about matters outside Unionville as well as goings-on in the community, and now she began sitting up nights reading the several magazines and daily newspapers she had subscribed to and which were now piling up. She also started taking newspapers to the hospital, reading there, and sharing them with Wendell. In addition to the *El Dorado Daily News*, the *Shreveport Times* from down in Louisiana, and the *Arkansas Gazette* from up in Little Rock, she also read *Life*, *Look*, *Newsweek*, and *Time* magazines. Many of her soon-to-be readers subscribed to some of these same publications. Others bought copies at the barbershop and newsstand. But Pearl imagined that most did not see anything except the El Dorado paper on any regular basis, and she believed that including a little national and international news in the *Unionville Times* along with the local items would help attract readers. She could not afford to subscribe to the big national wire services like the Associated Press, but she could get short items, along with columns, comics, and other filler from smaller syndicates. Lining all that up took another big chunk of time.

One weekday morning on her way to the office, Pearl stopped by Emmett's and asked him about the best time to catch Boomer Jenkins there. Boomer had no phone and she knew he liked to hang out at the café when he was in town. Emmett suggested she come back on Saturday morning. When it rolled around, she went there a little after eight o'clock and found the café filled with the usual loafers, including barber Odell Grimes and former night watchman Crow Hicks, all talking about the weather, sports, and such. Boomer was among them and knew she had asked about him.

"Hey, little lady," he called loudly when he saw her come in. He was drinking coffee alone at a booth in the back, his peg leg sticking out in the aisle. Nearly everyone turned to look at her and kept staring as she crossed the room, now suddenly quieter. She figured they all knew he was waiting for her and were bursting their guts wondering why. She felt blood rise in her cheeks and hoped it did not show.

"Hello, Mr. Jenkins," she said, sliding into the booth across from him. He did not get up for her.

"Hey, Emmett," he yelled. "Bring Mrs. Goodbar here some coffee."

A few folks continued to stare, but most returned to their food and talk. Pearl had seen Boomer around town lots of times but had never spoken with him or even been this close to him. He was a huge man with scraggly black hair and several days' growth of whiskers, and she half expected him to smell of fish and swamp, but he did not. He did smell of alcohol, though, and because of that and his manner, she wondered if maybe asking him to write a column was not such a good idea. However, being already seated, she reckoned she might as well go ahead and see how he regarded it. So, she came right out with it.

A grin spread over Boomer's face, his shoulders shook, and a growl-like laugh began way down in his chest somewhere, all as if she had said something harebrained. She feared he would break into a full-throated howl. "Hey, everybody," he shouted to the entire room. "This here woman thinks I'd be crazy enough to let her have all my fishing and hunting secrets to put in her newspaper. Ain't that a hoot? Any of y'all ever know me to say how I get more fish and critters than anybody?" Then to Pearl, "Goddamnit, woman, I ain't about to give away what puts food in my belly and money in my pocket. Besides, I ain't got time for no writing stuff. That's for you women—and for men that can't do nothing else." Now everyone was staring again. A few snickered but no one said anything. Some were embarrassed for Pearl and some were afraid of Boomer.

For a split second, Pearl wished she could disappear, but she pushed the thought away, got to her feet, looked down at Boomer, and said, also in a voice all could hear, "Mr. Jenkins, I have made a mistake. I came over here thinking you'd be pleased to share your vast knowledge of the outdoors with your friends and the rest of our community and see your name featured in my paper every week, but I didn't know how precarious your livelihood is or how challenging a task my little job would be for you. I'm sorry to have taken your time."Then she wheeled around and started for the door.There were more low chuckles and a lot of grinning, but otherwise, the onlookers sat quietly, most not sure what they had just seen and heard.

When Boomer was able to unclench his teeth, he stood and called across the room, "Hey lady, while you're here, how about you tell us what you're gon' be writing about coloreds? You gon' be on the right side of things?"

Pearl stopped at the door, turned back, squared her feet, and glanced around the room. Here was that question again but more in her face this time. Seemed like it was going to hang heavier over her than she had imagined, and maybe a lot of folks were going to expect her to take the same anti-black stances that her predecessor did when he owned the paper. In any case, here was an opportunity both to make a point and maybe also turn some of the gawkers' curiosity into sales, for at least a few issues, anyway. Maybe even into a few subscriptions. "Mr. Jenkins," she said, "I'm certainly gon' be on the right side as I see it.You'll just have to wait and see if you agree."

CHAPTER 8

Friday night after supper, Elton Washington could no longer restrain himself. He had known more girls than he could remember in Chicago. But he thought Priscilla was prettier than all of them and he wanted her. He also wanted to get her out of the clutches of Herbert Kramer somehow. Maybe help her run away, anything to keep the bastard's slimy white hands off her. Cleansed of the mill, Elton slipped away after supper and took up his hiding spot outside the Nobles' house. He did not know what exactly he intended to do, but he was confident he would come up with something.

Like the last time Elton watched Priscilla come home, after Kramer let her out, she turned and looked back toward the road before going inside. Also as then, Kramer pulled away, circled back, stopped, and stared for a while before moving on. After he was gone, someone in the house pulled back a window curtain and looked out, like the first time Elton had been there, except for a few seconds longer. He thought it was Priscilla and did not need long to convince himself of it. He wondered if she had heard him at the door talking with her granddaddy those two earlier times, or if Henry had mentioned him to her. Maybe she had noticed him at the store last Saturday. Or maybe she somehow sensed his presence tonight. Soon he satisfied himself of each of these things, too, and started for the porch.

This time when he knocked, Priscilla opened the door, but only a tiny crack and only for an instant. "Go through the gate over there in the alley," she whispered, before pushing the door shut again and clicking the locks. Elton wondered if he had heard right but he did not hesitate. He glanced back at the road then quickly crossed the porch, dropped to the ground, and in the dark found the fence in back of the house. The gate squeaked when he opened it, and he paused, afraid of making dogs bark. After a moment he saw a faint light under the door of a small enclosed shed. Being careful to make as little noise as possible, he walked over to it and pressed his ear to the door. Hearing nothing, he tapped softly on the cold wood.

The light went off and the door swung open, revealing only vague shadows. Elton stepped inside and felt the door close behind him. He could not see Priscilla but he could smell her, a musky mix of sweat and hand soap. Without waiting for his eyes to adjust fully to the dark, he stepped toward her and felt her palms against his chest. Thinking that she intended to embrace him, he put his hands on her waist, aiming to pull her closer. She had left her coat in the house, and for an instant he felt the curve of her hips and the warmth of her body. He leaned forward, ready to receive her kiss, blood rushing to his groin. Only then did he realize that her hands were pushing against him.

"No!" she whispered.

Surprised, he relaxed his grip, and she stepped back.

"Please. Don't touch me again," Priscilla said, her voice breaking.

Confused, Elton stood still, surprising even himself. "All right," he said. "But, I don't understand. Why'd you get me back here?"

His question brought only a muffled sob. Part of Elton wanted to grab Priscilla and draw her back to him no matter what she said. In other times and places he had not been so easily deterred. This time, though, he stayed where he was. He wanted now more than ever to hold her, but not like a few moments ago. Her beauty, her touch however brief, her smell, and her tears all tore at him inside somewhere, leaving him still wanting to make love to her, but also causing him to fear hurting her. He wanted to soothe her somehow, but he was uncertain what to do, or what to say.

"Elton," she said, in a quiet voice that further melted his heart, "I'm sorry. I heard you talking to my granddaddy, and I saw you watching me at your mother's store. I asked you to come back here because I need you to leave me alone, and I could see I was gon' have to tell you that myself, else you wouldn't do it. I can't let anything happen to Grandmomma and Granddaddy. If Mr. Kramer ever saw you anywhere near me, he'd hurt them bad. And like as not, he'd kill you."

Elton took a step toward her and she backed farther away. "Don't," she said, crying again. "You got to understand."

The fear in Priscilla's voice sent a chill up Elton's spine and kept him where he was. "Priscilla, there has to be some way around Kramer, some way to get you away from him."

"No, there ain't. It wouldn't do you no good anyway. He's done ruined me. I'm not fit for nobody. Lordy, you got no idea."

"He's been doing you like he done your momma, ain't he? If he has, I'll kill the son of a bitch."

"That ain't anything I'm gon' talk about. I'm just telling you that you got to keep away. Keep away from me and Mr. Kramer both. It's best for you and it's best for me and them in the house. Please, you got to."

"But Priscilla..."

"No. I got to get back inside. You wait till you hear the back door close, then you clear out of here and go across the railroad tracks before you get back on the road." Then she was gone.

Elton huddled in a ditch on the other side of the tracks for a long time afterward trying to puzzle through all that had just happened and think of a way around things. Unable to come up with answers, he made his way back to Sadie Rose's Place, which was still jumping as always on weekend nights. When no one was looking, he swiped a bottle, took it through the woods to his mother's still, sat on the ground with his back to a tree, and drank until he passed out.

All day Saturday, Elton kept trying to come up with a way he could get Priscilla away from Kramer, not only to fulfill his own desires but also for her sake. But he could not see how to do either without making things worse for her and probably getting a bunch more people hurt, including his mother. And he guessed he owed Sadie Rose better than that. Not wanting to hang around and be reminded of it all, he decided he ought to get on with his travels. He thought if he worked at the mill for another week and managed to win a few more dollars at pool, he could get by. He would not hustle anybody, but if any shooters wanted to challenge him for money, he would show them no mercy.

This time he did not try to fool folks by looking shabby. He put on a good pair of jeans and his bomber jacket, went over to the store a little after suppertime, and got a few fellows to play him with no money on the table. Big Sugar Smith was performing again, and by nine o'clock the music was blaring, the dance floor was filled, and drinks were flowing. A few better shooters showed up and even though most knew they could not beat Elton, they did not mind losing pocket change trying, and a lot of folks were enjoying watching him shoot. By around ten thirty he had won several dollars, not big money but helpful, and was enjoying the attention.

He was standing with his back to the door chalking his cue stick when a hand grabbed his neck from behind like a vice and a voice said, "You sneaky little bastard, you know you lucky to be alive, don't you? I'm gon' kill you one of these nights when I catch you without your momma around to help you, but tonight I'm gon' beat your ass at eight-ball." Elton did not need to turn around to know the voice belonged to Jewell Vines, the tall guy with the switch blade, though he did not know the man's name. Vines might have believed he was scaring Elton, but Elton's only thought was of a chance to make more money.

"All right, asshole," he said. "Put your bread on the table."

"Ten dollars a game, best two out of three, and then one more at double or nothing?" Vines asked.

"Fine with me," Elton said. He fished two fives out of his pocket and laid them on the lip of the table.

Sensing trouble, people began drifting over to watch, and Sadie Rose noticed and came over herself, her girth and orange-and-yellow muumuu parting the way. "I thought I told you to keep your sorry ass out of my place," she said to Vines. "Get!"

"Leave him be, Momma," Elton said, moving between them. "I'm fixing to take him to the cleaners."

"Yeah, Momma," Vines said in a mocking tone. "Leave me be. Besides, I ain't got no knife tonight. You got it."

"Nope," she said, "I give it to Elton."

Vines glanced at Elton, as if wondering whether he had it on him.

"Let them play," Leon Jackson, the dry-cleaning man, said, walking up with his thumbs hooked under his suspenders and his white shirt gleaming. He had been dancing with his wife Wanda and watching Elton at the same time. "I'll keep an eye on things." He gave Vines a cold stare. "There's not gon' be any fighting."

"You damn right, they ain't," Sadie Rose said, folding her arms over her massive chest. "I'm gon' be right here too. Y'all get on with it."

The players lagged for first shot at the racked balls, and Elton let Vines win, not to set him up for a hustle, but because he doubted Vines could run the table. Beating him after he got off to a good start would pull him down more. Vines took the solids, sank the first six balls and watched number seven hang teasingly at the edge of a side pocket before settling in place on the felt top. Without a word, Elton took his turn, sank all the stripes and the eight ball, picked up the ten Vines had bet, and motioned to him to put down another.

He did, and shaken now, he lost the lag and could only stand and watch while Elton ran the table and motioned to the money again. Vines looked around nervously, as if searching for a way out of the growing circle of onlookers. Leon pushed Vines' shoulder hard and said, "Put twenty dollars on the table, peckerwood! Double or nothing, remember?" Vines did and this game went exactly as the last one. Elton pocketed the bills, making forty dollars Vines had lost, then said, "You know, that goddamn checkered shirt you got on looks just right for a pile of dog shit like you."

Vines started to swing at Elton, but before he could draw back, Sadie Rose's open palm laid him on the floor, and she stood daring him to get up. Blood oozed across his lower lip, and instead of getting immediately to his feet, he slid backwards on his butt trying to get away from her. She was on him like a cat and about to smash him again when Leon stepped in and said, "I'll see the gentleman out." He was afraid Sadie Rose would send Vines to the hospital, or worse.

"You're a dead man, motherfucker!" Vines shouted at Elton as Leon took hold of him. "I live down here now and I'm gon' be looking for you."

CHAPTER 9

On Monday morning in the third week of March, Pearl arrived at the hospital to find Wendell's lead surgeon, Thomas Whitstock, a tree of a man with black-rimmed glasses and a stethoscope around his neck, standing at her husband's bedside with a tall, bony woman dressed in a white uniform without the sort of heavily starched cap that registered nurses wore to tell which school they graduated from.

"Just in time," Dr. Whitstock said. "Pearl, this is Helen Brunson, head of our physical therapy department. We've been telling Wendell that he's healing well and we believe in time he'll be able to get around on crutches. How soon and how much is going to depend on him and on Miss Brunson here. He's got a lot of hard work ahead of him, and he's gon' be in a wheelchair for a good while yet. It's gon' be even longer before he gets enough use of his right leg to drive, if ever, and he knows that, but we'll keep working with him on it. He's still gon' have some memory problems for a while, and he's gon' get irritated more easily than normal, but he hasn't been having any blurred vision and not much dizziness. Overall, things are looking much better than I expected."

Wendell winked at Pearl, and she took his hand and leaned over and kissed him. This was good news, but they were practical people with big financial obligations, and it was now clear that Wendell would not be working again for a long time, and most likely never at his old job. His employer could not keep it open indefinitely. He and Pearl had lots of questions, including where his therapy would take place, how long he would need it, what role Miss Brunson would have in it, and what it would likely cost. Whitstock and Brunson were not much help with the last question, but they explained that Wendell was fortunate that St. Joseph's Hospital had started a therapy program during the polio epidemic a few years back and had gotten good at it. He would have to do some work at the hospital before he was released, and someone would have to bring him back at least two times a week for sessions with Miss Brunson, but she could help them find ways to do some of the therapy exercises at home. She asked if there were any nurses in Unionville who would be willing to take some basic instruction from her and work with Wendell for an hourly fee and if there were any family members who could learn to help with such things as manipulating his legs. They all knew Pearl would not have time for it. She said they could talk to Paulette Franklin, a nurse for Unionville's only doctor, Aubrey Perkins, and see if she could take on the main tasks. Wendell thought Nancy and Alice could learn to help some.

When Whitstock and Brunson left, Pearl kept hold of Wendell's hand and dropped into the chair next to his bed. Each of them felt as if one cloud had been lifted—Wendell would be able to get around again—and another cloud had grown bigger—he would have to depend on other people for a long time and expenses would keep mounting. Tears rolled down his cheek. "I'm sorry," he said. "I've been remembering things. I should've been more careful on the dock. I was writing on my clipboard while I was walking. I let us down." Pearl got up and laid her head on his chest.

"Don't," she said softly.

⌒

With some clarity now about Wendell's future and Grady Atwell set to come on board in another week, Pearl threw herself into making further arrangements at home while continuing to push hard at work. She broke the news about Wendell to Nancy and Alice over dinner and thanked God for their determination to do whatever it took to make things work. Nancy, now old enough to get a learner's permit, had been looking forward to Wendell's teaching her to drive and knew her mother did not have time to do it. But instead of showing disappointment, she asked, seeing as how her daddy was not going to be able to drive for a long time, if maybe they should sell his car and use the money on medical bills. Pearl said that was sweet of her and a thoughtful idea, but Wendell's car was nearly as old as hers and not worth a whole lot. She felt they ought to hang onto it for now at least. Nancy said she understood.

Later in the week, Pearl asked Doc Perkins, as most everyone called him, for his blessing to talk to Paulette Franklin about working with Wendell, and he was all for it. Mrs. Franklin said she would be pleased to learn something new and help as much as she could. Her hourly fee and her charge for traveling to El Dorado for training were higher than Pearl expected, but she had no choice but to accept them.

At the newspaper, Pearl laid out typesetting specs for local advertisements already sold. Few required illustrations, and for those that did, she found existing images from which the *El*

Dorado Daily News could make papier mâché mats that Grady could then use as forms for casting hot metal for printing plates. She had already been selling space to national firms that bought advertising for their clients in newspapers across the country, and as mats for those began arriving in the mail, she set them aside for Grady to cast too. She also continued working with those firms and kept talking with potential advertisers in Unionville and El Dorado.

Pearl also called Arlan Tucker, the undertaker Hazel Brantley suggested she get to write about hunting and fishing. A stocky, clean-cut man, he looked like a walking Brooks Brothers ad when conducting funerals, but he was often seen around town in khakis and boots, and he wore them to the newspaper office early one afternoon. He also had on a seldom-cleaned hunting jacket with a game pouch that gave off the sharp outdoorsy smell of dead squirrels. In contrast with Boomer Jenkins, Tucker, whom nearly everyone called by his last name, liked Pearl's idea. He enjoyed telling fish tales and hunting yarns and was not above stretching the truth to amuse folks. "Of course. I'd be honored to do it," he said. "I'll swap you even, a free box ad for Tucker Funeral Home for every column I turn in and you print." This would probably cost more in lost ad revenue than Pearl had planned to pay him in fees, but believing she would likely get it all back, and more, in increased readership, she agreed.

When Elton Washington walked into Sadie Rose's kitchen after work on Wednesday night, five days after seeing Priscilla Nobles, Sadie Rose yelled, "Boy, I'm good mind to bust your head. I told you to leave that girl alone. Her grandmomma told me you was sneaking around over there again. After what I done told you, what the hell was you thinking?"

"Momma...," Elton started.

"You wasn't thinking, that's what. Dammit, Elton! What I got to do to get through to you?"

"You don't have to get through to me, Momma," Elton said, taking a chair at the table. "Priscilla Nobles already done it. She's about the prettiest girl I ever seen, but I ain't gon' bother her no more. She's messed up in ways ain't nobody can fix. That goddamn white man might as well have killed her. If I could get my hands on the son of a bitch, I'd stomp his damn guts out."

Sadie Rose walked over and put her hand on her son's shoulder. "Don't you go and do something else stupid now."

"I'm not, Momma," Elton said. "It's time I got going anyway. I got enough money for a little while, so I'm gon' quit the mill tomorrow and catch a bus Friday."

"I was getting sort of used to having you around again, son," Sadie Rose said. "But I expect that's probably best." She pulled him to his feet and hugged him for the first time in years.

CHAPTER 10

Sadie Rose insisted on driving Elton uptown to catch the bus late Friday morning, and he insisted she drop him off and not hang around to see him get on. He was afraid someone might remember him from a few weeks back, and he did not want to cause his mother any more trouble. Sadie Rose parked in an angled slot in front of the newspaper office, next to a large delivery van that blocked their view of Emmett's Café, and they sat there watching over their shoulders for the red-white-and-black Trailways until they saw it coming down the highway from El Dorado. After promising to send his mother a postcard when he got to Jackson, Mississippi, Elton, wearing his bomber jacket and his Fedora with the brim turned up, slid out with his duffle bag, and as Sadie Rose drove away, he headed for the bus, now stopped in front of the café. An elderly black woman was walking in that direction, too, expecting, like Elton, to buy her ticket from the bus driver after white passengers got on. If there were any of those, they would be waiting inside the café, now starting to fill with the lunchtime crowd.

When Elton got past the delivery van, he saw Herbert Kramer's pickup parked out front and next to it a beat-up gray Chevy with a Confederate flag painted on the tailgate. In a flash, any concern for Sadie Rose or for his own safety went out of his head. All he could think of was Priscilla Nobles, Kramer, and the driver of the last bus he had been on. By god, he thought, he might as well do here, right now, what he was going to Mississippi for, show white people that black folks were tired of being stepped on. Blacks were welcome in white stores in the South but never in white eating places, except in a few that had a separate "colored" room in the back, but then only there. Elton crossed the curb, sat his duffle bag on the sidewalk, went into the café, and stood looking for a place to sit down and order something to eat.

Emmett was the first to see him, and all he could think to do was yell, "What the hell!" That was enough to cause everyone to look around, and for a moment, things got so quiet Elton could hear sausage frying in the kitchen. Then someone said, "That's a nigger!" And someone else hollered, "Boy, get your black ass out of here!" Elton ignored them and started toward the counter where there was a vacant stool. Before he could take two steps, a large man grabbed him from behind in a bear hug, and someone else called, "Stick him, Boomer, stick him!" A skinny man in faded overalls came rushing over and punched him in the stomach, and another yelled, "Save some of the bastard for me, Crow!" Other men jumped up too. One kicked Elton a glancing but still painful blow in the groin. Another asked, "Who is he?" And another said, "I heard ole Sadie Rose's boy come home from up North somewhere. I bet that's him."

Then a big man with a deep tan and coarse white hair stepped up and spoke in a tone that commanded everyone's attention. "Take the son of a bitch outside," he said. "We'll teach him a lesson."

"We ought to cut his nuts out," said the man behind Elton.

"Mr. Kramer's right," Emmett said, having come around the counter. "Get him out of here."

The man holding Elton flipped him around toward the front as if he were no more than a broom, twisted one of his arms high between his shoulder blades, and hustled him to the door. Elton heard a thumping sound behind him and thought someone was banging a club against the floor. He drew in his head, as if that would lessen the blow he expected, and the man growled, "Stand up, asshole." He half pushed, half dragged Elton outside and across the sidewalk, forced him against the gray pickup, and spun him around again. As Elton was turning, he saw that the man had a wooden leg. Everything was happening lightning fast, but to Elton, it all seemed in slow motion, and for some reason that made no sense, he wondered what had happened to the man. Elton kicked at the artificial leg and both men fell to the ground. "Goddamn you black bastard!" Boomer yelled. Onlookers rushed to help, but Boomer righted himself with surprising quickness, pulled Elton up, and pinned his arms behind him.

"Hold him right there," Kramer said. "Let me at him." With Boomer keeping Elton in a vice grip, Kramer delivered another kick to his groin and this one found its target flush on. Kramer's boot tore into Elton's already throbbing testicles and sent searing bolts of pain across his abdomen. His knees buckled, but Boomer did not allow him to fall. Kramer then punched Elton in the mouth. Blood spilled down the front of his jacket and he gasped for air. Boomer let him drop to the ground then, and as he lay on his side, Kramer kicked him twice in the back. When he did not move, folks began backing away, but they kept on cussing and hurling threats.

At that point, Jesse Culpepper, chief of the Arkansas side's two-person police force, came running across the street hollering, "Hold up there! Police! Hold up there!" He had been parking his still-new blue-and-white patrol car across the highway in front of the combination town hall and jail right as the crowd finished spilling out of the café. A lanky redhead in his thirties, Jesse was a former Union County deputy sheriff and had been chief of police only a few months. Unlike Mr. Claude, the other member of the two-man force, Jesse wore a uniform and carried a pistol strapped to his waist in plain view. "What's going on here?" he asked, as Elton lay on the pavement not moving and still bleeding. Several men started talking at once, and Jesse pointed at Emmett and said, "You tell me."

"Damned colored boy tried to come in the café and the fellows here took care of it," Emmett said. "That's all."

By this time the crowd was growing, and Pearl Goodbar, Hazel Brantley, and Emma Lou MacDonald had rushed over from the newspaper office. They had heard the fuss while working on columns, and Pearl had grabbed her Blue Horse notebook and pencil on her way out.

"Anybody know who he is?" Jesse asked, having not seen Elton before.

"Yeah," Crow Hicks said, grinning. "We think he's ole Sadie Rose Washington's boy. Been living up North and done come back a real smart ass. You might've just saved us from killing the son of a bitch."

"And I might've gotten here in time to keep you out of jail," Jesse said. "Who busted him in the mouth? Was that you, Mr. Kramer? I saw you kicking him."

"You damn right it was," Kramer said. He was still red in the face and still had his fists clinched. "And I'm not gon' stand for you letting him press any charges either."

"Well, now," Jesse said. "That's not really up to you, is it? You need to calm down." He took a step back, motioned toward the crowd, and said, "All right, everybody get on about your business. Driver, get this bus loaded and get it out of here." As they began moving, he instructed a couple of men who had been looking on quietly to escort Elton across the street to the jail. Then he turned to Emmett and said, "Call Doc and tell him I need him to come as soon as he can." When Emmett did not move right away, Jesse said, "Damn it, Emmett, do it now."

Pearl's first thought was how gruesome and disturbing this all was. Her second was that everyone in town would want to know what happened and it would be two weeks before she could get anything in print about it. Nevertheless, she jotted down names of a number of folks in the crowd in case she wanted to talk with them later. As Hazel and Emma Lou headed back to the office, Pearl looked around for Kramer, did not see him, and decided he must have gone back inside. Boomer was still standing around, however. So, steeling herself against his foul mouth, she walked over and got his version of what had happened inside. After that she went into the café and, seeing Crow near the door, asked him how he knew the black man was Sadie Rose's son. Crow said he had heard several people talking about it. He thought maybe Herbert Kramer had found it out over in the quarters somehow but was not sure. He also said he hoped Pearl would tell how he and the others had shown "what happens to coloreds that don't stay in their place."

Pearl said, "Hardly," and while Crow pondered what that meant, she looked around for Kramer. He had left, so she made a mental note to talk to him later. By this time, Emmett was off the phone, but all she got from him was another crack like Crow's.

As she left the café to head to the jail and talk with Jesse, she noticed a duffle bag sitting on the sidewalk a few feet from the café door. Thinking it might be Elton's, she looked for identifying marks and saw "Washington" scratched into the leather handle. Surprisingly, the crowd had left it undisturbed. It was heavy but she managed to lug it across the highway.

The municipal building was a small white concrete block structure with a common room up front that doubled as an office and meeting space. Behind it a hallway ran between two supply rooms to the rear where there was a pair of jail cells, one for whites and one for blacks. A smaller hallway extended between them to an outside door in the rear. Doc Perkins was already heading into the cell for blacks when Pearl arrived with the duffle bag. A football player at Tulane University three decades earlier, Doc remained fit and always wore a black suit and tie. His gray hair gave him a grandfatherly look that most everyone liked. After a few minutes he came out front and took a seat in an armless wooden folding chair next to the desk that both Jesse and the mayor used. Jesse was sitting on one edge of it. Doc said Elton was badly bruised and missing two teeth but did not seem to have any broken bones. Said he was going to need some pretty strong pain pills, though.

Pearl showed them the duffle bag and told where she found it. "Pretty much proves he's Sadie Rose's son," she said, looking at Jesse. "You charging him with anything?"

"Disturbing the peace and entering a whites-only eating establishment," Jesse said. He did not have to explain the town's decades-old Jim Crow ordinance intended to ensure segregation of public facilities.

"Are you charging any of the men that beat him?" Pearl asked, only now pulling up another folding chair.

"I haven't decided," Jesse said. "The boy would have to press charges, and if he did, there'd be hell to pay. Probably cause an even bigger stink, and I don't remember any white man ever going to jail for beating up a Negro. The fellows all think he deserved it."

"Do you think he did?" Pearl asked.

Jesse looked at her and remembered that she owned the newspaper. "It doesn't matter what I think," he said.

"What are you gon' do then?" she asked.

"If you want my advice," Doc put in, "you'll slip him out the back door and take him to Sadie Rose and tell her to get him out of town. From what I gather from him, he was planning to leave anyway, and if he stays around here now, in jail or not, there's gon' be trouble of some sort for sure. And you don't need it, the town doesn't need it, and nothing good'll come of it." Doc was not only practical, he was one of the most respected men in Unionville, and few people discounted what he said without at least considering it.

"There's sense in that, Doc," Jesse said, "but I can't do something like that without at least getting Mayor Poindexter's okay. I ought at least to fine the boy. He can pay it. He had more than two hundred dollars on him."

"Wonder where he got that kind of money?"

"I asked him that, and he said he'd been saving for a long time so he could move to New Orleans."

"Do you believe that?" Doc asked.

"No. But I can't prove different."

"Did he have any weapons you need to charge him for?"

"No. Nothing on him but his billfold. Might be something in his bag there. I probably ought to look."

"Tell you what," Doc said, "I don't think there's any need for that. He didn't even bother to take it inside. What if you just go ahead and talk to Alan? Right now, I mean. I'll go with you."

Jesse said he could not leave Elton alone in the jail with tempers running the way they were.

"I have an idea," Pearl said. "Suppose I go get Mr. Claude and bring him back to keep watch for you?"

Jesse and Doc thought that was a good plan, and as Pearl got up to leave, Jesse said, "I need to get word to Sadie Rose before she hears about this and comes up here and makes things worse."

"I think she's too smart for that," Doc said. "But how about this? Leon Jackson's close to her. Let me walk down to his cleaning shop and ask him to go tell her what's going on and that she should stay put."

"Good idea," Jesse said. "Mr. Claude told me Leon knows how to keep his cool. Said he was a big help last year when we had those cross burnings. And how about you stop by the hardware store on your way back and tell Neal O'Brien what we're doing too? Better yet, see if he wants to go with us to talk to the mayor. Won't hurt to have the council president in on it, especially if he has any reservations."

Pearl wanted to talk to Elton and get his side of what happened, but she realized there was no time. On her way to get Mr. Claude, she wondered if her readers would care what Elton had to say anyway. It also occurred to her that even if any of them did care, printing it might cost her business when she could least afford to lose it.

After a long night of little sleep and a whole lot of fussing and fuming from Sadie Rose and arguing about getting even somehow, Elton climbed into his mother's panel truck early Saturday morning with his duffle bag and a bottle of pain killers from Doc. They drove south thirty-five miles in a chilling rain to Ruston, Louisiana, and there Sadie Rose bought her son a new bomber jacket, give him some more money, and put him on an eastbound bus for Jackson, Mississippi. As she stood watching it leave, she thought Elton was more like her than she had ever believed, leastways as far as backbone was concerned.

CHAPTER 11

For days after Elton Washington walked into Emmett's Café, all Unionville, white and black, buzzed with talk, questions, rumors, and threats. In the café and down the street at the barbershop and newsstand, white men fumed about Elton's getting out of town without jail time or worse. Some talked about burning crosses in the quarters to make sure no other blacks did what he did. In stores with clerks and at home with friends, white women swapped rumors to make sure each knew every version of what had happened. Black women working in white homes talked evenings among themselves and with their families about what white folks were saying, and black men argued at Sadie Rose's Place and elsewhere about whether Elton had done something stupid or something that took guts.

A lot of people, white and black, speculated about whether anything like this would happen again and when it might. Leaders in the White Citizens' Council schemed about how to make sure it did not. The ruminating even spilled into churches. At the Mercy Baptist Mission, Brother Spurlock railed against what he called "uppity coloreds," and at the Mt. Zion Baptist Church, Reverend Moseley preached about faith and courage.

The incident followed Sadie Rose Washington and Pearl Goodbar almost everywhere. In the black section of town, folks commiserated with Sadie Rose about her son's beating, and in the white section, everyone—at least it seemed to Pearl—wanted to know what she planned to write about it.

The questioning had started as soon as she returned to the office the day of Elton's beating. "Was this the same Negro that caused all that fuss three weeks ago?" Hazel asked.

"Looks like it," Pearl said.

"Is he really Sadie Rose Washington's boy?" Emma Lou asked.

"Yes."

"What do you reckon is gon' happen now?" Hazel asked.

"You think Crow Hicks and them will try to take this out on Sadie Rose somehow?" Emma Lou asked.

"I don't know," Pearl said.

"What're you gon' put in the paper?" Hazel asked.

Grady never stopped working and did not appear to notice all this questioning, but Pearl called him over with the others. She told them what she knew and reminded them that whatever was said in the office about this, or about anything else down the road, had to stay here. She also said she had not decided what she would write about it.

⌒

Either the *El Dorado Daily News* never got wind of the matter or did not consider it important to report, and by Monday morning, Pearl realized that whatever she wrote in the *Unionville Times* would likely be all that people ever saw in print about it.

That afternoon, Elmer Spurlock came by to try to make sure she gave it the right slant as he saw it. Pearl noticed him when he parked out front in his white pickup with a gaggle of painting ladders lashed in the back. He was a balding man pushing sixty, but he had a barrel chest, bulldog face, and deep voice, and although he was a minister, he always seemed to Pearl more sinister than preacher-like. As he came through the door in paint-splattered overalls, he tried to strike a neighborly tone, calling out, "Afternoon, Mrs. Goodbar. I wonder if I could have a word with you?"

"Good afternoon, Brother Spurlock," Pearl said from her desk, using the title whites preferred for their preachers and showing the respect most everyone afforded them in public. "Come in and have a seat. What can I do for you?"

"I was hoping we could talk about what kind of stance you're gon' take on the nigger question," he said, pulling up a chair, "especially seeing what happened over at the café last Friday, and how that's likely to cause some of the rest of them to try it, or worse. As you know, your predecessor, Mr. Upshaw, took a strong position against integration, and we need you to do that too."

Even though Pearl still had not decided what to write about Elton Washington, she had been thinking about her editorial policy on blacks and integration generally. She leaned back in her chair, folded her hands together, and rested them on the desk. "Mr. Spurlock, she said after a moment, "First of all, I do not like the word 'nigger.' It's meant to demean and we do not use it in this office. Likewise, I do not like the word 'colored,' and you will not see it in this newspaper. Thirdly, I am not Preston Upshaw, nor do I intend to follow in his footsteps. I do not favor integration, but I believe that everyone, white and black, deserves to be treated with dignity."

Hazel, Emma Lou, and even Grady stopped what they were doing to listen. Spurlock's face grew red, but to his credit he waited for her to finish. Then, right as he opened his mouth to speak, Pearl added, "And according to my reading of the Bible, Brother Spurlock, that is what the good Lord expects from all of us."

Spurlock pushed his chair back and got to his feet. "Mrs. Goodbar," he said, "you can believe whatever you want, and you can write whatever you want, at least as long as folks put up with you, but don't you lecture me on what the Bible says about coloreds. They are cursed by God. Genesis 9:25. You can look it up. He don't mean for us to lower ourselves to them, and if you don't support that point of view, you ain't gon' be in business long." He shoved his chair against Pearl's desk, said, "Good day, madam," and walked out.

Pearl looked over at her employees. "We're not gon' have any disagreement about this in the office, are we?" she asked.

"Nope," Emma Lou said. "Not from me."

"I'll go along," Hazel replied. "I just don't want no integration."

"I'm fine with it," Grady said.

⌒

Neal O'Brien felt pretty sure Pearl would write even-handedly about the row at the café, but having taken a lead role in getting business leaders behind her, he wanted to know more about her thinking. He dropped by one afternoon mid-week and found her in her new private office in the back. She liked working out front in the big room among all the type and machinery when she could, but other times she needed quiet.

"How're you doing?" he asked. "Everything coming along okay?"

"Yes, we're doing fine," she said, noticing his spiffy sport shirt and slacks. "Did you meet Grady Atwell out there? He started Monday and he's got the Babcock ready to hum. He says if we have copy ready in time—and we will—we shouldn't have any problem getting our first issue out when we told everybody we would. It's less than two weeks now."

"Yeah, I saw him," Neal said. "The guy in the funny hat, right? He was up to his elbows in something or other when I came in."

"That's a newsboy cap. He wears it all the time. Come on," Pearl said, getting up. "I'll introduce you."

"All right," Neal said, and moved toward the door. "You got your angle on the Elton Washington thing yet?"

"You're gon' question me about that too? I'll say one thing. If everyone who's asked me about it or tried to tell me what to write about it would subscribe to the paper, I'd get out of debt a lot sooner."

⌒

The next morning, when Pearl got back from visiting Wendell, instead of going to the newspaper office, she drove on impulse through the short commercial district, crossed into Louisiana, rode around both the white and black sections, then crossed back into the Arkansas side and ended up on the dirt road to Sadie Rose's Place. Pearl had driven over most of Unionville many times but never out to Sadie Rose's and was not sure why she was taking that road now. Almost everyone in Unionville knew everybody else, black and white, or knew of them. Pearl knew who Sadie Rose was and had seen her numerous times uptown. But the two women had never spoken. Most whites thought of Sadie Rose as operating somehow on the edge of the law and decency, and Pearl was no exception. Last year, when Governor Orval Faubus fought school desegregation in Little Rock and Preston Upshaw stirred emotions about it in Unionville, she did not like all the hate she saw. Still, she had not thought much about how black people lived. Now, however, she pictured Elton lying on the ground bleeding and his mother at home all the while thinking that he was safely on his way somewhere on the bus. That night earlier in the month, when she came home from the hospital trying to decide what to tell Nancy and Alice about Wendell, flashed through Pearl's mind, and she wondered what happened with Sadie Rose when Jesse Culpepper took her son home to her.

When Pearl got to Sadie Rose's Place, she was walking up the front steps to her house, having come from the store. She turned when she heard Pearl's car. Pearl parked on the side of the road, reached out of habit for her Blue Horse notebook and pencil, got out, and walked toward the house.

"Good morning, Mrs. Washington," Pearl said, extending her hand. "I'm Pearl Goodbar, editor of the newspaper."

Both what Pearl said and what she did surprised each of them. White people never said "Mister" or "Missus" to blacks. They called black people by their first names while expecting blacks to address them by title and last name. This applied even to white children. Something, she was not sure what, made Pearl do different here.

The two women stood looking at each other for a moment, one in her shirtwaist dress and the other in her muumuu, each uncertain what to say or do next.

"Yes, ma'am," Sadie Rose said after a moment, polite but wary. "I know who you are." She came back down the steps and briefly shook Pearl's hand. "What do you want?"

"I was wondering if I could talk with you for a minute about what happened to your son."

"Why you want to know?" Sadie Rose asked. "White folks don't care nothing about him."

"Well," Pearl said, growing increasingly uncomfortable, "I didn't like what I saw those men do to him. People have been asking me what I'm gon' put in the newspaper about it, and I'm trying to decide."

"How do I know you not gon' be like that man that had the newspaper last year and just use Elton to get people all riled up?" Sadie Rose asked, her tone tinged with anger.

"I don't guess you do," Pearl said, taking a step back, "but I assure you that's not my intention. Could we sit and talk about it?" She realized at once that, without meaning to, she had invited herself into Sadie Rose's home.

"All right, yes ma'am, Mrs. Goodbar, let's do that. Y'all come on in and let's talk," Sadie Rose said. She led the way up the steps and held open the front door.

Pearl had never been in a black person's home before, and the first thing she noticed was Sadie Rose's quilts. There were two draped over the back of the sofa and two more on chairs, all in colors as bright as Sadie Rose's flower-splashed muumuu. Pearl did not quilt and did not recognize any of the patterns.

"You're a quilter," Pearl said, still uncomfortable and still standing. "We're gon' be printing quilt patterns in the paper."

"Yes, ma'am," Sadie Rose said. "Go ahead, you can sit on them." She was eager to get this over. "What do you want to ask me?"

"To tell you the truth," Pearl said, taking a chair as Sadie Rose went to the sofa. "I'm not really sure. Mostly, I guess, I wondered if your son's all right." When Sadie Rose did not answer right away, Pearl continued. "And I was wondering what made him do it. I mean, why here, why right now, and why by himself? Negroes who're doing things like this in most other places are doing them in groups, not generally by themselves."

Sadie Rose wondered if Pearl really did not understand that Elton did it simply because he was tired of the way black people were treated and could not stand it any longer. But she was not about to say that. The time for it might come, but right now she figured it would only cause more trouble than she wanted to deal with. "I don't know exactly what Elton was thinking," she said, choosing her words carefully. "I didn't know he was gon' do it. I lit into him about it when Chief Culpepper brought him home. Anyway, he's done left town, and he ain't gon' be doing it again."

"Is he all right?" Pearl knew Sadie Rose was not about to tell her what she really thought, and there was nothing else to ask.

"He's hurting some but he'll be fine."

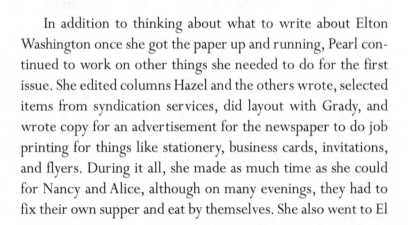

In addition to thinking about what to write about Elton Washington once she got the paper up and running, Pearl continued to work on other things she needed to do for the first issue. She edited columns Hazel and the others wrote, selected items from syndication services, did layout with Grady, and wrote copy for an advertisement for the newspaper to do job printing for things like stationery, business cards, invitations, and flyers. During it all, she made as much time as she could for Nancy and Alice, although on many evenings, they had to fix their own supper and eat by themselves. She also went to El

Dorado to see Wendell at least every other day and was glad he understood why she could not see him more often.

Sadie Rose threw herself into her work as well, but after Elton had been gone for a week, she thought of him every time the mail came. He had promised to send her a postcard when he got to Jackson, and when two weeks dragged by without one, she began to worry. Having no address for him, all she could do was wait.

CHAPTER 12

By Tuesday, April 1, Pearl and the others had almost everything ready to print their first issue, which was not due out until Saturday, and she was feeling good about where things stood. Then, early in the afternoon, Grady came to her desk in the big room wearing a grim look and holding a small metal rod.

"Connecting rod on the receiving fork broke," he said, referring to a set of twelve four-foot-long arms that collected pages coming off the large printing cylinder on the Babcock press. He had been doing test runs on it. "Welding won't fix it and we don't have a spare."

Pearl sagged against the back of her chair. Just when things seemed to be falling into place, she thought. "Can you find one somewhere in a hurry?" she asked.

"I don't know," Grady said. "These things don't usually break, and there's not many of these old presses around anymore. I can call folks I know at a few papers around close and see if anybody's got a dead one we can cannibalize, but it's not likely. The only other thing is to try to get a rod from a parts warehouse in Chicago. Either way, it's gon' take some time."

"Longer than we have to make the print run on Friday?"

"Probably," Grady said, turning the broken part over in his hands as if looking at it again would fix it somehow. "We might be able to get one flown into El Dorado by tomorrow, but it'd cost a bundle. There's bad weather coming this way too. Might affect the flying. Bus wouldn't be fast enough."

"How much?"

"Don't know. Never did it before. Hundred dollars at least, probably more."

The thought of another expense that large took Pearl's breath away. She started to say this was money she could not spare, but that was not something she wanted to share with Grady. "Can we print the paper without using the fork?" she asked.

"Yes, ma'am, but it'd take forever. You'd likely miss your deadline anyway and you'd have some crappy-looking papers. Excuse my language."

"All right," she said. "Make the calls, but if any of your contacts aren't available this afternoon, or they say they'll have to spend a lot of time looking, go ahead and call the warehouse. I don't want to miss the deadline if we can help it."

The next morning Grady found a connecting rod in Chicago. The plane carrying it beat the heavy rain that rolled in on the heels of the afternoon flight, and by Thursday night he had the Babcock up and running. The whole business cost nearly a hundred and seventy-five dollars. Early Friday morning, he, Pearl, Hazel, and Emma Lou were all on hand and prepared to go as late into the evening as necessary to make sure the paper got out the next day. To operate the press, Grady stood on a two-foot-high step-stool that enabled him to look over a five-by-five-foot shelf holding a stack of newsprint above the machine. Each sheet was the width of two printed pages. With fingers that he moistened periodically in a bowl of glycerin mixture, he fed the sheets one at a time onto a large, slightly wider rolling cylinder that turned counter-clockwise beneath the shelf. The cylinder passed the paper over a bed of type that slid underneath each sheet then back again to wait for the next one to come rolling down. On each slide backwards, the type was inked by smaller rollers that drew the black liquid from a tray at the front of the press. Then the bed was ready to slide forward again and print the next page of paper passing above it. The big cylinder fed the printed sheets onto other, much smaller rollers behind it, and these passed the sheets to the collector arms on the back side. The collector arms laid the finished sheets onto a table.

When all the sheets were printed, Grady replaced the first bed of type with a different one for two new pages, moved the first batch of sheets back to the raised platform, and printed the other side of them. Each double run produced four pages of the newspaper. Pearl planned on having eight pages in each issue, so Grady made two double runs. After each of the sheets went through the press the second time, Pearl and Hazel took them off the table and carefully folded them using smooth wooden rods to crease the edges. Next, Emma Lou put each pair of folded, printed sheets together making a completed eight-page newspaper, and rolled each one into the shape of a tube. She then put a hand-written mailing label around each one that was going to the post office for placement in postal boxes or for delivery by rural carrier. Unionville had no in-town home mail delivery and Pearl had no hand-delivery system of her own. Emma Lou left some papers unrolled for sale in racks at Emmett's Café and the barbershop and newsstand.

Pearl expected that next time they could manage without Emma Lou, who had not signed on for this sort of work, but she was a huge help this first time through.

Before each batch run, Grady had printed a test sheet to see if he needed to make any adjustments to the machine. Then he and Pearl had kept an eye on the printed pages as they came out, and she had watched them during the folding. But with everyone working in a frenzy all day, she had not stopped to enjoy looking at a completed paper. When all the copies—several hundred for subscribers, a few dozen for the racks, and some to keep on hand—were ready a little after six o'clock, Pearl thanked everyone for their hard work and saw them off to their homes with souvenir copies. With Grady set to come in and take the completed papers around early the next morning, she locked the front door and sat down at her desk to look over what they had done.

The congratulatory ad from Unionville merchants and other community leaders filled the middle two pages. Across the top, a big three-line headline read, "Welcome Back & Best Wishes to the *Unionville Times*," and underneath it, a five-line message in only slightly smaller type read:

We the undersigned Citizens, Businesses, and Professional Men of Unionville, having the interest of our community at heart and believing in the future of our town, extend wholehearted congratulations to Mrs. Pearl Goodbar and wish for her and the *Unionville Times* every success. We pledge our cooperation in every possible way to help make it a credit to the community.

Two boxes beneath the message carried the names of twenty-four businesses and individuals who had joined together to contribute a sum far greater than what the same amount of space would normally bring for advertising. Flanking the boxes were large ads for City Hardware and Farmers State Bank, indicating the major roles of Neal O'Brien and Horace Bowman in helping make it all happen.

Pearl already knew this content, of course. She had copyedited the message provided by the merchants and helped set the type. But seeing it in the middle of the paper—her paper—brought tears of joy and relief, and at the same time a sense of dread. She had a lot to live up to.

She looked next at her editorial in the upper left portion of the front page, where she expected to have a standing column called "Editor's Corner." Her piece there was titled "Our Intentions" and was short and to the point:

> We are pleased to restore the *Unionville Times* to the service of Unionville and its surrounds under new ownership. For encouragement and support in this effort, we are grateful to the members of the Arkansas-side town council, to the businesses and individuals who sponsored the banner of congratulations in the center of this inaugural issue, and to our advertisers. We are also grateful to our subscribers and readers. This newspaper would not exist without all of you.
>
> We believe an informed populace is essential to community pride, economic growth, and quality living, and to those ends we are dedicated. We

will be Unionville boosters where appropriate and Unionville critics where needed. In both, we pledge truth, honesty, and fairness.

We ask you to share your community news with us in order that we may share it with others to the extent that space permits, and we respectfully call your attention to our advertisement for other community printing services we are prepared to provide.

Pearl Goodbar, Editor

Deciding how to sign the editorial had taken almost as long as writing it. Pearl owned the paper, or at least owned it with Wendell. She managed its business side and decided its editorial policy and therefore was its publisher. But she was also its editor, choosing what to print and writing and editing the content. She liked this role most and chose it to go with her signature. On the masthead of the paper at the top of page three, which carried the paper's address, subscription price, day of publication, and official second-class mail designation, she dispensed with titles and listed only the names of those responsible for getting the paper out every week. They appeared in the order of the importance of their roles as she saw them and read simply, "Staff: Pearl Goodbar, Grady Atwell, Hazel Brantley, Emma Lou MacDonald, Arlan Tucker, Gerald Roberts."

The story everyone had been waiting for about the Elton Washington incident appeared in the upper right corner of the front page under the headline, "Calm Restored Following Disturbance at Eatery."

Decisive action by Arkansas-side police chief Jesse Culpepper restored calm following fisticuffs in uptown Unionville on March 21. When Elton Washington, a non-resident Negro, entered Emmett's Café shortly before noon, patrons forcibly removed him from the premises. He was struck several times and received lacerations and bruises. Chief Culpepper took him into custody and dispersed a crowd gathered at the scene. No charges were filed, and Washington has left the area.

Pearl knew there was more to it than this. She did not like what Elton Washington had done, but she also did not like how he was treated or the heated talk she had heard. He was gone, however, and she hoped people would let the matter drop.

⌒

On Saturday morning, Pearl could hardly wait to show the first issue of the newspaper to Nancy, Alice, and Wendell. She wanted all of them to see it at the same time, and she and the girls left home as soon as they cleared the breakfast dishes. Even though there was still some rain around, this was a day to celebrate, and they dressed like they were heading to church. When they got to the hospital, Pearl handed each of the girls and Wendell a copy.

"It looks great," Wendell said. He was feeling better these days and grinned broadly as he flipped through the pages. "I see you've got C. G. Hall's 'Arkansas Capitol News.' That's good. He just gives the facts and doesn't waste words." Wendell turned another page. "And you've got the 'International Sunday School Lesson' too. Preacher will like that."

"Yeah, I hope so," Pearl said, looking over his shoulder. There are some other good ones too. Etta Haley's 'Woman's World' and Kathleen Norris's literary column are on the next page over."

Wendell turned the pages. "Yeah, I see them."

"Wow, Momma," Alice said. "I didn't know you were gon' have comics. *Mutt and Jeff*'s my favorite. I like *Jitter* too."

"Where'd you get all these national ads?" Nancy asked. "I see Clabber Girl Baking Powder and Van Camp's Pork and Beans. And here's St. Joseph Aspirin and Prince Albert Tobacco. And that stinky Ben-Gay stuff. How'd you get them?"

"They're from advertising agencies," Pearl said. "Same as a lot of the classifieds. If you look, you'll see ads in there for jobs in Tennessee, woodworking patterns from Wisconsin, oil heater parts from Missouri, and lots of other stuff like that. I don't think anyone around here's gon' be interested in any of it, but I surely don't mind selling the space to let them know about it."

"I like seeing all these El Dorado ads," Wendell said, "specially that big one from Arkansas Power & Light. I'm really proud for you, honey, and I've got a thought. When I get home next week, how about I start helping you with some of this? I can make phone calls and help with the books and stuff. If this keeps up, we're probably gon' be all right with money."

"Well," Pearl said, "you better take a good look at everything before you get too excited."

CHAPTER 13

While Pearl Goodbar was considering what to write about Elton Washington, and his mother was waiting for him to send her a postcard from Mississippi, he was in Monroe, Louisiana. A city of some 50,000, it was the first major Greyhound stop east of Ruston, where Sadie Rose had said goodbye to him. As his bus had rolled through North Louisiana hill country that Saturday morning on US 80 heading toward the Delta, Elton could not stop thinking about Priscilla Nobles, the way Herbert Kramer treated her and her grandparents, and the beating he, Elton, took in the café' and on the street in Unionville. When the Greyhound crossed the Ouachita River and pulled into the station in Monroe, he got off with his duffle bag.

Elton did not know where anything was in Monroe, but he knew that strange black men in the South caused suspicion that could lead to harassment or worse and he needed to be careful. He was not unprepared, however. He fished into his duffle bag for a year-old copy of *The Negro Traveler's Green Book*, an annual guide to the few places where blacks could find food and accommodations in southern cities, and he found the address of a hotel on Desiard Street. Now all he needed was to find out exactly where that was. He had enough street smarts from his years in Chicago to get a quick sense of how to get around and whom he could talk to for directions. He picked an older black man who was wearing a suit, hat, and no tie and was carrying a small suitcase and standing off to one side smoking a cigarette. Elton did not smoke, but he walked over, set his duffle bag down, brushed off the front of his jacket, and said, "Whew! Man, I'm glad to be off that bus."

"Long trip?" the fellow asked, giving Elton a quick glance before taking another draw on his cigarette.

"Yeah," Elton said. Then, "That cigarette sure smells good. I smoked my last one in Ruston."

The smoker reached in his pocket, pulled out an open pack of Camels, shook it to make a cigarette pop up, and extended the package.

"Thanks, man," Elton said. He took the Camel, held one end against the hot ashes on the fellow's smoke, caught a light, and in a few minutes was on his way to Nunley's Hotel, which lay ten blocks east of the river and seven blocks south of the highway. It was a brick building situated among several other black-owned businesses on the edge of a residential neighborhood that covered several blocks. The area appeared likely to have everything he was looking for.

Elton took a second-floor room for a week with the understanding that he could stay longer if he decided to. It had a pull-chain overhead light, a single bed with a lone pillow, a low chest-of-drawers, and a window overlooking an alley. A shared bathroom stood at the end of the hall. He set his duffle bag on the bed, put his spare clothes in the chest-of-drawers, and emptied the remaining contents onto the bed. A folded brown towel tumbled out last. He spread it out and removed a roll of bills, the pearl-handled knife Sadie Rose had taken from Jewell Vines, and a loaded snub-nose .38 Smith & Wesson he

carried when running numbers part time in Chicago. He had
taken a huge risk traveling from the Windy City with a gun
and an even bigger one traveling across Louisiana with two
weapons, but he had gotten away with it. He also knew he
had behaved especially recklessly on the last two legs of his
bus trip to Unionville and been lucky both times, and he did
not plan to make any such mistakes in Monroe. He pulled the
bed away from the wall, used the knife to cut a slit in the back
of the mattress, slipped both weapons inside, and put everything back in place. The bills he put in his pocket. He had more
money than he had let on to his mother, and like the weapons,
he had not wanted it on his person when he was traveling. He
figured any cops who stopped and frisked him along the way
would think he stole it, toss him in jail on suspicion, and keep
it even if they ended up letting him go. He expected he would
see cops here, too, but he needed the money with him for
what he had in mind, plus he thought leaving it in the room
was a bigger risk than carrying it around.

He went downstairs, talked to the desk clerk, and learned
there was a café around the corner, a pool hall in the next
block, and another one three blocks south and two blocks east.
This was better than he had hoped. His new plans required
more money, and he expected to get it in his usual way. When
he started out the door, the man called him back and warned
him to watch out for gang members. He explained that half a
dozen gangs had started up in the last year, and a bunch calling
themselves the Untouchables sometimes prowled this neighborhood. You could recognize them, he said, by the white
jackets a lot of them wore. Elton mumbled thanks, said he
had forgotten something, and went back upstairs and got the
switchblade.

The café was small, clean, and inexpensive, and after a supper of red beans, rice, and gravy, Elton walked down the street to Elmore's Billiard Parlor. It did not have any tables for billiards, a game played with only three balls and no pockets, but it had three pool tables, a sizeable bar, and lots of guys shooting eight ball. Elton sat at the bar, nursed a beer, and watched the tables. After a while, he asked to play with a couple of men, shot a few games, and lost as many as he won. He left after only an hour, intent on returning the next evening, even though the bar would be closed because selling liquor was against the law in Monroe on Sundays. He hoped there would still be players even with the liquor locked up. In any case, he did not see any white jackets all evening and that was good.

Elton planned to follow a similar routine every day, assuming that the other pool hall, named simply "Joe's Bar," worked out as well as this first place. He would go every afternoon to one and every evening to the other, start to look like a regular, win only a little more than he lost at first, make it seem like he was getting better with practice, gradually up his game, and let others ask him to play for higher stakes. He planned to win only as much as he needed to pay for his time in Monroe plus a couple hundred dollars more, maybe three if his luck held.

By near the end of the week, Elton saw this would take a few more days, and he made the necessary arrangements at the hotel. He was confident, though, that he would end up with enough money to buy a vehicle, and on Friday morning, March 28, he started looking. Having kept his ears open and asked a few well-placed questions, he had already learned about two black-owned garages that were nearby and were said usually to have a few used vehicles for sale. He believed he would attract less attention at these than at a traditional used-car lot and also save money. When he went to the garages, however, he found the pickings slim and the prices no better than listings he had seen for similar vehicles in the *Monroe Morning World*.

Both garage owners told him they might have other cars after the weekend, so Elton spent the rest of the day and the weekend adding to his stash, then went back to both places on Monday. Because he wanted something that was reliable insofar as he could tell and did not look flashy, he settled on a nine-year-old light-green International Harvester pickup that had decent tires and an engine that sounded okay. It cost three hundred twenty-five dollars. All he had to do to drive it away with temporary tags was show his driver's license and pay the money. He could complete the registration by mail anytime within the next sixty days.

Elton intended to shoot pool the rest of Monday and all day Tuesday and leave town Wednesday afternoon. He arranged to keep the truck at the garage until then. All his stay here, he had been cautious. In order to reduce the chance of running into gang members, he ate all of his meals at the same little café around the corner and went only to the pool halls. Before Tuesday evening he never saw any gangs and was beginning to doubt that they ranged this far north toward Desiard. However, this time when he left the café after supper, several Untouchables were milling about on the corner a few doors east of the hotel entrance. Instead of taking his usual route back past the hotel to Joe's Bar, he headed in the opposite direction, took the first street to his left, went south several blocks, then cut over east. A block from Joe's, he saw more Untouchables. They were standing out front of the bar smoking, gesturing, and looking up and down the street. He wondered if they had gotten wind of a new face in town and planned to rob him. He

ducked into an alley and started trying to pick his way back
to the hotel and find a rear entrance. He got only a little way
before bumping into a pile of garbage cans, scraping his shins,
and raising a racket. Someone's dog started barking and he
heard what sounded like gunshots and people running. Unsure
where he was, he hid as well as he could behind the cans,
took out his switchblade, and waited. Then he heard footsteps
moving in the opposite direction and, a minute or two later,
police sirens. He thought the gang members must have been
on the lookout for someone else, but to be safe, he stayed put
until long after quiet returned. When it did, he hurried to the
hotel, found the back door, climbed the stairs to his room, and
started packing his things.

Elton left for Unionville early Wednesday afternoon wearing old jeans and his denim jacket and driving west on US 80.
A bank of storm clouds loomed ahead of him, but he had a
full tank of gas and a paper bag with a ham sandwich he had
bought at the café. He also had four uncooked pork chops he
had stolen from the café kitchen and wrapped in pages from
the *Monroe MorningWorld*. He had managed to sneak to the back
and grab the meat while the cook was taking out trash and the
owner was busy near the front door making a pass at a woman
who seemed to welcome his attention. Most of Elton's little
remaining money, his knife, and his gun were stowed in the
bottom of his duffle bag on the floor of the passenger side.

Being careful to stay under the speed limit, he crossed
the Ouachita River into West Monroe and drove through the
small towns of Calhoun and Choudrant. When he reached
Ruston, he turned north on US 167. By this time a steady

rain had set in, and he took his time going through two more small towns—Dubach and Bernice—and two bayous where water-filled bar-pits lined the narrow highway. He reached the outskirts of Unionville shortly after dusk gave way to night. While at Sadie Rose's earlier, he had never gone far from her place except the day he arrived in town and the day before he left, but he remembered the black sections on both sides from when he was a kid, and as soon as he could, he turned east on the Louisiana side and then north again to avoid the Unionville business district. He crossed into the Arkansas side and continued several more blocks north, turned back west across US 167, and found Newton Chapel Road.

Elton did not remember ever going very far on Newton Chapel Road, but he counted on spotting the big sign his mother said Kramer had at the entrance to his farm. Several miles out, he noticed a white frame church on his left, but with worn wiper blades struggling to beat back the rain, he missed the farm sign. When he thought he might have gone too far, he turned around where another road branched off to parts unknown. Coming back, his headlights caught "Kramer Farm" spelled out in a large wrought-iron banner on his right. From ends that rested on tall brick pillars, the sign extended over an access road that appeared to go straight for a hundred yards or more before bending out of sight to the right. He turned under the sign, cut his lights, and stopped to give his eyes time to adjust to the dark.

Elton had been thinking about this moment for days, but other than bringing raw meat to attract the attention of any dogs, he still did not have much of a plan for how to do what he came for. Which was to kill Herbert Kramer. He had, however, carefully weighed getting rid of one white racist alone,

and freeing three people right now, against joining a whole
bunch of other black folks, and trying to change things for
everyone a little at a time. Making something happen immediately had won out.

Kramer's access road proved long and winding beyond
the first bend, and after several minutes of moving slowly but
steadily, Elton still could not see any lights down it. Fearing discovery if he kept driving, he began looking for a place to hide the
truck. When he came even with a stand of trees and bushes off
to his left, he pulled into them as far as he could. He killed the
engine, fished the knife and gun out of his duffle bag, unwrapped
the pork chops, and put them and the knife in his jacket pockets.
With gun in hand, he slid out the driver's door, left it unlatched
to avoid making noise, and started walking through the rain.

Elton smelled the dairy operation before he saw it and
wondered how anyone could live near it. He thought for a
moment if there were any dogs around, they would not be
able to smell him for the stench of cow manure, but soon he
heard barking and two hounds came running toward him.
Before now, he had not been afraid, but bile came up in his
mouth, and he almost dropped his gun as he hurried to get
out two of the pork chops. He tossed them onto the ground in
front of him and resisted the temptation to turn and run. The
dogs stopped, gobbled the meat, and walked up to him with
tails wagging, tongues hanging out, and noses twitching at the
smell of the two chops still in his jacket. Wishing he had either
brought more or not eaten his sandwich on the drive from
Monroe, he walked on slowly, afraid that hurrying would start
the dogs barking again. His two new pals followed.

After what seemed like half an hour but was only a few
minutes, Elton came around a bend, and light from two

fixtures mounted on poles revealed a darkened, two-story white house and a detached garage some distance ahead, a large unpainted barn a hundred feet or more off to the left, a small white building on the right not far from the house, several covered sheds of different shapes and sizes, and half a dozen tractors and other pieces of equipment scattered about. Squatting in the sparse cover of a large corner fence post with blackberry vines clinging to it, he saw Kramer's pickup parked near the small white building. Lights shown from its windows, suggesting someone was likely inside.

The thought of that brought up another batch of bile. Elton choked it down and wondered if he had allowed enough time for Kramer to take Priscilla home after her work was done and get back to the farm. Maybe she was still here, possibly inside somewhere with him now. If so, then Elton would either have to shoot Kramer in front of Priscilla or wait for them to leave and for Kramer to return alone. That would risk Kramer's seeing the International Harvester on his way to town or back. Or maybe, there being no car in sight, Kramer was at this very moment using it to take Priscilla home. In that case, he might spot Elton's truck on the return trip.

Given what Elton knew of the man, he calculated that if Kramer were currently on the road somewhere and did see the International Harvester in the trees coming home, he would not go back to Unionville for the authorities. He would drive on into the farm and investigate himself. So, Elton could hide, wait for him, and shoot him when he got out of his vehicle. But what if Kramer had not left for town or had already been there and come back? If that were the case, Elton wondered, would he more likely be in the little white building with the lights, or in the darkened house farther on? Or maybe in the barn or one of the sheds? If he were in the house or in the little white building, hours might pass before he came out, and meanwhile, the dogs might get restless and start barking again. Also, there might be other dogs on the property and, if so, they would likely come around before long. Because there were no lights in the barn or any other outbuilding, Elton decided that if Kramer were here, he must be either in the little white building or in the house. The former, being lit and closer, seemed the logical place to look first.

Gambling that there were no other dogs, Elton took out the two remaining pork chops and tossed them to the hounds, now lying on the ground near him. Soaked and shivering, he began inching toward the smaller structure, keeping low and in the shadows as much as possible and counting on the sound of rain on the roof to prevent Kramer from hearing him. When Elton reached the building, he chanced raising up enough to glance inside, and he saw the big dairy farmer sitting at a desk facing away. He was wearing overalls, a plaid work shirt, and rubber boots. It would be easy enough to aim through the window, Elton thought, but it was not a close-up shot, and if he missed and Kramer had a gun anywhere about, this might not turn out well. Unable to think of a better option, Elton eased around to the front. He would knock on the door and, when Kramer opened it, empty the pistol at him. Elton did not see how he could miss pointblank this way, even if Kramer did not pull the door back fully, or even if he managed somehow to push it closed. One or more shots were bound to penetrate the door and find the target.

As soon as Elton stepped onto the small porch, things started going wrong. A third dog, way off somewhere, possibly in the house, started barking in a yipping, high-pitched tone that carried across the farmyard. Elton froze, his mind working, his body not. If he ran, he would not be able to kill the son of a bitch he was hunting; if he stood his ground, he might. Seconds ticked by like minutes. Then, as he reached with his free hand to knock, the door flew open, and there stood Kramer with a shotgun. "Well, look who's here," he said, grinning. Then he shot Elton in the chest.

The blast knocked Elton off the porch and he was dead when his back hit the ground. "You black bastard," Kramer said. He stepped down in front of his victim, raised the .12-gauge, and shot Elton twice more, once in the face and once in the groin.

A light went on in the house, the front door opened, and a slight, dark-haired woman looked out through the screen. "Go back inside, Lorraine," Kramer shouted. "This don't concern you." He knew his wife saw the body but he also knew she would not say anything about it—to him or to anyone else, ever.

⌒

Kramer had already been to town once this evening, driving Priscilla, and sometime after midnight he pulled back onto Newton Chapel Road, this time driving Elton's truck to the town dump.

The vehicle had not been hard to find. For a while, Kramer had thought about calling the sheriff then decided against it. The killing was clearly self-defense, but either the head shot or the chest shot would have been enough to do the job, and the other of those and especially the shot to Elton's genitals would likely lead to questions and possibly even raise some hackles. Kramer did not much care about ticking a few people off, but what he could not chance was someone putting Elton with Priscilla Nobles, then nosing around, finding out, and telling what he, Kramer, had been doing to her, or how he was connected to her in the first place. He did not think anyone would prosecute him for any of that. After all, she was black. But that was also why it might cost him at least some of his standing in the community, and maybe even hurt his business. For the same reasons, he could not risk burying the body on the farm somewhere, or being seen trying to get rid of it someplace else without having a way to mask what he was doing and avoid other scrutiny.

Kramer calculated that Elton had come out to the farm on his own. Sadie Rose was too smart to have driven him, and no one else would have dared even to think about doing it. Before going to look for whatever Elton was driving, Kramer put away his shotgun to clean and reload later, picked up Elton's pistol, and went through his pockets and took out his knife and wallet. He then parked a large tractor near the body to keep anyone who might come up the access road from seeing it before he could move it. He had two hired men living on his property a few miles farther out Newton Chapel Road, but he doubted the sound of the gunshots would have carried that far. And if they had, the men would likely have thought he was shooting at a varmint of some kind. Kramer did not cover the body because it was bleeding all over the ground, and he wanted the rain to help the blood soak in. If it did not, he would do something about that later. All the while, Lorraine stood in a dark upstairs bedroom watching behind slightly parted window curtains.

When Kramer located Elton's truck, he drove it up to his office building and rifled through Elton's duffle bag. Then he went to the dairy barn, brought back a piece of canvas, rolled the body up in it, and using a forklift on a second tractor, hoisted it into the back of the International Harvester. After that, he drove the truck over to what he regarded as his junk shed, hid the duffle bag behind a pile of boards, and threw a bunch of old tires, bails of rusty wire, odd lengths of used pipe, and near-empty paint cans over the canvas-covered body. All of it was stuff anyone might haul to the dump.

Although Kramer doubted that anyone he knew would see him at this hour, let alone stop him, he hosed off his boots and the floorboard of the truck before leaving. If anyone asked him tonight about his driving the International Harvester, he would tell them he had bought it to fix up, never mind that he would never do it. And if anyone asked him later about having seen him in it, he would say they must be mistaken. If anyone asked him about hauling stuff to the dump at night in the rain, he would tell them his cows did not give him enough time off from tending them in the daytime and they did not care whether it was raining or not. It was thin but he believed it would work. In any case, this all seemed better than anything else he could think of. Besides, he did not reckon anyone would be at the dump on a night like this, or that after the body was discovered, anyone would waste much time trying to find out who killed a black man.

Rain was still coming down hard when Kramer got to the dump, and he worried about getting stuck in the middle of it, but it was too late to turn back. He found a spot way in back, tossed the tires, wire, and other stuff out, then drove a bit farther, stopped again, put down the tailgate, and rolled out the canvas. Because Kramer had not taken time to bind up the canvas, Elton's body slid out of it and landed face up. To leave open the possibility that the authorities might think Elton had been shot at the dump, Kramer gathered up the canvas and hefted it back into the truck bed.

As far as he could tell, he got back to his farm without being seen. He stopped at the shed where he had hid the duffle bag, slid the canvas out of the truck bed, and loaded a dozen concrete blocks, several rusty tire rims, and more lengths of rusty pipe into it. After tossing in a heavy chain and some rope, he drove over to the forklift tractor, pulled up behind it, and hitched the two vehicles together with the chain. Then he removed the temporary paper license tag from the truck and tied down the steering wheel with the rope. That done, he used the tractor to pull the truck around the dairy barn, down a rutted service road, and onto the wide earthen dam of his fishpond. Kramer had dug the pond himself with a rented bulldozer. It was arguably the largest in the county, more than fifteen feet deep at the big end, was fed by a spring, and thus far had stayed full year round. After unhooking the tractor, he turned it around on top of the dam, and used the forklift to shove the truck down the steep incline and into the water, where it disappeared within seconds. Kramer did not allow any swimming in the pond, and with his only kid off in the navy somewhere, only he fished it. No one, not even his hired men, even knew he had stocked it. He was confident, therefore, that the truck would not be found if he continued to maintain the dam. If someone did find it years later, he would not be around to care.

Once the rain stopped, he would repair the gouges he made in the dam, smooth over any suspicious tracks not washed away, find some gravel to put over the dirt in front of his office, and burn the canvas, duffle bag, temporary tag, and Elton's wallet with other trash. No one except Lorraine would ever know that Elton Washington had been here, and Kramer was not worried about her telling it. In the meantime, he could not have been happier that the man he considered nothing but a no-good uppity bastard had come after him.

CHAPTER 14

At church on Easter Sunday and at the post office on Monday, people congratulated Pearl and told her how happy they were to see the *Unionville Times* up and running again and how much they liked what she had done with it. Arkansas-side mayor Alan Poindexter, council president Neal O'Brien, and Louisiana-side mayor Eddie Dunn each stopped by to see her and wish her continued success. Bailey's Floral Shop sent over a green plant for the office.

Hazel was still beaming about people at church saying they had seen her name on the masthead, and Emma Lou, who had been out of town visiting over the weekend, called and reported that several friends had phoned to thank her for her date nut cake recipe. Arlan Tucker called, too, and said he had heard good things about his story on training squirrel dogs. Even Grady was in a talkative mood. As soon as he came in, he asked Pearl how her family liked the paper.

By mid-morning, Pearl was at her desk working on her second cup of coffee and one of the chocolate chip cookies she had brought in, when they heard tires squealing in the street and a horn blaring. Pearl and Hazel went to the front windows expecting to see a near accident, but all they saw was Crow Hicks's old gray truck sitting catawampus on the curb, apparently having narrowly missed Jesse Culpepper's police car parked in front of the town hall. Black skid marks trailed behind the crosswise vehicle, and it was so mud-splattered that even Crow's crudely painted Rebel flag on the tail gate was obscured. Crow let off his horn and started climbing out when Jesse came running out of the building. Pearl did not know if all the fuss was anything important or only Crow drunk or just plain acting strange, as he often did. But she grabbed her Blue Horse pad and pencil and hurried over anyway, her mind racing through possibilities while thinking how convenient it was to have an office across from the town hall.

"I found a dead nigger! I found a dead nigger!" Crow was shouting. Other people had heard the racket, too, and were coming out of Emmett's Café and the Ford place and the two nearby gas stations and gathering around.

Jesse grabbed Crow, pulled him inside the building, went back out alone, and said, "All right, y'all go on now. There ain't nothing to see. Crow's probably drunk or all mixed up about something. I'll take care of it." He waited a moment then said again, "Go on now."

Having gotten to the town hall ahead of most of the others, Pearl was at the front of the crowd, and when Jesse started back inside, she pushed in behind him, saying, "Wait for the press."

He locked the door to keep the others out and was about to tell her she would have to leave, too, when Crow started jabbering in his high-pitched voice, "Ain't nothing left. Ain't nothing left." Pearl could not discern if he was upset about what he was telling or happy about it. He kept running a bony hand across his face, and she thought he might be trying to hide a grin.

"All right," Jesse said. "Settle down and take it slow. What're you talking about?" All three of them were still standing. Pearl flipped open her Blue Horse pad, ready to make notes.

"I done found a dead nigger," Crow said, passing his hand across his face again. "He's plum blowed to pieces."

"Where?" Jesse asked. "Where'd you find him?"

"Out at the dump," Crow said. "He's out at the dump." On certain days Crow hauled garbage to the town trash heap. The Arkansas-side council had set him to that after removing him as night watchman. They figured this was one job he could not mess up and everyone would be better off if he had something to do occasionally.

"Who is it?" Jesse asked.

"I don't know. He ain't got no face. You got to see it, man. You got to see it. He ain't got no face." He ran his hand across his own face again while Pearl scribbled in her notebook.

"Was there anyone with you? Did anyone else see him?" Jesse asked.

"I don't know. I didn't see nobody else."

"Did you move the body? Did you touch it?"

"Nah. Come on, man. You gotta go out there."

"All right," Jesse said, "but you're coming with me. I have to call the sheriff's office over at Farmerville first, though. And if you're making this up, your ass is gon' end up in jail."

"It's the truth, I swear."

"Sit down," Jesse said. He pushed a chair toward Crow and turned to Pearl. "Mrs. Goodbar, I'm afraid you're gon' have to leave now. If he's right, this is gon' be a formal police matter, and I'll fill you in when I get something we can share with the public."

"With all due respect, chief," Pearl said, "I'm not going anywhere except with you out to the dump." Startled by her pushback, Jesse started to tell her she was not, but she spoke again first. "You know very well that as soon as Crow gets a chance, he's gon' talk to everyone who'll listen—unless you lock him up, and you don't have any legal reason to do that. So, people are gon' hear about it whether I go with you or not. I promise I won't print anything that I don't run by you first. Besides, it's four days till the next paper comes out."

"Okay, you have a point," Jesse said. "But I can't say the sheriff's boys won't make you leave when they get there."

"I guess they can try, can't they?"

With Crow still seated, arms now folded across his bib overalls, Jesse called the Tonti Parish sheriff's office. Like the way that part of Unionville sat in Arkansas and part in Louisiana, a portion of the Louisiana side sat in Tonti Parish and a portion in Claiborne Parish, with US 167 as the dividing line. The entire community shared the garbage dump, which lay about three miles southeast in Tonti Parish. Any crime committed there was out of Jesse's jurisdiction. When someone finally came on the phone, Jessie asked to speak to Sheriff Harvey Overstreet directly. The sheriff had been in office for years, thanks to a well-honed knack for back-slapping during elections and avoiding attention at other times, and he did not like anything that might cause a stink. Overstreet was not in, so Jesse settled for the dispatcher, told him he had a report of a body, and gave the location. The man said they had a deputy on the road somewhere south of Unionville who could probably get to the dump in about thirty minutes and Jesse should meet him there and bring whoever reported the matter. Pearl heard both ends of the conversation.

"What are you gon' do about them?" Pearl asked, motioning toward the door and a few die-hards still standing around outside.

Jesse ran a hand through his thick red hair then walked over and looked through a window blind. "First, I'm gon' get Crow's truck off the curb before somebody runs into it. Then I'm gon' stretch the truth a little and see if I can get folks to go back to whatever they were doing. But I'm gon' need your help." He explained what he had in mind, and when Pearl agreed, he told Crow to stay put then went out front and said, "Y'all go on now, like I told you. Crow's a little mixed up this morning. Y'all know how he is. Looks like he might've got a nip of hooch somewhere. I'm gon' hold onto him for a spell."

People walked away shaking their heads and laughing. Jesse moved Crow's truck, took the keys, and came back inside. "If he's right," Jesse said, pointing to Crow, "I reckon they're gon' be pretty put out with me. But better that than let them mess up a crime scene."

With Jesse having called ahead, Mr. Claude was standing on his porch when Pearl stopped in front of his house. He was wearing his usual khaki pants, black hat, and black suit coat. They exchanged a quick hello when he got in the car, and Pearl headed east for the Rock Island depot, where the railroad crossed State Line Road. "Jesse said to wait in the parking lot till we see him pass and then follow him," Pearl explained.

"That was a slick trick," Mr. Claude said, as they drove, "him making people think Crow was drunk then sneaking him out the back and not letting anybody see us all together. Some folks are gon' be mad when they find out, though. That is, if there really is a body."

"Yes," Pearl said. "I've seen Jesse in action twice now, and I think he's pretty smart."

"Yeah, me too," Mr. Claude said.

They reached the depot and sat talking about the newspaper until they saw Jesse go by with Crow in the back seat. Then Pearl fell in behind. As they turned off State Line Road and onto the dirt track leading to the dump, Pearl looked into her rearview mirror and saw a sheriff's car coming fast a quarter mile back. After a couple of hundred feet, Jesse maneuvered into a makeshift turn-around created over the years by hormone-charged teenagers pulling off the dump road onto an old logging path on dark nights. He got out and waved Pearl down, and she rolled in behind him and put down her window.

"You better ride in with me," Jesse said, walking up. "It's gon' be real muddy back there and you don't have the tires for it. If you don't mind, we can use your car to block the road—just in case somebody saw me leave town with Crow and comes nosing around."

"It's all right with me," Pearl said, getting out, "long as I don't have to stay with it."

Mr. Claude got out, too, and they waited for the deputy to roll up. He came to a stop, climbed out, and said, "I'm Deputy Quinn. What've you got here?" He was a tall, red-faced man pushing sixty, with his belly hanging over a brown gun belt that matched the pocket flaps on his khaki uniform. Jesse told him what Crow had said and introduced Mr. Claude and Pearl. "I remember Mr. Claude, but what's she doing here?" Quinn asked, staring at Pearl.

"She's with me," Jesse said. "She helped us get out here without a bunch of folks following."

"Aw, all right, but keep her the hell out of the way," Quinn said, as if Pearl could not hear him. "Let's get on up there and see what we've got."

Jesse explained his idea about blocking the road, and they moved Pearl's car and headed for the dump. She and Crow rode with Jesse in the lead and Quinn followed and brought Mr. Claude. The dump was an old corn field of twenty-plus acres surrounded by a barbed wire fence thrown up in slap-dash fashion to mark the public property line. It was flanked on two sides by a thick hardwood forest and on the other two by random patches of pine trees and thick underbrush. The unpaved access road ran all the way around the inside edge of the dump, and two other dirt roads crisscrossed it, dividing it roughly into quarters. In every section, household garbage, yard trash, and junk sat decaying in haphazard piles that ranged from a few feet around to mounds the size of small house trailers. Pearl could see stoves and refrigerators, lawn mowers and automobile tires, cardboard boxes and bundles of old newspapers, sofas and chairs, worn-out carpets and old clothing, and grocery containers of all sizes and descriptions. A sulfur-like stench hung in the air and mud covered every bare patch.

Crow showed where to stop the cars, and when every-one started getting out, Pearl sank to her ankles in black slush and almost dropped her notebook and pencil. "Damn!" she blurted without thinking, and the men looked at her in sur-prise. "Well, I ruined my shoes," she said, thankful that at least they were tight enough not to come off. Crow led the officers and Pearl between two large mounds, and despite the stink of everything else, they smelled what they were looking for before they saw it, several feet from the road.

"Holy shit!" Jesse said. A bloated human form lay sprawled in the mud with arms flung out to its sides, most of its face missing, and jagged holes the size of volleyballs in its chest and groin. Maggots were crawling in the openings, stark white against rotting flesh in various shades of black, brown, gray, and green. Whatever clothing the person had been wearing and was still there was soaked with rain and body fluid and had turned similar colors.

Pearl barely got her head turned before vomiting, and when she looked around again, Jesse was throwing up too.

"Looks like it's been here three or four days," Quinn said. "Take that long to bloat up like that. The maggots ain't that far along, but that's probably because of all the rain we had." Pearl noticed that he did not seem at all bothered by what he was seeing.

"What makes you think this is a Negro?" Mr. Claude asked Crow.

"Just look at him. What's left anyway. He's black."

"That happens to all bodies left out like this," Mr. Claude said.

"What about his hair? Looks like nigger hair to me."

"I don't know. Doesn't appear he had much. Anyway, it's hard to tell for all the mud and stuff in it."

"Well," Quinn said, looking around, "we've for sure got us a crime scene here. Or what's left of one. Whatever happened to him, he didn't get like this by hisself. Problem is the rain's washed away any useful sign of anybody else being here. There ain't no clear tracks except what us and your man there made. What'd y'all say his name is?"

"It's Waylon Hicks," Jesse said. "Folks call him 'Crow.' How do you want to proceed here? Mr. Claude and I'll be glad to help however we can."

"I'm gon' get on the radio and let the sheriff know and get the coroner up here. And we're gon' need a statement from Mr. Hicks. Let me call in, then I'll talk to him while we're waiting." Until then, Quinn had not noticed that Pearl had been taking notes. "This is an active investigation, Mrs. Goodbar," he said. "You can't print anything about it till the sheriff says it's okay."

"Oh, yes, I could," Pearl said, closing her notebook, "but we don't go to press till Friday, and I've already told Jesse I'll let him comment on any story before we run it. Meanwhile, I want to know who this person is as soon as you find out and can tell it."

CHAPTER 15

Because the coroner would likely take the rest of the day to arrive, examine the scene, and remove the body, Pearl got Deputy Quinn to promise her an official statement as soon as his office could give one. Then she asked Jesse to take her to her car so she could go clean up and get back to her office. He said okay and told Quinn he would keep the access road blocked until the coroner and the sheriff or other deputies came. Quinn and Mr. Claude stayed with Crow and the body. As Jesse drove Pearl to her car, she told him how she thought Crow looked like he was grinning when he talked about the body. Jesse said he noticed it, too, but it was most likely nothing but nervous excitement.

"You're probably right," Pearl said, "but I was thinking, seeing how he thought the body was a Negro, he might've been grinning because he liked the idea of it."

"Could be, I suppose," Jesse said. "Depending on what the coroner says, and how much Sheriff Overstreet lets me be involved, I'll keep that in mind. Since the Louisiana side doesn't have a marshal or anything, they might want me to help, unofficial like."

Pearl asked him to keep her posted on anything he learned and could share, and he promised he would.

As usual, when Pearl got back to the office after being gone a long time, Hazel wanted to know what had happened.

Unsure how the Tonti Parish authorities would proceed, Pearl repeated what Jesse Culpepper told the crowd outside the town hall and said she had gone home because her feet were giving her trouble and she needed to put on some different shoes.

⁓

Late in the afternoon, Jesse took Mr. Claude home and returned to the town hall. To avoid raising questions by being seen going to the newspaper office, and also to keep from risking someone other than Pearl hearing what he had to say, Jesse called her on the phone. He told her the coroner, a Farmerville doctor named Nolan Ruggleman, had examined the scene and taken custody of the body for an autopsy. The sheriff's office was holding Crow overnight for further questioning, and Jesse planned to go on letting folks think he was in jail in Unionville. That would keep rumors from flying for at least a little while. Jesse said he did not know when the sheriff's office would have a statement, and he asked Pearl to keep all of this to herself for now. After hanging up, he got in touch with mayor Poindexter and council president O'Brien and told them what was going on.

⁓

Deputy Quinn called Jesse from Farmerville Tuesday morning and said they had not gotten anything more out of Crow Hicks. The coroner and the sheriff's office hoped to have a joint statement ready by mid-afternoon, and they expected to release Crow then and bring him back to Unionville. Jesse phoned Pearl to let her know.

Quinn called her around two o'clock and read the statement to her: "Deputy Sheriff Bud Quinn and Tonti Parish

Coroner Nolan Ruggleman responded to the discovery of an unidentified body at the Unionville, Louisiana, town dump on Monday morning. An autopsy is being performed, and further information will be forthcoming."

"That's all?" Pearl asked.

"Yes and no," Quinn said. "We know it's a homicide and the victim's a male, but we still don't know if he's a white man or colored, and we can't say any of that till Dr. Ruggleman files an official report. He has to hold a coroner's inquest first. It's state law for any suspicious death."

"How long do you think that's gon' take?"

"Couple of days probably."

"Why can't the coroner determine if he's white or black?" Pearl asked.

"I already told you too much, "Quinn said. "You're just gon' have to wait."

"You know what Mr. Hicks is gon' tell everybody, don't you?"

"Yeah," Quinn said, "but there ain't nothing we can do about that."

Around the same time Pearl was on the phone with Deputy Quinn, another member of the Tonti Parish sheriff's department was bringing Crow Hicks back to Unionville, and shortly before four o'clock, he walked out of the Arkansas-side town hall and straight across the street to Emmett's Café.

Looking and smelling even more than usual like a man not on good terms with soap, water, or razor, Crow walked in the front door feeling half a foot taller because he knew he was about to be the center of attention. "Hey, Emmett," he said loudly, making sure all the handful of customers heard, "Gimme a cup of that there high-test coffee! I found a dead nigger!" As everyone turned to look at him, he took a seat at the counter.

Boomer Jenkins, who moments before had brought Emmett a mess of fish, got up from a corner booth, walked over, and sat next to him. "You did what?" Boomer asked.

"I found a dead nigger," Crow repeated. "You ought to seen it. Somebody near about blowed his head off."

"Yeah?" Boomer asked, folding his arms across his chest and looking around the room, like maybe he was ready to take credit for it, if only in present company. "Now, who would've gon' and done something like that?"

Emmett came over empty-handed, wiping his fingers on his dirty apron. "We heard you yelling about that outside yesterday," he said to Crow. "We thought you was drunk."

"I wasn't drunk," Crow said, "but I'm gon' be. Goddamn deputies had me in jail all night just 'cause I found the son of a bitch. Get me my damn coffee."

With Emmett's special blend finally in hand and the other customers huddling around, Crow told everything he had seen. By Wednesday morning, everyone in Unionville had heard a version of Crow's story, and all were speculating about who the dead man was. Almost everyone thought it was grisly business, but some folks, especially black residents, found it much more troubling than others. Most of them knew stories about black men being mutilated or coming up missing over in the Delta and other places for little or no reason except their color. But no one, white or black, knew of anyone missing around Unionville. Therefore no one felt the body had anything to do with them specifically. Besides, there were no reports of any other crimes or attempted crimes to put with it and worry about.

⌒

Late Thursday afternoon, Jesse called Pearl and asked her to come over to the town hall. He had the results of the coroner's inquest.

"That didn't take long," she said, after walking over and taking a folding chair. Jesse was sitting behind the desk.

"Nope. All Ruggleman had to do was get six people together for a coroner's jury and have it sign off on his findings. Make them official and all," Jesse said. "It's pretty quick when there aren't any witnesses or any facts to question."

"What are the findings?" Pearl asked, opening her notebook.

"There aren't many," Jesse said. "It's a homicide. The victim is a male, shot three times up close with double-aught buckshot. Once each to the face, chest, and groin. He'd been dead about four days when Crow found him. There wasn't any identification on the body, or anything else that'd tell who he is. Body's too decomposed for fingerprinting. Teeth are blown to bits, and there's no way to know where to send what's left to find a match. Can't even tell if he's white or black. Sometimes jawbones can be indicators, but both of his are all busted up, and Ruggleman says he can't tell anything definitive from the hair. He thinks the guy's most likely black, but he's not gon' say that, and he's not gon' spend any more time trying to find out. I asked if he wasn't at least gon' send a hair sample to the state lab in Baton Rouge, but he said he didn't see the need because it wouldn't help determine the man's name and next of kin. Also, there aren't any missing persons reports that look like they might fit. I think he just doesn't want to make the effort. He's like a lot of Louisiana coroners. Nothing but a political appointee and don't care a hoot about forensics. But don't quote me on that. One thing we do know is that the fellow wasn't killed at the dump. There's too little evidence of blood, even considering the rain. He was shot somewhere else and dumped there, no pun intended."

Pearl finished making notes then asked, "Okay, what happens next?"

"Well," Jesse said, "Deputy Quinn will ask around some, see if anyone living near abouts over there saw or heard anything. And if no one claims the body in the next few days, they'll bury it in a pauper's grave down at Farmerville. They may already have. I'm not sure."

"What about personal effects?" Pearl asked. "Did he have anything on him I could put in the paper that someone might recognize?"

"Quinn didn't mention anything, but I can ask. Thing is, if there's nobody missing around here, then it's not likely anybody's gon' recognize anything he had on him."

"That's true," Pearl said, "but would you ask anyway?"

"Okay. You gon' be able to get something in the paper this week?" Jesse asked.

"Yeah, probably," Pearl said, "if I get on back across the road. If you can't get me something on personal effects today, though, that'll have to wait till next week."

"What if I get on the horn right now and find out if Ruggleman's got anything?" Jesse asked.

"All right," Pearl said, getting up to leave. "But I'm going on back. You can call if he has something."

"Wait. There's one more thing. Maybe you ought not to print about the shooting happening someplace else. Quinn didn't say I shouldn't tell you that, but I'm thinking if we just keep that quiet for now, it might help somehow. To find who did it, I mean. Same thing about where on his body he was hit too."

"Okay," Pearl said. "I've got to run."

⌒

This was going to be another flat-out sprint to get the paper out on time. Pearl had already saved space on the front page and drafted some copy for a story, and now she revised it and added stuff from the coroner's inquest. She hated to call on Emma Lou to help with the printing again, especially because in addition to writing up two more recipes, she had been working this week on finishing the first quilt pattern to print. But Emma Lou said she would be happy to come in the next day anyway and get in on what she called "all the fun" again.

Pearl was still working on the story about the body when Jesse phoned around five thirty with news about personal effects. Grady was still there, too, waiting to help with the typesetting. Pearl wrote out the headline she wanted, they settled on how long the story would be in inches, and she made a quick change in her draft then banged it out on the Linotype machine while Grady set the headline by hand.

By the time they finished, all the stores were closed, and Pearl went next door to Emmett's and had a waitress pack a half gallon of chocolate ice cream in a carry-out box. At home, she ate warmed-over casserole with Nancy and Alice, opened the ice cream, and over spoonfuls told them what she learned when she went to see Wendell that morning. His doctors said he could come home next week. They would let him know which day on Monday and work out a schedule for his twice-a-week trips back to the hospital for therapy with Helen Bronson. Pearl planned to call nurse Franklin on Monday night and arrange for her to meet with Wendell and work out home therapy times. When the ice cream was gone, Pearl left the dishes to the girls and went to bed to rest up for a long Friday.

CHAPTER 16

Because of how and when the story unfolded, the headline in the upper right corner of the front page of the *Unionville Times* was small for its importance, but few people missed it: "Unidentified Body Found in Town Dump." Talk about the incident had died down some over the last day or two, but Crow Hicks was still rattling on to anyone who would listen. Folks could not recall anything this grisly ever happening in Unionville, and nearly all of them wanted to know more. Pearl printed sixty additional copies of the paper for rack sales.

Scarcity of both space and information made the article short:

> On Monday, April 7, Waylon Hicks of this community reported finding a body at the refuse dump on the Louisiana side of town in Tonti Parish. Arkansas-side Police Chief Jesse Culpepper and Officer Claude Satterfield verified the report and called parish authorities. Deputy Sheriff Bud Quinn and Coroner Nolan Ruggleman responded to investigate. Coroner Ruggleman removed the body, conducted an autopsy, and assembled a coroner's jury as required by Louisiana law, and the jury signed off on his findings. The deceased was a male who died

of multiple shotgun wounds approximately four days before his body was found. Neither his race nor his identity could be determined from available evidence. The only personal effect recovered was an Indian head penny the deceased was wearing on a chain. The sheriff's department is continuing to investigate and asks that anyone who has any potentially helpful information please come forward.

The appearance of issue number two of the *Unionville Times* ignited another round of chin wagging about the murder, especially in the white section of town. Loafers and diners at Emmett's talked about it nonstop. Men getting haircuts at the barbershop and newsstand and women getting perms at the town's three beauty parlors speculated about who the murdered man was and who might have killed him. In the black section of town, people talked about it at Sadie Rose's Place. And whites and blacks alike ruminated about it with family members at home and with others of their own race at work.

With Wendell set to come home next week, Pearl decided to stay in Unionville on Saturday, catch up on some paperwork, and call on a couple of potential new advertisers she hoped would come on board now that she had gotten out another good issue. The morning did not turn out as she planned, however.

Hazel Brantley was out running errands, saw Pearl's car in front of the office, and stopped in to see if she needed any help. That part was fine, but they had been so busy on Friday, Hazel had not been able to ask as many questions as she wanted about all the week's excitement, and she chewed up a lot of time doing it now. Because Hazel had been exceeding expectations and apparently keeping her mouth shut outside the office, Pearl indulged her for too long and, as a result, fell behind in the paper shuffling she was doing. Hazel finally took note of the time and offered to take over whatever tasks she could while Pearl went to make her sales calls.

Pearl accepted and soon got her second surprise of the morning. People in Unionville had always been friendly toward her but never like today. While not everyone she saw wanted to talk about the murder and ask her what else she knew, and was not telling, that surely seemed the case. She realized for the first time that being the editor of the town newspaper carried not only the sort of responsibility for true and honest reporting and analysis she expected to provide and had written about last week, but it also meant people looked at her somehow differently than before. It was not that they liked her more, but rather they paid her more attention. It was like she had become more important to them, though she did not feel that way herself. And there was something unsettling about it, something she could not put a finger on. It did not seem entirely real, and she wondered how they would act if she ever wrote something they did not like, which, given human nature, was sure to happen sometime. She had seen her last boss, Preston Upshaw, get people really mad at him, lots of them, but he seemed to like it. She knew she would not.

There was yet another surprise when Pearl got back to the office a little before noon. A black panel truck she did not recognize was parked out front, and she was still pondering who it belonged to as she walked in and saw Sadie Rose Washington waiting for her. Sadie Rose was wearing a scowl and a yellow-and-red-flowered muumuu and matching head wrap and sitting stiffly in a chair way too small for her bulk. A quilted bag in the same material as her dress lay on her lap. Hazel Brantley was sitting across from her in Pearl's desk chair and nervously saying something about how she liked dresses in flowered prints too.

Pearl said, "Good morning, Mrs. Washington. What can I do for you?" Hazel frowned on hearing Pearl's use of "missus."

Sadie Rose said, "Good morning, Mrs. Goodbar. I'm sorry to trouble you, but I need to talk to you, if you please. I won't take but a minute of your time." She was holding a white hand-kerchief and dabbing it to her nose.

Unable to imagine what Sadie Rose wanted, Pearl wondered if it had something to do with their conversation from a few days ago. Or maybe Sadie Rose wanted to advertise. That possibility had never occurred to Pearl because she did not have a lot of black subscribers, and as far as she knew, no whites ever went to Sadie Rose's Place. Now Pearl wondered if maybe she should have at least asked Sadie Rose. "Let's go back to my office," Pearl said.

She left the office door open and was pleased to see Hazel stay where she was. When they were seated, Pearl asked again, "What can I do for you?" She was surprised when tears began rolling down Sadie Rose's cheeks.

They sat in silence for several minutes. Pearl did not know what to say, and Sadie Rose, now wiping her face, seemed to be searching for words.

"I'm sorry, Mrs. Goodbar," she said eventually. "I ain't used to acting like this. I got a reputation for being tough and I am. I may even be mean, like some folks say, but right now I don't rightly know what to do. Me and the law don't always get along too good, and I thought maybe you could help me with what I got to know and maybe, seeing as how you was nice to come out to my house and all, you might be willing to."

This was not getting any clearer for Pearl, but she could see that Sadie Rose was doing something that was hard for her. "I'll help if I can," she said.

"I'm afraid that body they found might be my boy Elton," Sadie Rose sobbed, her body now heaving under the muumuu. Then she made a loud wailing sound that brought Hazel to the door with a worried look on her face. Pearl waived her back to the front and waited for Sadie Rose to gather herself and speak again. "I need to know, and if it's him, I need him home."

Pearl's thoughts flashed to Nancy and Alice, and she reached in her shirtwaist pocket for her own handkerchief. "I thought he had left town," Pearl said. "What makes you think it's him?"

"That Indian head penny you wrote about," Sadie Rose said. "He had one he wore on a chain. His granddaddy gave it to him when he was just a little thing. He showed it to me once while he was home, so I know he was still wearing it."

"But, if he left town," Pearl said, "why would he come back?"

"Well, ma'am, you see," Sadie Rose said, "that's the thing. That's why I come to you. If I go to the law, the first thing they gon' do is think Elton done come back to get even with some of them men that beat him up, and they ain't gon' listen to anything I got to say. All they gon' see is a big old colored woman they don't like, and I won't never find out nothing. I hear you've got kids and I figured you'd understand. And you own the newspaper. Folks gon' listen to you."

Pearl took a deep breath and leaned farther back in her chair, trying to take in all she was hearing. "The Indian head penny could be a coincidence, you know. There's still a few of them around."

"Yes, ma'am," Sadie Rose said, "but if the one they found is the same year as my Elton's, then I'd know. It don't seem likely that two of them with the same date and a hole in them would turn up around here about the same time. And there's something else too. He promised to send me a postcard when he got to Jackson. He should've done that the same day he left, and that was three weeks ago, and I ain't got one yet."

"He told Chief Culpepper he was going to New Orleans," Pearl said.

Sadie Rose realized immediately that Elton had not wanted them asking questions about why he was heading to Mississippi. No matter what he told them about that, they would likely come to their own conclusions, and those would make things go harder for him. Caught off guard this way, the only thing she could think to do was back up his story. To her mind, it was simply the safest way out. "He was," she said, "but he planned on visiting some folks over in Jackson first. His daddy's people come from over there."

Pearl was not sure where to go next. She could feel her visitor's misery, but she did not want to believe the officers would disregard Sadie Rose's information and her need to know whether the dead man was her son. Bud Quinn maybe. But not Jesse Culpepper. "You said how you think the authorities will look at you and what they'll think about Elton if you go to them, but why do you think he might've come back, if, in fact, he did?"

Sadie Rose answered without hesitating. "I figure if he came back, it was to do what I said the law's gon' think. That's 'cause Elton's a lot like his momma. I ain't saying that's what I would've done, but it sure might've crossed my mind to."

This sent a chill up Pearl's spine, but it did not keep her from seeing a mother who may have lost her child. If Sadie Rose had said that to almost any other white person in Unionville, there would have been hell to pay in one way or another—a threat, a slap, a call to Jesse Culpepper, or worse. But Pearl only asked, "What's the year on Elton's penny?"

CHAPTER 17

Hazel asked all kinds of questions after Sadie Rose left the office, but Pearl told her only that it was complicated and she would share more about it when she could. The next day she drove Nancy and Alice to Sunday School, picked them up afterward, and in between worked at getting things ready for Wendell to come home. She had already gotten the front porch steps replaced with extra-wide planks and taken up all the throw rugs inside to make things easier for him to get around on his crutches. Now she wanted the whole house spotless. The Goodbars had never had household help, but Emma Lou MacDonald had put Pearl together with a black woman she knew named Doreen Dykes, and she was set to start doing cooking and cleaning as soon as Wendell came home. It was another expense they had not counted on, and one Pearl had not told him about, but she saw no way around it and was confident he would agree. Nancy and Alice helped for a while after church, and in mid-afternoon Pearl drove them to the hospital to see their daddy. She shared copies of the newspaper again, and, like many people had done on Saturday, Wendell asked Pearl if she knew more than she had written about the body at the dump. When she said, "Not much," he grinned, winked, and said, "Okay," and she loved him for it.

Pearl was back in El Dorado by nine the next morning making sales calls for ads, and at eleven, she went to the hospital to meet Wendell and his surgeon to find out when the doctors planned to release him and if there were any more instructions about his care at home. Dr. Whitstock told them that Wendell could leave the hospital Wednesday morning but warned that he must make certain to keep up with his therapy. Wendell said he had no intention of slacking, and after Dr. Whitstock left, Pearl and her husband shared a long hug and kiss, each relieved that this part of his ordeal was over and each thinking about sharing a bed again.

All Monday afternoon Pearl kept looking up from her desk in the big front room of the newspaper building, trying to spot Jesse Culpepper's patrol car at the town hall across the street. When she saw it a little after three o'clock, she walked over and told him what Sadie Rose had said about Elton Washington's Indian head penny.

"Well, I'll be damned," he said. "If the dates match, she's gon' have to talk to the parish boys whether she wants to or not. They'll have to get a statement from her."

"I'm sure she knows that," Pearl said. "If it's him, she's gon' want the body. Can she get it?"

"I don't know," Jesse said. "I'll have to ask what the law is on that in Louisiana. But I'm not sure they'll think the matching dates would be proof enough it's him. If it is, though, that's likely gon' make the killing an even bigger problem."

"How's that?"

"If it's him, seems to me like that pretty much confirms that whoever did it is from around here somewhere," Jesse said. "We already know it's not very likely that somebody from somewhere else would dump a body out there. They could've, of course, just to get it out of their own neck of the woods. But if it's Elton, there's a whole lot of possible suspects—like all those fellows that beat him up and threatened him that day at Emmett's, and might've done even more to him if I hadn't stopped them. If one of them did it, I don't see how we'll ever find out which one it was. Unless somebody saw something and comes forward, there's nothing to go on."

"Right now," Pearl said, "I'm more concerned about something else. If the coroner says this is enough to prove it's Elton, whose responsibility is it to tell Sadie Rose?"

"Probably Deputy Quinn's, but I'd likely have to go along, seeing as how she lives over here on the Arkansas side."

"Do you reckon he'd let me go too?" Pearl asked.

"I can check," Jesse said, "but let's don't get ahead of ourselves. I need to talk to Quinn and maybe the coroner too. I don't want to do it on the phone, because they may need to talk it over, and I'd like to be there when they do. Maybe put a little pressure on them. I'll go down there as soon as I can tomorrow."

Pearl and Jesse were sitting, and as she got up to leave, he said, "I thought Elton had gone. Did Sadie Rose say anything about him still being here, or if he left, why he might've come back?"

"Yes," Pearl said, "she did. Elton left, like you thought, and she said she was afraid you all would think he came back to try to get even with the men that beat him up. What she didn't say, and what I'm pretty sure she was also afraid of, is that you and the sheriff would think he got what he had coming, or something like that, and y'all wouldn't try to find out who killed him, or even let her have the body."

"She doesn't have any cause to think that," Jesse said.

"I'm not so sure about that," Pearl said. "I'm guessing that from where she's sitting, she believes she does. And it's not about you or the sheriff personally as much as it's about y'all being white and her and Elton being Negroes."

"Yeah, maybe so," Jesse said.

When Pearl got back to her desk, she picked up where she had left off sorting through material for the next issue of the *Unionville Times*. To avoid having to rely solely on short, syndicated blurbs for national news content, she sometimes summarized stories she found in one of the daily papers or weekly news magazines she subscribed to. She was always careful to assign credit, of course. One story she had only skimmed earlier came to mind now, and she retrieved it from items she had saved and read it again, more closely this time. It told how a twenty-two-year-old black man named Jeremiah Reeves had recently been executed in Alabama after being tried and convicted a second time for raping a white woman six years earlier. Before the first trial, authorities apparently got Reeves to confess by strapping him to an electric chair to scare him. Thurgood Marshall, lead attorney in the *Brown v. Board of Education* school desegregation decision, took up his cause and got the US Supreme Court to overturn the conviction because the judge kept the jury from hearing about the shady business with the chair. But Alabama tried Reeves again, convicted him again, and sent him to the chair for real. On Easter Sunday, civil rights supporters held a rally on the steps of the Alabama State Capitol, with Martin Luther King, Jr. among the speakers, and protested unequal treatment of whites and blacks in the courts. Ku Klux Klan members showed up in white robes and disrupted the event, and afterward, thirty-nine white ministers from Montgomery put out a letter criticizing King and the others for exaggerating wrongs and grievances.

When Pearl finished reading, she put together a summary of the story to print in the *Unionville Times*, along with a short front-page editorial with the headline "Fair and Equal Treatment." Under it, she wrote, in part, that "two of the greatest strengths of the United States are the rule of law and freedom of speech, and the application and protection of these must be the same for all citizens, white and black." The deaths of Jeremiah Reeves and Elton Washington were different in nearly every way, and Pearl made no attempt to connect them. Nor did she even mention Elton Washington. But the concerns of the protesters in Montgomery and the fears of Elton's mother were similar. Even after completing her editorial, Pearl continued thinking about both incidents.

On Tuesday morning Pearl sat with Grady Atwell and went over the growing list of job orders coming in for business forms, stationery, invitations, flyers, and such, thanks in no small way to Hazel's nose for what was going on around town and her lack of shyness in drumming up business. A little before noon Emma Lou MacDonald brought in two recipes, one for sausage-onion squares and one for lemon chess pie, and asked about getting a head start on organizing the quilt show she had suggested earlier. She said they should make it a contest with cash prizes. Pearl wanted to tell her to get with Hazel and put a plan together, but Hazel was now too busy with other things.

"What kind of help do you need for that, Emma Lou?" Pearl asked. They were sitting in Pearl's back office, where she kept her business records and now did most of her writing and editing. Emma Lou was wearing her flowered burgundy dress again and her matching quilted bag was lying on Pearl's desk.

"I don't really need any help to plan it out," Emma Lou said, "but if we got one or two more quilters involved in it, they could help promote it."

"Do you have somebody in mind?"

"Yeah, I do," Emma Lou said. "I know someone that'd work hard, but she can grate on a body's nerves sometimes, and she loves gossip. I don't know if you'd like having her around much."

"You're talking about Almalee Jolly, aren't you?" Pearl asked.

"Yes. How'd you know?"

Pearl said she knew the two of them were good friends but she also knew they were not at all alike. She agreed that Almalee would tell everybody about the show if she helped organize it. But she admitted she did not want Almalee at the newspaper on any regular basis, or even much at all. Emma Lou said that would not be a problem. She said they could work at her house until time to put on the show, which would be way down the road sometime. First, they had to give people time to make the quilts.

"You really think people are gon' be interested in this?" Pearl asked. "I don't think I've ever heard of anyone displaying quilts for any kind of show except at the county fair."

"That's just it exactly," Emma Lou said. "The fair only comes around once a year. Trust me. People are gon' like getting another chance to let other folks see what they can do."

"Tell me about your quilted bag," Pearl said, as Emma Lou was leaving. "I'd never seen one till you brought that one in here a while back, then I saw another one the other day."

"It's just something that occurred to me," Emma Lou said. "I had a square I decided didn't go in a quilt I was making, but I still liked it and didn't want to get rid of it. This seemed like a fun thing to do with it." She turned the bag over. "The back's just plain." Then, "Where'd you see another one?"

"A Negro woman I saw had it."

"Well, I'll be doggone," Emma Lou said. "Small world, ain't it?"

Wendell's doctor was not ready for him to get in and out of cars or try to get up and down steps or stairs on his crutches and insisted he go home in an ambulance Wednesday morning. Arlan Tucker, fresh off a second well-received newspaper column, this one on deer hunting, went and got him in the converted hearse he used for emergency runs. Wendell, happier than he had been in a long while, joked that this was fine as long as Tucker did not drop him off at the cemetery on the way back to Unionville instead of taking him all the way to his house. Tucker had heard it before, but he laughed and teased Wendell most of the way. When they arrived, Doreen Dykes was waiting there with Pearl to help get Wendell inside and settled. Pearl was pleased that he noticed the new front steps.

Jesse Culpepper got back from Farmerville in mid-afternoon and went straight to see Pearl, who was working in the back office again. She motioned him in, and he closed the door behind him, sat across from her, and put his western-style uniform hat on his knee.

"They near about threw a fit down there," Jesse said, turning the Stetson slowly, "because they already did all the paperwork, and there still aren't any missing person reports or any leads about who did the killing. Dr. Ruggleman has already filed his report with the state, and he doesn't want to go to any more trouble about it. Neither does Sheriff Overstreet. 'Dead, gone, and nobody cares,' he said. 'Case closed.' And that's just from me telling him I had something that might help identify the body. When I told him it's likely a Negro, he really got going. Said he sure as hell didn't care about any 'nigger.'"

"He can't just leave it like that, can he?" Pearl asked.

"No," Jesse said. "When they got through blowing off and got out the penny and saw that the date on it matched what Sadie Rose told you, the sheriff said he guessed he'd have to look into it some more, but he wasn't gon' waste very much time on it. Ruggleman thinks the matching dates are enough for him to say the body is Elton Washington, but he'll have to reconvene the coroner's jury and get them to sign off on it."

"Will that be a problem?"

"He didn't think it'd be, but Sadie Rose is gon' have to give Quinn a statement about the penny first. Normally, she'd have to give it in front of the jury, but Ruggleman doesn't want to take time for that, and apparently coroners in Louisiana have so much discretion, he doesn't have to."

"What about the body?" Pearl asked. "Will they let Sadie Rose have it?"

"Yeah, they have to," Jesse said. "But they've already buried it, so she'll have to pay for digging it up. I asked about that, too, and they said the Negro funeral home down there could take care of it for her."

"What about telling her?" Pearl asked. "Who's gon' do that?"

"Quinn will. He'll come up tomorrow and I'll go with him. He'll ask her some questions, write up a summary right there on the spot, and get her to sign it."

"Did you ask if I can go along?"

"No," Jesse said. "They'd have only said you couldn't. But when Quinn gets here, I'll tell him I asked you to come with me since you know Sadie Rose and I don't. He won't like it but he won't stop you. You have to remember, though, you can't print that the dead man is Elton Washington till the coroner's jury says it is."

CHAPTER 18

An elderly man with a cane was going into Sadie Rose's store when Deputy Quinn and Jesse Culpepper, with Pearl in his passenger's seat, drove up a little before eleven o'clock in their separate patrol cars. When the man told Sadie Rose that "the law" was out front, she knew at once why they had come. She put down the package of Gold Metal flour she was holding, went out on the porch, and stood there in her blue-flowered muumuu as the visitors walked over. She did not wait for them to speak.

"Y'all got my boy, ain't you?" Sadie Rose asked. They stopped at the bottom of the steps, looking up at her. She did not ask them to come inside.

"Yeah, looks like it," Quinn said, "but I need to ask you some questions about that penny." He was carrying a clipboard in one hand and resting the other on his billy club. It hung from a gun belt buckled under the paunch straining his uniform shirt.

"That date I give Mrs. Goodbar must've matched up, else you wouldn't be here," Sadie Rose said. "What else is there?"

"Don't you get uppity with me, nigger," Quinn said.

Sadie Rose's eyes narrowed but she did not move and did not say anything.

This was not the way Pearl had imagined the conversation going. She had come along because she thought her being here,

another woman and a mother, would make things easier somehow, but Sadie Rose seemed not even to notice her.

"Sadie Rose," Jesse said, stepping in front of Quinn and
taking charge, "what did you say was the date on that penny?"

"It was 1895, like I done told Mrs. Goodbar there," Sadie
Rose said, nodding toward Pearl but not looking at her.

"When did you last see your son with the penny?" Jesse
asked.

"It was about six weeks ago, right after he come back
home. He had it on a chain around his neck."

"Any way you could be mistaken that it was an Indian head
penny and not something else?"

"No, sir. Them things is near about big as quarters, but
quarters ain't copper colored. Ain't got no Indian's head on
them neither."

"Is that enough for the coroner?" Jesse asked, turning to
Quinn.

"Yeah, I reckon," Quinn said. Then to Sadie Rose, "I'm gon'
write down what you said, and you're gon' have to sign it. I'll
do it right now."

While Quinn went back to his car to write up the statement, Jesse explained what Sadie Rose would have to do to
claim Elton's body.

Pearl told Sadie Rose she was sorry for this outcome, and
all Sadie Rose said in reply was, "Yes, ma'am." When Quinn
came back with the clipboard, Sadie Rose signed the statement and asked, "Ain't y'all gon' try to find out who killed
my boy?"

"Ain't no use. We ain't got nothing to go on," Quinn said.

"You ain't looking for nothing neither, are you?" Sadie Rose
said evenly. "You ain't even asked me who I think done it."

"Who the hell do you think you're talking to, you black bitch?" Quinn shouted. "You want to cool your fat ass in jail?" Jesse put his hand on Quinn's arm and the deputy jerked away.

Sadie Rose stayed still. "No, sir," she replied. "I just want you to look for who killed my boy."

Quinn was red in the face now, and beads of sweat popped out on his forehead. He glanced at Pearl, holding her Blue Horse notebook and pencil, and said, "All right, not that I give a good goddamn myself, but who do you think killed him?"

Sadie Rose clinched her fists but did not move otherwise. "You send somebody around that does 'give a good goddamn,' and I'll tell him."

Quinn took a quick step forward, but Jesse grabbed his arm again and said, "Sadie Rose, we're leaving, and you best go back inside."

⌒

"I don't believe what I just saw," Pearl said, as she and Jesse drove back uptown.

"I'm surprised Quinn didn't take his billy club to Sadie Rose," Jesse said. "He's not used to being talked to like that, especially by a Negro. I think he was a little scared of her, or maybe it was what you might write about him."

"What do you think is gon' happen now?"

"I expect he'll ask me to see if she has anything that might be a lead. Make extra sure they're not missing something obvious."

"I've heard about officers acting like that other places, but that's the first time I've actually seen it," Pearl said.

⌒

The *Unionville Times* staff printed their third issue on Friday, April 18. Pearl looked forward to spending most of the weekend with Wendell and their girls, but first she went to the office on Saturday morning to help Grady Atwell catch up on their job printing orders. They had a "Closed" sign on the front door, but a little after ten o'clock, Elmer Spurlock knocked on the glass.

After his last visit, Pearl had no desire to talk with him, but she let him in and greeted him politely. She was used to seeing him in his spattered painter's clothes, but today he was wearing a denim shirt, bib overalls, and rubber boots caked with mud. She had never been to one of his services at Mercy Baptist Mission, and she struggled to imagine him behind a pulpit. She started to ask him to come to the back and have a seat, despite his boots smelling like a hog pen, but he did not give her time to. As soon as he stepped inside, he said, "Mrs. Goodbar, I just got my copy of your newspaper and saw your smart-aleck editorial, and I wanted to do you the courtesy of letting you know that tomorrow morning I'm gon' be preaching about how this community don't need you lecturing us about no equal treatment for coloreds. And while I'm gon' keep subscribing to your little rag so I can keep track of you trying to stir up trouble, I'm gon' ask my congregation not to subscribe. And I'm gon' do the same thing at the next White Citizens' Council meeting."

Pearl reached for the door and pulled it open before Spurlock could continue. "Good day, Brother Spurlock," she said, jolting both her visitor and herself. He drew a deep breath as if getting ready to reply but then only scowled and stomped away, his face and neck turning a bright shade of red. Pearl wondered for a moment if she should have said something more, maybe tried to reason with him somehow, but the notion passed. She knew it would have done no good. She was not surprised he did not like the editorial, but she was surprised by how deeply his anger ran, and she wondered if he really could sway people.

The next morning, in the simply furnished white frame home of the Mercy Baptist Mission on Newton Chapel Road, Spurlock carried out the first of his threats. House painting and pig farming stood aside when he took to a pulpit. He wore a suit and tie when he was preaching, though once he got rolling good and started to sweat, he would toss the coat away, loosen the tie, and roll up his sleeves before alternately fuming, shouting, and whispering in ways that seduced his listeners. He took every word of the Bible literally and had a congregation that, though small, tended to agree with almost everything he said, except when he came down too hard on things like drinking and fornicating.

He had favorite songs he liked to use when he wanted to stir folks to action, and his members seemed never to tire of them. The little church had no organ and no choir, but it had a piano player who could improvise and add chords to any song in ways that made people's hearts jump and spirits soar. Today, Spurlock led the congregation in singing "Stand Up for Jesus," "Rise Up, O Men of God," and "Onward Christian Soldiers." Then he used the songs and the story of Noah's curse on his grandson Canaan—twisting its meaning like untold numbers of other avid defenders of segregation—as calls to action against the *Unionville Times*.

"Last year," he told his listeners, "we could count on the editor to stand up to the growing forces of integration in our country and our community, but I can already see this new editor is misguided and ain't gon' do that. It's clear she's heading down a different path. Women ain't got no business running newspapers, and there ain't no telling what kind of stuff she's gon' be writing next. We've got to nip this in the bud right now. We've got to stop buying her newspaper. I'm gon' keep getting it so I can keep an eye on her, but she ain't got nothing in it you can't live without. So you need to quit taking it. And if any of y'all are advertising in it, you need to quit that too."

Spurlock went on to get in a few usual licks about sinning and repenting, then he closed the service with a repeat singing of "Onward Christian Soldiers" to further inspire his flock about the urgency of his request.

> Onward Christian soldiers,
>
> Marching as to war,
>
> With the cross of Jesus
>
> Going on before!

On Monday morning, the *Unionville Times* received four calls from people canceling their subscriptions. Hazel Brantley answered the phone each time, and after the fourth one came in shortly before noon, she told Pearl about them and asked what she made of it all. Pearl said she guessed Spurlock had done precisely what he had said he would do. She told Hazel not to worry about it, but she had to admit he had not threatened her idly.

CHAPTER 19

Because he wanted to be done with the whole matter, Nolan Ruggleman wasted no time getting the question of the body back before a Tonti Parish coroner's jury, and on Monday afternoon, it made the identification of Elton Washington official.

Jesse Culpepper learned of it by phone and called Pearl to let her know. Then he drove out alone to tell Sadie Rose. This time no one saw him coming. Assuming she would be in her juke joint, which was how he thought of her place, he parked out front and went inside. Having never had occasion to go in before, he was surprised to find what looked like a well-run business with lots of sidelines. Sadie Rose was standing behind a counter filling a paper sack with grocery items for a customer, and Jesse waited near the door for her to finish. When she did, he walked over, told her the news, and saw her shoulders slump under her orange muumuu. A tear rolled down her cheek and she flicked it away.

"Thank you for coming to tell me," she said. "I see that deputy ain't with you this time. Are you gon' be the one to try to find out who killed my boy?"

"I guess it's come to that," Jesse said. "They asked me to tell you again what Deputy Quinn said about not having anything to go on and how they're short-handed right now and all. But they said I could ask around and let them know if I turned up anything. They said if I do, they'll take a look at it." He glanced around to make sure no one else was within earshot. "So," he said, "I've got a couple of questions for you. I need to know anything you can tell me about Elton leaving. How he was traveling, where he was going, why you think he came back. Then I need to know what you were thinking when we were out here the other day and you said we ought to ask you who you think might've killed him."

Sadie Rose told how she put Elton on the bus to Jackson and watched it leave, and how she had no idea why he would come back, because he never intended to stay long in Unionville in the first place. She also said he had enough money to live on until he could get a job somewhere. So, he would not have been coming back because he ran out of money or anything like that. Jesse asked the same question Pearl had posed earlier about New Orleans and got the same vague explanation.

"Okay," Jesse said. "If you don't know what he was doing back over here, what makes you think you know who might've killed him?"

Sadie Rose told Jesse about Jewell Vines and how he threatened to kill Elton over the pool games and how Leon Jackson had heard him say it. Then she asked, "And what about those men that beat him up?"

"Are you suggesting one of them might've killed him?" Jesse asked.

Sadie Rose wanted to say she was. She had come to think more and more that Elton most likely came back to kill Herbert Kramer. After all, she had told Elton she would do it herself if she thought she could get away with it. It was something she now regretted saying, though she did not feel at all sorry about thinking it. But she did not believe she could bring Kramer into the matter directly without the possibility of putting Priscilla Nobles and her grandparents in danger. Plus, she was afraid that even appearing to accuse a white man, any white man, would make her, Sadie Rose, a target and probably get people so riled up that blacks all over town would pay a price. "No, sir," she said. "I can't afford to be saying nothing like that. I'm just asking what about them."

"Sounds to me like you're suggesting," Jesse said.

"No, sir. I ain't. But Elton did tell me them men was threatening to do more than beat him up."

"Maybe Elton came back to get even with one of them and it backfired on him," Jesse said. "You think that's what happened?"

"Chief Culpepper," Sadie Rose replied, "that's you saying. It ain't me."

Sadie Rose was in Farmerville first thing on Tuesday morning, and by late Thursday afternoon the Blanchet Funeral Home had Elton Washington's body in Unionville, resting in Mt. Zion Baptist Church's largest Sunday School room. Raymond Blanchet, who, in addition to being an undertaker, was also a Baptist preacher, told Sadie Rose she was moving too fast to get Elton in the ground and not giving enough time for people to mourn. "It's not how us folks do things," he said. She told him she was not aiming to let whoever killed her boy see her taking on over it a long time and have them get a kick out of it. Blanchet could see better than to argue with her, and he got busy doing as she asked.

People started gathering at the church around seven thirty. Unlike what Elton had told her about what Emmett Till's mother did in Chicago three years earlier, Sadie Rose kept her son's casket closed. Possibly fearing she might be thinking about opening it, Blanchet told her the body was too badly decomposed to let anyone see it. He had no need to worry, however. She had no intention of putting her son on display like that. She had Blanchet wrap him in one of her favorite quilts, a log cabin pattern she associated with her daddy and her land, and place him in the most expensive casket the funeral home had. She also put in a huge order for flowers for the wake, with more to come for the funeral service in the church sanctuary on Friday morning and the burial that afternoon in the Unionville black cemetery. She even managed to get a mourning muumuu made.

Even though Sadie Rose did not get to church often, and few Mt. Zion members had seen Elton in the short time he was home, church members and other black folks in Unionville turned out in force to pay their respects. They came in part because Sadie Rose was a fixture in their community and in part because they thought it right. And even though this was a time for grieving, it was also a time for fellowship. That the church ladies laid out a potluck feast did not hurt the turnout. At the end of the evening, after most had gone home, some of the men took turns sitting through the night with Elton's body. Most were sad they had been unable to do it from the moment he died.

The next day, many of the same folks and scores of others were back for Elton's funeral service. It started at ten o'clock and ran into the early afternoon. Reverend Moseley handled the preaching, and even though Sadie Rose told him not to drag things out, he went on long enough to get in a ton about sinning and salvation, in keeping with tradition. There was enough lively singing punctuated by electric guitar and drums, in addition to piano, that women had plenty of time to shout, jump, and fall out praising the Lord. Sadie Rose appreciated their being moved this way but did not join in. There were soulful going home songs, too, as the church choir sang "Take My Hand, Precious Lord," asking God to lead them to the next life, and "Sweet By and By," looking forward to meeting again "on that beautiful shore." Leon Jackson, who had saved Elton's hide twice, was there, as was Henry Nobles. But Priscilla Nobles was not. Having known better than to ask for the day off, she was at Herbert Kramer's dairy farm.

That afternoon, following another potluck feast for the mourners, Sadie Rose laid Elton to rest with a bank of flowers around the grave site and with his Indian head penny good luck charm in the casket with him. The floral display included a large wreath from Pearl Goodbar.

⌒

By this time almost everyone in Unionville had heard that the man found dead at the town dump was Elton Washington, and in addition to Unionville's black residents, many whites knew his funeral was taking place. Herbert Kramer was among them, and he took pleasure in the knowledge. He also noticed that Priscilla Nobles, who had been acting more nervous and frightened than usual for several weeks, seemed especially anxious today. He always watched her closely, and even though she tried to keep quiet and not show any emotion, he had learned to detect even the slightest changes in her manner. He wondered if she had some sort of connection to Elton Washington and decided she must. The idea of it both angered and excited him.

Kramer liked to have Priscilla bring his dinner out to his detached office most days so he could have sex with her if he felt like it. She did not give into him willingly, but he had terrorized her grandparents so much and beaten her so many times that she generally did whatever he told her. Today, he thought that having her while folks in town were putting the bastard he shot in the ground would be especially enjoyable.

Kramer was already aroused when she set his tray on his desk, but when he ordered her to take off her clothes while he watched, she turned away from him. "Goddamn you, bitch!" he yelled. He grabbed her by the shoulders, turned her around, and slapped her across the face, knocking her down. Instead of staying down and silent, as she had come to do in order to escape further blows, she got up and screamed in a way he had never heard her do before, even during the first few times he assaulted her. He recognized it as more anger than fear and it made him want her even more. He bellowed like a bull, raked the food and dishes off the desk, forced Priscilla onto it, yanked up her dress, ripped off her underpants, and thrust himself into her. She cried out the whole time, and he loved it and never gave a thought to anyone maybe hearing her.

Kramer's wife had known what he was doing with Priscilla almost from the start. Lorraine had confronted him about it more than once, but all she ever got for it were beatings and threats that he would kill her if she told anybody or tried to do anything about it. She believed him because she had scars to remind her. So, after a while she tried to ignore what was happening. Today, though, she could not shut out what she was hearing. Like on that rainy evening a few weeks back, she stood behind a curtain, looking out the window toward the little white building. She wanted to cry but could not.

CHAPTER 20

Pearl Goodbar did not go to Elton Washington's funeral. She thought about it, as it was not unheard of for whites to attend the funerals of blacks they knew well, particularly those who had worked for a long time in a white home. But it did not happen often, and in this instance of a violent killing, Pearl did not feel comfortable going to the church. She did not want her presence affecting grieving that was sure to be even more highly charged than usual, and further, she felt she needed all the time she could muster to get the fourth issue of the *Unionville Times* printed and out the door. The work went faster than she expected, however, and she made it to the grave-side service. The mourners there treated her with politeness, but she felt she was intruding, nevertheless. She kept to the rear of the crowd and did not press through it to speak to Sadie Rose after. But she knew Sadie Rose saw her, and she was glad for that.

Meanwhile, the newspaper was packed with copy—eight pages again—and Pearl was pleased that Coach Roberts over at the high school had come up with a lot more sports and club items this time. Also, Hazel Brantley had lined up additional volunteer correspondents to write about things happening in various little communities out a ways from Unionville. Most of them consisted of only a few scattered houses and farms situated near a rural store or church, and none was incorporated.

However, each one had a name—Larson Springs, Shady Creek, Hickory Center, Taylor Crossroads—and the residents of each one had a strong sense of place and togetherness. Pearl believed that highlighting them and their doings in the paper would bring more subscribers and that would bring more advertisers.

Emma Lou MacDonald and Almalee Jolly had made progress on plans for a quilt show, too, including collaborating on an announcement, which Pearl edited. They set the show for mid-October, four weeks after the Union County Fair so women could enter quilts in both. Pearl put the announcement at the bottom of page one:

First Annual *Unionville Times* Quilt Show

Saturday and Sunday, October 18-19, 1958

The *Unionville Times* is pleased to announce its first annual quilt show. It will be held during two days, October 18-19 of this year, in the newspaper building on Main Street.

First and second prizes will be awarded in two categories. Quilts in each category will be judged on a combination of workmanship and general aesthetics. The two categories are quilts made from patterns appearing in the newspaper and quilts made from other patterns. Crazy quilts are welcome, too, and will be judged in the latter category. First prize is $25, and second prize is $15. Judges will be announced later.

There is no fee to enter, but all entries must be turned in by Friday, October 3. Those wishing to enter should attach their name, address, and phone number to their quilts and bring them to the newspaper office no later than noon on that date.

Admission to the show will be free on both days.

The top of page one carried a brief story about the identification of Elton Washington's body with the notation that he was the son of "Mrs. Trudell Washington." The piece went on to say that the authorities were still seeking leads that might help them find the party or parties responsible.

Jesse Culpepper did not go to Elton Washington's funeral or burial, but he drove by the church and the cemetery several times during both, in case someone involved in the incident at Emmett's wanted to make more of it now. He did not like what Elton did that day, but he also did not like what had happened to him in the street. On Friday night Jesse continued to think about both the beating and the murder. He was engaged to a teacher in El Dorado, and because she had a school event that evening, he spent it at home, a few miles up the highway from Unionville. A native of Rison, over near Pine Bluff, he lived with a widowed aunt, helping her around her home place in exchange for the Union County address he had needed to become a deputy sheriff prior to his Unionville job. Like his fiancée and like his parents, who were also teachers, Jesse opposed integration. But he had served with blacks in Korea, and his older brother and his wife were Methodist missionaries in Nigeria. Pearl's piece about fair and equal treatment under the law rang true for him as long as schools and public facilities remained segregated.

On Saturday morning, Jesse drove out State Line Road well past the turnoff to the town dump, then doubled back to the access road, and went down it to the place where Crow Hicks found Elton's body. When he had been at the dump earlier with Deputy Quinn, Jesse had wondered out loud why someone would shoot Elton somewhere else then bring the body to the dump and risk being seen, but Quinn had shown no interest in the question and Jesse had let it go. The only logical reason he could come up with himself was that the murderer needed to get the body away from where he did the shooting. But that did not explain taking it to the dump and leaving it where it would be easy to find instead of throwing it into a ravine or creek or hiding it in the woods somewhere.

Getting nowhere with this line of thinking, Jesse decided to stop at houses along State Line Road near the turnoff and ask if anyone had seen anything out of the ordinary on any of the three or four nights before Elton was found. He did not believe the killer would have dumped the body in the daytime and doubted anyone would have seen anything at night, but it would not hurt to ask. He was surprised when both an elderly woman, who said she liked to sit on her porch and listen to thunder and watch the rain, and an old man, who said he had been out walking around looking for a lost puppy, told him they saw a light-colored pickup turn down the road to the dump sometime well after dark on Wednesday, the night the big storm rolled in. Both individuals thought it strange but neither could tell him anything more.

Remembering what Sadie Rose said about Jewell Vines threatening Elton in front of her and Leon Jackson, Jesse drove back to town. He parked in front of the bank and walked past it down the alley to Leon's dry-cleaning shop. It was a small corrugated-tin structure that backed up to the rear of the bank and the south side of the City Hardware building, which extended much farther back from Main Street than the bank did. Sawed-off broom handles propped up top-hinged wooden window shutters facing the alley, and a sliding tin door stood open to let out heat and humidity caused by steam coming from the pressing machine. The place smelled of cleaning fluid, and Jesse wondered how Leon could see what he was doing in the dim light from a trio of over-matched lightbulbs dangling from the ceiling.

The big man was hanging a freshly pressed suit coat over a pair of pants when Jesse walked in. "Hello, Chief Culpepper," Leon said. "You here to ask me about Jewell Vines? Sadie Rose told me you'd probably be around." Despite Leon's having helped him and Mr. Claude look into cross burnings a few months back, Jesse did not know Leon well, but he knew that he was an army veteran, that he was well-respected in the black community, and that he was at least as well-thought-of as any black man could be among whites. Jesse did not know that Leon's wife Wanda worked at Unionville's black school, or that Leon made extra money shooting craps at Sadie Rose's Place and lending it to other black folks at high interest, or that he used those earnings to send his and Wanda's daughter to Southern University in Baton Rouge, where she was studying to become a teacher.

"Yeah," Jesse said. "I understand you heard this Vines threaten to kill Elton."

Leon hung the finished suit on a rack. "Yes, sir. Heard him do it twice, on different nights."

Jesse glanced around the shop. It was crammed with equipment and racks filled with clothes. "You get a lot of business, don't you?" he asked.

"Yes, sir, I do," Leon said proudly. He picked up a pair pants and started arranging them on the pressing machine. "Lots of people bring stuff to me. I do good work." He assumed Jesse took his cleaning to the Taylor sisters' shop over near the town hall.

"I understand their set-to had something to do with Elton beating him at pool," Jesse said, getting back to whatever was between Elton and Vines. "Was that all?"

"Elton beat him bad. Showed him up."

"Was there money involved?"

"Now, Chief Culpepper, I don't mean no disrespect," Leon said, grinning, "but I expect you know the answer to that, don't you?" Leon knew from things he and other blacks overheard here and there that plenty of hustling and betting went on at the white pool hall and domino parlor across State Line Road from the Liberty Theater, and he thought surely the chief knew those same things must happen at Sadie Rose's Place.

"Do you think Vines was mad enough to kill Elton?" Jesse asked.

Leon held down the pressing machine lid, gave the pants a shot of steam, raised the lid, and said, "I think he was mad enough when he threatened it. He'd already come at Elton with a switchblade, but I don't know if he'd have stayed mad enough to shoot him later."

"What happened with the switchblade?"

"Sadie Rose took it off him."

"She took a switchblade off Vines?" Jesse asked, surprised.

"Yes, sir, she did. Big old pearl-handled one. She's not afraid of much of nothing."

"Yeah, I'm seeing that," Jesse said. "What happened to the knife? Depending on what else I find out, we might need it."

"She gave it to Elton."

"Hmm. Do you happen to know what kind of vehicle Vines drives? You can save me from having to check records."

"Yeah, as a matter of fact, I do," Leon said. "Saw it out at Sadie Rose's. It's an old gray Ford pickup. I don't know what year. Early fifties sometime."

Before Jesse left, he asked Leon if he knew where Vines lived, and Leon said he had heard it was on the Louisiana side somewhere near the Bowman Lumber Company, where the man worked.

Late in the afternoon, when Vines would most likely be done for the day, Jesse went looking for him. Horace Bowman was building a new combination chip and lumber mill on the site of his former sawmill near where State Line Road crossed the Rock Island Railroad tracks. Jesse stopped by the company's temporary office, situated in a back room of its old commissary, now a general store for the neighborhood, got the location of the house Vines was renting from the company, and drove there.

It was one of several unpainted shotgun houses lining an unpaved street. A dented-up gray pickup was parked in front, and two elderly women were sitting in straight chairs on the narrow front porch. Jesse stopped behind the pickup, got out and looked it over, then walked up to the porch. One of the women had a basket in her lap and was stitching a sock stretched over a darning tool of some kind, a gourd Jesse guessed, and did not look up. The other woman was fanning herself with a cardboard church fan with a picture of Jesus on it. Jesse nodded to her and asked if Jewell Vines lived here. When she said he did but offered nothing more, Jesse asked where he was. She said he was inside sleeping, and Jesse said, "Wake him up and tell him Chief Culpepper is out here and wants to talk to him." Jesse had no jurisdiction on this side of town but was confident his badge was enough to get Vines to come out.

The woman pulled herself up, fan in hand, crossed in front of her companion, opened a sagging screen door, and went inside. In a minute or two, she came back out, nodded as if to confirm that Vines was coming, and resumed her seat and fanning. Vines appeared a moment later, pushed open the screen, and leaned against the doorframe, wearing only a pair of jeans. Although clearly not happy about being awakened or about being questioned, he did not resist. Jesse told him he knew about his threatening Elton Washington and asked him where he was on the several evenings when Elton's body might have been dumped, especially Wednesday, April 2. Vines said he was home every night and said Jesse could ask his aunt, sitting there with the fan. Jesse figured she would vouch for him whether Vines was home or not. So, he asked Vines if he owned a shotgun. He said he had one he used for squirrel hunting and Jesse could see it if he wanted. Jesse asked him to go get it and bring it out holding it by the barrel, which he did. It was a single shot .12-gauge.

"Did you shoot Elton Washington?" Jesse asked. He expected Vines to say no, which he did, but Jesse wanted to see his reaction.

"No, sir," Vines said evenly and without hesitation, "but I might've done it if I thought I could get away with it. I'm glad somebody else did it for me."

⌒

After Jesse finished with Vines, he drove around for while trying to remember who else besides Crow owned a light-colored pickup and looking to see if he could spot one anywhere. Near dark, when he expected Mr. Claude was likely done with the daytime sleeping he did for his night watchman's job, Jesse went to see the former marshal. As a courtesy, Jesse had been keeping him up to date on developments in Farmerville, but they had not discussed them in much detail. Now, however, with the Tonti Parish authorities having washed their hands of the matter and Jesse's having allowed Sadie Rose Washington and Pearl Goodbar to believe that he would make at least some effort to find out who killed Elton, he wanted to talk it over with Mr. Claude and see if he had any additional thoughts about it.

Irene Satterfield, a slight woman with white hair rolled into a bun, answered the door and invited Jesse into a spotless living room filled with furniture and mementoes from fifty years of marriage. She explained that her husband was getting dressed and would be out in a minute or two. "We're gon' be having supper in a little bit," she said. "Would you like to eat with us? It's beef stew and we've got plenty. Got fresh bread too. Baked it myself this morning." Not wanting to intrude, Jesse said he could not stay because he had other calls to make, but Irene told him she knew he had to eat sometime, and he and her husband might as well talk over supper. "You're not gon' say anything I'm not gon' hear about later, anyway," she said. Jesse looked around the room and realized she was right.

When Mr. Claude came in, they talked about the weather and Bowman's new mill until Irene called them to the table. After they helped their plates, Jesse asked Mr. Claude if he'd given any more thought to who might have killed Elton, and he threw the question right back. Jesse told what he had learned about Elton's go-around with Vines at Sadie Rose's Place, about Leon Jackson's having seen it, about the light-colored truck spotted near the dump, and about his conversation with Vines.

"Well," Mr. Claude said, buttering a piece of bread, "you've got quite a bit on Vines. He threatened the Washington boy, he owns a .12-gauge, and witnesses saw a truck that could have been his going to the dump at about the right time. But that's still thin and you say he's got an alibi."

"I don't think his alibi would hold up if I checked around some more, but there's something else in his favor too," Jesse said. "The tires on that old truck of his are near about bald. If he had driven it in the dump, he wouldn't have gotten it out without somebody helping him. I don't think he's very smart but he's likely not dumb enough to have tried that."

"Who else are you thinking about?" the old lawman asked. The only individuals other than Jewell Vines they could think of who might have wanted to kill Elton were either men who had gotten into it with him when he went into Emmett's Café or men who might only have heard about it but were angry enough about integration in general to have shot him over hearsay. The two officers went over the list. Crow Hicks, Boomer Jenkins, Odell Grimes, Herbert Kramer, Emmett Ledbetter, and Elmer Spurlock came quickly to mind. Grimes did not own a truck, and Jenkins, Kramer, and Ledbetter drove dark-colored trucks. Jesse and Mr. Claude agreed that would make Hicks and Spurlock the most likely suspects based on what the two witnesses living on State Line Road reported seeing. But even assuming both witnesses saw the same truck, there was no proof it was carrying the body.

"Crow was acting strange that whole morning he reported the murder," Jesse said, "and Mrs. Goodbar thought she saw him laughing about it, but I don't know. He seemed pretty shook up to me." Jesse reached for a second piece of bread, and Irene smiled at him, happy to see him eating and pleased to see her husband caught up in the puzzle.

"There's one other thing about Crow," Mr. Claude said. "He's just plain crazy. Crazy enough to do it and crazy enough to think if he reported the body before anybody else, no one would suspect him."

"I like him for it better than Spurlock," Jesse said. "I can't see a preacher doing it."

"I don't know," Mr. Claude said. "He may be a preacher, but he's as conniving as anybody I ever saw, and there's nobody that hates Negroes more."

"Personally, I'd like Kramer for it best, if the truck fit," Jesse said. "I think he would've kicked that boy to death right there in the middle of the street that morning if I hadn't stopped him. Now that I think about it, that's the kind of rage that might make a man put a mutilated body where people would see it."

"I never cared for the man," Mr. Claude said, "but he's president of the school board. Seems like he'd be smarter than to risk his reputation and that farm of his just for spite. I think Spurlock might be capable of wanting folks to see the body, too, and if Crow really was laughing, that would fit him."

They talked for a while longer, and before Jesse left so that Mr. Claude could start his evening rounds, they agreed Jesse should keep looking for other light-colored trucks, though they doubted he would find any. Jesse said he also wanted to check the tires on Crow's truck, and on Spurlock's, and ask everyone on their list where they were for several nights before Elton's body was found, starting with the evening when the two witnesses on State Line Road said they saw the truck. Maybe the witnesses were wrong about the color of the truck, unlikely as that seemed. Because all of the suspects probably owned shotguns, checking on that could keep for now.

"You know you're probably gon' piss off a bunch of people, don't you?" Mr. Claude asked. "I expect most folks think Sheriff Overstreet's right to just step back and let this go away. Not make a fuss over a Negro."

"Yeah, I know," Jesse said. "I'll take it slow and not push too far, but I tell you, I'm having a hard time with how cold-blooded this was."

CHAPTER 21

In the week after Elton Washington's funeral, Sadie Rose and a few folks close to her continued to mourn his death, and many in the black community worried that his killing had something to do with his color and that they or someone they loved might be next. Jesse, Mr. Claude, and Pearl—all of whom had seen the brutality of Elton's murder up close— and to a lesser extent mayor Poindexter and council-president O'Brien—who were concerned about general public safety— were still thinking about Elton too. But about the only other white people doing any ruminating about him or his murder were those who stayed riled up pretty much all the time about civil rights protesters, no matter that none other than Elton had ever been within a hundred miles of Unionville.

A lot of whites were still mad about the feds forcing the desegregation of Little Rock Central High School last fall and were hoping Governor Faubus could find a way to turn back the clock this coming September. With several other Arkansas districts already integrated, it seemed likely that if he failed, Unionville—where students from both sides of town went to school on the Arkansas side—would soon be targeted for desegregation too. Nearly every white person in Unionville was either opposed to it to some extent as a matter of personal belief or was at least concerned about its disrupting ways of life they were accustomed to. Consequently, almost any news about desegregation got their attention. When that happened, they talked about it at home, at work, and almost everywhere else. And some whites, those who made fighting integration a near-about-twenty-four-hours-a-day crusade, chewed on it up and down and back and forth, over and over, whether it was in the news or not. They talked about it over meals and coffee at Emmett's, during haircuts at the barbershop and newsstand, while playing eight-ball at the pool hall and domino parlor, and while whittling on sticks and chewing tobacco under a giant sycamore tree that stood across from Emmett's Café, between the town hall and the Esso station. They also talked about it at meetings of the White Citizens' Council the last week of each month and at the Mercy Baptist Mission almost every Sunday.

On Monday, Hazel Brantley took five more calls from people canceling their subscriptions to the *Unionville Times*. She asked each one why they no longer wanted the paper, and each said they would not read anything that used "Mrs." with the name of a black woman. These made nine cancellations, and when Hazel told Pearl, she thought immediately of Elmer Spurlock.

The next day, Gerald Roberts called from the high school, asked for Pearl, and told her he would no longer be able to write up school and sports news for the paper. When she asked why, he said, "I think you can figure that out for yourself." After he hung up, Pearl asked Hazel if she knew where Coach Roberts went to church.

"Mercy Baptist Mission," Hazel said.

"Figures."

On Wednesday, she stopped by the high school, which also housed the district offices. Bypassing both superintendent

Vernon Appleby—who everyone knew operated under the thumb of board president Herbert Kramer—and principal Jordan Cage, she went to see Margaret Rainwater, a young teacher who had taken her place a few years back and said at the time she often thought of working at a newspaper herself. When they finished talking, they had a plan for a school journalism club whose student members would gather and write a biweekly mimeographed school newspaper with Margaret as their sponsor. She would give a copy to Pearl, along with weekly updates on athletic events, and Pearl would use that information to produce school news for the *Unionville Times* with no byline. Margaret would have to get Cage's approval for the club, but she thought that would be easy if she promised to provide the supplies herself at no cost to the school. She did not plan to tell him that Pearl was behind the idea and would be reimbursing her. It was too late to put everything in place this term, but it would be ready come fall.

Meanwhile, Jesse Culpepper worked his way through his and Mr. Claude's list, looking into where those who were on it had been on each of several nights before Elton's body was found. The checking did not go well from the start. Jesse began with Crow Hicks because of the peculiar way he acted about the body, because his truck was the right color, and because he had already shown he could get it in and out of the dump in the mud. Jesse caught up with him on a garbage run, and when he asked Crow where he was on those nights, he seemed to think it was funny and said he already told Deputy Quinn he was home by himself every night. "Ain't that good enough?" he asked.

Jesse flagged down Boomer Jenkins on the highway and expected him to raise hell about being asked, but he laughed too. Said he had been waiting for Jesse to get around to it because he had about choked the boy to death in the café. Said he was by himself the whole time Jesse mentioned. Said he dared Jesse to prove different. Then he laughed again and said, "I wish I had got a chance alone with him, but it wasn't me that did it, and I don't think you or them parish boys are ever gon' catch who it was. From what I hear, you've done been outfoxed." There was no reason to look at Boomer's tires. He had his truck in back-road mud every time it rained.

Even though Odell Grimes did not own a truck and it would have been nearly impossible for anyone to get in and out of the dump in a car during a big rain, Jesse decided to talk to him anyway. He hung out a lot with Crow Hicks, and it was not far-fetched to imagine their acting together. Jesse waited until he saw Odell alone at the barbershop and newsstand before questioning him. He laughed too. "Whoever killed that boy has got you stumped, don't he? I ain't got no alibi, if that's what you're looking for, but you ain't got no reason to suspect me except I don't like coloreds, and that sure ain't no crime. You're just pissing in the wind."

By the time Jesse found Emmett Ledbetter alone, the crusty café owner had already heard from Crow, Boomer, and Odell, and he started laughing as soon as he saw Jesse coming. "I'll hand you one thing," Emmett said. "You don't give up easy, but there ain't no point in you asking me. I was home by myself every night after I locked up here, and you can't convince anybody I wasn't."

Jesse waited to talk to Spurlock last, not only because he was a preacher, but also because he was not at the café the morning Elton went inside and got beat up. Other than Spurlock's well-known views about blacks, the only thing remotely

183

connecting him to Elton was some members of the White Citizens' Council being at Emmett's the night Elton came into
town on the Trailways. Further, because Elton had slipped
away during the commotion that the driver's yelling kicked
up, those who were there could only assume after the fact that
Elton was the one who set the fellow off.

Spurlock was painting a porch over on the Louisiana
side when Jesse found him. Jesse parked his cruiser on the
street behind the preacher's truck and looked at the tires on
it before crossing the yard. They had plenty of tread. Jesse
said he was sorry to interrupt the work but he was tying up
some loose ends on the Elton Washington killing for the Tonti
Parish authorities. Without saying when, he told Spurlock a
truck resembling his had been seen out at the dump not long
before the body was found, and therefore as a matter of routine he had to make a note of the preacher's whereabouts
on several nights around that time. He expected Spurlock
would be offended, or at least pretend to be, but he was
measured in his response.

"Chief Culpepper," Spurlock said, paint brush in one hand
and bucket in the other, "it ain't no secret how I feel about
uppity niggers, and I'm glad somebody sent that one to hell
before he would've got there otherwise, but you ain't got no
cause to be going around harassing good God-fearing folks
when you ain't got one shred of evidence about nothing. I
know you're just trying to do your job, but what you really
need to do is start coming to our White Citizens' Council
meetings and get on the right side of this colored business.
As for my whereabouts on nights that week, I was conducting
prayer meeting on Wednesday night and a deacon's meeting
on Thursday night, and when I wasn't doing that, I was either

taking care of my hogs or having biblical relations with my wife. If that ain't enough for you, I don't much care."

Things went worse with Herbert Kramer. Jesse drove out to his farm early one afternoon and saw him coming out of the little white building near his house. He had a work jacket under one arm and was using both hands to hook up one side of the bib of his overalls. That done, he stepped off the porch and walked out to meet his visitor. "What can I do for you, Culpepper?" he asked, putting on his jacket and glancing back toward the building. Jesse took the same approach he used with Spurlock.

"Ain't you a little outside your jurisdiction?" Kramer asked. He folded his arms across his chest. "The town line's a few miles back yonder way," he said, nodding toward the road.

"Like I said, I'm only clearing up a few loose ends for the parish boys."

"Well, I don't think I have to answer any questions from you, and as far as I'm concerned, you can tell the parish boys I said they know where they can put their loose ends."

When Jesse left, he drove slowly past Kramer's pickup, which was parked in front of a large, open-front shed. The tires looked almost new.

Late Friday, Jesse waited at the town hall for Mr. Claude to come by before his rounds then told him he had gotten nowhere. Bald tires seemed to rule out Vines, and there was no good reason why Elton would have come back and confronted him anyway. According to Leon Jackson, Elton had already gotten the best of the man by taking his money and making him look bad in front of the juke-joint crowd. No one on the list had a believable alibi, or even one at all, except Spurlock for the first part of Wednesday and Thursday nights. Further, as with Vines, it seemed unlikely Elton would have come back for Spurlock, because insofar as Jesse could determine, they never even saw each other when Elton was in town. With nothing more to go on than the sighting of a light-colored truck on that one night, Jesse and Mr. Claude could not think of anything more to do except wait and see if anyone came forward with something else or if whoever did it talked about it somewhere.

They had been sitting on folding chairs in front of Jesse's desk, and as Mr. Claude was putting his chair away, he said, "You know, we haven't talked about how Elton got back to Unionville after Sadie Rose put him on the bus to Jackson. I wonder if she lied about that, and he was around all the time waiting for a chance to do some payback for getting beat up?"

"I guess I could ask her about that," Jesse said, "but I don't think she'd tell me if he was."

"No, I doubt she would either. But if he really did leave, how'd he get back? It's not likely he hitch-hiked, him a Negro, and he couldn't have expected to come in on a bus again without being seen. If we knew where he'd been and how he got back—if he was actually gone—maybe that would get us somewhere."

"I'll think about it some more," Jesse said.

CHAPTER 22

While Jesse was asking around about Elton, Pearl Good-bar and her staff were settling into more of a routine as they worked on their fifth issue of the newspaper, and Pearl, Wendell, and their girls were doing pretty much the same at home. Weekdays and Saturdays, Nancy and Alice helped get breakfast, and Doreen Dykes cleaned up afterward then looked after Wendell the rest of the day while doing the remaining housework and making dinner and supper. Like many people who had house help, Pearl drove to Doreen's home and picked her up most mornings. Unless it was raining, in which case Pearl tried to leave the office long enough to come get her, Doreen walked home evenings, as did all but a handful of other black women working in white homes.

Pearl drove Wendell to El Dorado two mornings a week for his therapy sessions at the hospital, and while he was there, she made advertising sales calls and dropped off orders for papier mâché mats and printing plates and picked up finished ones at the *El Dorado Daily News*. Nurse Franklin came by the house to work with Wendell for an hour on two other days, and Nancy and Alice helped him stretch his leg muscles after school and on weekends. He was bored, though. Tired of sitting around in his plaid shirts and khakis reading, watching daytime television, and doing crossword puzzles. He kept asking Pearl to come up with something he could do to help her with the paper. They decided she would bring home bills and the financial ledger each weekend, and he could spend some time writing checks and making entries.

~

Pearl started taking the bills and ledger home the very next Friday as planned, and the *Unionville Times* went out in the mail and on sale in racks the next morning. With one exception, the content was routine. In her "Editor's Corner," Pearl returned to a chord she had struck earlier about the law:

Why Are Tonti Parish Officials

Giving Up on Murder Investigation?

In a telephone interview with this newspaper, Tonti Parish Sheriff Harvey Overstreet said his office has no leads in the murder of Elton Washington, and no one in his department is actively investigating the case. It is a fact of life, the sheriff said, that not all crimes can be solved, especially when law enforcement agencies are strapped for resources, as he claims his is. Overstreet said he has told Unionville, Arkansas, Chief of Police Jesse Culpepper that if he comes across anything new that might be pertinent to the case, the sheriff's office will look into it. Until such time, the sheriff said, they will devote no further effort to the matter. We have to wonder if the sheriff would take such a position if the victim were white. Is this fair and equal treatment under the law?

~

The Unionville White Citizens' Council held its regularly scheduled monthly meeting the following Tuesday night, May 6, returning this time to the Mercy Baptist Mission. The experiment of gathering at the high school had not helped attendance much, and meeting at the church required less work. All Elmer Spurlock had to do to get ready was turn on the sound system, hang a big Confederate flag in front of the baptistery, and tape a round cardboard sign to the front of the pulpit. The sign had the words "Citizens' Council" printed in black around the top edge and "Unionville, Arkansas" hand-lettered around the bottom. The middle had a printed picture of crossed US and Rebel flags.

When Spurlock took to the pulpit to start the meeting, he saw an invited but unexpected guest in the audience. However, Jesse Culpepper had not come to "get right" on the Negro business, as Spurlock had put the invitation to him. Jesse was familiar with White Citizens' Councils in general but had never attended one of their meetings. He knew they had sprung up in several Southern states after the Supreme Court's school desegregation ruling in 1954 and had gotten started in Arkansas the next year in Pine Bluff, near where he came from. He also knew that people saw them a couple of different ways, depending on who was doing the looking. Some folks considered them civic organizations watching out for what they called "community interests." Other folks looked at them as sort of a slicked-up version of the Ku Klux Klan. Jesse thought it might be useful to see one of the Unionville meetings firsthand. He wanted to find out what Spurlock and others were saying in them and who was hearing it.

He came in uniform, sat in the back, and eventually saw every man he had talked to about Elton Washington's body being left at the town dump. The crowd was not large, maybe fifty or so, and was almost all male. Jesse recognized three or four businessmen, about the same number of farmers in addition to Herbert Kramer, several men who worked at various other occupations in Unionville or El Dorado, school superintendent Vernon Appleby, and coach Gerald Roberts. He noticed that no members of the Arkansas-side town council were there, nor was mayor Alan Poindexter.

Spurlock had everyone stand for recordings of "The Star Spangled Banner" and "Dixie" then announced that there would be no outside speaker for this evening. He said he wanted to talk about "a disturbing and dangerous new trend in the community." He then spent half an hour lambasting the *Unionville Times* for editorial policies that he said, "if not stopped will lead to colored kids in our schools and colored men in our bedrooms." Like he had done from the same pulpit for mostly different listeners two days earlier and on a previous occasion as well, he declared that there was nothing in the newspaper that anyone really needed and folks ought not subscribe to it or advertise in it. Applause and cries of "Amen" interrupted him several times.

⌒

The next day, Hazel Brantley took six more calls from people canceling their subscriptions to the paper and three from people canceling their advertisements in it. Those who cancelled ads included Lester Grimes, the brother of Odell Grimes and co-owner of the barbershop and newsstand. The other two ad cancellations came from the owners of the town's ice plant and a radio and television repair shop. Each call alarmed Hazel more than the one before, and after she started running to tell Pearl each time one came in, Pearl said, "Just wait and give me a tally at the end of the day."

"We're up to fifteen subscription cancellations altogether," Hazel reported a little after five o'clock. "We're losing them faster than we're getting new ones."

Pearl told her not to worry because they still had plenty of opportunity to get more. She wished, though, that she felt as confident as she tried to sound.

She had not told Wendell about the cancellations, but she knew she would have to soon. They would start showing up on the books, and more to the point, the two of them were in this together. That night, after Nancy and Alice had gone to bed, Pearl brought Wendell a cup of hot chocolate in the living room. He was sitting in his wheelchair, which he still used occasionally when he was tired. She sat on the sofa, took off her shoes, pulled her feet up under her, and spread the skirt of her blue shirtwaist over her legs.

"How many total?" he asked, when she finished telling him. She grimaced and gave him the number. He took a deep breath, let it out slowly, and said, "Tell me again what they said about why they were canceling." She repeated what she had told him about the calls. "Geez, Pearl," he said, frowning, "maybe you better back off some on this race stuff. We could get upside down on money pretty quick. Brother Spurlock is a fanatic. People up in El Dorado have even heard about him. He's like a dog after a bone about anything favorable to Negroes, and he's not gon' stop gnawing."

Pearl sat quietly for a moment then shifted her body, put her feet on the floor, and said, "I can't do that, Wendell. What kind of newspaper editor would I be if I didn't stand up for what's right?"

"One that's still got three squares a day," he said, color rising in his face. "Dang it!"

"Dang it to you too." She leaned over the coffee table, picked up his still half-full cup of hot chocolate, took it into the kitchen, and poured it down the drain. She did not care right now whether it was money concerns or lingering effects of his accident that got him upset this quickly. She expected him to support her and was angry that he did not. And more than that, she was disappointed with him and with herself. She wished she had not stomped out the way she had, but she was not about to go back and apologize. She was working her butt off, she believed she was on the right side of an important social matter, and he could apologize first.

Neither of them said anything more about the cancellations or her editorial positions that evening or at breakfast the next morning, but when she left for the office, they both still felt the tension hovering over them.

CHAPTER 23

The next few weeks passed without the *Unionville Times* receiving any more cancellations. Pearl was able to make the loan payments. Wendell apologized for yelling at her. And she apologized for making him worry, but not for her editorial stances. A few new subscriptions drifted in, mostly from women who went on at length about how they liked Emma Lou MacDonald's column on recipes and the quilt patterns she came up with, often with help from Almalee Jolly. Some of the patterns were common, and some less so, but quilters among *Unionville Times* readers seemed to love seeing all of them and, Pearl hoped, picking ones to make for the October show. She liked the names of the traditional patterns Emma Lou selected, especially Hidden Sisters, Dresden Plate, Sandhill Star, Carpenter's Wheel, Triple Irish Chain, and Birds in the Air, as well as the names of patterns she and Almalee made up, particularly Apron Strings, Hummingbird Wings, and Scarecrow.

School ended in the middle of May, and Nancy got a job working at the refreshment counter at the Liberty Theater. Alice got one helping the Taylor sisters in their dry-cleaning shop, after their niece got picked by the American Legion Auxiliary to represent Unionville at Girls State in Little Rock for a week and her proud mother told her she could take the rest of the summer off.

Jesse Culpepper went to see Sadie Rose and asked her to tell him again about putting Elton on the bus to Mississippi, and she did not say anything different. He asked her pointblank if she was sure Elton was not still in Unionville all that time, which was the same as suggesting she might not be telling the truth. Instead of getting huffy about it, as he thought she might, she not only said she was sure, but also that she knew Jesse had to ask and she was glad he was still trying to find out who killed her son.

Jesse guessed Elton could have gotten off the Jackson bus anywhere along the route and taken another bus back to a nearby town and made it from there to Unionville by some other means, but he could not think of a way to check on it. He asked Sadie Rose if Elton had enough money to buy a car or truck of some kind. Jesse remembered the amount he found on Elton after the café incident, but he figured she might have given him some more, which, of course, she had. Sadie Rose said he did not have enough to buy a vehicle but he might have earned enough somewhere to go with what he had. Jesse called the Louisiana and Mississippi motor vehicle registration departments in Baton Rouge and Jackson to see if they had anything related to an Elton Washington and they did not. Then he wondered if maybe Elton stole a car or truck to get back, but there were not any unaccounted-for cars or trucks around town anywhere, nor could he find any stolen vehicle reports he could tie Elton to.

Eventually, Jesse told Sadie Rose, Mr. Claude, and Pearl separately that he did not know anything else to do unless something new turned up somehow, and he did not think that was likely. None of them was surprised. Pearl told Jesse she had bumped into Sadie Rose outside the bank a couple of

times and they had said hello to each other but little else. Sadie
Rose had thanked her for sending flowers and coming to the
cemetery, but other than that, she had not mentioned Elton.

May folded into June, the weather went from warm to
hot, and people in Unionville busied themselves with the usual
activities of the season, from gardening to fishing and from fixing stuff around home to skiing on Corney Lake over in Claiborne Parish. Jesse Culpepper bought a used boat, and he and
his fiancé skied as much as his duties would allow. Stores closed
on Wednesday afternoons so that owners and others working
in them could have an extra half day to work or play. Teenagers
took over Emmett's Café weekday evenings as well as Saturday nights, and amped-up music from Sadie Rose's Place carried for blocks over that end of town. Except for Sadie Rose
and Pearl, most everyone, including Jesse, either forgot about
Elton Washington, or stopped thinking about him.

On June 3, despite some worry from Wendell about the
cost, Pearl drove to Little Rock, spent the night at the Mar-
ion Hotel, and went to a dinner honoring Harry Ashmore
of the *Arkansas Gazette* for receiving the 1958 Pulitzer Prize
for Editorial Writing. The award cited "the forcefulness, dis-
passionate analysis and clarity of his editorials on the school
integration conflict" in the capital city. Ralph McGill, editor of the *Atlanta Constitution* and a previous winner, was the
guest speaker. Neither man supported whole-cloth race mixing, but both men wrote about treating everyone fairly and
obeying federal law on integrating schools. Segregationists
despised both of them. Ashmore regularly received hate mail
and threats on his life, and the *Arkansas Gazette* was losing
circulation to its rival *Arkansas Democrat* in Little Rock and
around the state. Pearl, operating on a much smaller stage

and having gotten only a small taste of that kind of pushback, found the two men and their work inspiring. She knew that some other Southern editors were taking similar positions, including Hodding Carter over in Greenville, Mississippi, which was immediately across the river from Lake Village, Arkansas, less than three hours from Unionville. But reading what they wrote was not the same as seeing Ashmore and McGill in person and hearing them speak.

Around the same time as the dinner, statewide elections were getting in full swing with school desegregation at their center. Governor Orval Faubus, who had used the National Guard to block the desegregation of Little Rock Central High School until President Eisenhower sent federal troops to force the admission of nine black students the previous September, was running for a third term. Jim Johnson, his chief opponent in the last election, was running for the state supreme court. Both were segregationists, as were the governor's two opponents. Even so, because winning the Democratic primary pretty much guaranteed a win in the general election in November, there was plenty of arguing and speculating about what the candidates thought ought to happen at Central High when school resumed in the fall. Pearl ran a few straight-forward stories about what they were saying on that and other issues, but she did not publish any more race-related editorials until the Fourth of July.

What led her to it then was another incident in Alabama.

During the early hours of Sunday, June 29, in Birmingham, a bomb exploded outside the Bethel Street Baptist Church, the pastor of which, Reverend Fred Shuttlesworth, was a leading opponent of segregation. Members had been taking turns standing watch at the church since another bomb went off there a year earlier. One of the men found this one, a paint can containing more than a dozen sticks of dynamite, sitting against a church wall. He moved the can into the street before it exploded, but there it blew a hole several feet deep and shattered windows in the church and nearby houses. No one saw anyone leave the can next to the church. However, a car carrying several white men was observed nearby not long before the blast.

Pearl wrote a story about the bombing and posted a related editorial in the next issue of the *Unionville Times*, which came out on Independence Day.

The Need for Tolerance

This newspaper does not advocate full-fledged across-the-board integration of the races, but it opposes hate and supports tolerance and respect for human life and dignity and equal treatment under the law. The recent attempt to bomb a black church in Birmingham, Alabama, mere days before our country celebrates the Declaration of Independence, with its proclamation that everyone has the right to life, liberty, and the pursuit of happiness, was cruel and inexcusable. There is no basis in our great nation for such a heinous act of hate or any other act of intolerance based on the color of a person's skin. There is also no basis for defying federal law and denying anyone access to education for that or any other reason. The Fourteenth Amendment to the Constitution of the United States guarantees equal protection under the law to all our citizens.

Since Wendell's return home, publication of the paper had become even more routine, and Pearl did not go over every issue with him and the girls after it came out. This week she pushed hard to get it printed a day early because July 4 fell on Friday and she wanted to give Grady and Hazel the day off. When she brought copies home Thursday night, she put them on a table in the front hall without comment and went looking for Nancy and Alice to give them the birthday cards that had come in the mail from her Aunt Myrtle. Every year on Valentine's Day and Independence Day, like she had always done for Pearl when she was growing up, Aunt Myrtle sent each girl a greeting card with a $25 savings bond. She always said she never could remember their birthdays but she could remember Uncle Sam's and that was always a good time to celebrate. Like they usually did when they heard from Aunt Myrtle, they got to remembering stories Pearl liked to tell about how every summer from the time she was ten until she finished college she spent a week or two with her aunt out in the country. With all the talking and celebrating, the copies of the newspaper remained untouched.

On Friday, puffy white clouds in a bright blue sky combined with an occasional light breeze to make a beautiful day for being outside, and the family put together a picnic-style dinner and ate on the back porch. Afterward, Nancy and Alice put the leftovers aside for supper and walked down the street to visit friends, and Pearl settled in for a nap in the porch lounge chair. Left to himself, Wendell went inside, picked up a copy of the newspaper, and read it while having another glass of lemonade. Pearl was dozing lightly when he came back out on the porch. "I see you've decided we can afford to lose more money," he said.

"What's that?" she asked, coming awake and turning toward him.

"I said I see you've written another editorial that's gon' get everybody's hackles up and cost us more money. You know things are tight. Why did you go and do this again? What happened over in Alabama doesn't even have anything to do with Unionville."

Pearl set up, clinched her teeth, took a deep breath through her nose, and let it out slowly. "Wendell," she said, getting to her feet and heading for the back steps, "I'm gon' assume you didn't read that very closely, and I'm gon' go for a walk while you do that and see if you can't figure out the answer for yourself."

"Aw, Pearl, doggone it. Come on back."

"No. Read it again and think about it."

⌒

"There ain't but one way to read that woman's editorial," Elmer Spurlock railed during his sermon at the Mercy Baptist Mission on Sunday. He had his white suit coat off and his shirt sleeves rolled up but sweat was still pouring off him despite three ceiling fans going full tilt. He was holding his Bible up in the air and jabbing it toward the congregation with almost every word. "She wants us to integrate our schools," he shouted, "and if we do that, if we have white boys and girls going to school with colored boys and girls, then someday down the road—and I'm telling you it won't be long—we're gon' end up with mongrelization of the races. That's what she's really after."

⌒

The next day at the *Unionville Times*, each ring of the phone sounded like a cash register to Pearl, but it was the sound of money going out, not money coming in. By the end of the day, there had been seven more subscription cancellations and another dropped ad. When Pearl went home that night, she did not tell Wendell.

On Tuesday, segregationists attempted to blow up the home of L. C. and Daisy Bates in Little Rock. He was the founder and editor of the black weekly newspaper *Arkansas State Press*, and she was the head of the state chapter of the National Association for the Advancement of Colored People, whose acronym NAACP was a red flag to opponents of integration everywhere. Working both separately and together, the couple had helped lead the effort to integrate Little Rock Central High School. The bomb exploded on their lawn, leaving a huge crater and wrecking part of the house, but no one was hurt. News about what happened swept over the state. After Pearl read about it in multiple dailies, she kept thinking about what she saw and heard on the street in Unionville, and later in Emmett's Café, on the day Elton Washington was beaten. She also thought about his mother's visit to the newspaper office, about Nancy and Alice, and about the dinner she had attended in Little Rock. On Thursday she wrote another editorial and squeezed it into Friday's paper.

Hate

What we saw in the bombing of the home of L. C. and Daisy Bates in Little Rock this week can be called many things. Destruction of property, attempted physical assault, psychological intimidation, a criminal act, senseless, useless, heinous, un-hinged, and un-Christian all come readily to mind, and all apply. Above all, however, this was an act of hate—hate based on skin color, hate based on the unfounded fear that guaranteeing equal rights and equal opportunity for all will somehow limit those things for people who already enjoy them. There is no place for that type of thinking in a free society.

⌒

Several times on Saturday, Wendell started to say something to Pearl about the piece, but each time she said, "I don't want to talk about it." So, they did not. On Monday, the *Unionville Times* received additional cancellations. As with the last ones, Pearl did not tell Wendell. She knew he would learn about them soon enough, when he worked on the books, and she did not have any solutions for the loss of revenue or any intention of changing her mind about doing what she thought was right. She was also about to the point of spending her nights on the sofa.

CHAPTER 24

Wendell Goodbar was getting along well enough by mid-July that Pearl no longer had to take him to El Dorado for therapy, though she still made at least two trips a week to the county seat for newspaper business. He was attending church occasionally, too, on Sundays that Pearl went. Also, after repeated requests from Nancy, Wendell was teaching her to drive. She was a good learner and hoped that if she got her license before her senior year started in September, her daddy would let her take his car to school. She was popular without trying to be, or even much caring, but driving to school earned kids who could do it a little more notice and gave them a nice grown-up feeling to boot.

As July wound down, politicians all over Arkansas ratcheted up their campaigning for state and local primary elections. Despite its size, Unionville not only straddled the line between two states, but the Louisiana side also straddled the line between two parishes, and that line marked the boundary between two congressional districts. The Tonti Parish part of Unionville lay in one district and the Claiborne Parish part lay in another. Townsfolk sometimes boasted about having two mayors, two governors, four US Senators, and three members of the US House of Representatives. About the only office seekers not on ballots in Unionville this summer were members of the Unionville school board, the Arkansas-side mayor and town council members, and statewide candidates in Louisiana. Elections for those positions fell in odd-numbered years.

Candidates for governor of Arkansas had come to Unionville occasionally during previous elections, but this time they did not get closer than El Dorado. Other candidates came, though, and walked around the business district going into stores, talking to people on sidewalks, shaking hands, and passing out matchbooks, fingernail files, cardboard fans, pins, and flyers with their photographs and slogans. Their comings and goings sometimes seemed like a carnival. Some parked sound trucks on Main Street, played country and gospel music until a crowd gathered, then climbed onto car fenders or truck beds and made speeches lambasting their opponents and promising voters everything from better roads to lower taxes, never mind that the two things usually did not go together. A lot of folks found all the politicking and speechifying entertaining. A few found it annoying. But nearly all of them talked about it in the usual places they gathered to swap news, gossip, and tell tall tales. All the campaigners called on Pearl as editor of the local paper, and some took out ads with her, but other than the governor's race, she did not write much about the candidates except that they had come to town and made a lot of pledges. She even resisted editorializing about whether the candidates lucky enough to get elected would actually do what they said.

On July 29, Faubus won the Democratic gubernatorial primary by a landslide. Pretty much assured now of a third term, he claimed that his win proved that the people of Arkansas did not want integrated schools. Jim Johnson barely squeaked to victory in the state supreme court race, however, and in Pulaski County, home to the capital, no segregationist candidate won anything, though one forced a runoff for a seat in the state legislature. With these mixed results overall, speculation about what would happen with school desegregation in Little Rock shot up all over the state. The *Arkansas Gazette* asked NAACP leader Daisy Bates what she thought, and she declined to guess.

Even with the statewide races, Pearl remained on the sideline. Contrary to how Elmer Spurlock and some others had taken her editorials about tolerance, equal treatment, and respect for federal law, she had stopped short of saying straight out that schools should be integrated. Several things held her back. She knew federal law required integration, she believed black children deserved the same education as white children, and she was against mistreating people because of their color. When she looked ahead, though, and tried to imagine what other changes school integration might bring, she had difficulty seeing past the likelihood of a lot more violence and turmoil. Further, she was not sure she could accept the kind of race mixing some segregationists argued it would eventually bring. She was also worried about losing more business and maybe even the newspaper itself and how that would hurt her family. And she worried about finances coming between her and Wendell.

In addition, the situation in Little Rock remained muddled, and it was unclear what impact any elected official in the state might have on it. Back in late June, a federal district judge had granted the Little Rock school board—whose members feared more incidents of violence like those at Central High last year and therefore wanted time for tempers to cool—a two-and-one-half-year delay in desegregating schools in the capital. The NAACP had appealed the decision, and a federal appellate court was set to hear the case in a few days. Like everyone else who was following closely, Pearl was waiting to see how the court ruled.

At the end of the week, she brought home her accounting ledger, a stack of invoices, and other business records covering most of the month, put them on the hall table, and braced herself for the argument she knew would come at some point before Sunday evening. It did not take long. Wendell started pouring over the materials after supper, and he was still working wordlessly at it when Nancy and Alice said, "Good night," and headed off to bed. A couple of hours later, Pearl put down the book she was reading in the living room and went into the dining room, where he had everything spread out on the table. She told him she was turning in, too, and finally he spoke. "Wait a minute. We need to talk."

"Okay," she said, and pulled out a chair and sat down.

He tossed his pencil onto a pile of papers, leaned back, and asked, "Do you have any idea how much trouble we're in?"

Pearl did not like the question, or the way he asked it. Her first thought was to tell him that of course she did because she was not stupid and she resented his attitude. But she held her tongue. She could not stop her eyes from narrowing, though, and she saw that he noticed. "Yes, Wendell," she said, stiffly. "I have a pretty good idea."

"All right, then. Do you have any ideas about how to get out of it?"

"No. Do you? And don't tell me to back off my editorials, because I won't," she said, crossing her arms like his. "Besides, we agreed when we bought the paper that I'd decide those things. Remember? And anyway, changing them now wouldn't help us make the next mortgage payment."

"You know we don't have the money for it, don't you?"

This time, she could not resist. "Yes, Wendell. I'm not stupid."

He stretched his arm toward her and, unable to reach her hand, laid his on the table. "I'm sorry," he said. "I didn't mean to suggest you are. But I'm really worried."

"Well, that makes two of us," she said, staying where she was, arms still folded across her chest.

"Tell you what," he said. "We'll sell my car. I can use yours to teach Nancy on weekends. I know she's been counting on driving to school, senior year and all, but if I was working, she wouldn't be able to anyway. She'll be disappointed but she's young. She'll adjust."

"I hate to do that," Pearl said, and unfolded her arms. "I could go talk to Mr. Bowman. See if we can get an extension or something."

"Better hold off on that. We're probably gon' need to ask him sooner or later, but if we've done everything we can think of before then, there's a better chance he'll do it."

"All right, but I'm not gon' stop writing what I think needs to be said."

"Yeah, okay," Wendell said. It was not exactly what Pearl would have liked to hear from him, but it was a concession of sorts. She got up, went around behind his wheelchair, leaned over and kissed the top of his head, and put her arms around his.

The next day, Pearl and Wendell told Nancy what they planned to do and why, and she reminded Pearl about having suggested selling his car back in March if they needed money. Wendell told her he was sorry they had to do this but said he was proud of her for being so grown-up about it. He got on the phone Monday, and by the middle of the week, they had what they needed to pay the bank for this month and a little left over.

⌒

Two weeks later, on Monday, August 18, the Eighth US Circuit Court of Appeals overturned the district court's approval of a delay in integrating Little Rock schools. The court stated that holding off on integration there would be an open invitation to segregationists in other towns and cities to also use violence to defy federal law and stop desegregation. Some newspapers in the state wrote that they were disappointed with the decision. Some of those said it would likely lead to exactly the type of turmoil that the Little Rock board feared. Others said it flew in the face of the majority of Arkansans, who voted for Faubus. It was the notion of potential violence in towns and cities all across the state that moved Pearl. After agonizing for several days over what she wanted to say, she penned an editorial in the nick of time for her August 22 issue, alongside a front-page story about the circuit court decision. She wrote:

School Integration

Is a Better Choice

Than Violence

We, the citizens of Arkansas, are facing a choice between obeying the law of the land or opposing the integration of our schools. The issues surrounding this choice are multifaceted, but in the view of this newspaper, the choice itself is simple. We stand with the federal circuit court of appeals and for obeying the law of the land. We stand against the use of violence in defying federal law. It is time to stop expending resources of intellect, energy, and money trying to find a way to continue discriminatory and hurtful practices. It is time to use those resources to find ways to do what is legal, just, and in the best interest of the well-being and future prosperity of our country and all its people.

All through the spring and summer, no one working on the newspaper other than Coach Roberts, who had quit in protest, had said anything to Pearl about her editorials, and she assumed they either agreed with her or had no problem with them. After getting the type tray ready for this one, however, Grady Atwell had said, "Miss Pearl, I reckon you're sure about this, or you wouldn't have written it, but I wonder if you're ready for what's gon' come on you now. It's gon' be lots rougher than those subscriptions and ads you already lost."

"Grady," she said, "I honestly don't know, but I think I am. I hope so, anyway. The thing is, I'm pretty sure I'll sleep better this way than if I didn't follow my conscience." She did not tell Grady that she would still be lying awake plenty.

"Well," Wendell said, when he saw her piece on school integration Friday night. "You've done it this time. You may as well have gotten a can of gasoline and set fire to the place."

CHAPTER 25

On Saturday morning, scattered clouds and occasional light wind from the west proved weather forecasters sometimes got things right. This gave folks more faith than usual in the forecast for rain on the upcoming Labor Day weekend, and they tried to cram all the chores and playing they could into this one. With school set to open the first week of September, Pearl already planned to take Nancy and Alice to El Dorado to buy school clothes and supplies they could not get in Unionville. Now they made a day of it, but not only because of the weather. Pearl did not want to hear any more from Wendell, and spending the whole day with her daughters made a good excuse. They went to Samples Department Store on the south side of the courthouse square to see the latest fashions then went to West Department Store on the north side to buy clothes that cost less. At noon they had open-face roast beef sandwiches with mashed potatoes at Woody's Grill, and in the afternoon, they took in a matinee at the Rialto Theater and followed that with a visit to F. W. Woolworth's to buy school supplies and get strawberry milkshakes at the soda fountain.

They were not much hungry when they got back to Unionville. For supper they made do with leftovers from the dinner Doreen Dykes made for Wendell and a peach cobbler she made for all of them, and Nancy and Alice told him about their day. They were starting to clear the table when Hazel Brantley called. She had come only moments before from the Taylor sisters, who kept their dry-cleaning shop open late on Saturdays so folks could pick up their church clothes for Sunday. Hazel said Lucille Taylor told her Jesse Culpepper had been in a skiing accident on Corney Lake. According to Lucille, he was doing sharp turns to throw up sheets of water, and on a pass through the pull-boat's wake, he lost his grip on the towrope, went under, and got hit by another boat that was following too close.

"Lucille told me she heard that the propeller cut him up bad." Hazel said. "There were some Claiborne Parish deputies down there, and they didn't even wait for an ambulance. They put him right in a patrol car and took him to El Dorado."

"I think we met them when we were coming home this afternoon," Pearl said. "They were flying—siren, lights, and all. Alice said she thought it was a Claiborne Parish patrol car, and we wondered why it was driving over here like that. Is that all you know? Did Lucille or Mae Vinnie hear anything about how Jesse's doing?"

"No, and I don't know who we could call and ask, unless Alan Poindexter might know something. You'd think somebody would've let him know, him being mayor and all. I don't know who else was down there, but it was probably pretty much the same bunch as always. I could make some calls."

"No. Don't do that," Pearl said. "I'll call Alan, and if I don't get him, I'll go to Mr. Claude's or see if I can find him uptown somewhere and see what he knows. Then I may go on up to the hospital. I like that boy, and I've got a good idea what his family's going through right now. I'd like to interview those deputies too."

"Would you like some company?" Hazel asked.

"That'd be nice. I'll swing by in about ten minutes."

⌒

Pearl told Wendell and the girls what she knew then called the mayor. His wife Lily said he was on his way to the hospital and may already be there, but she did not know any more about the accident than what Hazel had heard from Lucille Taylor. In a few minutes, Pearl was speeding up US 167 with Hazel holding onto the seat with one hand and bracing against the dashboard with the other. "I don't see too good at night anymore," she said, hinting for Pearl to slow down. "I'm always afraid I'll hit something."

"That's okay," Pearl said. "I'll let you know if I run into anything."

When they got to St. Joseph's, Jesse was in surgery, and Alan Poindexter was waiting in a lounge with Jesse's fiancé Deborah Barnes, her parents, and their minister. The two Claiborne Parish deputies who brought Jesse were also there. They and Deborah, a blond woman of medium height, were wearing white lab coats over their clothes because her swimsuit and the deputies' uniforms were covered with blood. Jesse's parents were on their way down from Rison. No one had thought to call Jesse's aunt. Alan made introductions, and Pearl and Hazel said how sorry they were. As people always do at such times, they asked if there was anything they could do to help, although they knew there likely was not.

"Pray and give blood," Deborah's mother said.

Pearl and Hazel told her they would, and while Hazel went off to find out how and where in the hospital to donate blood, Alan Poindexter pulled Pearl aside. A fleshy balding man in his mid-fifties, his day job was keeping books for Bowman Lumber Company. He usually wore a pleasant smile but tonight his face was lined with worry.

"It doesn't look good," the mayor said. "The hospital folks haven't said anything except he's gon' be in surgery a good while. The deputies said his chest and his right arm and shoulder were all torn up and his face was cut up pretty bad too. I don't like the sound of it."

"I'd like to talk to the deputies," Pearl said. "For the paper. Would you mind asking them to come over here for a minute? I don't feel comfortable doing it in front of Deborah and her folks."

Alan returned to the family and sent the deputies over, but Pearl did not learn much more from them. Delbert Payne and Jerry Miller were both tall, beefy, and in their thirties, and both looked self-conscious in their white hospital coats. They explained that their department did not have a patrol boat on the lake because it was too small to justify the expense, but deputies took turns stopping by the parking and picnic areas and the boat launches on weekends in the summer. By chance, Payne and Miller ended up there in separate patrol cars at the same time, right as the boaters were getting Jesse to the shore. They said they knew right then they could not stop the bleeding and he would die before an ambulance could get to the lake and then get him to a hospital. So, they wrapped a bunch of towels around the wounds, and took off, one driving, one in the back with Jesse, and his fiancé riding up front and hanging over the seat. There was nothing more to tell.

After the deputies talked to Pearl, they left to go back to Claiborne Parish, and shortly after that, Jesse's parents arrived and phoned his aunt. Pearl waited with them and the others.

Hazel returned in a little while and reported that they would have to come back another time to give blood because the hospital had enough on hand at the moment and the staff was too busy to take more tonight. A little after twelve, one of the doctors came out and told those waiting that Jesse was stable but would need several more operations over time to repair all the damage. He would likely lose some function in his arm and might have some vision issues, but it would be impossible to determine how much in either case until later, maybe even for weeks. The doctor also said before anyone could ask, "I know you're wondering if he will have scars on his face, and he will, but we think with time and additional surgery, they'll be minimal."

Pearl imagined that Jesse's family felt the same mix of relief and dread she had when Wendell's emergency surgery was over. After quietly expressing her good wishes and saying goodbye, she waited for Hazel and Alan to do the same, then walked out with them. As they were going down the concrete steps out front, Pearl asked Alan whether he had been giving any thought to what he would do if Jesse could not come back to work for a while. Alan knew she was asking for something she could put in the paper.

"Yeah, I have," he said, stopping on the sidewalk. "I don't want you to quote me, but I don't mind telling you, I'm worried. Jesse was absolutely the right man when we hired him, and he's done a good job—you can quote that part—but if he'd turned us down, we'd have had a hard time finding somebody else. I noticed the doctor didn't say whether he'd recover enough to come back to work. Nobody in the family asked and I certainly wasn't about to. I guess we're gon' have to get somebody temporary, but I sure as heck don't know right now who'd be willing to do it, or able."

"What about Mr. Claude?" Pearl asked.

"He can't drive, for one thing. You know that. And even if we were okay with him doing nothing but walking around town for a while like he used to, he probably wouldn't want to go back to it. And if he did do it, we wouldn't have a night watchman."

"Well, I'm gon' need something from you for the story—by Wednesday evening if possible. Thursday latest. Will you let me know when you have a statement I can use?"

"Yeah, sure."

"You think you might get the council together this week to discuss it? I know your monthly meeting isn't till the eighth, because of Labor Day."

"If we meet, it'll probably be informal, not anything official," Alan said. He started for the parking lot, Pearl and Hazel alongside.

"Yeah, I figured," Pearl said. "So you can keep everybody else out of the way, me included."

"Aw, come on, Pearl. How would it look if we discussed this in public before we know how Jesse is? Anyway, we have to have a formal meeting to take any action."

"How about you call me or come see me Monday and let me know how he's doing and what y'all are thinking?"

"Okay. "I'll talk to you Monday."

"Weren't you a little hard on him?" Hazel asked, when they got in Pearl's car.

"No. I don't think so."

CHAPTER 26

O
n Sunday, Pearl slept in and Nancy drove Wendell and
her sister to church. After they got home, they helped
rustle up a dinner of fried chicken, mashed potatoes, corn
bread, and warmed-over field peas. While they ate, Nancy and
Alice told what they had heard at church about Jesse's accident, including someone saying the man driving the boat that
hit Jesse had been drinking. Pearl told them as much as she
thought they needed to know of what the deputies said. No
one mentioned last Friday's editorial.

Pearl heard plenty about it Monday morning, though. In
what was getting to be all too common, another dozen people
called and cancelled their subscriptions to the paper. Plus, two
businesses in El Dorado—a building supply place and a jew-
elry store—called and cancelled ads. Hazel said both owners
belonged to the White Citizens' Council up there. When Pearl
asked how she knew, Hazel said she had a third cousin on her
mother's side whose husband was a member, and she was so
mad at him about a whole bunch of things that she was about
ready to kick him out of the house. After the cancellations
came in, Hazel was suspicious and called her cousin and asked
if she knew the men, or had heard her husband mention them.
The cousin had and was happy to tell about them.

"You never cease to amaze me with all your connections," Pearl said. Still feeling the effects of little sleep on Saturday night, they were standing at the office hot plate getting a second cup of coffee.

"It's nothing, hon," Hazel said. "Like I told you when you hired me, I like to know what's going on, and I like talking to folks."

"For someone who likes to talk, and the Good Lord knows you do, you haven't said how you feel about what I've been writing."

"Okay, I'll tell you," Hazel said. She tugged at the belt on her flowered dress as if doing so would help her get the words out. "You asked us all one time if we were on board with your thinking. Remember? It was right after you told Brother Spurlock not to say 'nigger' or 'colored' in here because they were hurtful. I was a little surprised, but I liked the way you stood up to him. I've always been against integration and I pretty much still am. It's the way I was raised and how I've always been. But ever since that day, I've been watching what you've been writing, and I've been thinking about a lot of the things that are going on, not just around here, but all over the place, and I see the points you're trying to make. I know I'm probably not making any sense, and that's partly why I hadn't said nothing. It's complicated."

"Yes, Hazel, it is. In lots of ways," Pearl said, and headed back to her desk.

⌒

Things were complicated another way for Alan Poindexter and Neal O'Brien. The mayor went to see the Arkansas-side council president at his home Sunday afternoon after

Jesse's accident. Dressed in the white shirts and dress slacks they had worn to church that morning, they sat in the shade on Neal's back porch, drank iced lemonade his wife fixed for them, talked about Jesse, and tried to figure out what to do about his being out of commission for a while. Until the last couple of years, Unionville had never had much trouble with people breaking the law, other than an occasional fist fight or someone getting publicly drunk every now and then, or even less often, someone shoplifting or soaping store windows on Halloween. Then last year, after some cross burnings and a couple of other incidents put a spotlight on Mr. Claude's age and inability to drive, he and the Arkansas-side council had a meeting of the minds about the desirability of his retiring and their hiring Jesse so they could have a lawman with wheels. Now, with an unsolved murder on their hands, never mind that most white folks seemed to have forgotten about it, a younger officer in a patrol car seemed more desirable than ever.

After going over the names they and other members of the council had talked about last year, they were nowhere. "I'm glad for Norm Patterson," Alan said, referring to one of their other leading possibilities from the first time around, "but it's too bad for us he got that promotion up at Ark-La-Tex Oil. Otherwise he might be our answer now."

"Nah, not for a temporary appointment," Neal said. "He wouldn't have quit Ark-La-Tex under any circumstances for something like this."

Alan poured himself another glass of lemonade from the pitcher sitting on a small side table. "I've got a feeling we're not talking short-term," he said, "but that's part of the problem. We don't know yet."

217

"What about seeing if Mr. Claude will do it?" Neal asked. "Like you said, we can't decide anything permanent, and if he'll do it for a little while, that'll give us more time to see how Jesse comes along and what our options might be then. We might even be able to recruit some other deputy sheriff if it turns out Jesse can't come back at all."

"Pearl Goodbar mentioned Mr. Claude last night up at the hospital. But what about him not being able to drive?"

"We live with it," Neal said. "At least till we can think of something else. Why don't we go ask him? Tell him it'd be subject to council approval, and if he says yes, we can get the boys together and see if they'll go along."

"We can't take any council action without a public meeting," Alan said. "Pearl will roast us. And by the way, I told her I'd give her some sort of statement by the middle of the week."

"Yeah, you're right. Speaking of Pearl, what do you think about these editorials she's been writing? Lots of people know we helped her buy the paper, and some of them are complaining to me that she's meddling in stuff she ought to leave alone. You know what I mean?"

"Yeah, I do," Alan said. "I've been thinking about that. There's two things. One is I believe the way she sees it she's doing what we wanted her to, and that means writing what she thinks is in the best interest of the town down the road. The second is, and you know this as well as I do, school desegregation is coming, and no matter how anybody feels about it, there isn't anything anybody can do to stop it, lawfully or otherwise. I don't like it, but if it's gon' happen anyway, I'd rather see it happen peacefully than with a lot of people getting hurt, white or black. And that's sure as heck what's gon' happen if Elmer Spurlock gets his way. I'm not convinced that

Washington boy's murder wasn't tied somehow to what happened to him up at Emmett's that day. And if he left town, then came back to get even some way, and then one of them good ole boys killed him and everybody finds out about it, then it won't be long till blacks and whites are coming at each other out in the open."

Neal took a deep breath, let it out slowly, then leaned forward, rested his elbows on his thighs, and touched the tips of his fingers and thumbs together between his knees. Neither man spoke for a few seconds, then Neal sat up, turned to Alan, and said, "I'm glad to hear you say that, 'cause it's how I see it too. But you know we're in the minority, don't you?"

"Yeah, that's for sure. Look, it's about supper time. Mr. Claude ought to be up now. How about we call him and see if we can go over there and talk to him after he eats? He only makes one or two rounds on Sundays, so he ought to have time enough to sit with us a spell before he goes uptown."

The Satterfields were waiting for Alan and Neal when they drove up out front a few minutes after eight. "Y'all come on in," Mr. Claude said, holding open the door. He had on his night watchman's garb, except for the black hat and coat. Irene had made a fresh pot of coffee and put out half a pecan pie with plates and utensils. She said a quick hello and headed off to a back room to read. "So you boys can fuss and cuss all you want," she said, with a wink. The men sat down at the dining room table and helped themselves to the coffee and pie. As they were filling their plates, Mr. Claude asked his guests if they had any more word on Jesse. Alan said he had spoken with Jesse's fiancée on the phone after supper and there was nothing new.

"So, what can I do for you boys?" Mr. Claude asked, flicking his fork at them with his wrist. "Don't tell me you're gon' ask me to stand in for Jesse till he gets well. We had that conversation before, you know, and I'm a year older and still can't drive. And I'm not gon' start now." He took a bite of pie and said as he was chewing, "Irene makes good pies. Y'all go on. Dig in."

Alan loaded his fork then laid it back on his plate. "We just want to see if you'd be interested in talking about it," he said. "You know, get a read. If you was to be interested, we'd have to take it up with the council." Alan assured him they were only thinking about his working on foot, like he did all those years before and the way he was doing now as night watchman.

"How long you reckon Jesse's gon' be laid up?" Mr. Claude asked. "I understand the doctors haven't said, but what do you guess?"

"I imagine it's gon' be several weeks," Alan said. "Maybe a couple of months, possibly more. So, is this something you'd consider?" He glanced at Neal and took a bite of pie. Neal returned the look and loaded up his own fork again. Both men were eager to hear Mr. Claude's answer but they knew better than to rush him. Besides, both feared they would not like what he had to say. For several minutes no one spoke. The only sounds were those of forks against plates and cups against saucers.

Then Mr. Claude pushed his plate away, rested his forearms on the table, and looked first at Alan and then at Neal, as if taking further measure of them. "I pretty much knew this was what you had in mind when you called," he said. "Matter of fact, I was already ruminating on it. And I tell you what. I've got a proposition for you. I don't think you're gon' like it, but it's the only way I'll do it. And I'm only willing to do it even this way because I've got a hunch some of these hotheads are close to going off the deep end again."

"You know something we don't, Mr. Claude?" Neal asked, shifting in his seat.

"I like to drop in on Emmett's place once or twice every evening to rest up some and hear what folks are talking about. And I can tell you that Pearl Goodbar's editorials have got a bunch of the boys pretty riled up. They're doing a lot of popping off and they don't mind me hearing it. Pearl don't go in there much and I don't blame her. I expect they think I tell her what they're saying every time I stop over at the newspaper office to say hi to Irene's cousin Grady. They'd like to scare Pearl off what she's writing somehow."

"What're they saying?" Alan asked.

"Their usual sort of stuff, about how they want to shoot Negroes and such. How the Klan used to deal with blacks. It's mostly hot air, of course. They know there's not any Klan around here. Hasn't been for thirty years or more. But if a couple of them get liquored up enough together sometime, and somebody else eggs them on, they could hurt somebody."

"Who's doing most of the talking?" Neal asked.

"It's mostly the same bunch that ganged up on the Washington boy that day. Boomer Jenkins, Crow Hicks, Odell Grimes. Emmett, too, some days. And some other ones too."

"You didn't mention Herbert Kramer," Alan said.

"Nah, I don't see him in there as much. He's a little different sort of fish. He's got more sense than the others, and he don't pop off as much. Seems like it takes something particular to set him off."

"What's the proposition you think we won't like?" Neal asked.

"I'll go back to being marshal till Jesse gets well if you let me get Leon Jackson to be my deputy."

For a moment, the only sound in the room was Mr. Claude's Seth Thomas shelf clock ticking. Alan and Neal looked at each other then back at their host. "You're not serious, are you?" Alan asked.

"Good god, man!" Neal said. "Don't you think that'd just make things worse? Giving a black man a gun and a badge, especially right now? Somebody's liable to shoot him then we'd have a real mess on our hands. Not to mention that he's got his dry-cleaning business to run and doesn't have any qualifications. I like Leon fine for a Negro, but I'm sorry, I can't see it." Neal looked at Alan as if to urge him to say something else, but Alan only sat with his mouth open.

"That's because you're not looking," Mr. Claude said. "Let me lay it out for you."

"Yeah, you do that, please." Alan said.

"All right," Mr. Claude said, "but you ought to get yourselves some more coffee first." He waited while they poured. Then he said, "I've thought about all of that. First off, it wouldn't be a full-time job. It'd just be to drive me around town a couple of times a day and take me places I might need to be and can't get to easily on foot. And if I was to get into some kind of scrap, he'd come in handy for that too. I don't see him doing any patrolling or anything on his own. That might be too much. He'd have plenty of time to do his dry-cleaning stuff when he's not out with me. As far as qualifications go, you remember how he helped me on stakeouts last year?" Alan and Neal nodded, and Mr. Claude continued. "Well, me and him spent a lot of evenings together that nobody saw, and he told me a lot about his time in the army. He wasn't drafted. He enlisted. And he wasn't driving trucks like a lot of folks think. He was in an all-Negro infantry division, the 92nd I think it was. Fought in the mountains in Italy. His unit was the first one across the Arno River north of Rome before the Nazis surrendered up there. And he earned a Purple Heart."

"And you take him at his word about all that?" Alan asked.

"Yeah, I do. Me and him talked a good amount, and I can tell when a man's lying to me. He wasn't bragging about it. He was just saying it. And here's the other thing. He's got a way about him that's different too. You've seen him around town. Think about it. He knows what white folks say about Negroes having a place and needing to stay in it, and he's careful to do that, but he's not somebody you could push around much about it, and I think everybody knows that, blacks and whites. You don't see anybody messing with him. He doesn't have to say anything. Folks just see it in him. They respect him. They probably wouldn't call it that, but that's what it is. Well, a lot of it might be fear, I guess, but that's not a bad thing either."

Neither Alan nor Neal said anything. Mr. Claude could see they were mulling it over. "He can drive too," he said, grinning.

"But he's a Negro," Alan said, and looked at Neal.

"Have you ever heard of anything like this, a black officer anywhere in the South?" Neal asked. "Seems to me this'd just be asking for trouble."

"There's one in Little Rock right now," Mr. Claude said. "I met him at the state police association. He's a Pulaski County deputy sheriff. He was in the army, too, like Leon. Seems to me if it caused very much of a problem, we'd have heard about it, what with all the school fuss they've got up there."

"Hmm," Alan said. He rubbed his hand across the bottom half of his face and grasped his chin between his thumb and forefinger. "I guess if we did this, it'd at least help keep the Negroes from starting something."

"It might," Mr. Claude said, "but if you ever put it to him like that, there's no way he'd take the job."

"Mr. Claude," Neal said, "I remember hearing you cuss black folks lots of times, even remember hearing you tell more than one to get back where he belongs. Saw you bust a couple of black heads with that noggin-knocker you carry too. Some of this stuff you've been saying here is pretty different. How'd you come to it?"

Mr. Claude did not answer right away. He pulled his arms back and folded his fingers together on the table and seemed to study them for a minute or two. "Time," he said. "Time brought me to it. Experience too. And age. Things are changing, and there's some things coming we can't stop, no matter how we might feel about them. What we can do is try to make the best of it. That's what my daddy was doing when he sold our farm and moved us to town when I was a kid." He unfolded his hands, put his palms on the table, and pushed his shoulders back. "A while ago I was cleaning out some things, and I came across some old newspapers I'd saved from back then, and I've been looking through them. In 1910, the year me and Irene got married, the *Unionville Advocate* had an anniversary issue where they wrote about all the merchants and other businesses in town and the bright future they were all expecting. And in one of the pieces they said, 'All good people are cordially welcomed.' They were talking about white people, of course, but I'm thinking that if Unionville is gon' keep growing and being prosperous, like it was doing then, and like you want Pearl Goodbar to help it do now by putting out a good paper, it's gon' take everybody, white and black, working together and not fighting with each other. To put it plain and simple, we don't have but two choices. We can tear up our nest, or we can keep trying to build it up."

"Hmm," Alan said, again. "You sure you're not aiming for my job, Mr. Claude?" They all chuckled, then Alan said, "All right, you've given us a lot to think about. We'll sleep on it."

CHAPTER 27

Late Monday afternoon, Alan Poindexter and Neal O'Brien stopped by the newspaper office and asked Pearl if they could talk with her privately and off the record. They went to her office in the back, closed the door, and all three of them stood in front of her desk. Alan told her about talking to Mr. Claude and what he suggested.

"Well, I'll be John Brown!" she said, calling up from somewhere what her late mother and her Aunt Myrtle had always used for "I'll be damned." She walked around the desk and sat down. "Are you really considering that?" she asked.

The men took chairs in front of the desk. Alan told Pearl that he and Neal had slept on Mr. Claude's idea, gotten up early this morning and talked about it some more, and managed to see most members of the council during the course of the day. It looked like a majority would approve it. None particularly liked it, but they did not see any other option than Mr. Claude for town marshal, and they knew he meant what he had said. There was no other way to persuade him to take the job except to agree to what he was proposing.

"Maybe they just need more time to think about it," Pearl said.

Alan said that might be, but Mr. Claude was going to talk with Leon tomorrow. They expected he would want to discuss it with his wife. But if he agreed in time, they were looking to have a special council meeting Wednesday night.

"We want to get it done quick so we can cut down time for people to do a lot of worrying and speculating," Neal said. It would be an official public meeting, and they expected Pearl to be there and write about it, but they also expected her to keep at least the Leon part under her hat until it was over. Alan emphasized again they did not see any other solution and they did not want to have any public fuss over it before they could make it official.

Pearl said she understood and that she kind of liked both the Mr. Claude part and the Leon part, but she thought a lot of people would have a hissy fit about it, if not worse. "And how do you plan to deal with things that come up before you get all of this approved and in place?" she asked.

"Sheriff Eubanks is gon' have a county car down here at least once every day, maybe twice, pretty much like he did during all that trouble last year before we got a police car," Neal said.

"Have you thought about the night watchman's job? Who you could get to take that on?"

"No, not yet. We might have to see if Mr. Claude will work in the afternoon and evening and not worry about morning and overnight. When Crow Hicks was night watchman, he napped in the town hall most of the time anyway, till we caught him at it."

Leon and Wanda Jackson lived in a year-old white frame house not far from the Mt. Zion Baptist Church. He waited till after supper Tuesday night to bring up Mr. Claude's idea.

Some evenings, weather permitting, they liked to sit for a while on the front porch, drink iced tea, and listen to kids playing around the neighborhood. This evening, Leon said he wanted to stay in the kitchen because there was something they needed to talk about.

Wanda was a slender brown woman who worked in the principal's office at the black school and was fussy about her appearance, even at home, and Leon loved her for it. She put two glasses of tea on the table, took off her apron, sat down, and said, "Okay, what is it? Is it something I'm not gon' like?" Leon reached for his glass and spun it around on the table with his fingers a few times. "It is, isn't it?" she asked.

"It may be," he said. Then he told her about what had happened to Jesse Culpepper and what Mr. Claude was proposing.

Like Leon, Wanda regularly read the *Pittsburgh Courier* and kept up not only with things happening with school desegregation in Little Rock, but also with things happening with voting rights and bus riding and such in Mississippi, Alabama, and other places. "I guess I can see how this might fit with the movement," she said, "but do you really want to take a chance on going through what happened last year all over again?" Their previous house had been destroyed in a fire set by a white man who hated black people and the prospect that Unionville schools might be desegregated sometime soon. And apparently all Leon had done to set the fellow off was carry himself well, run a successful business, and get along with most everybody, black and white. Members of Leon's and Wanda's church, along with others in the community, some of them white, had contributed money, materials, and labor to help the Jacksons rebuild, but they had lost personal things

they could not replace, and Leon, working evenings and weekends, had only recently finished up the inside.

"I'm not a hundred percent sure," Leon said, "but I'm close
to it. I was thinking about something I said to Reverend Moseley once. It was about keeping an eye out for the right time to
do things. You know, watching for when there's a real chance
to make something work. We were talking about what Mrs.
Bates is doing up in Little Rock and how what happens up
there is gon' affect things down here, maybe not this year, but
pretty soon. This business with Mr. Claude seems like it could
help pave the way for that a little bit here."

"How do you think it's gon' do that?"

"This would be integrating law enforcement. Mr. Claude's
not looking at it that way, and I'm pretty sure the mayor and
Mr. O'Brien ain't either. They're just thinking about getting
done what they think is needed for public safety. But it'd be
integration just the same. And maybe it'd help a few white
folks be more open-minded about desegregating the schools."

"Yeah, I guess, but seems to me it's just as likely to make
things worse. Might be even more likely to. You know there's
a whole bunch of white people that'd get hopping mad. One
of them might even shoot you. I don't know how I'd live if
something happened to you, Leon. I don't even know if I could
take worrying about it all the time." She pushed her tea away,
looked down at the table, and fiddled with her wedding ring.

"That's possible, sure. But I don't think it's likely, because
this'd be something Mr. Claude and the town council are
doing. It'd be coming from them, not from black folks. I'm
not asking for this. They're asking me. I think that makes a difference. And when I do a good job—and I will—that could

help change a few minds about things. Wanda, I think we have to take the risk."

"Are you sure you can keep up with the shop and do this too?" she asked. Leon said he did not think that would be a problem. Then she asked, "Will you have a uniform, like Jesse Culpepper?"

"No, I'll do like Mr. Claude. I'll just keep wearing my white shirts and black pants, and I'll find an old suit coat to wear. But I'm not gon' go traipsing around without a gun like he does. And I'll have a badge, of course."

"Leon, some of them crackers see you with a gun, that'll be like waving a red flag in front of a bull."

"I'm not a fool, woman. I ain't gon' carry it so's they can see it."

Wanda got up and came around the table, and Leon rose and took her in his arms. "I'm awful proud of you, Leon," she said softly, "but I'm gon' be worried half to death. You got to promise me you're gon' be careful."

"I will, baby. I will."

In a rare small-town instance of everyone who knows something keeping their mouths shut about it, the Arkansas-side council members got together for a special meeting on Wednesday night without tipping their hands. Neal O'Brien posted the required public notice on the front door of the town hall, but as he had sometimes done in the past, he put it on the inside of the door instead of the outside, and no one noticed it. When he called the members to order, Alan, Pearl, and Mr. Claude were the only other people there. Neal sat at the only desk in the small front room and the others sat on folding chairs. American and Arkansas flags drooped in floor stands in the back, and an oscillating table fan struggled to cool the warm late-August air.

Neal stated for the record that he had confirmed with Jesse Culpepper's family that he would not be able to work for a long while. He then called on the mayor to summarize what the two of them were proposing. Alan did so, stressing that Mr. Claude's and Leon's appointments would be temporary, and they would work as a pair, with Leon patrolling and responding to emergencies alone only when absolutely necessary.

Even though Alan and Neal had already talked to everyone individually, the discussion, which flowed along the same lines as their earlier conversations with each other and with Mr. Claude, took longer than the two leaders expected. Several members complained that Alan and Neal had laid the idea on them too quick-like and they had not had enough time to consider it. Some who had said earlier that they were okay with it now said they were no longer sure it was a good idea. They worried that it would cause more problems than it solved. After a lot more discussion, Neal came to believe that every member of the six-man council might accept it simply because none could come up with a better solution to the town's need for some kind of ongoing law enforcement presence. He went around the room once more and asked each council member to say how he was feeling about the matter. Five of the six said they would support the proposal, but each of those emphasized again that he had serious reservations and was going along only because he did not see any workable alternative. Each also said he wanted his statement to that effect put in the minutes of the meeting. The only person who remained solidly against the proposal was Lawrence Perkins, son of Doc Perkins. Citing his experience as an insurance salesman, he repeated the argument he had already made, that hiring a black law officer would make the town less safe instead of more and was therefore reckless. "What's gon' happen," he asked, "if somebody kills him? Or, the good Lord forbid, he shoots a white man?" They had been over that before, but raising it again was enough to keep them debating and to turn one other member against the idea, as he was already more on the fence than the others. In the end, however, the council approved Leon's appointment by a vote of four to two.

With that done, they set to arguing about how best to let the town know what they had decided. Eventually, Pearl asked to be recognized and told them she could put their official announcement in Friday's paper, which people would first see on Saturday morning. That is, she said, if the council decided tonight that they wanted her to. Alan said he was afraid if they went that route, someone at the newspaper might talk about it before the paper was distributed. Pearl came back with, "My folks won't talk. I'll see to it. What about y'all?"

⌒

After deciding, wisely Pearl thought, to let her publish their announcement and to make it short and to the point, the council members left the writing of it to Neal. He delivered it to Pearl's office early Thursday morning. After he left, she called everyone together, including Emma Lou MacDonald, who had brought in a new recipe for the following week. Pearl told them about the council's decision, the reasoning behind it, and the need to keep it quiet until Saturday. Each one assured her it would not be a problem.

"All right, then," she said. "We've got to work fast. Emma Lou, we need you to help tomorrow if you can." Emma Lou said she could, and Pearl asked if anyone had any questions before they hopped to it.

Grady tipped back his newsboy cap and said, "I ain't got a question, but I sorta wish I lived closer to town so I could hear the fireworks Saturday morning."

"It ought to be interesting," Emma Lou said.

Remembering how Deputy Quinn had treated Sadie Rose the day he and Jesse Culpepper went to tell her that the body found at the dump was her son, Pearl wondered how she and other black people would feel about Leon's hiring and whether they would attach any potential benefit to it.

CHAPTER 28

Earlier in the week, Pearl had saved space in the upper right corner of the front page, and now she put the Arkansas-side council's announcement there so readers would see it first thing when they got their papers on Saturday morning. She used the simple headline requested by the council.

Official Announcement

The Town Council of Unionville, Arkansas, announces that Police Chief Jesse Culpepper has been placed on medical leave for an indefinite period of time not expected to extend past the end of this calendar year, and until he returns, Claude Satterfield will return to duty as Unionville Marshal and Leon Jackson will serve in the newly created position of Unionville Deputy Marshal. These appointments are effective starting August 30, 1958. The council calls upon all citizens of Unionville to give Marshal Satterfield and Deputy Marshal Jackson their full support and cooperation.

In her lead front-page story, Pearl reported on Jesse's accident, gave an update on his condition, which was encouraging, noted the action taken at the special council meeting, and quoted the mayor trying hard to put a spin on it that would appeal to as many people as possible. He said, "We are confident that this pairing of an experienced officer, who patrolled our streets for many years, with another man we all also know and respect, and who saw combat duty in World War II, will ensure an efficient and effective continuation of our recently added mobile law enforcement capacity."

For her "Editor's Corner," Pearl wrote a short piece, under the headline "Town Council Shows Backbone," to address head-on the thing she thought everyone would focus on: The new deputy marshal was a black man. On a hunch, she had called the sheriff's department in Pulaski County and learned that Atlanta and Miami each had several black officers. Pointing to them and the Pulaski County deputy, she wrote:

> This newspaper applauds the members of the Unionville, Arkansas, Town Council for having the courage to join three of the leading metropolitan areas in the South—Little Rock, Atlanta, and Miami—and break with tradition to meet the policing needs of this community. The council members know, as do we, that everyone may not support their decision to hire a black officer like local governments in each of the aforementioned places has done, but they hope, as do we, that everyone will respect it and extend every courtesy to Marshal Satterfield and Deputy Marshal Jackson.

Pearl did not get home in time for supper Friday night because the late additions she made on Thursday disrupted their typesetting schedule and caused the printing to run late. Feeling it important to tell Wendell, Nancy, and Alice about Mr. Claude and Leon as soon as possible, however, rather than have them read it in the paper or hear it from someone else, she gathered them in the living room before they went to bed. The girls, already in their pajamas, sat on the sofa, and Pearl and Wendell sat in upholstered chairs. His crutches lay on the floor beside him.

"This is a pretty big deal," she said, after she gave them the details, "and there's probably gon' be some people setting up a howl, and some of them are probably gon' be mad at me for supporting it. I thought you ought to know that ahead of time, and know what the council's reasoning is, too, and how it's all gon' work." She looked at Wendell but Nancy spoke first.

"Momma, you've all but come right out and said you're for integrating the schools, so how's this gon' be any different?" She pulled her legs up under her, put her feet together, and rested an elbow on the arm of the sofa, getting comfortable for a long talk.

The question surprised Pearl. She crossed her legs, smoothed the skirt of her shirtwaist, and took a minute to gather her thoughts. She and her family had talked generally about what was happening around the country and the world over supper and on other occasions ever since the girls were old enough to understand and join in. These conversations had included the civil rights movement. In a broad way the Goodbars were sympathetic toward it almost from the outset, at least as far as things like voting rights and, to a lesser extent, equal access to certain types of public accommodations were concerned. They

also reluctantly accepted that eventually schools would be integrated everywhere as a matter of law, though until the last year
or so that did not seem like something close at hand for Unionville, even with all that had been going on in Little Rock. Before
Pearl's editorials, none in the family had done or said anything
that might be considered advocating for any of these changes,
even though they disliked the violence some folks used to try
to stop them. And Pearl had not said much about her pieces at
home, other than when she and Wendell talked about the negative financial effect they were having. For one thing, she was busy
with a ton of work and not home a lot, and for another, she did
not want the girls to see their parents fussing with each other.
She realized now that holding back might have been a mistake.
All Nancy knew about her mother's current feelings came from
the newspaper. Pearl wished now she had talked more with the
girls about her work.

"I haven't said I'm for integrating the schools exactly,"
Pearl replied. "I've said I'm against mistreating people because
of the color of their skin, and I'm for complying with federal
law, with *Brown v. Board of Education*.

"I don't see what the difference is, Momma," Alice said.
She was sitting with her legs crossed beneath her on the sofa,
hands in her lap.

"Girls, maybe there isn't any difference in the long run,
but at least for some folks I think hearing me say, 'Obey the
law,' somehow seems more reasonable than hearing me say,
'Integrate the schools.' They hear 'integrate the schools' and
that makes them think of integrating eating places, theaters,
rest rooms, and such, and they get a whole lot more riled up."

"Momma, are you sure those people really think that way?"
Nancy asked. "I mean that you're only saying, 'Obey the law.'

Or are you just hoping they do, because you believe if you can get them to look at it that way, it's gon' make everything go easier?"

"Probably some of both, I guess."

"Well, are you for integrating the schools, or not?" Alice asked.

"How do you girls feel about it?" Pearl asked.

"I don't spend much time thinking about it," Nancy said. "Seems like we're gon' have to anyway. I don't believe it'll bother me any, if that's what you mean."

"Yeah, same here," Alice said. "But what about you? Are you for it, or are you against it?"

Wendell, sitting with his hands on the arms of his chair, had been resisting interrupting the back and forth, but now he said, "I think what your mother has been trying to do is express her opinions in relation to specific events. So maybe she can kind of move people's thinking along a little at a time." Pearl looked over at him, her eyes registering her surprise.

"So, Momma," Alice asked again, "are you for integrating the schools or not?"

"Yes," Pearl said. "I've come to that. I think it's the right thing to do, and not only because of *Brown*."

"All right, then," Alice replied, "why don't you just say so?"

Pearl did not answer. Instead, she brought the conversation back to the starting point. "Some people are gon' think that's exactly what I'm saying by supporting Leon Jackson's appointment. They're gon' collapse the two things together and see me as getting in their face, and when you go back to school next week, some of the kids might try to get in your faces about it too."

"That's all right," Alice said. "We can handle it."

"Yeah," Nancy echoed. "We can handle it."

After Nancy and Alice went off to bed, Pearl said, "Wendell, those are really good kids. And smart too."

"That they are," Wendell said. "I only hope you and I can handle it."

"Now don't start in again about the money," Pearl said. "It's not gon' help. I'll figure something out."

"I'm not. I'm with you. I want you to keep on speaking your mind. In the meantime, I have an idea I'm gon' look into."

"What is it?"

"I'm not ready to say."

⌒

As expected, rain blew in before dawn Saturday morning. Grady Atwell had planned to finish re-painting his barn, but being unable to, he let his curiosity get the best of him and drove into town to see what folks at Emmett's Café were saying about the big news. Grady did not go to Emmett's often, even during the week, but he was there enough that a lot of folks knew he worked at the newspaper. Not wanting to call any more attention to that than necessary today, though, he left his newsboy hat at home and wore a faded John Deere baseball cap.

When he got there a little after eight, the place was packed, partly on account of the weather he reckoned. He took a seat at the end of the counter but near a row of booths, out of the center of things but still, he thought, where he might hear a lot. A couple of men he knew said hello to him on his way to sit down, but no one said anything about the paper. Not even Emmett, who came over and took his order for pancakes and coffee.

As Grady waited for his food, he found that although he could make out some of what people were saying, all the noise from talk, laughter, and dishes made it impossible for him to follow anyone closely. Folks who were not swapping fish tales about the big ones that got away had more than town council news to talk about. Governor Faubus had been busy all week angling for ways to keep Little Rock schools segregated, and since Wednesday there had been two big developments.

First, Faubus got the state legislature to pass a bill allowing him to close any school federal courts ordered integrated, if he believed that opening it with black students in attendance would lead to violence or hinder learning. The law also authorized him to call an election allowing parents in a district with a court-affected school to vote on whether or not they wanted integration in their district. He also got approval to withhold state support from any schools he closed and to use that money to fund private segregated schools. And as he had done the previous year, he questioned the authority of the federal government to decide matters he thought states had the right to determine.

Second, Chief Justice Earl Warren postponed a decision in the US Supreme Court about whether to uphold the federal circuit court of appeals ruling that integration of the Little Rock schools should go forward.

For those and other reasons, no one in Little Rock seemed sure when the school year would begin or under what circumstances. Pearl had included some of this news in this week's *Unionville Times*, but some of it had happened after she went to press. This meant most folks in Emmett's were getting their information from the *El Dorado Daily News*, from the *Arkansas Gazette*, from radio and television, and from each other, all of which led to a variety of understandings with aggravation being the only shared ingredient.

From the snippets Grady heard, most everyone thought Faubus was some kind of hero, and there was a lot of popping off about never letting black kids go to the white school in Unionville. He could not make out everything that customers were saying about Leon Jackson being made a deputy marshal, but he could pick up enough to know they did not like it. If he had any doubt about how deep the feeling ran, that cleared up for him when he overheard someone say, "Somebody ought to do him like they done that Washington nigger."

Grady had almost finished eating when Boomer Jenkins, who had come in sometime after he did, spotted him, came stomping over with Crow Hicks trailing behind, and bellowed, "Well, I'll be damned. We got us one of them nigger-loving newspaper jaybirds sitting right here. Grady, looks like you'd be afraid to show your face in here with all these good ole boys after what that boss of yours wrote." Boomer turned back toward the middle of the café and said, "Begging the pardon of all you ladies in here, but ain't that right, boys?"

There was a chorus of, "Yeah," and, "You're damned right," around the room. Grady, having already swung around on his stool to face Boomer, waited until things quieted down and said, "Things ain't always what they look like, are they, Boomer?" Then he turned back around and took up where he had left off with his pancakes.

Having failed to get the rise he wanted, Boomer glared at the back of Grady's head for a moment then gave him a shove in the back and said, "You tell Pearl Goodbar we're tired of reading that shit she's writing and we ain't gon' keep putting up with it." With that, he turned, pushed Crow aside, and headed back to his own stool at the end of the counter.

"Yeah, dickhead," Crow said to Grady before following along, "you tell her she better wise up."

Across the room, someone shouted, "That's telling him, boys!" Then, everyone started talking at once, and no one said anything more to Grady until he paid his bill.

"If I was you," Emmett told him, "I'd do like they said."

"Let me ask you something, Emmett," Grady said. "I'm curious. If you feel that way, why are you still advertising with her?"

"I got a business to run," Emmett said. "I ain't against having a newspaper. I'm against what she's writing in it. You just tell her what them boys said. It's for her own good."

CHAPTER 29

Pearl had been noticing for several weeks that a few First Baptist folks seemed less friendly on Sunday mornings. At first, she thought it was because she had not been going to worship regularly. This Sunday, though, even some members she knew better than others appeared to push out their "Hello" and "Morning" greetings like saying the words put some kind of strain on their vocal chords. Anna Louise Thornton, whose husband worked for an oil well service company in El Dorado, did not speak at all. Sue James, a widow who clerked in Lawson's Dry Goods, said while passing in the aisle before preaching started, "I'm really disappointed in you, Pearl Goodbar." And Janelle Ferguson, who was a teller at Farmers State Bank, made a point of coming over to where Pearl was sitting in the back of the sanctuary with her family and whispering in her ear, "I always liked you, Pearl, but now I'm just plumb ashamed of you."

As the service went along, Pearl could not stop thinking about how these worshipers had reacted to her. She realized that she had been so caught up with her family, her employees, and a few others in the community, like Alan Poindexter, Neal O'Brien, and Mr. Claude, that she had too often been regarding her readers and others in the community as either people who agreed with her or could be persuaded to, or as people like Elmer Spurlock, Crow Hicks, and Boomer Jenkins, who so vehemently disliked blacks that nothing would likely change the way they behaved. She had even been looking at her business cancellations more as dollars lost than as individuals she was ticking off. Today had felt a lot more personal, and it brought Pearl back to what Hazel Brantley said a few days ago about how complicated this all was for her. People and their views did not fit neatly into one box or another. Things spilled over. Pearl also recalled how the men in Emmett's Café had talked about Elton Washington after his beating and how Deputy Quinn had talked to Sadie Rose after her son was killed. Today's remarks did not feel as bad as those seemed, but they did not feel good.

<hr />

Pearl, Grady, and the others at the paper had done enough advance work on the next issue of the *Unionville Times* to be able to take Labor Day off. They did not have to listen to any complaints on Monday. However, people who took exception to the town's having a black deputy marshal and Pearl's defense of it had plenty to say about it on Tuesday.

The day started with Grady sharing what he had heard at Emmett's on Saturday morning. Pearl feared a rash of additional cancellations would follow as the hours wore on, but there were fewer than after some of her earlier editorials. One caller, when asked why she was cancelling her subscription, said it was because Brother Spurlock had told her, "Nobody should put up with having a Negro marshal, or with any idiot who thinks it's a good idea." Pearl quipped to Hazel and Grady that nearly everyone out at the Mercy Baptist Mission who was going to stop taking the paper probably already had, else there would have been more calls, because it was pretty clear Spurlock had lambasted Leon Jackson—and her again too—from the pulpit.

Grady said the White Citizens' Council was meeting tonight and he was thinking about going to hear what Spurlock had to say there. Pearl said she appreciated that and thought she ought to go, too, especially since she had never attended one of their meetings. Hazel said that would be tempting fate and she ought not do it. Grady seconded that thought, and Pearl knew they were right.

Tuesday was also the first day of school in Unionville, and over supper Pearl learned about a different kind of reaction to her editorials. Nancy and Alice both said several students asked them why their mother wanted them to go to school with black kids, and a boy in Nancy's homeroom told her not to talk to him because, "Your mother is a nigger lover." Another student got up and moved when Nancy sat down at the table where he was working on something in the library during study hall. Alice said she was walking in a hallway with a friend, and when they passed Coach Roberts and said, "Hello" to him, he said, "Goodbar, your mother better be careful."

Pearl and Wendell were livid and neither could keep it from showing. She felt guilty for causing her daughters to have to go through what they did. Wendell said he had a good mind to go see Superintendent Appleby and complain. But he admitted that this was a kneejerk reaction and would not do any good because the superintendent made no secret about his unwavering opposition to integration. Nancy and Alice both said, "No way," because it would make things worse all around.

Then Nancy made them laugh by asking her father how he thought he would get to the school anyway, because she certainly was not going to drive him there so he could embarrass her by making a fuss. They talked a long while about the meanness in the things said to them and about ignoring the coach and the bullying students as much as possible.

"We told you," Nancy said finally. "We can handle this."

"Yeah," Alice said.

But they did not sound as sure about it as they had last Friday night—especially Alice—and it hit Pearl hard.

Grady thought about asking his cousin, Mr. Claude, to go with him to the Citizens' Council meeting but decided that the marshal's being there would probably only get everybody more stirred up and make Mr. Claude spitting mad for nothing. As he had when he went to Emmett's on Saturday, Grady again left his newsboy hat at home and wore his faded John Deere cap. He hoped to arrive early enough to find a seat in the back where he could slip out without being noticed. But when he pulled into the Mercy Baptist Mission's gravel parking lot at twenty minutes to seven, it was already filling up. He parked his pickup under a tall pine tree where he would not be blocked in, and climbing out, he heard a recording of a John Phillip Sousa march blaring over a loudspeaker through the open church windows. As he walked across the lot, the music changed to "When the Roll Is Called up Yonder" with a gospel quartet singing about doing the work of God in order to be ready when Gabriel blew his horn. Grady calculated right then that Elmer Spurlock intended to turn the meeting into some kind of call for Citizens' Council members to go out and smite the enemies of segregation in the name of the Lord. Shortly after Grady got inside and grabbed a seat way over in a back corner, the music switched to "Onward Christian Soldiers." Spurlock's big Confederate flag hanging on the wall behind the pulpit completed the scene.

There were a lot of men in the audience whom Grady did not know, but he saw Boomer Jenkins, Crow Hicks, Emmett Ledbetter, Odell Grimes, Herbert Kramer, Vernon Appleby, and a few others whose names he did not remember but whom he had seen in Emmett's from time to time. As far as Grady could tell, no one paid him any attention.

In a few minutes Spurlock, founder and president of the Citizen's Council, came out of a side door wearing a suit with a coat too small to button over his corn-bread-and-mashed-potatoes belly. He laid a Bible on the pulpit as if he intended to preach then asked everyone to stand for the usual playing of "The Star Spangled Banner" and "Dixie." When folks sat down, Spurlock dispensed with anything resembling any sort of business meeting. He asked God to bless the members of the Citizens' Council and its mission to "save the white race." Then he lit in on Alan Poindexter, Neal O'Brien, and Leon Jackson and what he called "the absolute folly and downright sinful wrong-headedness of giving a black man a gun and the authority to shoot white people." He also had a few choice words about Mr. Claude, whom he called "a senile old fool too far gone to recognize he was being played for a pawn in a liberal-inspired war against good law-abiding white people."

Those and similar comments sparked repeated applause from his sixty-some listeners, and Grady was more than ready to leave when Spurlock dialed his spiel up another notch, heading into his call to action.

"I tell y'all right now," he said, "we've been blessed in this community to have people like our school board president, Herbert Kramer, and our superintendent of schools, Vernon Appleby, that've stood up against integrating our classrooms, and if we want to keep them segregated, you and me have got to stand up against politicians who think having a colored law officer is okay and a newspaper editor who thinks black folks ought to be treated just like they was white. Like I already told my congregation, if we don't stop this kind of wrong-headed thinking now, we're gon' end up with black kids sitting with our white kids in school, eating with them in the cafeteria, and riding with them in school buses, and then the next thing you know, they'll all be sleeping with each other and we'll be overrun with a bunch of yellow mongrels. I ain't lying. That's exactly what's gon' happen, and y'all know it. So, y'all have got to let them holier-than-thou idiots on the Arkansas-side council know you don't like what they've done and you ain't gon' vote for them come next election. And like I've told you before, you're gon' have to stop patronizing that Goodbar woman's newspaper in any way, shape, or form."

Applause erupted all across the room, and when it died down, Spurlock leaned over the pulpit and said in a lower tone, but still loud enough to be heard, "And I expect some of you can think of some other ways to let all of them know we ain't gon' lie down and let them put this kind of red Commie crap over on us."

There was more applause, and down front somewhere there were several catcalls of, "Right on," "We hear you, brother," and "We got it." Some in the audience were still hooting when Grady slipped out the back door.

CHAPTER 30

As Pearl pulled into her usual parking place Wednesday morning, she saw a knot of men standing in front of the café. Early in the day like this, there were always a good number of folks going in and out, but they did not usually hang around outside this way. If Emmett's regulars did not head off to work somewhere, they generally stayed inside to shoot the breeze or, in good weather, they crossed the street to the whittler's tree.

Because she was looking toward the men, she did not glance at her building until she got out of her car, and then she saw why they were standing outside. Across both of her large front windows someone had used bar soap to scrawl "Nigger Lover" in large, uneven letters. Seeing the graffiti stopped her in her tracks, and she heard thinly muffled guffaws from the direction of the café. The men had been waiting to see her reaction. Although curious about who they were, she resisted looking back at them. Instead, she unlocked the front door, went inside, put her purse on her desk, got a camera, came back out, and took pictures of both windows. Then she turned the camera toward the gawkers and snapped their photograph. If she had it enlarged, she could eventually identify each of them. She would not know which, if any, of them did the writing, but at least they would be wondering what she intended to do with their picture. Put it in the paper maybe? A couple of the men yelled at her, but she turned away from them and walked back inside and closed the door as if nothing out of the ordinary had happened. Then she kicked her desk chair so hard she hurt her foot. A few seconds later she was on the phone to Mr. Claude.

"Aw, crap," he said, after she told him what happened. "I'll be there in a few minutes."

"I'm not sure I want you to do anything about it," she said, "but I'd like them to know you've seen it before I wash it off. Give them something to think about."

Mr. Claude was wearing his usual marshal's get up when he arrived at the newspaper office. "Did you get a good enough look at them to see who they were?" he asked.

"No," Pearl said, "not really. I think I caught a glimpse of Crow Hicks's faded overalls, and I'm pretty sure I saw Odell Grimes in his barber's smock, but I don't have a clue about any of the others. I didn't want to give them the satisfaction of more than a glance."

Pearl told Mr. Claude about the photograph she took, and he said if she got the shot of the men blown up enough for him to see who they were, he could talk to them, but there would be no way to prove any of them did the writing. At best, all he could stick anyone with would be a misdemeanor and a fine. Pearl said she understood and he should just let it drop.

"Yeah, I agree," he said, "but I'm gon' walk over to Emmett's and tell him and whoever else is in there that if this happens again I'm gon' be inclined to put the whole bunch of them in jail on suspicion and throw away the key till I can find out whichever of them's guilty."

"They know you're not gon' do that."

"Yeah, but they'll still puzzle over it a bit. To tell you the truth," he said, grinning, "it'll be fun just to yell at them. The dadblamed peckerwoods! Are you gon' put a picture of the window in the paper?"

"I don't think so. Why give whoever did it that satisfaction?"

⌒

By the time Mr. Claude left, Grady, Hazel, and Emma Lou, who was back with more quilt patterns that she and Almalee Jolly had put together, had seen the writing. Their reactions ranged from surprise and irritation to concern.

"I'd bet a dollar to a doornail," Hazel said, "that Crow Hicks had something to do with it. He's got pig slop for brains."

Emma Lou said, "I'll put my nickel on Odell Grimes. He's just goofy enough to do something this juvenile."

Grady got a mop and a bucket of water and washed off the windows, and when he came back inside, he found Pearl in her rear office and told her about the White Citizens' Council meeting. "It wasn't exactly what I expected," he said. "It was more like some kind of revival meeting. Spurlock's really good at pushing people's hot buttons, and he sure has it in for you. I expect before all the bile he was spewing wears off, we're gon' see a lot more of this fool stuff."

Pearl watched Grady when he left to go back to his type-setting, his newsboy cap jutting at a perfect angle, and thought that for someone who did not say much the day he came to see about working for her, he was becoming downright talkative. She also counted herself lucky to have found him.

Later in the day, they saw some of the additional fallout he predicted, as more cancellations came in, especially for subscriptions and for printing invitations and such. Only one advertiser cancelled, but it was a good-size loss, Unionville Feeds. Things were getting to a point where Pearl feared she might have to cut down the number of pages in each issue from the usual eight to six, and she hated the thought of it. That was partly because of pride and partly because she did not want to give any quarter to people who did not like what she was doing. But it was also because she still had enough content and advertising for nearly seven pages. After thinking about it for a while, she decided she would stay with eight by stretching some of her local stories, providing larger ads at no additional cost to her biggest advertisers, and offering discount pricing to new advertisers and also to current ones willing to renew for extended time periods. She also started thinking again about going to see Horace Bowman and asking if she could get some sort of deal that would lower her mortgage payments, even if that meant spreading the debt over a longer period and even if Wendell did not want to. Maybe she would not tell him until after she got Bowman to agree to it. Then it would be harder for Wendell not to go along.

Whoever soaped Pearl Goodbar's windows was not the only person whose buttons Elmer Spurlock pushed with his ranting. His rancorous outpouring also moved Herbert Kramer, but in a different way. He could not stop thinking about what the preacher said about black people and white people sleeping with each other and making what he called "mongrel" children. Kramer had done it and loved it years ago with one black woman, and now he had another one he could sleep with any time he wanted to. He knew other white men got it on with black women, or at least some liked saying they did and bragging about it. He expected a lot more of them fantasized about it but were afraid to do it themselves. He never talked about it, however, because he liked doing something people did not know about and he could get away with. And, of course, if people knew about it, it would hurt his position in the community. Mostly, though, he liked the sex. All the way home from the White Citizens' Council meeting, all he could think about was Priscilla Nobles. She had a near perfect body, just like her mother, and doing her never got old. He could barely wait for the next day.

Normally Kramer went into town after the morning milking, picked up Priscilla, brought her to the farm, and left her with Lorraine to cook and do housework until noon. Then, if he were in the mood, when Priscilla brought him dinner, he took her in whatever way he wanted. He did not like how—except for that one time several weeks back—she no longer put up a fuss in the exciting way she did the first time or two, but he still enjoyed her. By noon on the days he wanted her, he made sure the hired hands were off in the fields someplace out of the way, and they never knew a thing. He was not afraid of someone dropping by unexpectedly and catching him at it either. A truck from the processing plant in El Dorado picked up the milk dependably between eleven and noon. The mailbox was down by the main road, and if anyone sent him a package that was too big for the box, the mailman always left a form saying it was at the post office and Kramer had to come pick it up. And he had a closet in the back of his office where he could hide Priscilla if someone happened to drive up for some other reason. Early on, she had learned better than even to think about calling out to anyone who showed up unexpectedly, as she feared not only for herself, but also for her grandparents.

Wednesday morning Kramer found some fencing work for the hired men to do way over on the back of his property as soon as the milking was done, and when he got back from town with Priscilla, he took her straight to his office. When he told her to get out of the truck and go inside, she did as he said, and he stood watching, undressing her with his eyes as she went up the steps and through the door. Then he followed, closed it behind him, started taking off his clothes, and ordered her to, "Get naked." Like the time a few weeks earlier, on the day of Elton Washington's funeral, Priscilla did not do what he said. On that occasion, however, she had merely turned away. Now she looked at Kramer without flinching, and in her eyes he saw a flicker of something different. Rather than the mix of hate and resigned submission he had become used to seeing, this seemed more like defiance. He wondered if she were going to put up a fight. He thought of her hollering and screaming for him to stop, the way she did those first couple of times and again the day of Elton Washington's funeral. Kramer's anticipation of that happening again aroused him almost to the point of pain. He grabbed the front of Priscilla's dress and ripped it off with two powerful yanks, popping buttons and tearing cloth. She kicked at him, and he pushed her to the floor, penned her down, and hit her with his fist. When she did not scream, he hit her again, and when she still did not, he hit her a third time. Now she cried out like he remembered, a long piercing yell from somewhere deep down inside. He got the rest of her clothes off and rammed himself into her, and she screamed again, even louder than before.

Lorraine Kramer had been expecting her husband and Priscilla from town and heard the truck when it came up the gravel access road, but after a few minutes, she realized they were not coming to the house. She went to the front door, lifted a curtain from the edge of a side panel, saw the truck in front of the office, and knew at once what her husband was up to. With no intention of going through it, she cracked the door. Then she heard Priscilla's screams. They came a second time, then a third, and she thought of her own bruises and fractures from Kramer's rages, inflicted over the years for one kind of offense or another he had imagined, or during the many times he had forced himself on her. Lorraine had heard Priscilla screaming a few times before and had managed on those occasions to shut it out, but this time some combination of pain and anger drew her out the door, across the yard, and toward the little white building. She crouched against the wall under a window and heard, as she knew she would, the thumping of bodies against the floor. She sat for a moment, wringing her hands in the folds of her housedress, listening. Then she raised her eyes above the windowsill, looked in, and saw Priscilla on the wood floor, blood around her head with Kramer on top of her, having his way. Even though Lorraine knew her husband had been beating and raping Priscilla like this for what seemed forever, she thought for a moment about rushing inside now and yelling at him to get off her. But fear took over, and she ran for the house, went to the rear, grabbed a broom, and started sweeping. She would pretend as always that she had not seen or heard a thing, and she hated herself for it, just as she hated her husband.

Later, when Kramer came through the house and saw Lorraine filling a dustpan with a pile of sweepings she had been saving until she heard his footsteps, he said from the kitchen door, "Priscilla's had an accident and ruined her clothes. Go find something she can wear and put it on the kitchen table. I'll take it out to her after I eat that leftover corn bread and buttermilk."

CHAPTER 31

Pearl told Wendell about the newspaper windows being soaped, but she did not tell Nancy and Alice. She did not see how their knowing would accomplish anything. If they heard about it later and asked, she would tell them she was ignoring it. Wendell got angry about the soaping, but he agreed that they should not let the girls know that it bothered their parents.

At the office, Pearl pulled out syndicated material left over from last week about how to get kids ready to start school. She calculated that if she used all of it, plus went ahead with her plan to stretch her other stories and give top customers bigger ads without charging more for them, she could come up with an eight-page issue for the holiday-shortened week. With that settled, on Thursday morning she put on one of her best shirtwaist dresses, and shortly before noon, she walked down to Farmers State Bank to see Horace Bowman.

His office door was partly open, and his secretary was standing at his desk waiting for him to finish signing some papers. She saw Pearl through the crack and waved her in. Even though it was after Labor Day, Bowman was still wearing his sky-blue seersucker suit to work several days a week. His jacket was hanging on the back of his chair, his red tie was loose, and he had a cigar going. He looked relaxed.

"What can I do for you Mrs. Newspaper Woman?" he asked, as his assistant left and closed the door. He waved Pearl to one of the low chairs requiring visitors to look up at him. "I hear you've been having a rough time of it," he said, not giving Pearl a chance to answer his question.

"What have you heard?" she asked, as he took a puff of his cigar. She sat down on the front edge of one of the chairs, put her purse on the floor, and folded her hands in her lap.

Bowman took another drag on his stogie and leaned back. "Oh, stuff about that writing on your windows, what ole Spurlock's been saying, and more to the point, that you're losing business. Is that why you're here? You're getting squeezed and you're gon' ask me to bail you out?"

"Well, sir..." Pearl started.

"No need to beat around the bush," he interrupted. "I figured you'd be around, and I'm gon' tell you something. I don't like Elmer Spurlock. The Bible-thumping son of a bitch gives me the creeps, and he don't have sense enough to know he's beating a dead horse. Not that I disagree all that much with his position on integration, mind you. I gotta say, though, you got me thinking some. I've got a lot of coloreds working for me, and in one way—probably the biggest one—they're not much different from white folks. Some of them aren't worth a damn and some of them are good people. Anyway, I like your spunk. Frankly, I didn't think you had it in you, you being a woman and all. But you've jumped into the frying pan with both feet for what you believe. I'm a contrary enough old bastard myself to admire that sort of thing. I think you've gone at things too fast, though. You ought to have held off some."

"Mr. Bowman, I have to write what I think is right. I..."

"Don't do no good to write it if you don't have a place to print it, now does it? You have to stay in business, don't you?"

"Yes, sir, but…"

"There's no but to it. That's the way it is." He set up straight and tapped ashes off the cigar. "Tell you what I'm gon' do. I'm gon' personally lend you the money at no interest to make your September payment on your mortgage. I'll write up a note you can pay at the end of the mortgage or when you sell the paper if you sell it before you've got it paid off. But that's it. That's the only concession I'm ever gon' make to you on this thing. You've got to go figure out some way to turn things around. And this here personal arrangement has got to be kept between me and you. If anybody finds out about this, they'll start thinking I'm not the money-grubbing snake-in-the-grass I'm made out to be, and every Tom, Dick, and Harry in four states will be in here looking for a handout, and I don't have time for that. You hear what I'm saying?"

Pearl did not know whether to be grateful for Bowman's unusual gesture or try to press on and get some sort of longer extension on the loan, and in the few seconds she was trying to think which to do, he decided the matter for her.

"That's it. That's all," Bowman said. "Go on, now. I've got work to do."

Pearl mumbled some words of thanks. Then she realized Bowman was no longer listening and she got up and left. She guessed she was supposed to feel good about having gotten something from the crusty banker that most likely few, if any, other people ever had. But she felt like he had won. And she was still in a tight spot. She wondered how much he really knew about her losses—and how he knew it exactly, other than Brother Spurlock and members of his flock popping off—but that was of no importance now.

⌒

Pearl did not print anything in her next issue about her windows being soaped. Nor did she print anything about the White Citizens' Council meeting or about school desegregation. Plenty about the latter had appeared in the various daily papers during the week.

On Thursday, too late for Pearl to include a story about it in the *Unionville Times*, one hundred high school students in Van Buren, Arkansas, not far from previously integrated schools in Bentonville and Fayetteville up in the northwest corner of the state, walked out of classes in protest against letting in thirteen black students. Then they sent a telegram to Governor Faubus asking him to do something to keep their school segregated. A few days later, pushing and shoving by white high school students in Ozark, a little east of Van Buren, caused the superintendent of schools there to send home three black students trying to integrate that district. Faubus went on television and said, again, that there was more opposition to integration in Arkansas this year than last, when President Eisenhower had used federal troops to force it in Little Rock.

⌒

Heading into the weekend, nearly everyone in Unionville, including Pearl, expected Bobcat football would be the major topic of conversation on Saturday morning, at least among white folks. As in most other small towns, nothing created more excitement year after year than high school football games on Friday nights in the fall. Some people talked about pigskin rivalries, game highlights, and their favorite helmet-wearing heroes all year long. Memories—some accurate and some dressed up by wishful thinking—about past touchdowns, band shows, trips to away games, homecoming celebrations, sweethearts, and even injuries gave adults a convenient way to remember their youth and feel like they remained in tune with old classmates even as they grew farther apart in daily life. Each new season gave them and current students something to look forward to all summer long and then from week to week as leaves turned from green to shades of red, yellow, and brown.

Several hundred people attended each home game, filling all the school parking spaces and lining neighboring streets with their cars and trucks, overflowing the wooden bleachers on each side of the field, and standing along the sidelines and end zones. When the Bobcats played in other towns, parents and fans followed the team and band to the games in motorcades of cars and trucks decorated with black-and-gold streamers.

Union County Sheriff Floyd Eubanks always divided his available deputies and patrol cars among the towns hosting home games to direct traffic, help with emergencies, and discourage mischief by fans carried away by the competition on the field, or in some instances bored with it. Throughout his first stint as town marshal, Mr. Claude attended the home games too. Even without a patrol car, he could help direct traffic, walk the grounds, and watch out for the cash boxes at the ticket gate and concession stand.

This year the Bobcats opened their season at home against the Prescott Wolves, from way up near Hot Springs in Nevada County. The day started off sunny and warm but by dusk a light wind had brought low clouds and cooler air. Still, it was a fine evening for football. As expected, a huge crowd turned out in their not-quite-Sunday-go-to-meeting-but-generally-better-than-everyday clothes looking for a good time. Mr. Claude was back to perform his usual duties, but without his new deputy. At first, Mr. Claude wanted Leon to come with him so people would see them working together and get used to the idea. Also, Mr. Claude thought those who did not like Leon's being a deputy would be less likely to show their displeasure here and disrupt what was supposed to be an evening of fun and good sportsmanship. But Leon thought some people might find safety in numbers and therefore be more likely to sound off or even try to start a fight, which would only make things harder down the line. He said he would rather ease into things. So, he asked to stay at the town hall with the patrol car during the game, and Mr. Claude agreed. If anything happened and Mr. Claude needed wheels independent of the sheriff's deputies, one of them could radio Leon.

After what happened at church last Sunday, Pearl did not want to go to the game and hear more of the same snide remarks. But as editor of the local newspaper, she felt she needed to be there even though, in keeping with arrangements made at the end of last school year, Margaret Rainwater, sponsor of the new high school journalism club, would provide a write-up about the game like she was now doing for other school events. It did not matter that stories about Bobcat games would appear a week late. Parents always liked seeing their kids' names in the paper.

Pearl and Wendell talked about parking along the sidelines and watching the game from their car, but she could not leave work early enough to grab one of the few available spots, and he did not think he could sit through the entire game anyway. So, Pearl got Hazel Brantley to go with her. They sat with Neal O'Brien and his family, and although a few people gave Pearl angry looks, no one said anything to her about the paper. Some, Alan Poindexter's wife Lily among them, were as friendly as always and asked her how she was doing. Most who did that, however, asked in the way people have of being polite without really expecting an answer other than okay, and Pearl obliged them in the customary manner.

Nancy and Alice went to the game with friends and sat with other students but planned to go home with their mother afterward. Ordinarily, Nancy would not have done that. She had been dating the Bobcats' star running back Ronnie Metcalf and had been looking forward to going with him to Emmett's Café after the game to hang out, drink milkshakes, and listen to Elvis Presley and Pat Boone on the juke box. But yesterday Ronnie had told her he could not go out with someone whose mother wanted him to "go to school with coloreds." She was not crazy about Ronnie, but she liked him because he was fun to be with and was probably the most popular boy in school. What he said both hurt her and made her mad. Plus, after the things some of the other kids had said to her during the week, she did not want to face the likelihood of hearing more at Emmett's. Alice, who was not old enough to go hang out, told Nancy that Ronnie was not good enough for her to waste time on, but that did not help.

During the game, Nancy cheered along with everyone else every time Ronnie made a good run, and he made a lot of them. But secretly she hoped he would fumble the ball or get the crap knocked out of him. He did neither, as he gained 225 yards and led Unionville to a 36 to 14 win. When the game ended, all the Goodbars left together, and after dropping off Hazel, they went home to have pie with Wendell and tell him about the game. Unaware of Ronnie's snub, Pearl described every big play he made. Nancy sat for as long as she could while trying to block it all out, but finally she said, "Momma, do you really have to keep talking about Ronnie Metcalf? I'm tired of hearing about him." Then she stormed off to her room leaving her parents exchanging glances that silently asked, "What was that all about?"

When they asked Alice if she knew anything about it, her "Who me?" response pretty much confirmed that things had gone sour between her sister and her sometimes boyfriend. Had Pearl known the cause of it, she might have gone to bed more worried than she already was about how the controversy surrounding her editorials was affecting her family.

Unaware, however, of why Nancy reacted the way she did to talk about Ronnie, Pearl went to bed thinking about him and football in another way. Based on what she knew second-hand from previous football seasons, she expected that the next morning the first thing that most people all over town—especially those that went for haircuts at the barbershop and newsstand, to Emmett's for breakfast, or to the pool hall and domino parlor to play games of their own—would be talking about was the Bobcats. Instead of spending all day and the rest of the weekend fuming and griping about her editorials, they would spend at least a sizeable portion of their time talking, fussing, and arguing about what they did and did not like about the play-calling and officiating at the game and even the performances of the two bands at halftime. Pearl hoped this would distract at least a few of her critics enough for them to ease off a bit on her.

CHAPTER 32

When Alice came running into Pearl's and Wendell's bedroom early Saturday morning in her pajamas screaming, with Nancy close on her heels, Pearl scrambled to reach a lamp on the side table and instinctively looked at the clock. It read twenty-five minutes after two.

"Momma, Daddy, there's a fire!" Alice yelled.

"Oh, my god! Where?" Pearl asked, springing out of bed and trying to step into her slippers.

"We gotta get out!" Wendell said. "Hurry!" He was reaching for his crutches.

"No! It's outside!" Alice said, grabbing at Pearl as she snatched her housecoat from the foot of the bed.

"What? It's where?" Wendell asked, maneuvering his crutches under his arms.

"It's outside!" Nancy said. "Someone's burning a cross in our yard!"

"I'll go look. Y'all stay here," Wendell said. Wearing only a t-shirt and pajama bottoms, no slippers, he held up one of his crutches for a second as if to bar the others from following then hobbled through the door toward the front of the house. The others ignored what he said and followed only inches behind. "Stay back," he ordered again. "Who knows who's out there or what else they might do." Pearl, Nancy, and Alice kept coming, though, and they all got to the double living room windows and saw the thing at the same time.

Standing about thirty feet from the front porch, it rose seven or eight feet above the ground, was engulfed in orange-and-yellow flames from bottom to top, and smelled like a huge kerosene lamp. Small burning pieces that looked like cloth of some kind were rising in the air and floating into nearby trees whose browning leaves made them potentially giant torches.

"God almighty!" Wendell said.

"I'll call the fire department," Pearl said, and rushed to the phone.

"Better get ahold of Mr. Claude too," he called after her. Then, "Stay back from the window, girls."

"Who do you think did it, Daddy?" Nancy asked.

"Cowards, honey, that's who. Ignorant cowards. Some-body stupid who wants to shut your mother up and is afraid to say it to her face."

Within moments after Pearl called, they heard the fire siren go off on the water tower behind the Arkansas-side town hall. It made a shrill whining noise that rose and fell, over and over again, waking everyone in the community and summon-ing members of the all-volunteer department that served both sides of town. Not long after, they heard the town's only fire truck, an aging La France pumper that sounded like it had no muffler, leave its garage next to the town hall and roar toward them. When it arrived with two men in the cab and three rid-ing on the back, other men, including Arkansas-side council president Neal O'Brien, were right behind it in their own trucks and cars. Within minutes they turned a hose on the cross and put out the flames. Then they sprayed water into the nearest trees for good measure. Caught now in the spotlight of the engine and the headlights of some of the firefighters' own vehicles, the cross stood black and wet with wisps of smoke still rising from it and the whole of it stinking now of burned wood and wet burlap, which someone had wrapped around it in thick layers and tied with wire.

When the truck's whining water pump shut down, the loudest sounds in the neighborhood, other than the vehicle's idling engine, were dozens of dogs barking and howling. By this time, nearly all the neighbors had come out of their houses and were standing on their porches and in their yards watching. Dozens of other onlookers had arrived in their cars and trucks and were standing in clumps a short distance behind the fire truck. While the firemen busied themselves rolling up their hose, they kept people from walking onto the Goodbars' yard and approaching the charred remains of the cross. Pearl and Wendell threw on some different clothes, and after telling Nancy and Alice again to stay inside, they came out onto the porch. Mr. Claude and Leon Jackson arrived about that same time, left the patrol car in the middle of the street, and walked over to the cross. Neal came over and joined them, along with mayor Alan Poindexter, who had pulled in right after them.

Pearl, armed with a camera and flash, walked out to meet them. She saw now that the cross was leaning toward the house at a nearly thirty-degree angle. A couple of neighbors standing closest said hello and that they were sorry someone did this. Mr. Claude was walking around looking at the ground. "Whoever put this here sure wasn't afraid of being seen," he said. "It took a while to dig that big a hole. Used a shovel instead of posthole diggers. That's why the thing's leaning that way and the ground's all busted up. They couldn't have hauled it in a regular pickup without it sticking out in the back either. It's clear they didn't much care if somebody saw them."

"Yes, sir. Might even have been as many as three of them," Leon said. "That way, one of them could stay in the truck in case anybody came along and they had to get away in a hurry." Everyone in the little group turned and looked at him as if making sure Unionville really did have a black officer. It was not that most of them seemed to mind Leon personally. It was that for all of them except Mr. Claude, the whole idea of a black man in a position of authority was taking a lot of getting used to.

Mr. Claude said, "Pearl, can we come in and talk to y'all for a minute? Then we'll go see if anybody else around here knows anything about this."

Pearl told them that of course they could, and Neal and Alan said they would stay outside and help keep everybody backed away. As the others went inside, Neal heard a woman who lived down the street from the Goodbars tell another gawker, "Look at that nigger going into the Goodbars' front door just like he belongs there. The way she's been acting, she's brought all this on herself."

The Goodbars told Mr. Claude and Leon all they had seen and heard, but it was nothing that would help identify the culprits. The two officers then went back outside and, together, talked to all the near neighbors, asking if anyone had heard or seen who set the cross or anything else unusual around that time. None of those they talked to said anything about Leon's being along with Mr. Claude as they caught up with them outside or knocked on their doors. But both men could tell that nearly all of them did not like it.

No one knew anything except Charlie Abrams, who was pushing ninety and lived alone four doors north of the

Goodbars, in the opposite direction of downtown. He had gotten up to go to the bathroom and was walking back to his bedroom when he saw headlights coming down the street. Suspicious because of the time, he watched until they passed his house and he could see who it was. "It was that goddamn Crow Hicks," Charlie said. "He's still driving that beat-up old truck he run over my dog Buddy with last winter. The sorry piece of shit. I couldn't see him or tell if there was anybody in there with him, but I'd know that truck anywhere. Still has that Confederate flag painted on the tailgate. I saw it in the streetlight. Had to be him. Who else would be driving it?"

Mr. Claude and Leon told Neal and Alan what they found out. Then Mr. Claude reminded them that even if Crow did it, since there was no law against cross burning and there was only limited property damage, about all they could do to the man was yell at him and write him up for trespassing and disturbing the peace. Mr. Claude also explained that to Pearl and Wendell, and they said they understood. Wendell said he would call someone to take the cross down and repair the yard in the morning.

When the sun came up, football now had plenty of competition for people's Saturday attention after all. At the barbershop and newsstand, Crow Hicks's pal Odell Grimes and his fleshy, near-look-alike brother Lester, who was chief of the volunteer fire department, did not want to talk about anything else. At Emmett's, while not admitting to anything, Crow and his cousin Luke Fenton, a fellow who drove up from Lillie, Louisiana, a few miles down US 167 every Sunday to go to the Mercy Baptist Mission and could have passed for Crow's brother, asked almost every man and woman who came in if they had seen the big fire last night. Every time anyone uttered anything that sounded like approval, Crow said, "Sure is nice to see that old biddy get her come-upping's, ain't it?"

He was still holding forth, even though the breakfast crowd had thinned out, when Mr. Claude came in a little after nine. The pint-sized marshal ordered coffee and listened a while before walking over to where Crow was sitting on a counter stool. Crow swiveled around to face him and grinned. "Hello there, Mr. Claude. Sure is a fine morning, ain't it?"

Mr. Claude put his left hand on Crow's right shoulder and said loud enough for everyone to hear, "Crow, I reckon since you were night watchman all those years, you might know burning a cross ain't no crime, but vandalizing somebody's private property is, and if this ever happens again, I'm gon' hold you responsible for the one last night and the next one too. Then I'm gon' haul your sorry ass off to jail, even if it's not for but one night. And on the way there, I'm gon' beat the crap out of you for resisting arrest."

"Aw, Mr. Claude," Crow said, "you ain't gon' do no such thing cause then you'd be breaking the law yourself. You just talking. What you better do is leave me alone." Then in a single motion he got to his feet and raised his right arm up and back in a quick sweeping manner that bumped hard into Mr. Claude's arm, pushing it away.

In the next instant, the sound of Mr. Claude's right fist colliding with the side of Crow's nose was sickening, like someone had dropped a ripe cantaloupe on the floor. Blood gushed down the taller man's face and bib overalls.

Mr. Claude turned to the stunned onlookers and said, "You saw it. Crow assaulted an officer of the law, but I'm not gon' arrest him, leastwise not right now. I don't want the son of a bitch bleeding all over my jail. One of y'all better get Doc Perkins."

Then he turned, walked out of the café, cut quickly around the next corner, and stood smiling while rubbing his throbbing hand.

CHAPTER 33

Hazel Brantley, Emma Lou MacDonald, Grady Atwell, Margaret Rainwater, and several others called Pearl during the course of the day on Saturday to tell her they were sorry about what happened and ask if they could do anything to help. There was not, of course, but she appreciated the calls. In between a couple of them, Wendell got on the phone long enough to arrange for someone to haul the charred cross away and repair the yard, but not before a number of rubberneckers drove by to see it. In the afternoon, the Goodbars decided they needed to get away from the whole mess for a few hours, including avoiding El Dorado where they might run into people they knew. So, they piled into Pearl's car and she drove them to Ruston, Louisiana, about thirty-five miles south, and there they watched Andy Griffith, Nick Adams, and Don Knotts in the hit comedy *No Time for Sergeants* at the Dixie Theater. After the picture show they splurged on steak dinners they could not really afford but thoroughly enjoyed.

Back home, they talked about staying in on Sunday to avoid more sniping like Pearl got the previous week, but with the air cleared somewhat by lots of laughter and a satisfying meal, she decided she would go to church. "I'm not gon' let a bunch of narrow-minded fools and bigots determine what I can and cannot do," she told her family.

All of them went, and like last week, some folks avoided Pearl before the service started, but to her surprise most of the people who spoke to her this time told her they hated she had been threatened. Even more surprising, before she thought back on it later, the pastor, Brother Walter Byrd, preached about violence. He was a tall, thin man who had curly brown hair, was always neatly turned out, and could preach hellfire and damnation with the best around. He also never backed away from anything. He had grown up in the North but graduated from the seminary in New Orleans and lived in the South for years. Last year, when crosses were burned in the black section of Unionville during the Central High standoff in Little Rock, he had rankled more than a few First Baptist Church members by speaking his mind against prejudice and intimidation. Some even talked about getting rid of him. The church kept him on, though, mostly because of his outgoing personality and his moving stories about how as a younger man he let the devil make him commit near about every sin there was short of murder and how after winding up in the gutter on Bourbon Street he found Jesus Christ. It did not hurt, either, that he could fish with the best of the men and that the women liked his wife.

Even before Byrd, wearing a navy pinstripe suit, took his seat next to the pulpit, some in the congregation who remembered those sermons of a year ago knew that today was not going to be a normal service. But even those folks did not expect as much as they got. Byrd had a gifted baritone voice and always led the choir and congregational singing, and today, instead of asking everyone to rise and sing the first song listed in the bulletin, he turned his back on the crowd and led the choir in singing "The Old Rugged Cross." He followed that with a normal opening prayer then said, "We will not be following our usual order of worship today. You may disregard your bulletins."

Over the next twenty minutes or so, with one pause for church announcements and another for taking an offering, he led the congregation in singing "The Nail-Scarred Hand," "Beneath the Cross of Jesus," "When I Survey the Wonderous Cross," and "At the Cross." If at that point anyone did not know what Byrd intended to preach about, they had somehow managed to sleep through the singing. When he finished leading songs, he picked up his Bible and said, "Listen now to the word of God." He flipped open the pages but did not read from them. Rather, he spoke from memory. "In the third chapter of Luke, verse fourteen, the Holy Word says, 'Do violence to no man, neither accuse any falsely,' and in Zechariah, chapter nine, verse seventeen, it says, 'And let none of you imagine evil in your hearts against his neighbor.'"

Byrd closed the Bible on his index finger and pointed the Holy Book toward his listeners. "Someone," he said, "or, more likely, several someones in our community did all of those things last Friday night when they burned a cross on the lawn of a member of this church. They committed an act of violence and falsely accused a neighbor of evil when, in truth, they are the ones that had evil in their hearts. I'm here to tell you today that they not only sinned against their fellow man but also blasphemed the cross of Jesus and sinned against the Lord."

For the next thirty minutes, Byrd lambasted not only whoever burned the cross in the Goodbars' yard, but also anyone who sympathized with the message of hate and intimidation it was intended to send. "Cross burnings are the devil's work," he said, wrapping up, "and so is anything that supports them, encourages them, or celebrates them in any way whatsoever. When I preached about this sort of thing last year, I hoped it was gon' be put behind us, but obviously it isn't. So, I ask each of you to go home and think and pray about this reoccurrence, about all the issues in our society that surround it, and what your Christian response to them ought to be in accordance with the Scriptures."

In place of the usual hymn of invitation for sinners to come forward and repent, Byrd had the congregation sing "At the Cross" a second time, and during the last verse he walked to the back of the church and there delivered the benediction himself, instead of having one of the deacons do it as was his usual practice. He asked God to, "Please protect and bless the Goodbar family and Mrs. Pearl Goodbar in particular as she stands up for what is right and decent in Your sight."

The entire service, and especially the prayer, not only surprised Pearl, it embarrassed her. She appreciated Brother Byrd's support and the sentiments he expressed, and she drew encouragement from them. But she did not like being the center of attention. She looked down during much of the time Byrd was speaking, and more than once she felt her face and the back of her neck redden. When he mentioned her family and her work in his closing prayer, however, she had to brush tears of gratitude from her eyes.

When he finished, she was glad she always sat in the back, as she felt self-conscious and did not know how people would treat her as she left. As it turned out, no one said anything much at all to her. A couple of the people who voiced their disapproval last week gave her a look of disgust, but most of the few worshippers with whom she made eye contact nodded and smiled at her, and some put an arm around her shoulders or gave her a pat on the hand. When she went past Brother Byrd, he whispered, "I'll be praying for you," and, choking up again, she managed only to mumble, "Thank you."

Once the family got in the car to go home, Wendell said, "Wow, honey, wasn't that nice?"

"Yeah, Momma," Nancy said, "that was great."

All Pearl could get out was, "He's good people."

———

The cross burning came up in at least two other Unionville churches that morning. At Mt. Zion Baptist Church, with Leon and Wanda Jackson and Sadie Rose Washington among the worshipers, Reverend Hosea Moseley also preached about hate and violence and said it did not matter whether someone burned a cross in a black neighborhood like last year or in a white neighborhood like last Friday, it was an ugly act and a sin in the eyes of God. Like Brother Byrd, Reverend Moseley also prayed for Pearl Goodbar. After the service he said privately to a few people as they were leaving that he wished she would come right out and support full desegregation but that they all should be grateful she was doing as much as she was.

Out at the Mercy Baptist Mission, Brother Elmer Spurlock was overjoyed about the cross burning, and he fell back on songs that, to his mind, suggested his flock was soldiering for God: "We're Marching to Zion," "Onward Christian Soldiers," and "When the Saints Go Marching In." He was in such a rush to gloat about the cross burning that he cut short the singing and put off taking collection until after his message. As soon as the congregation sang the last "go marching in," he reached for his Bible, waved it over his head, and said, "Folks, if you have your Good Books today, open them to the thirty-second chapter of Deuteronomy, verse forty-one and read along with me." Then he opened his and read, "'If I whet my glittering sword, and mine hand take hold on judgment; I will render vengeance to mine enemies and reward them that hate me.' My friends," he said, "some good citizens of our community whetted their glittering swords last Friday night and smote that hateful *Unionville Times*. It did my heart good, and I can tell you, the Lord above is smiling down on His brave soldiers today. I don't know who they were, but I know they were the kind of good, God-fearing, right-thinking men we've got right here with us today, men like Mr. Herbert Kramer sitting over there, and Mr. Vernon Appleby there in the back, who're doing such a fine job of heading up our still-segregated Unionville schools, thank the good Lord."

Neal O'Brien stopped by the newspaper office in mid-morning on Monday and told Pearl what he had heard about Mr. Claude slugging Crow Hicks, and they snickered about it like a couple of high school kids. "I know I shouldn't be laughing about someone fighting," Pearl said, "but Crow's so dadburned mean, I can't say I'm sorry about it." Hazel Brantley and Grady Atwell overheard.

"I wish I'd been there," Hazel said.

"Yep, that's puredee Claude Satterfield," Grady said. "He always was a feisty son of a gun."

A little before noon, Mr. Claude came by with Leon Jackson and said, "We're just walking around letting folks see we're both on the job. Showing our badges, you might say, and we thought we'd check and see how you're doing."

"We're fine," Pearl said, "and I heard what you did. You come on over here and let me hug your neck."

Leon, who had never been in the newspaper office, said, "You know, Mrs. Goodbar, I haven't ever needed to advertise my dry-cleaning shop, but if you don't mind, I'd like to take out a month's worth of ads."

"That's wonderful, Leon," she said, "We'll fix you right up."

That afternoon Hazel received three more subscription cancellations, which took a little shine off the morning. Around three o'clock, however, another visitor brought it back. Sadie Rose Washington appeared wearing a bright orange-figured muumuu and carrying a cardboard box with "Carnation" in red letters on two sides and a large piece of yellow cloth folded several times across the top. She asked for Pearl, and Hazel took her to the back office, where Pearl was talking with Emma Lou MacDonald about the quilt show.

"Begging your pardon, Mrs. Goodbar," Sadie Rose said as soon as she and Hazel got to the door of the back office, "I hope y'all don't mind me stopping in, but I wanted to say thank you for the way you've been writing about things in your newspaper, and I brought y'all a pecan pie for the office. It ain't been out of the oven but barely long enough to cool off." At that point, Sadie Rose saw Emma Lou standing off to one side and hesitated before holding out the box. Pearl took it and introduced her to Emma Lou. "How do, ma'am," Sadie Rose said, now uneasy about a gesture she thought some other white woman would consider inappropriate for a black woman to make. The last thing she wanted to do was cause Pearl another problem.

"How do you do?" Emma Lou responded, to Sadie Rose's surprise. "I love pecan pie. Pearl, don't you have some paper plates around here somewhere? Let's cut that thing while Sadie Rose is still here." That surprised even Pearl, but she set the box on the desk and removed the covering. As she looked inside, the office filled with a sweet aroma that only the right blend of sugar, butter, and Karo syrup cooked to perfection and topped with toasted pecans could deliver.

"Mrs. Goodbar," Sadie Rose said, before Pearl could speak, "I don't want to be no bother, but I know how them crosses makes a body feel, and I just wanted to say please don't let them that burned it get you down. Like Reverend Moseley said when he was praying yesterday, we're all mighty grateful to you."

Pearl came around the desk, patted Sadie Rose on the arm, and went to the door. There, she called, "Hazel, would you see if you could find those paper plates, a knife, and some forks so we can eat this pie. Ask Grady if he wants some too."

Up front Hazel went about doing what Pearl asked but whispered to Grady, "I reckon we better do what she wants, but I don't know what she's thinking. If somebody comes in here and sees us eating with that Negro, there's just gon' be more trouble."

"Well, I'll tell you," Grady said, wiping his hands on his apron, "there ain't nothing I like better than pecan pie. Let's go."

CHAPTER 34

Nancy and Alice had a much rougher Monday than their mother, as several students made ugly comments about Pearl and about them. Some kids in groups whispered things under their breath loud enough for Nancy and Alice to hear when they walked by, but not loud enough to give themselves away. A girl who was Alice's partner on a prize-winning science project at the end of last school year told her with a sneer, "I see all you Goodbars got what you deserved." In the girls' locker room during gym class someone wrote "Nigger Lover" in Magic Marker across the front of Nancy's new zippered notebook.

At supper, both girls talked about their day, and Pearl and Wendell tried to find words to make them feel better. There were not any, though. Pearl knew how some white students had taunted and even spit on and hit the nine black kids who integrated Little Rock Central last year, and she thought about mentioning that as a way of somehow bracing up her daughters. But those things, while they might not seem like it to Nancy and Alice, were much worse, and she did not bring them up. It hurt her, however, to see her girls being treated the way they were.

Pearl thought about that most of the day on Tuesday, along with a well-publicized speech Governor Faubus had made at

280

the Arkansas State Democratic Convention in Little Rock on Saturday, three days earlier. In what was, for all practical purposes, his acceptance of the party's nomination for another term as governor, he repeated a theme he had been sounding for more than a year and a half as a way of both putting off school desegregation and staying in office. She found a copy of highlights she had saved from the *Arkansas Gazette* and read it again, twice.

"People need more time to get used to the idea of integrating the schools," the governor had said, "and if it is not postponed, not only in Arkansas, but in other sections of the country, there will be more disorder and violence which may result in bloodshed." What is needed, he claimed, is "moderate thinking and common sense," and he called again for the US Supreme Court to overturn the current federal circuit court of appeals ruling that Little Rock schools must integrate. The Supreme Court was scheduled to consider the matter in a rare special session at noon on Friday. Unwilling to stop there, Faubus said that when the court handed down its *Brown v. Board of Education* decision in 1954, it was influenced by psychologists who, according to a US House of Representatives committee investigating un-American activities, belonged to Communist organizations bent on destroying American democracy.

A little after four o'clock, Pearl went to the office hot plate for her fourth cup of coffee, and on the way back to her desk, she muttered, "This is bullshit!"

"What's that you said?" Hazel asked from her desk.

"What?" Pearl asked, turning around. "I didn't say anything."

"Yes, you did. You said something about bullshit."

"I said that out loud?"

"You sure did. What were you talking about?"

"Hmm. Give me five minutes then find Grady—I don't
see him anywhere—then come back to the office, and I'll tell
you."

Ten minutes later, Hazel and Grady, both wondering if
they should be worried about something, appeared in Pearl's
doorway.

"I have a huge favor to ask," she said, getting up and coming to meet them. "Would you be able to work all night Friday
if necessary? So we can get something in the paper that's not
gon' happen till that afternoon sometime? I just got off the
phone with Emma Lou, and she said if you can do it, she'll
come in and help too."

Hazel and Grady said they could, and after some conversation about why Pearl needed them to do this and how they
could adjust the order of production to make everything work,
they went back to what they were doing. Pearl called Wendell
and told him something had come up that she needed to attend
to and she would be late getting home. Then she closed her
door and sat down to write a draft of her editorial for this
week. As she wrote, she knew she was writing to herself as
well as to her readers and the piece probably sounded that
way. If so, she hoped that would make it more effective. The
draft read:

Time to Get on with It

Four years have passed since the United States
Supreme Court ruled in *Brown v. Board of Education*
that segregation of public schools is a violation of
the Fourteenth Amendment and must be ended.
Implementation of that decision has proven difficult

for almost everyone—white citizens, black citizens, parents, students, teachers, administrators, government officials, law enforcement officers, members of the press, and others—for myriad reasons, some legitimate in terms of money and logistics and some not legitimate in any truly defensible way. During that time, we citizens have fought among ourselves with words, with fists, and with worse, all the while using up precious resources of time, money, energy, and intellect. And the only thing all this has accomplished is to postpone both what is inevitable under the law and what is right morally, ethically, and for the long-term best interest of our nation.

There are those who argue, and this paper has been among them we now regret to say, that all we need is more time and then the integration of our schools will come about gradually and peacefully. Some who make that argument have said, and we also regret that we have been among those to some extent too, that it is sufficient in the meantime merely to assure equal and fair treatment, including equal access to educational resources, as such a course will eventually make integration of the schools acceptable for all and enable it to occur without opposition.

But whether that is true is not the point. The point is not even that integration is the law of the land. The point is that all the while that we are fighting over this matter, we are hurting our children, white and black, by stirring and promoting hatred and violence and depriving them in one way or another of the resources and opportunities they need to achieve the full potential of their individual lives in ways that accrue to everyone's greatest benefit. The complexities of the matter are large and numerous, but they do not change that overarching truth. Getting on with integrating our schools will help us begin to overcome negative perceptions and misguided traditions, and the time for us to do it has come.

Pearl took the draft home and after supper, when they were alone in the living room, she showed it to Wendell. "We agreed at the beginning," she said, "that the editorial policy of the paper is up to me. We said it again a little while ago, too, but I need you to see this draft so we can talk about it if you want to. I'm planning to publish it this weekend and I hope you agree with it. Anyway, it's likely to affect all of us and I don't want it to be a surprise. I'll make some hot chocolate while you read it."

She went into the kitchen, stayed more than long enough for him to read the piece several times, then returned with two steaming mugs of chocolate with marshmallows on top.

"I didn't have enough time to get all the way through it," Wendell teased. He was sitting on the sofa with a leg that was still troubling him propped up on the coffee table. He laid the paper on a side table and took one of the mugs and a sip of hot chocolate.

"Well?" Pearl asked and sat down next to him.

"I haven't been thinking about much else since we got home from the picture show Saturday," he said, and took another sip of his drink before setting his mug on the coffee table.

"And?"

"And I think you're right about getting on with it. I wouldn't change a word."

"You know this is gon' make things even harder for us—all four of us, them too," Pearl responded, asking as much as saying, and glancing toward the girls' bedrooms.

"If you recall," Wendell said, "Nancy asked you the other night why you didn't just come on out and say this."

"Yeah, I remember. I wasn't ready then but I am now. I'm also ready for something else," she said, shifting to reach her arms around him and put her lips to his.

⌒

Lacking a news wire, Pearl got word of the Supreme Court decision from the radio on Friday afternoon, and Grady slipped pre-set type into the printing tray a little after five fifteen. Pearl had written two short pieces of equal length, one for whichever way the court ruled. The Supreme Court upheld the appellate court's decision that the Little Rock district should proceed with desegregation in compliance with *Brown v. Board of Education*. Pearl had already decided that no matter which way the court decision went, she would run her getting-on-with-it editorial exactly as she had drafted it. As Wendell had suggested, she did not change a word.

Pearl, Grady, Hazel, and Emma Lou completed the printing in the wee hours of Saturday morning, and Grady dropped bundled copies in front of the café and the barbershop and newsstand. Emma Lou said her husband Purvis had an early morning errand, and she volunteered him to take rolled-up copies to the post office before it opened for carriers and other postal workers to sort all the mail for pick up or delivery. Pearl thanked them all, promised them a chocolate pie next week, and headed home thinking it would be both nice and smart to head out somewhere for another picture show over the weekend.

⌐⁓⌐

While Pearl and her staff were still running their press, Faubus, angry with the Supreme Court decision, signed the recently passed bill allowing him to close Central High School—currently scheduled to open on Monday, integrated like last year—if he thought it necessary to prevent violence. Under that new state law, he then issued a proclamation closing not only Central High but all four public high schools in Little Rock and ordering a special election in which parents in the district could vote on whether they wanted integration. He set the election for October 7.

News of the court decision and the governor's actions was all over radio, television, and the daily newspapers on Saturday morning, and in Unionville that coverage, along with Pearl's editorial, raised the blood pressure and neck hair of a whole heap of folks. There was almost no place where people were talking about the Unionville Bobcats' 17 to 7 win over the Strong Bulldogs on the road the night before and how Ronnie Metcalf had not only run the ball for nearly two hundred yards but had also thrown a halfback option pass for a touchdown. Elmer Spurlock called Herbert Kramer and Vernon Appleby and asked if he could meet with them before he prepared his Sunday sermon. He said he wanted to get a statement from them about what he called Pearl's "outright campaign to put black kids in Unionville classrooms before the school year was over." Boomer Jenkins, Odell Grimes, and several others got so loud in Emmett's Café that even Emmett was moved to tell them, "Can it or take it out on the street!"

Mr. Claude became worried that someone might soap the *Unionville Times* windows again, or worse, break them, and he thought about calling Leon and asking him to park the patrol car in front of the building, sit there, and keep an eye on it. But then it occurred to him that having Leon there might make things worse. Besides, it would take Leon away from his shop on a day he had customers wanting to pick up their cleaning for Sunday. So, figuring that even if he could not drive the car, he could sit in it and keep watch as well as Leon, Mr. Claude called Neal O'Brien and asked him to get the car and bring it over. By the time Neal got there with it, however, Mr. Claude had yet a different idea. He said he still wanted the car there, but he wanted to be more visible himself, and he asked Neal if he would mind getting an empty nail keg from City Hardware. When Neal brought the keg, Mr. Claude was leaning on the car and holding a foot-long stick he had picked up around at the side of the building. He took the keg over to the newspaper building's double front doors, turned it upside down, sat down on it, took out his pocketknife, and started whittling on the stick.

"Did you tell Pearl Goodbar you were gon' do this?" Neal asked.

"Nope."

"Are you gon' sit here all day?"

"Might."

CHAPTER 35

Pearl slept late on Saturday morning, and with Wendell's encouragement, Nancy and Alice brought her breakfast in bed. That started a weekend of ignoring the outside world, including forgetting about going to another movie. Because getting the paper out the night before had gone into the wee hours, Pearl had not brought home bookkeeping records. This left Wendell with no paperwork to do. All weekend except when getting their meals and cleaning up after themselves, the four of them napped, read, played Rook and Scrabble, and baked cookies. In the evenings they sat on the back porch watching the sun go down and listening to mockingbirds sing.

They even skipped church on Sunday and did not know that Brother Walter Byrd included Pearl in his prayers again. They also had no way of knowing that Reverend Moseley had too. And Pearl tried not to think about what Brother Elmer Spurlock might be saying at the Mercy Baptist Mission.

⁓

"I want to talk to you this morning about infidels," Spurlock said in an unusually calm voice after he led his congregation in some of the same marching-to-war-for-God songs they had sung the week before. Sweat was starting to run off his near-bald head, even here in mid-September with the windows open, but he still had his white suit coat on, his collar buttoned, and his red tie tightly knotted. Because he was mad as the devil, he knew he would get carried away before he finished and do plenty of yelling, but he wanted to try something different and start out in what he thought was a more scholarly manner. He said he was "tired of that holier-than-thou newspaper hussy"—a name he had long been using for Pearl when talking with his wife—and the way she used fancy words and arguments trying to get people to do what she and Chief Justice Earl Warren—whom Spurlock considered a Communist—thought was best for them. Spurlock had preached a lot about how he thought integration would lead to mongrelization of the races, and he did not feel the need to repeat that this week. Today, instead, he intended to go Pearl Goodbar one better. He would use a fancy argument too. He had a good concordance, he had used it, and he was good at reading into almost any Scripture whatever he wanted it to mean.

With his left hand he lifted his King James Bible, thumb marking the page he wanted, and tucked it under his armpit. Then he stretched out his right arm, palm up, and made a slow sweeping motion across his view of the gathered faithful, as if to bind them together with each other and with him. At the end of the sweep, he held his pose for a moment. Then, bringing his hands together under the Bible, he said, "Turn with me now to the second epistle of Peter, chapter two, and follow along with me on verses one and two: 'But there were false prophets also among the people, even as there shall be false teachers among you, who privately shall bring in damnable heresies, even denying the Lord that bought them, and bring upon themselves swift destruction. And many shall follow their pernicious ways; by reason of whom the way of truth shall be evil spoken of.'"

He knew the congregation might not be able to decipher that passage. He was not sure he could either but he did not care. The only things he cared about were certain words and phrases in it.

"Look now at verse nineteen," he said. "Verse nineteen is referring back to verses one and two, and it says these false prophets and false teachers are servants of corruption. These, my friends, are what Earl Warren and Pearl Goodbar are. They are false prophets. They are false teachers. They are servants of corruption. What Warren and Goodbar are saying and writing are damnable heresies. Don't be swayed by them. Don't even listen to them. Tell your friends and neighbors not to be swayed by them. Warren and Goodbar and their kind are also infidels. Turn back with me now to Paul's first epistle to Timothy, chapter five, verse eight. Read what the Bible says here: 'But if any provide not for his own, and especially for those of his own house, he hath denied the faith and is worse than an infidel.' Warren and Goodbar ain't true to their own house. They ain't true to their own kind, to white people. They want you and me to mix with coloreds."

By now, Spurlock had kept an even tone for as long as he could. He put his Bible on the pulpit, shucked his jacket, and yelled, "They want to put black kids in our schools and black men in our bedrooms." Then he went on from there, ranting for nearly an hour and calling as he had before, for members of his congregation to shun the *Unionville Times* and do whatever they could think of to "fight anybody and anything" that advocated for or might lead to the integration of Unionville schools. He said Herbert Kramer and Vernon Appleby had pledged again to him that they would do everything in their power to ensure continued segregation, and what Unionville needed was more men like them. For good measure at the end, Spurlock added a dose of hellfire and damnation about sin in general and issued his usual invitation to sinners to come forward and repent. Then he closed with a prayer that included a plea for protection of what he called "good God-fearing white folks." Afterward at the back door, he soaked up the praises of worshippers who told him how much they loved his sermon.

On Monday, Pearl went to work expecting more cancellations, and she got a dozen of them, including three from local merchants stopping their ads. One of them told Hazel he was cancelling partly because he did not like the paper's editorial policies but mostly because some of his customers told him they were going to stop buying from him if he kept advertising with Pearl. "Enough is enough," he said. "Your boss is flat out wrong."

At school, no one said anything to Nancy or Alice. Instead, students who disagreed with their mother or, maybe more likely whose parents disagreed with her, ignored them in the several ways people have of saying with sly glances and gestures, "I know you're there but I don't want anything to do with you."

Herbert Kramer liked how Spurlock singled him out in his Sunday service, same as he liked being the president of the school board, presiding at its meetings, and influencing decisions on the budget, facilities, and a host of other things. He had won election to the board three straight times, and his fellow members had voted him to be president each time largely because no one else much wanted it. Also, because he owned a big farm and lots of timber, they figured he knew a thing or two about money and property. Horace Bowman might have been a better fit if he had any kids and wanted the position, but he did not. Kramer had a grown son, Bobby Lee, named for Confederate general Robert E. Lee, and he had been an outstanding quarterback and basketball player in high school, raising his father's profile even higher. Under different circumstances he might have gone on to star for some college, but Kramer worked him like a hired hand and hassled him so much about his play on the gridiron and the basketball court that after he graduated from high school, he joined the navy to get as far away from his old man as he could as quickly as possible. He was now an airplane mechanic on an aircraft carrier on some ocean somewhere. Kramer did not know which carrier or which ocean and did not much care.

About the only things he cared about these days were power, screwing Priscilla Nobles, and running over to Bossier City down near Shreveport every now and then and playing poker in the back rooms of dives that thrived on taking advantage of servicemen from military bases in the area. He could not stand his wife and hated being around her. Plus he had all the money he would ever need, and he enjoyed taking chances with some of it. Looking back, he could not remember what he ever saw in Lorraine except that in high school she had a great body, doted on him, and would let him do anything he wanted. Now she was frail, and, in his view, mousy. He never stopped to think that he made her that way by slapping her around, even over minor disagreements. She no longer held any appeal for him physically, but she was good for taking to church now and again to keep up public appearances. He did not have to worry about her ever telling his secrets, as she had no other family around and no money of her own except what little she kept back from what he gave her for groceries and such every month. She did not know he had caught on to her spending a little on other things now and then, but the amounts were so small he did not care. He knew that no matter how badly he treated her, she believed she had no choice except to stay with him. She did not have enough money or any place to go to get away.

Ah, but Priscilla. She was something else to Kramer, now even shapelier and prettier than her mother Yulanda had been. It amused him how accommodating people could be, especially black people he thought, when they had no alternative except yielding to his will. Yulanda was not much more than a girl when she came to work for his momma and daddy, both now dead, and he was not much older than she, and it had been easy to get her to give him what he wanted and then to keep her quiet about it. He did not especially enjoy beating on old man Nobles and his wife, but then he did not mind it much either. They were nothing to him. He had not counted on getting Yulanda pregnant and her running off, but after she did, he had contented himself with Lorraine, and a short time later they got married and Bobby Lee came along. When the boy got old enough to play sports, that and the farm were plenty to pass the time with. Then, not long after Bobby Lee joined the navy, Kramer came across Priscilla living with her grandparents. He finagled her into coming to work for Lorraine, and then used the same methods as before to keep the old people quiet. They needed money and wanted to stay alive. He did not really think he would kill either of them, but they could never be sure of that. He had certainly shown them that he would beat the hell out of them. And Priscilla too.

All the way home from Spurlock's sermon and all the rest of Sunday, Kramer reveled in the power he had over people, how he could fool those who were not close to him, and how he could make those who were do whatever he wanted. By nightfall his desire to have Priscilla again pushed all other thoughts aside. On Monday morning, like on the day following the last White Citizens' Council meeting, after Kramer and his hired hands finished the milking, he sent them off to do work that would keep them away for a few hours. Then he picked up Priscilla in town, brought her back to the farm, and took her to his detached office. There he told her to take off her clothes—all of them, shoes and socks too.

This time she did as he told her without hesitating. He stood watching, admiring her body, and fondling himself through his overalls. Then he took them off, along with his boxers and boots. Clad only in his socks and blue checked shirt, he sat down in his office chair, rubbed his hand across his erection, and told her to take him in her mouth. But she did not move. She only stood where she was, looking into his eyes, as if deliberately trying to irritate him. She did not look as scared as he liked, and he thought he might have to beat her again, but he was ready for her and kept seated. Still, anger began to wash across his face, and Priscilla saw it. Knowing he might spring out of his chair at her any moment, she moved toward him, shaking her shoulders to jiggle her breasts and keep him aroused. Then she got down on her knees, put her hands on his thighs, and put her mouth around him like he had forced her to do many times before. But this time she snapped her jaws together, biting as hard as she could and drawing blood, lots of it. That she might do something like this had never occurred to Kramer. He thought he kept her too afraid. He hollered in pain and rage and swung wildly at her head without thinking that his striking her might do as much damage to himself as to her. His fist collided with her cheekbone and nose, and as she fell away, her teeth ripped away a huge chunk of his engorged flesh.

Gagging, Priscilla spit and let out a guttural roar, and they scrambled to their feet, blood flowing from both of them. "I'll kill you, bitch!" Kramer yelled, and started toward her. She turned and tried to get the door to the porch open, but before she could, he grabbed her shoulder, spun her back toward him, and swung at her again. As he did, he slipped on the bloody floor and managed only a glancing blow to Priscilla's mouth. It drew more blood but did not knock her down, and she ducked around him before he could pin her to the wall. Still yelling, she retreated to the center of the room and picked up the first heavy object she saw—a rusty tractor gear he used for a paperweight—and turned to face him. Afraid to get close enough to swing the gear at him, she threw it instead. The unwieldly weapon went wide of the mark and struck a window, leaving shards of glass on the floor. As she turned away to look for some other way to defend herself, her eyes fell on the closet, and she rushed to try get inside it and shut Kramer out. He was still bleeding like an animal at slaughter and moving slower, but right as Priscilla managed to get the closet door open, he grabbed her by her hair from behind and yanked her toward him. As she fell backward, she pushed against the floor with her legs and feet, hoping to knock him off balance and somehow jerk free. The broken glass cut her soles but she kept pushing. Kramer crashed against his desk, sending papers, books, and more flying. As he went down, his head struck a sharp corner, opening a long gash. He slumped to the floor, rolled onto his back, and lay still, his eyes searching wildly for Priscilla then glazing over. She stumbled for the front door, but before she reached it, she slipped in her own blood and went down hard. Her head hit the floor with a thud and everything went black.

~

Lorraine had heard Kramer's truck when it came up the graveled drive and stopped short of the house. She did not want to see him and Priscilla go into the office or even think about what she knew was about to happen, yet the loathing and disgust she felt for her husband lured her to a living room window to confirm her suspicions. Once there, she could not pull herself away, even after Kramer and Priscilla disappeared inside. When Lorraine heard Kramer's yells—a mix of anger and pain—and Priscilla's primal screaming, she slipped through the front door like before, made her way to an office window, and looked in. By this time the two were fighting, and seeing them whaling away at each other froze Lorraine with fear. If she tried to run back to the house, he might glimpse her through the window. If she stayed put until they stopped fighting and then ran for it, he would be even more likely to see her. Either way, he would surely come after her when he finished here. Then Kramer suddenly went down, followed by Priscilla, and both lay still. Lorraine went around to the front door, opened it, and stood looking at them. Kramer did not seem so menacing now. She walked over to where he was lying, her shoes making crunching noises in the shattered glass, and then she saw the wound that started the fight. For a long while, she stood staring at the shock still registering on

Kramer's face and at what was left of his manhood. She did not move to help him.

When Lorraine finally turned away, she noticed the open closet door and saw Kramer's .12-gauge pump leaning against the back wall. Without pausing, she walked over, picked up the gun, went back to where her husband lay, and shot him twice, once in the chest and once in the face. She started to shoot him in the groin, but the recoil of the weapon hurt her shoulder, and she decided it would be even more satisfying to leave that part of Kramer the way it was, with a sizeable piece no longer there. She used the hem of her housedress to wipe her finger-prints off the shotgun then laid it on the floor next to Priscilla, who was still bleeding but not as much as before. Using her shoe, Lorraine moved the gun around in the blood enough to smear the stock and fore-end. Next she bent down and used the inside edges of her index fingers to flip the weapon over. Then, with her shoe again, she slid that side of the gun around in the blood too. That done, she walked around Priscilla and Kramer a couple of times more to leave additional footprints so that the ones she had made nearest to the gun would not stand out to anyone looking around the room later. She then walked out the door and up to the house. There she took off her shoes, left them on the porch, went inside, looked up a number, and called the home of Claude Satterfield. His wife would know how to reach the acting marshal. Lorraine then put on a different dress and some different shoes, went to a bedside table, took out a loaded .38 Smith & Wesson, went back out to Kramer's office, and sat down on the steps to wait.

CHAPTER 36

Ed Bonneville, a deeply tanned, muscular man of medium height, and Roy Bill Gatewood, younger, wiry, and a shade taller, heard the two shotgun blasts. They were wearing overalls and faded Allis-Chalmers equipment caps and cleaning a drainage ditch next to a cornfield way west of the house. They thought the shots sounded odd, more muffled than sharp, as if they came from over toward the milking barn somewhere, but there should not be anyone shooting near the cows. After deciding that Kramer must have come upon a varmint of some kind, the men went back to work. The out-of-place blasts gnawed on Ed, however, and eventually he said they ought to take the tractor and go see about them.

They drove around the edge of the field, came out on Newton Chapel Road, and took it to the main entrance drive to the farm. As they approached the cluster of farm buildings, they saw Lorraine sitting on the steps outside Kramer's office, but they did not see that she was holding a pistol until Ed stopped the tractor in front of the porch. The gun startled them, but even stranger was Lorraine's expression. She was staring off into the distance somewhere and did not even seem to notice them. Ed looked past her, through the open door, and saw Priscilla on the floor. "Good god almighty!" he said, and ran inside with Roy Bill right behind.

When they saw Kramer, Roy Bill said, "Aw, shit!" and walked around Priscilla and over to his boss. "Aw, man! Aw,. man! He's shot all to hell!"

Ed circled Priscilla and stood looking at her, uncertain what to do. Although he could see she was breathing, he crouched beside her and felt her neck for a pulse. He did not know why he did. It was something people always seemed to do in picture shows when they came across somebody who looked like he might be dead or dying.

"She hurt bad?" Roy Bill asked, stepping over to where Priscilla lay.

"I don't know. Can't tell. I wonder what the hell happened."

"Seems pretty clear to me," Roy Bill said, staring at Priscilla. "Old Kramer was trying to get him some, and it didn't turn out the way he thought it would. Looking at that gal, I can't say as I blame him."

"Shut up," Ed said. "Gimme that dress off the floor over there so I can cover her up. I wonder if Mrs. Kramer called anybody. This gal could use a doctor, and we need to get the sheriff or somebody."

Both men went back outside, and Ed kneeled next to Lorraine, away from the hand holding the pistol, and asked, "Mrs. Kramer, are you all right? Did you call anybody?" When she did not answer, he reached out and touched her on the elbow and asked again.

She flinched and said, "Don't touch me. I called Mr. Claude. His wife leastways. She said she'd fetch him."

"What about an ambulance?"

"Nope. I reckon Mr. Claude will see to it if the girl needs one. She don't seem bad hurt. Just beat up a little."

"This here ain't in the town limits, Mrs. Kramer. Did you call the sheriff?"

"Nope. I reckon Mr. Claude will do that when he gets here."

"Ma'am, Mr. Claude don't even drive."

"He don't need to," Lorraine said. "He's got that colored boy to drive him around now."

"Ma'am, don't you want to give me that pistol? That girl ain't going nowhere and ain't nobody gon' hurt you none."

"Nope. I reckon I'll hold onto it."

⌒

Because on most days Mr. Claude started his morning late so he could stay on duty into the early evening and shake locks and such after the stores closed, he was at home when Lorraine phoned. She did not stay on the line long enough, however, for Irene to hand off the receiver. Lorraine said only, "Mrs. Satterfield, this is Lorraine Kramer. Herbert's been shot dead. Tell Mr. Claude to come."

"That's all she said?" Mr. Claude asked Irene.

"That's all. Didn't sound upset or anything. Just said it and hung up."

"All right." He called City Hardware and was relieved when Neal O'Brien answered the phone. "Neal, I need you to go around the corner and tell Leon to come get me, right now." Leon did not have a phone in his shop.

"Okay," Neal said. "What's wrong?"

Mr. Claude said only that he had gotten a suspicious phone call he thought he should check out and he would get back to

Neal when he knew more. Then he called the Union County sheriff's office and asked to have a deputy meet him at Herbert Kramer's farm. Next, he called Pearl Goodbar and told her she might want to drive out to Kramer's place for a story. She asked what story, and he said he would tell her when she got there but bring a camera and wait for him in her car when she arrived. "In the meantime," he said, "don't tell anyone where you're going." Within minutes after Mr. Claude got off the phone and finished dressing, Leon was out front with the patrol car. They drove without lights and siren, and on the way, Mr. Claude told Leon what little he knew.

When they got to Kramer's place, they saw Roy Bill sitting on the tractor, still pulled up to the office steps. Ed was leaning against one of the rear tires, and Lorraine, having moved in order to distance herself from the hired men, was sitting sideways in the open office door. She was still holding the pistol. Leon parked the patrol car off to one side, and he and Mr. Claude got out and walked up to the porch. Mr. Claude nodded to the men, looked at Lorraine, and saw Priscilla through the door beyond her, and Kramer beyond Priscilla. She had regained consciousness but was still lying on the floor, now in a fetal position, knees drawn up to her breasts, and clutching her dress in a way that left much of her body still uncovered.

"Mrs. Kramer," Mr. Claude said, his eyes on the pistol, "what's going on?"

Lorraine did not look up. "Herbert's dead and that girl shot him," she said, nodding her head in the direction of Priscilla.

"How about you give me the gun?" Mr. Claude asked. He mounted the steps and crossed the porch toward Lorraine while trying to avoid the web-like array of bloody footprints she and Kramer's farmhands had tracked there. "I've got this now." Near the steps, Leon had his hand resting on his pistol under his coat in case Lorraine tried to shoot.

"Okay, you can have it," she said, handing over the gun. "I don't need it with you here. I'm going to the house." Then she got up, climbed down from the porch, and started walking away.

"Mrs. Kramer," Mr. Claude called after her. "The county's got a deputy sheriff on the way, and he's gon' want to talk to you. Why don't you go sit in our car and wait for him?"

"All right," she said. She went over, got in on the passenger side, and left the door open.

Mr. Claude squatted down in the office doorway and asked Priscilla, who seemed to be breathing all right, "Are you hurt bad?"

She tightened her grip on her dress but otherwise did not move. "I don't think so, but I ain't good neither."

Not wanting to disturb the scene any more than necessary before someone from the sheriff's office saw it, Mr. Claude asked her if she would be okay staying where she was for a few more minutes until a county deputy arrived and they could get her some medical attention. Afraid to do otherwise, Priscilla said she guessed she would. Mr. Claude made his way off the porch and asked Ed and Roy Bill if one of the overhead utility lines he saw running to the dairy barn was a phone line like he thought. Ed confirmed that there was a phone in the barn. He said his boss liked the convenience and could afford the extra cost.

"All right," Mr. Claude said, "I want you to take Deputy Jackson over there so he can phone Doc Perkins to come out, then I want you to come back here and talk to me. Roy Bill, you stay right there. I'll get to you in a minute." As Leon and

Ed started for the barn, Mr. Claude said, "Tell Doc I said to make it quick."

While they all waited, Mr. Claude walked up on the porch again and looked through the door, trying to take in as many details as possible without going inside. When Leon got back, they walked around the building and looked in all of the windows. In addition to Priscilla, Kramer, and lots of blood, they saw the shotgun, the open closet door, and clothes, desk items, and broken glass scattered all around, along with footprints that looked like they were from at least four people.

"So, what do you think, Leon?" Mr. Claude asked out of earshot of the others.

"Well," Leon said, "it looks to me like he was attacking the girl and she shot him."

"Yeah, and you know how else it looks? It looks a lot like when Elton Washington was shot, everything except Kramer's not shot in the balls."

"Guess there wasn't no need."

"Yeah. And that and everything else about this is gon' stir up a mighty big stink. Look, this is not our jurisdiction. So, I'm not gon' ask anybody a whole lot of questions. I'm gon' leave that for the deputy, but I want us to get in there and look around as soon as he'll let us. I reckon he'll take pictures, or bring somebody to do it, but in the meantime, do you think you could get some paper and make some kind of sketch or diagram of where everything is right now, before the county gets here and starts moving things around—just in case they don't bring a camera and won't let Mrs. Goodbar get in there with hers? It don't have to win no prizes. It just has to show where things are relative to other things."

"Yes, sir. I think I can do that."

"Be sure to show how the shotgun's lying next to the girl, where the stock is, and where it's pointing.

"Mr. Claude, couldn't we find her some more clothes somewhere and get her out of there?"

Mr. Claude explained that he wanted the deputy to see what he and Leon were seeing, plus he did not trust sending Lorraine Kramer up to the house for clothes by herself because they still did not know what had happened or who did what. He agreed that Leon had a point, however, and he said he guessed if Leon could remember where they had found Priscilla well enough to show it accurately on his sketch, they could go ahead and move her. Mr. Claude got everyone away from the front of the building and waited while Priscilla put on her dress without anyone watching. Then he got Lorraine out of the police car, put Priscilla in it, and told Lorraine, Ed, and Roy Bill to go sit on the edge of the porch, leaving the steps clear. While they waited for everyone who had been summoned, Leon sketched.

Union County Deputy Sheriff R. C. Munford, Doc Perkins, and Pearl Goodbar all got to the Kramer farm within minutes of each other. The two men got out of their cars, Munford in his khaki uniform and Doc Perkins in his usual suit and tie, and approached the porch. Pearl, in a shirtwaist as always, stayed in her car as asked, but Mr. Claude waved her over and made introductions all around.

"This looks like a goddamn circus," Munford said. "Got enough people out here to skin a mess of polecats." He was a giant of a man with short brown hair under a big straw Stetson and had so many things hanging off his pistol belt that he squeaked like a new saddle when he walked. He gave Leon a sharp look of disapproval and took charge right away, telling Doc Perkins to see after the girl but not to ask her any questions except where she was hurt, and telling Pearl to stay back with her notepad and her camera until he got through talking to the witnesses. Disregarding the bloody footprints on the porch, Munford climbed up, walked across it, and looked through the door but did not go inside. Then he came back and said to Lorraine, Ed, and Roy Bill, with Mr. Claude and Leon looking on and listening, "All right, tell me what happened. Just give me short answers, no bullshit. You first, ma'am." Mr. Claude thought it was unusual and not helpful to question them all together this way, but he did not say anything.

Lorraine told them she had heard a ruckus and come out to her husband's office and looked in the window. She said she saw Priscilla shoot Kramer before she passed out or fainted or whatever it was that made her drop to the floor.

Munford nodded back toward the front door. "Ma'am, your husband ain't got no pants on. Did you notice that?"

"Yeah, I saw," Lorraine said. She was staring straight ahead and speaking quietly, like when Ed and Roy Bill first came up on her. "Ain't nothing new," she said. "He's been fornicating with her for years. I guess she got tired of it."

"What about you? Wasn't you tired of it?"

"No. I didn't care as long as he left me alone."

"Hmm," Munford said. He turned to Ed and Roy Bill. "Boys, what's your story?" They gave an accurate account of what they heard, what they saw, and what they did when they arrived on the scene. "All right," the deputy directed, "Y'all stay here while I go inside. Mr. Claude, you and him," Munford said, avoiding using Leon's name or title, "might as well come with me. Looks like the room's pretty much already trampled up. Don't matter none, though. It's pretty clear what happened. The nigger gal killed him. She's probably gon' claim it was self-defense, but it sure looks like murder to me."

Mr. Claude and Leon pushed through the door behind Munford. Leon kept his thoughts to himself, but Mr. Claude asked, "How can you say that? You haven't even talked to her."

"Don't need to," Munford said. "He's dead. She's not. The missus said she saw her pull the trigger, and you can see that the gun's right there where she was lying before y'all took her out. There's sorta an outline in the blood. We'll have somebody talk to her when we get her up to the jail, but it's a white woman's word against a nigger's, because that poor bastard over there sure can't say nothing. Case closed is the way I see it." He headed for the door. "I'm gon' see if the doc's all done out there then I'm gon' radio up to the office. See how the boss wants to wrap this up, find out if he wants any pictures, and get the coroner down here—all that good stuff. Then we'll get the witnesses' statements. Probably ought to get one from you too. Meantime, y'all are welcome to keep looking around if you want to. But if I was you, I wouldn't take too long. There's likely to be a bunch more reporters down here pretty quick like, and I expect you're gon' want to miss them. I know I sure as hell would."

"Goddamn!" Mr. Claude said, when Munford was outside. "I'm sorry about that, Leon."

"No need," Leon said. "I've heard it plenty." Then, "Here, look at this." He pointed to a pearl-handled switchblade knife sticking out from under a wooden box that was upside down on the floor with pens, pencils, and paper clips scattered around it. Leon bent down and used his own pencil to push back the box and uncover more of the knife.

"What about it?" Mr. Claude asked.

"See that 'J.V.' carved into the handle? Sadie Rose took a knife like that off Jewell Vines and gave it to Elton. And I heard Vines tell her that it had his initials on the handle. Don't seem like there'd be two like that floating around. It's gotta be the same one."

"Well, I'll be damned. Maybe Elton came back to Unionville to get Kramer, they met up somewhere, and Kramer killed him and took the knife off of him. I tell you, though, both of them being shot pretty much the same way is a helluva coincidence."

"You don't think Priscilla Nobles shot Elton for some reason, do you?" Leon asked. "She might've had access to a shotgun, but she didn't have any way to move the body."

"Nope. I bet that boy was shot right here somewhere," Mr. Claude said. "I doubt there'd be any way to prove it, though. Besides, if Kramer did it, he's damn sure already got what he had coming for it. Stay right here and don't let anybody come in here and touch the knife. I'm gon' get Mrs. Goodbar. I'm not waiting for anybody else from El Dorado."

Mr. Claude found Pearl taking pictures outside, told her he would catch her up on details later, and asked her to go inside and shoot the room, the body, and the knife, and do it quick while Munford was on his radio. Mr. Claude did not know if he could persuade Munford to take the knife and hold it as crime-scene evidence, but he intended to try.

CHAPTER 37

Wile Doc Perkins cleaned Priscilla's wounds and stitched up her cuts in the Unionville police car, Deputy Munford paced around fuming about how long it was taking. "Dammit Doc, that could've waited till I got her locked up," he said.

"Some of these need tending to now," Doc said. "If you'll go on and leave me alone, I'll get through quicker. Besides, she's not going anywhere."

Pearl got all the pictures she and Mr. Claude wanted, and he and Leon filled her in on as much as they knew about what happened before she arrived. Mr. Claude asked Deputy Munford about the knife, and he said, "I don't give a damn about it. It don't have nothing to do with what happened today. If you want it, take it." Mr. Claude wrote out a receipt on a piece of paper he borrowed from Pearl's Blue Horse notebook, and Munford signed it.

After Doc finished with Priscilla, he told Munford she was going to need a dentist. Munford grunted by way of reply, put her in the back of his own patrol car, told everyone to stay away from her, and continued his pacing. Doc went over to Mr. Claude and Leon, related what he could about her injuries, and said Priscilla told him she did not remember shooting Kramer. "It was the oddest thing," Doc said. "She just volunteered it.

Real quiet, matter-of-fact like. Right out of the blue. I wasn't even saying anything to her about what happened. I can't put my finger on it, but something about how she put it made me want to believe her."

$\sim$

Union County Sheriff Floyd Eubanks sent another deputy down to help Munford wrap up the scene and take official statements, and after Mr. Claude, Leon, and Doc gave theirs and Doc looked in on Lorraine Kramer to see if she needed any medical attention or wanted him to call anyone for her, they saw no reason to hang around for the coroner or any news people from El Dorado to arrive.

"I'm afraid this is gon' cause some folks to go off half-cocked," Doc observed as the three of them and Pearl were leaving.

"Me too," Mr. Claude said. "Pearl, it's too bad you can't print those pictures of Kramer lying there with his britches down, but we can sure as heck tell what he was trying to do. That'll put a quietus on some of them."

"I'm glad I've got a few days before I have to write about it," Pearl said. "Right now, I might be tempted to include more than is needed."

Before leaving with Leon, Mr. Claude had him point out the phone in the dairy barn then called Neal and asked him to get Alan Poindexter and meet them at the town hall in half an hour. As they were driving back, Leon said he would like to go tell Priscilla's grandparents as soon as they finished up with the mayor and council president. Mr. Claude told him to go ahead, and take the patrol car.

$\sim$

At the town hall, everyone sat in folding chairs pulled up close to the desk, and Mr. Claude gave Alan and Neal the highlights of what had occurred out at the Kramer place.

"I'll be damned," Alan said. He took a deep breath and let it out slowly. "I never cared much for the man, but this is hard to believe. He's president of the dadgum school board, for Pete's sake. What a holy mess!"

"Yeah, whew!" Neal said, frowning as if still trying to take it all in. "Hard to believe is right. And him a big wheel out there in the Mercy Baptist Mission and the White Citizens' Council too."

"There's more," Mr. Claude said. "I'm not sure Priscilla Nobles did the shooting. There's some things about it that don't quite add up. I can understand that Lorraine Kramer wouldn't be sorry to see the son of a bitch dead, but she was altogether too calm about it to suit me. That girl told Doc she didn't remember shooting Kramer, and Doc said she sounded believable. He couldn't say why exactly; it was a gut feeling he had. And then there's the shotgun. It was a .12-gauge pump. They hold at least three shells. Five, some models. Kramer was shot twice. Maybe the gun only had two shells in it when the person who fired it first picked it up. I don't know if it had any more in it after Kramer was shot. I didn't handle it. But if Priscilla fired it, and it was empty when she dropped it, Mrs. Kramer couldn't have known that unless she picked it up, and she told Munford she never touched it. When she left the office to go up to the house to call us, she didn't take the shotgun with her, but she brought back a pistol. Her sitting out front there with it made it look like she thought she needed some way to protect herself or make sure the girl didn't run off once she came to. But if either one of those was the case, and Mrs. Kramer didn't know whether or not the shotgun was still loaded, why didn't she remove it? She'd certainly been in there walking around, so it's not like she was trying to preserve the crime scene."

"That's not the only thing about the shotgun," Leon said. "There was blood all over the stock and the fore-end, and..."

"What's a fore-end?" Alan asked.

"That's the wood grip under the barrel," Leon said. "Where you hold the gun with the hand you don't have on the trigger." He held up his arms as if shooting an imaginary shotgun. "Anyway, there was blood all over both of them, but it was even-like. Seems like if somebody was holding it with bloody hands when they fired it and then just dropped it, or if someone else had picked it up later and dropped it, it wouldn't have looked that way. There'd have been handprints of some kind."

"You saying somebody was trying to make things look different from what really happened? Cover it up?" Alan asked.

Before Leon could answer, Neal asked, "Won't the county boys check for fingerprints?"

"I doubt it," Mr. Claude said. "Munford made up his mind right quick that it must've happened the way Mrs. Kramer told it. He said there wasn't any need to do any investigating. Said he considered the case closed. Used those exact words, 'case closed.'"

"Huh," Neal said.

Mr. Claude said, "Tell them about the knife, Leon, and how Kramer was shot in the same places, with one exception, that Elton Washington was."

"My god!" Neal said, when Leon finished. "You don't think the same person shot both of them, do you? I mean, if you don't think the girl shot Kramer, then who do you think might've shot him and the Washington boy both? Who'd have wanted both of them dead? I don't see any connection other than Kramer hated the boy, and the boy had good cause to hate Kramer."

"I don't think the same person shot both of them," Mr. Claude replied. "Like Leon said to me earlier, it doesn't make sense, the girl killing the boy. I think Elton Washington came back to Unionville, how I don't know, looking to get Kramer somehow, maybe even to kill him, and pay him back for the beating. And him and Kramer met up somehow and Kramer killed him. Kramer having the knife wouldn't prove that in a court of law, but it's pretty close to enough for me."

"Mr. Claude," Leon said, "do you think it's possible Elton went out to the Kramer place, Kramer shot him, and Mrs. Kramer saw him do it, and that's partly why she shot her husband in the face and the chest today, if in fact she's the one that did it? Because she saw Kramer do that to Elton?"

"I don't know," Mr. Claude said, "but may the Good Lord forgive me, either way I think justice got done."

"Are you gon' take any of this to Sheriff Eubanks?" Neal asked. "I mean, for the sake of the girl?"

"Yes, sir, are you, Mr. Claude?" Leon asked.

"I'm not sure. I guess I think we ought to keep all this to ourselves for right now. I don't like the idea of anybody sitting in jail for something they didn't do, but we don't actually have any proof about anything. I'd like to give it a little time and see if anything more happens with the county boys. See if the sheriff goes along with Munford or digs a little deeper. For instance, I wonder if the prosecuting attorney will insist on them checking for fingerprints. Is this okay with everybody?"

Everyone nodded their agreement. Mr. Claude said the only thing he wanted to tell around town was the part about how Kramer got caught with Priscilla Nobles with his britches down. He said he knew that information would be embarrassing for her grandparents, but he hoped it would help keep hot-heads like Elmer Spurlock and Crow Hicks from starting trouble of some kind over Kramer's murder. Everyone agreed with that too.

When the meeting broke up and Leon started for the car to drive over to the Nobles' house, Mr. Claude said he would like to go along unless Leon thought it would make things harder. Leon said he had been thinking he ought to go tell Sadie Rose first, and maybe she should be the one to go see the Nobles because she knew them better. Mr. Claude seconded that thought. They went to Sadie Rose's house but she was not at home.

"She's most likely across the road in the store," Leon said. "I should have thought of that."

There were not many people in the store, but there were enough for Leon and Mr. Claude to feel a hush fall when they walked in. Mr. Claude couldn't remember when he was last inside Sadie Rose's Place, and Leon had never been there in his new law officer capacity. Having no idea why they had come, Sadie Rose's first reaction was pride in Leon's being the first black law officer she had ever seen or even heard of. "Well, well, just look here," she said, coming to the front in her bright green muumuu to greet them. She said, "How do, Mr. Claude." Then, "Come here, Leon, and let me give you a hug." After Leon obliged her, she asked, "What can I do for you gentlemen?" When neither answered immediately, she asked, "Something's wrong, ain't it?"

Leon said there was and they needed somewhere to talk. She led them through a side door to some benches under tall pine trees. "Thought I might make this a place for people to eat outside some nights," she said, motioning for her guests to sit, "but it didn't work out. So, what's happened?" She sat down across from the two officers and folded her arms, bracing for bad news.

Leon told her that Kramer had been killed and the sheriff had Priscilla in jail and things did not look good for her. He said he hoped Sadie Rose would break the news to her grandparents.

Sadie Rose closed her eyes, and Leon and Mr. Claude watched as her shoulders slumped and her arms slid into her lap. The men waited for her to cry out, but she gathered herself and brushed her hand under one eye to catch a tear. What happened next was even more surprising.

"I sure am sorry to hear about Priscilla," she said, "but I'm glad to know that mean bastard finally got what's been coming to him." Mr. Claude had almost never heard a black woman, or a black man either, speak about a white person this way, and he had never let it pass before. But he agreed with Sadie Rose. Plus, he had grown comfortable enough with Leon that the remark did not much faze him.

"Sadie Rose, you said, 'finally,'" Mr. Claude observed. "We know from Mrs. Kramer that her husband had been taking advantage of Priscilla before, but you make it sound like there's a lot more to it. What else do you know?"

"I know he was doing it for years and he had her too scared to say anything about it. Her grandparents too." Sadie Rose was not about to tell about Yulanda and about Kramer's being Priscilla's daddy. She was afraid it might make it harder for Priscilla to defend herself with the law.

"So, will you let her grandparents know?" Leon asked.

Sadie Rose said she would but, "Lord, I don't know how them two old people are gon' live now. They depend on Priscilla to support them."

"We can do something for them at Mt. Zion," Leon said.

"Yeah, and I'll help them too," Sadie Rose said, "but this is near about gon' kill them."

CHAPTER 38

Unlike the way no one beyond Unionville paid much attention to the earlier murder of a black man that many considered a troublemaker, the story of the white president of the Unionville school board found shot dead, his face blown away, his pants down, his private parts all torn up, and a near-naked black woman beside him grabbed the attention of news organizations all over Union County, the two neighboring parishes, and beyond. Thanks to all the media coverage and the eagerness of Kramer's hired hands to tell all that they knew, plus the willingness of Mr. Claude, Leon, Pearl, and Doc to confirm basic facts when asked about them, by Tuesday morning nearly everyone in town knew most everything that had happened. Mr. Claude and the others were careful not to say that Priscilla shot Kramer. They only confirmed that she was in custody and the sheriff was investigating. Sheriff Eubanks put it that way in interviews, too, but Deputy Munford, enjoying the attention, was freer with his remarks and had Priscilla all but convicted.

Almost everyone in Unionville was talking about it. Some, it seemed, talked about nothing else. Reactions ranged from shock and disbelief to disappointment and anger. White people who knew Kramer mostly as the president of the school board were stunned and disappointed that a man with such a huge responsibility for the education of their children had been cheating on his wife, and with a black woman to boot. Black people were sad for the Nobles family but not much surprised by Kramer's behavior. They had seen similar things more times than they wanted to remember, and they were angry at seeing it again. Then there were whites like Elmer Spurlock, Crow Hicks, and others whose hatred for blacks was almost unmatched. They had the hardest time believing all this happened the way it was being told. Mostly they were embarrassed that a man they admired and considered one of them had fallen this way. They did not regret what he had been doing; they regretted that he got caught at it.

Beyond distant curiosity, not many people gave much thought at all to Lorraine, not even most of the women at Mercy Baptist Mission. When she entered their minds at all, they were sad for her, but years had passed since she last attended services regularly, and even those church women who had once known her best did not know what to say to her. So, they left her alone.

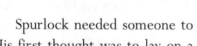

Spurlock needed someone to blame and he chose Pearl. His first thought was to lay on a huge funeral at the Mercy Baptist Mission regardless of what he had begun to call Kramer's "unfortunate adulterous fornicating with a black woman." But no one knew when the coroner would release the body, and Lorraine Kramer said all she wanted to do was stick her husband in the ground over at the Mercy Baptist Mission cemetery as soon as she got possession of the body and their son Bobby Lee could get home. She told Spurlock he could pray over the "low-down scum-sucking rascal" if he wanted to, but she was not going to allow anything more than that. "He's shamed me enough, and I don't want nobody looking at me and blaming me or pitying me. And I don't want nobody making a fuss over his sorry carcass."

With his opportunity for speaking out at a big funeral gone and nearly a week left until Sunday, Spurlock thought about calling a special meeting of the White Citizens' Council, but then he hit on another idea. He could use Wednesday night's prayer service for what he had in mind. He got on the phone and started calling members of his church and members of the Citizens' Council and asked each person he caught up with to call several others. There would be overlap, he knew, but that would only spur interest. He told the church members the prayer meeting would be about forgiveness for Herbert Kramer's soul, and he told the Citizens' Council members it would be about seeking the Lord's guidance on how to turn the tide against the growing threat of integration and the way blacks were getting pushier and pushier in going after it.

⌒

On Wednesday afternoon, Mr. Claude told Pearl he had learned that the Union County prosecuting attorney had ordered the shotgun checked for fingerprints and found only unusable smudges but had decided to charge Priscilla Nobles with murder anyway. A trial was likely before the end of the year. Mr. Claude also told her that he and Leon thought Lorraine Kramer may have done the shooting, but they did not have anything concrete to go on. He said they would keep chewing on it and asked Pearl not to say anything about it in the meantime. He did not tell her about the knife.

By this time Pearl was already drafting a story on the murder for Friday's paper. There was little she could say that others had not already reported, but this was the biggest local news story in years, and she felt the *Unionville Times* should carry a solid account. She added Mr. Claude's information about the prosecuting attorney, completed the piece, then wrote a related editorial:

A Time for Decency and Compassion

Based on information available at this time, it seems possible that we will never know everything that happened at the Kramer Farm last Monday, or everything that led up to it. What we do know is that a man is dead, one woman is widowed, and another woman is charged with murder. We also know that deceit, brutality, fear, and hatred all played a role. These kinds of actions and feelings never lead to positive outcomes. Yet they are all too common in our society today, especially in regard to the biggest question of our time, the integration of our schools. Let the events of last Monday demonstrate to everyone the need for decency and compassion in all our human interactions, whether between individuals or groups of individuals. Let us put aside differences, recognize the value of all human life, and treat others—all others—with respect. Let us pull together for the common good. And, let us not, as we have heard some among us urge, rush to judgement about guilt or innocence in regard to what happened last Monday. Let us show compassion there also and await the gathering of all the facts and the outcome of the judicial process.

When Wednesday evening rolled around, Elmer Spurlock walked onto the Mission Baptist Church's modest podium wearing his white suit again and looked out on the largest crowd ever to attend a Wednesday prayer meeting or a White Citizens' Council meeting at the church. Unlike in his recent Sunday services, he went with songs like "Amazing Grace" to set a tone of sadness and sorrow—sorrow for the sinful fall and death of one of their number and sorrow for the coming end of their segregated way of life unless they could find a way to head it off.

The singing done, Spurlock prayed for the deliverance of Kramer's tortured soul and for the preservation of the white race. He intended after that to make his points calmly, make his listeners feel despair, and use that to push them into action. Once again, though, after he got started, he could not stop himself from yelling, prancing, and punching the air with his fists in his usual manner as he blamed Kramer's death and potential school desegregation in Unionville on Pearl and her editorials.

"This red Commie stuff Pearl Goodbar's been writing to promote integration is what gave that colored gal the gumption to kill Herbert Kramer in cold blood," Spurlock shouted. "He was sinning, that's true, but that didn't give her the right to shoot him. She got the gall to do that from Pearl Goodbar, and if we let her keep writing that bile she's been spewing, we're gon' wake up one day and find coloreds marching on our streets and overrunning our schools right here in Unionville, no matter how hard Governor Faubus is fighting to keep that from happening anywhere in Arkansas. I've told y'all before and I'm telling you again now," Spurlock said, "the only way to stop Pearl Goodbar is not to patronize her paper or the businesses that advertise in it. You got to quit doing that, and you got to let them know why you're quitting."

⌒

On Thursday, as Pearl, Hazel, and Grady worked through their normal routines getting ready to put out the paper for the third week of September with all the usual content—comings and goings, school news, births and deaths, syndicated pieces, comics, a quilt pattern, more of Emma Lou's recipes, and local and national advertisements—they felt like the phones would never stop ringing. Before they did, the *Unionville Times* got another dozen subscription cancellations and three more advertising cancellations. Betty Sue Perry, co-owner of Perry's Grocery, asked Hazel to put Pearl on the line then said she was sorry to have to drop the ads, but half a dozen regular customers had called her complaining about her advertising in the paper and threatening to take their business elsewhere if she did not stop. Dalton Bailey, owner of the flower shop, said much the same thing. Neal O'Brien called and reported that he had gotten several complaints at City Hardware and wanted Pearl to know about them. He said he assumed other merchants were getting similar calls, and when Pearl confirmed it, he told her he would talk to them about it, but in the meantime, he wanted to increase the number and size of his ads.

Pearl appreciated Neal's call, but she went home after work wondering what she would do, and what her family would do, if she could not keep the paper going. She certainly would not be able to go back to teaching, not in Unionville anyway, and probably not anywhere close around.

CHAPTER 39

Bobby Lee Kramer got home late Thursday night, the Union County coroner released his daddy's body on Friday, and Bobby Lee and Lorraine buried him on Saturday. She let Elmer Spurlock say a prayer over the grave but kept everyone else away, and when Spurlock tried to give her an envelope filled with money he had collected for a marker, she refused it. "But, Mrs. Kramer," Spurlock said, "the congregation wants to do something for him, and for you."

"He doesn't deserve a marker," she said. "Let the son of a bitch lie there and rot. You want to do something with that money, take it and give it to that Negro girl's grandparents. I understand they depended on her to support them."

"What?" Spurlock asked. He was not sure he had heard right. "You can't be serious. Why would you do anything for them after what she did to you and Herbert?"

Lorraine was watching the grave diggers shovel red clay onto Kramer's coffin, the cheapest available from undertaker Arlan Tucker's inventory. "I don't know," she said. "I guess it's because he treated us both like dirt."

"I don't understand you," Spurlock said.

"No, you wouldn't," she said, and walked away.

Pearl took Nancy and Alice to El Dorado Saturday afternoon to buy groceries. Even though the big Kroger store there offered a wider selection at lower prices, she usually shopped for groceries in Unionville, spreading her business among her advertisers. Today, however, she told her family she was going to El Dorado because she did not want to hear any more about Herbert Kramer. She knew she would probably run into people she knew at Kroger's, too, but there certainly would not be as many as in Unionville. What she really wanted was to avoid thinking about the newspaper altogether for a little while. She half expected the girls to suggest another picture show outing, but they did not, and she did not feel like she had time for one anyway.

The family had already discussed the Kramers, and Pearl was pleased when on the drive up to the county seat and back, Nancy and Alice wanted to talk about Hollywood stars and the latest songs on the *Your Hit Parade* television show. They asked Pearl what actors and songs she liked during her high school days, and they all giggled and laughed the whole time in the car. The girls had heard of tunes like "Stardust," "Goodnight Sweetheart," and "Dream a Little Dream of Me," but they could not believe "Minnie the Moocher" and "Don't Take My Boop-Opp-a-Doop Away," or that Pat Boone's recent hit "Love Letters in the Sand" had first appeared more than 30 years earlier, with someone else singing it, of course. This was exactly the kind of afternoon Pearl needed.

When they got back to Unionville, a late-model pink-and-white Cadillac with huge tail fins and Arkansas plates was parked on the edge of the driveway.

"Wonder who that is?" Nancy asked.

"Oh, my goodness," Pearl said. "Aunt Myrtle's the only person I know who'd be driving a car like that, but it can't be her. She's past eighty now." Pearl pulled to the back of the driveway and said, "Y'all gather up the groceries and let me go see who it is."

Pearl went up the back steps, and as she crossed the porch, she noticed two cigarette butts and a pile of ashes on a saucer sitting on a small table near the kitchen door. Wendell did not smoke, but Aunt Myrtle did. In the kitchen, the countertops were cluttered with cooking utensils, and there were dirty pans in the sink and three pots simmering on the stove. Doreen Dykes had the day off and Wendell did not cook. The husky laughter of a long-time chain smoker was coming from the living room. It had to be Aunt Myrtle.

Myrtle Wilbanks was Pearl's late mother's sister, but despite all the summer days Pearl had spent with her while growing up, the savings bonds she now sent Nancy and Alice every Valentine's Day and July Fourth, and the huge turkeys she sent Pearl every Christmas along with money to put in the girls' stockings, they had not seen each other in several years. Pearl had been too busy and Aunt Myrtle was not much for visiting. Her only child had died of pneumonia at age three, and her husband had died nearly thirty years ago. He had left her with a fortune from his share of scores of wells drilled on his parents' farm north of Stephens during the South Arkansas oil boom in the 1920s, and from a slew of other investments he had made with his initial earnings, but she lived alone and generally kept to herself while contributing anonymously to a variety of charities, mostly around Camden but also in Little Rock. She loved cars and horses, though. Every other year she bought a new Cadillac, and every spring she rented a suite in a big hotel in Hot Springs for several weeks and spent every day at Oaklawn Park, finagling her way into the thoroughbred barns with sweet talk and tips, putting down bets in nearly every race, and winning more often than she lost.

"Aunt Myrtle!" Pearl said, as she came into the living room. She rushed over to give her aunt a hug, and Aunt Myrtle got out of her chair to return it. She was somewhere short of five three and a hundred pounds, and she had one of Pearl's way-too-large aprons wrapped around a smart navy dress.

"I hope you don't mind my busting in on you like this," Aunt Myrtle said. "Wendell told me you were grocery shopping, so I took the liberty of starting us some supper."

"I saw that," Pearl said, remembering that cooking was not one of her aunt's strong suits. "It's really great to see you. What brings you here?"

Before Aunt Myrtle could answer, Nancy and Alice burst into the room and started another round of hugs and how-are-yous. She took on over the girls, said how much they had grown and how pretty they were, and asked them the usual questions about school and boys. Then suddenly she looked at the clock on the mantle, said, "Oh, my, I've got to see to the peas," and got up and headed to the kitchen.

Pearl and the girls followed with Pearl protesting that Aunt Myrtle should not have gone to the trouble of cooking and Aunt Myrtle saying she did not know why not. The four of them bustled around for the next little while getting supper on the dining room table and talking about little else.

At the table Wendell said grace. For a few minutes after that, the only sounds were requests to pass one thing or another and the tinkle of serving spoons against bowls and plates. Then everyone except Aunt Myrtle sat looking at the undercooked black-eyed peas, watery cabbage, lumpy mashed potatoes, and scorched corn bread in front of them while trying to think how to eat enough of it not to give offense. The pork chops were fine because Pearl insisted on frying them herself, but after a platter piled high with them made it around to everybody one time, none were left.

"So," Pearl said, when all the dish passing and plate filling and liberal use of salt and pepper was done, "Aunt Myrtle, it's so good to have you here. What made you drive down?"

"Well, my dear, I've been watching what you're doing. I like it and I want in on it."

"You want in on what?" Pearl asked, cutting a pork chop.

"I want in on telling folks what a scoundrel that old bastard Orval Faubus is and how mean that whole crowd is being about this integration business."

"Aunt Myrtle!" Nancy said, surprised by her great-aunt's language. Alice giggled and Wendell looked down at his plate to hide a grin.

"What do you mean you want in on it?" Pearl asked. She put down her knife and fork.

"I want to buy an interest in the *Unionville Times*. I've been giving away money to the NAACP up in Little Rock, and to some others, but I don't know Daisy Bates or any of those folks personally, and I want to feel like I'm doing something useful with somebody I know, something where I can see kinda close up what's being done with my investment."

Pearl looked at Wendell. Her face was turning red. "This is your doing, isn't it?" she asked. "Is this the idea you said you had a while ago?" Wendell nodded and started to speak, but Pearl cut him off. "And you think it was okay for you to go ask my aunt to bail us out because you think I can't make a go of it by myself? Is that it?" Her voice was rising. "That is it, isn't it, Aunt Myrtle? Wendell called you up and you came down here to put us on your charity list."

No one was eating now. Nancy and Alice looked from their mother to their daddy then at each other, surprised by their mother's outburst. This was not going the way Wendell hoped. He started to speak again, and this time Aunt Myrtle cut him off.

"Yes, Pearl," she said. "Wendell called me, but before you go putting your foot in your mouth any farther, listen to me for a minute. I've been reading that paper of yours ever since that idiot you used to work for owned it. Somebody in Camden told me what an ass he was—excuse me girls—and I subscribed to it just to see. I was curious when it stopped coming for a while, then I saw you'd bought it. You could have told me, you know. Anyway, I get it and a lot of other papers and stuff at a post office box over at Magnolia because I don't like a lot of people knowing my business. It's close enough to home that I can run down there and check it every few days, and I told the postmaster if I ever heard of anybody knowing about it, I'd raise Cain with him. Didn't you ever notice the name "Will Banks" on your list and get curious about it and the subscription being paid with a cashier's check?

"Anyway, the point is this. I've got plenty of time on my hands, and I read a lot of editors—Harry Ashmore at the *Gazette*, Ralph McGill in Atlanta, Hodding Carter over in Greenville, Grover Hall down in Montgomery. I bet you didn't know Hall's been advocating for black police officers down there. He says he only wants them for black neighborhoods, but still, he's stirring a pot that needs it. I even read Hazel Bannon Smith for a while. She's a friend of Hodding Carter's and has two little papers over in Holmes County, north of Jackson. I saw an article about her in a magazine. Might've been *Time*. Anyway, I took both of them for a while. Same thing with Buford Boone down in Tuscaloosa."

"I didn't know about Grover Hall asking for black police officers," Pearl said, "but I read Ashmore and Gill and Carter, and I know about Buford Boone getting the Pulitzer for his piece on that black graduate student trying to get into the University of Alabama. Autherine Lucy, I believe her name was."

"Well, all right then," Aunt Myrtle said. "You haven't been at this newspaper business nearly as long as them, and you don't have anywhere close to as big an audience as they do, but in my book you're as good as any of them. And I'm tired of just reading stuff and donating to charities. I want in on the action. Before I die, I want to feel like I'm actually doing something."

"Aunt Myrtle..." Pearl began. She was still angry at Wendell and she was embarrassed to have Nancy and Alice hear all of this fussing.

"I'm not through yet," Aunt Myrtle stopped her. "Yes. Wendell called me. And he told me what's been happening. You need help, and if you don't get it, this community is gon' lose your voice, and that'll be too bad, because what you're saying is important. It's more than that; it's critical. And like

I said, I want in on it. I want to own a piece of the *Unionville Times*, and I need you to say okay to that, for both of us."

"I still don't understand," Pearl said. "I think it's important for Unionville, but I don't know why it's so important to you."

"Honey, people around home don't know me very well, and I like it that way. Keeps them out of my hair. Most of them think I don't do anything but buy a big new car every year or two and go up to Hot Springs every racing season and bet on the horses. But ever since I lost my baby Carol Ann, I've been trying to help folks that need it. I just don't go stand on street corners and ring bells. The other thing is I don't like bullies, I don't like hypocrites, I don't like blowhard politicians, and I don't like people who think they're better than other people, for whatever reason. I could tell you stories about how badly white people at Oaklawn treat the Negroes working in the barns there and the jockeys that're starting to come up from Mexico and South America. I see it every year and it makes my blood boil. So, what about it? Are you gon' do business with me or not?"

CHAPTER 40

Aunt Myrtle spent the weekend with Pearl and her family, but Pearl insisted on doing the cooking. Over Sunday breakfast of scrambled eggs, sausage, toast, blackberry jelly, orange juice, and coffee, Aunt Myrtle could see Pearl was weakening. "Look," Aunt Myrtle said, "Every Southern newspaper I know of that's taken positions like yours is losing readers and advertisers, and they're all bigger than you. Some of them can probably afford it, but some of them are gon' go under. Then what good are they gon' be?"

"How do you know all that?" Pearl asked.

"Well, for one thing," Aunt Myrtle said, buttering her toast, "I hear things when I'm up at Hot Springs. You'd be surprised who all shows up there for the mineral water and the gambling. Plus, I called up a couple of big shots your Uncle Edmund knew pretty well in the oil business. They don't think like I do, but they have connections, and I didn't tell them where I stood. I only told them I was thinking about investing in a newspaper and asked them what they knew about how certain ones were doing, or what maybe they could find out about their operations and standing that might help me make up my mind."

As Aunt Myrtle remembered the conversation later, by the end of breakfast, her life experiences and money had won out over Pearl's bullheadedness and, in particular, her anemic bank account. What finally persuaded Pearl, though, was when Aunt Myrle asked, "You don't really want to let bozos like that sleazebag preacher Sherlock or Skerblock or whatever the devil his name is put you out of business, do you?"

On Monday, Pearl, Wendell, and Aunt Myrtle drove up to El Dorado and met with a lawyer Aunt Myrtle knew from the oil business. He set in motion the paperwork needed for her to acquire a thirty-three percent interest in the *Unionville Times*, with the option to buy sixteen percent more at a later date if she felt it necessary to keep the paper afloat. Either way, Pearl and Wendell would retain majority interest and Pearl would control editorial policy. Meanwhile, she would have enough money to make the mortgage payments and keep the paper going.

⌒

Over the next few weeks, as daytime grew shorter, evenings started getting cooler, and trees began to lose their leaves, Herbert Kramer remained a big topic of conversation in Unionville, but most white folks finally got to talking more about Bobcat football than about him. The team continued its winning ways with Ronnie Metcalf gobbling up yard after yard every game and college scouts turning up in ever-increasing numbers to see him play. People still talked about integration a lot, too, however, because under the new state law engineered by Governor Faubus, the citizens of Little Rock voted by nearly three to one against allowing blacks to attend district schools, and that set off a chain of other actions. The city school board leased the district buildings to a group calling itself the Little Rock Private School Corporation with the understanding that they would reopen them, but to whites only. Within hours, the

Eighth US Circuit Court of Appeals ruled the leases illegal, and a few days later the US Supreme Court reaffirmed that *Brown v. Board of Education* was the "supreme law of the land" and labeled "evasive schemes for segregation" illegal. The private school group then leased another facility for a high school but was able to enroll only about seven hundred fifty students. Parents of more than three thousand five hundred other students arranged for their kids to attend schools in other Arkansas districts or out of state.

All this was more than enough to keep Elmer Spurlock ranting and raving about integration in Unionville. He worried that the school board would select someone to be president who had more moderate views than Kramer on the subject. Pearl wrote editorials urging them to do exactly that. She also criticized Faubus for continuing to defy federal law. Some additional cancellations came in, but for the time being anyway, they were no longer a significant concern.

What worried Pearl most at this point was the low number of entries coming in for the paper's first annual quilt show, now only a few weeks away. Emma Lou MacDonald's husband Purvis started putting up frames in the front part of the building to display the entries, but it appeared that the show might get only half the number they all hoped for. Pearl thought her editorials were keeping some women from entering, and Emma Lou's planning partner Almalee Jolly agreed, which made Pearl all the more pleased that Emma Lou was keeping her friend away as much as possible. Emma Lou said she was not sure the editorials were the problem, however. She thought that with the county fair now over, more quilts would come in soon.

On Wednesday, the eighth of October, ten days before the show, Pearl was coming back from an early morning trip to the *El Dorado Daily News*, when she saw Leon driving the patrol car and turning off the highway toward Mr. Claude's house. Leon was not going fast, but it was unusual to see him in the vehicle by himself. So, she turned off behind him. A couple of blocks later, she saw Mr. Claude standing on the curb in front of his house and Leon pulling over. She honked her horn, pulled in behind him, rolled her window down, and Mr. Claude walked over.

"You sure have a nose for news," he said.

"What's going on?" she asked.

"I just got a call from Ed Bonneville out at the Kramer place. Seems like Lorraine Kramer is dead. He said it looks like she shot herself."

"Oh, my god!" Pearl said.

"I called the sheriff," Mr. Claude said, "but we're gon' head on out there because the call came here first, and besides, I'm curious."

Pearl said she would follow the patrol car. They got there before anyone from the sheriff's office and saw Ed Bonneville and Roy Bill Gatewood standing on the front porch of the house. Leon parked, Pearl stopped behind him, and Ed walked over to the patrol car as Mr. Claude and Leon were getting out. Pearl joined them in time to hear Ed say, "She's in the kitchen. She left a note that says to call you, and it has your phone number on it. And there's a package on the table with another note that says, "Give this to Mrs. Goodbar."

"All right, show us the way," Mr. Claude said. "There ought to be a deputy sheriff here any minute, but let's go ahead and take a look."

Ed led them in the front door and through the house back to the kitchen. Pearl noticed that all the rooms she could see looked as if they had not been cleaned in a while. Not since Kramer's murder and Priscilla's arrest she guessed. Lorraine was lying on the floor near an overturned chair, her head resting in a mass of blood that had turned black and smelled like iron pipe. A .38 Smith & Wesson lay in the edge of the blood pool. Obviously, Lorraine had been there for some time. Much of her chin was gone and there were pieces of tissue and bone in her hair, where the bullet exited the top of her head.

"I found her when I came up from the barn to bring the last few days' receipts for the milk," Ed said. "When Bobby Lee was here, he told me and Roy Bill to keep on doing like we had been, so that's what we done. He said his mother would tell us if she wanted to change anything about the farm, but she didn't hardly say a word to us except when I brought up a batch of receipts or when she wrote out our paychecks every two weeks. She sure won't be doing that no more, but I reckon we can keep on taking care of things till Bobby Lee comes back and tells us what he wants to do."

"Did y'all touch anything?" Mr. Claude asked.

"No, sir. Didn't see no need to. Didn't even check her pulse. Wasn't no doubt she was dead."

"Okay," Mr. Claude said. "We'll sit tight and wait for one of the sheriff's boys." He asked Leon to go out to the front and show whoever was coming how to get to the kitchen, and he told Ed and Roy Bill to wait on the back porch.

Pearl looked around the room. It was dusty and there were unwashed dishes in the sink. "I'm really curious about this package," she said to Mr. Claude. "Is it okay for me to open it, or do I need to leave it where it is till somebody from the county gets here?" It was sitting in the middle of the table. About two and a half feet square and ten inches high but lumpy and uneven in shape, it was wrapped in back issues of the *Unionville Times* and tied with twine.

"Probably better leave it where it is," he said.

"Yeah, I guess so. Do you think it would be all right if I looked around the house while we're waiting? This whole business with the Kramers is really peculiar."

Mr. Claude said he did not think it would hurt, seeing as how there was not much doubt that Lorraine took her own life.

The rest of the house looked much the same as the rooms Pearl saw on the way to the kitchen. She found the upstairs room where Lorraine had been sleeping and saw that the bed was unmade, with the sheets looking like they had not been changed for some time. The bathroom nearest it was also untidy. Doors to nearly all of the rooms up there were standing open, like those on the first floor, but one door at the end of the hallway was closed. That seemed odd to Pearl, and for a moment she wondered if she should call Mr. Claude. Then she dismissed the thought and turned the knob.

The door opened into a small, windowless space that, unlike the other rooms, was, with one exception, clean and neat. A foot-tall pile of scraps from a number of types, colors, and designs of cloth lay in one corner. An old-fashioned Singer treadle sewing machine sat on a wood-and-iron table under the room's single window. A chair like the ones in the kitchen sat in front of the machine, and on the floor to the left of it, a large hand-woven wooden basket held bits of thread in random lengths and tiny scraps of cloth that looked as if they might have been cut from the bigger pieces piled in the corner. Pearl thought the stuff in the basket was clearly trash, and maybe Lorraine had not been able to decide whether to throw away the bigger pieces on the floor or hold onto them in case she needed them somehow later. To the right of the machine, a small table held a lamp, a pair of scissors, a pin cushion, and a ceramic dish with a couple of thimbles and several small packets of needles. The dish sat on top of a dog-eared Bible and what looked like a reference book of some kind. Pearl left everything as she found it.

A large oak armoire stood against one wall. It was closed, but having pushed this far into Lorraine's private life, Pearl opened its double doors. Inside, nearly a dozen quilts lay folded and stacked neatly on the left, and several drawers occupied the lower right side. The top of the uppermost drawer served as a shelf, and it held half a dozen copies of the *Unionville Times*. All were from several weeks earlier, as Herbert Kramer had been among the earliest to stop taking the paper.

When Pearl got back downstairs, Leon was showing Deputy Sheriff Munford through the front door. He filled the entranceway with his bulk and told Leon, "We don't need you no more. You can wait outside." Then he headed through the living room, calling as he went, "Mr. Claude, where's the stiff?"

He went past Pearl without speaking to her, and Leon kept coming. He caught Pearl's eye and she mouthed, "He's an asshole." In the kitchen, Munford took a quick look around, said the coroner was on the way, and said since there was no doubt about this being a suicide, they would have the body out of the house and the scene wrapped up in short order.

Pearl asked if she could take the package because it was clearly intended for her.

"Yeah," Munford said, "We've got her note here to call Mr. Claude. There's the gun and there's the body. The package don't matter none."

Pearl grabbed it before Munford could change his mind and told him to tell the coroner she would be in touch with him to get a copy of his report when he had it ready. As she walked out with Mr. Claude and Leon, she said, "I'm pretty sure I know what's in here, but I want to wait till I get back to the office to open it. Why don't y'all follow me back and come in with me, and we'll open it together."

Before they got in their cars to leave, Pearl remembered that Ed Bonneville had shown Leon a phone in the dairy barn on the day of Kramer's murder. She asked Mr. Claude if it would be all right for Leon to show her the phone so she could call Emma Lou MacDonald and ask her to meet them at the newspaper office. Mr. Claude said, "Sure," and when Emma Lou came on the line, Pearl told her she had a special quilt she knew Emma Lou would want to see.

"Count me in," she said.

CHAPTER 41

Everyone got to the newspaper office about the same time. Pearl put the package on a table behind the frames Purvis had been building for the quilt show in the big open space up front and called Hazel and Grady over and told them and Emma Lou what had happened. Grady only shook his head. Emma Lou said how sad she thought it was. Hazel said she had been shocked by Kramer's murder but was not surprised by the suicide. Pearl asked her why, and Hazel said Lorraine never came to town much and did not seem to have any friends. Hazel did not know anyone who was more than casually acquainted with Lorraine. She mostly called in her grocery orders to the Food, Feed, and Seed, and Kramer picked them up. If she ever needed a doctor, Hazel surmised, she must have driven to El Dorado or somewhere, because she never came to see Doc Perkins. Hazel also said the few times she had seen Lorraine in town she always seemed unhappy.

"Where in blazes did you get all that?" Mr. Claude asked.

"Oh, I see things," she said, "and I hear stuff. You know me."

"Yeah, I guess I do," Mr. Claude said. He took off his hat, ran his fingers through his hair, and put the hat back on. "Well, Pearl," he asked, "are you gon' open that thing or not?"

Pearl tugged on one end of the bow knot, the twine fell away, and she pulled back the newspapers, revealing a colorful crazy quilt. Penned to the top of it was a quilt show announcement clipped from the *Unionville Times* with Lorraine Kramer's signature in the margin. Pearl asked Emma Lou to help her, and after they removed all of the wrapping, they unfolded the quilt and laid it across the table, with part hanging off each side.

"Would you look at that," Emma Lou said, lifting one edge of the quilt so she could see more of it. "It's beautiful."

"There's no pattern to it," Mr. Claude said. "Irene's quilts all have some kind of pattern."

"That's why it's called a crazy quilt," Emma Lou said. She smiled and ran her hand lightly over it. "The pieces are supposed to be all sorts of shapes and all jumbled up like this, like these colors. Look at the light and dark shades mixed together, random like. It's got all kinds of cloth too. There's gingham, organdy, satin, even some silk."

"She must have got most of this in El Dorado or ordered it from Sears Roebuck or Montgomery Ward or someplace," Hazel said. "She sure didn't get much of it in town here."

"Yeah, maybe," Emma Lou said. "No telling how many old dresses she cut up too. Probably some of hers and maybe even some of her mother's, if she'd saved any of them. Anyway, people don't generally make quilts like this anymore. That's why I thought we ought to have a category for them in the show. Maybe get more people doing them."

"My grandmomma used to make quilts like that," Leon said. "Hers weren't sewed up as fine because she didn't have enough time. But we loved them. Wore them plum out."

"I saw one at Sadie Rose's house too." Pearl said. "She has a whole bunch of pretty quilts. You reckon Lorraine started this one after her husband was killed? I saw her sewing room, and there were some larger pieces like these in there. They were in a pile on the floor, and there were a lot of little scraps like them in a trash basket. From all that, and the mess the house was in, I'm guessing this might've been about all she was doing lately."

"She might have been working on it pretty steady since then, but she must have at least started it before that," Emma Lou said. "I don't believe she could've got this all done otherwise. What puzzles me about it, though, is the embroidery stitches on the edges of the pieces."

"What do you mean 'embroidery stitches?'" Grady asked. "Ain't they all quilting stitches?"

"I mean these decorative stitches she added across some of the seams where the quilt pieces are sewed together," Emma Lou said. "Looks like she sewed all her pieces together on a machine, then quilted the front, back, and batting together all regular like, and then took her time putting these herringbone stitches across most of the seams. The only way she could've done that was by hand, and look how they're all nice and even. Same thing for her work on the binding on the four outside edges. She did a good job all the way around. But now look at her embroidery work on the seams of the pieces that are closest to the binding. They're all jumbled up and crooked. Like maybe she was all in a rush."

"Maybe she got tired of working on it. Just wanted to get it over and done with and didn't much care how it looked anymore," Hazel said.

"No," Emma Lou said. "I think she knew she was running out of time to get it ready for the show, and she had to rush."

"Might be that," Grady said. "But might be something else too. Those stitches look to me like they could be letters." He leaned over for a closer look.

"I suppose they could be," Emma Lou replied. "I've seen quite a few crazy quilts in my day that had names and sentiments stitched on them, sometimes all over. But this don't look like nothing but bad sewing to me."

"Yeah, me too," Hazel said.

"I'd like to look at them with a magnifying glass," Grady said. "We got one around here anywhere?"

"Maybe in my old desk," Pearl said. "I never cleaned it all the way out when I bought the paper. Let me look." While the others continued to pour over the quilt and speculate, she went through all the desk drawers and came back empty-handed. "Sorry," she said, "I don't have one."

"I've got a big one at home," Grady said. "I'll bring it in tomorrow."

"Grady," Mr. Claude said, jumping in, "I think all this talking and guessing is probably a big waste of time and Emma Lou's probably right. But I have to admit, you've got my attention. If this is writing, I'd like to know what it says. If she was in a hurry like Emma Lou thinks, why'd she even bother with it? Seems to me she could've just left it off. If you've got time and Pearl don't mind, how about you take this thing home with you tonight, study on it, and see if you come up with anything?"

"Sure, I can do that if it's all right with the boss."

"Fine by me," Pearl said.

"If you find anything, give me a call first thing in the morning," Mr. Claude said. "This is all pretty strange."

"What about the rest of us?" Emma Lou asked. "I want to know too."

"Well, I guess that'd be all right," Mr. Claude said. "You all work for the paper. But if he finds something that means anything, everybody's got to keep it quiet till I say different."

Everyone agreed, and when Grady went home at the end of the day, he took Lorraine Kramer's quilt with him.

CHAPTER 42

The next morning, Grady got to the office before Pearl, let himself in, and made a pot of coffee. When Pearl arrived, he told her he had something, but he did not know what it was exactly and he thought she ought to call the others. She reminded him that Mr. Claude usually slept late because he was still doing early evening duty as night watchman.

"I think he'll want to see this," Grady said.

Pearl called everyone from the day before and told them Grady had something to show them as soon as all of them could get there. At a little after nine o'clock they gathered around the table again with the quilt spread out before them.

"I was right about part of this," Grady said. "There's letters here all right. But there's numbers, too, and it looks to me like they're arranged in nine groups. I made a list of what's in each group, and I wrote out copies for everybody." He handed them out, and everyone stood silently looking at a list with nine lines, one for each of the nine groups. Each group contained alternating sets of letters and numbers:

EXO2014HK

HOS411HK

EXO2120HKPNLK

EXO212324LKHK

EXO2013HKEWLKHK

GEN96LKHK

LEV247LKHK

NUM3531HKLKLKLK

REV218HKLK

"I don't get it," Pearl said after a couple of minutes, voicing what each of them was thinking. "What's it all mean?"

"I was hoping some of you would know," Grady answered.

"Can you show us where each of these came from on the quilt?" Emma Lou asked. "Maybe that'll help us figure it out."

"Since I couldn't tell one end of the quilt from the other, I picked that end as the top," Grady said, pointing to the one nearest Hazel, "and I started from there and wrote down the groups in clockwise order till I got all the way around. There's two groups on each of the first three sides and three groups on the fourth side."

Again everyone fell silent as they looked back and forth from Grady's list to the quilt.

"It ain't likely some kind of code," Mr. Claude said. "Has to be something simple, else why put it there if no one could figure out what it means. But it sure don't spell anything."

"Well, begging your pardon, maybe it does, sort of," Leon spoke up. "I think the first set of letters in each line is probably an abbreviation for a book of the Bible. They match what you see on a thumb index. 'Exo' for Exodus. 'Lev' for Leviticus. 'Gen' for Genesis. And so on."

"By golly, that could be right," Emma Lou said. "I've seen whole verses spelled out on crazy quilts."

"So then the numbers may be chapters and verses," Mr. Claude said, "but how do we know which are which, with them all run together that way. And what do the other letters mean?"

"Now that you say that," Grady responded, "I think there may be some punctuation marks between some of the numbers and some of the letters. There's stitches in there that are so tiny, I didn't see any meaning to them. I thought they were just something she had to put in when she was moving on from one letter or number to the next. But she might have meant some of it for periods, or commas, or something. I brought my glass, and if you give me a couple of minutes, I'll take another look. If I'm right, I can add whichever marks they seem like to my copy of the list."

"Begging y'all's pardon again," Leon said, "I believe I recognize a couple of these. Maybe more. If you've got a Bible around here somewhere, Miss Pearl, I'll be happy to look them up right quick and write them down while Mr. Grady's working with the magnifying glass. Reverend Moseley's got all us Mt. Zion folks trained to find scriptures real fast." Pearl said she had one she used occasionally in editing stories that had Bible references. She went and got it from her desk, along with a pen and a clean sheet of paper.

"Good. It's a King James," Leon said. He pulled up a chair opposite Grady. Based in part on his memory of some of the numbers and in part on guesses, Leon started looking up verses and copying first the citations and then the verses. Mr. Claude and Pearl looked over his shoulder and read silently while he wrote as quickly as he could:

Exodus 20:14. Thou shalt not commit adultery.

Hosea 4:11. Whoredom and wine and new wine take away the heart.

Exodus 21:20. And if a man smite his servant, or his maid, with a rod, and he die under his hand; he shall surely be punished.

Exodus 21:23-24. And if any mischief follow, then thou shalt give life for life, eye for eye, tooth for tooth, hand for hand, foot for foot.

Exodus 20:13. Thou shalt not kill.

Genesis 9:6. Whoso sheddeth man's blood, by man shall his blood be shed.

Leviticus 24:7. And he that killeth any man shall surely be put to death.

Numbers 35:31. Moreover ye shall take no satisfaction for the life of a murderer, which is guilty of death: but he shall surely be put to death.

Revelations 21:8. But the fearful, and the unbelieving, and the abominable, and murderers, and whoremongers, and sorcerers, and idolaters, and all liars, shall have their part in the lake which burneth with fire and brimstone.

"I think I know what all this means," Mr. Claude said, a few moments after Leon finished.

"Yeah, me too," Leon said.

"Is it what I think?" Pearl asked.

"What are y'all thinking?" Mr. Claude asked. He wanted to hear it from someone else first.

Pearl said, "I think the other letters are initials, and Lorraine was telling us who did the things in the verses."

"Well, I'll be John Brown!" Emma Lou said.

"Leon," Mr. Claude directed, "write the letters at the end of the verses and put a period after whatever looks like it might be a set for somebody Mrs. Kramer would have known." All watched as Leon added the letters and periods. When he finished, he handed the paper to Mr. Claude. He looked at it and handed it to Grady. "Is this what you're seeing too?"

"Yep." Grady said. "That's it exactly."

Mr. Claude took the paper back from Grady, handed it to Pearl, and said, "Lorraine left the quilt for you. Why don't you explain it."

With Hazel and Emma Lou pressing close so they could see, too, Pearl stood reading the list over again silently, this time with the other letters added to the ends of the completed verses and marked off in individual sets:

Exodus 20:14. Thou shalt not commit adultery. HK.

Hosea 4:11. Whoredom and wine and new wine take away the heart. HK.

Exodus 21:20. And if a man smite his servant, or his maid, with a rod, and he die under his hand; he shall surely be punished. HK.PN.LK.

Exodus 21:23-24. And if any mischief follow, then thou shalt give life for life, eye for eye, tooth for tooth, hand for hand, foot for foot. LK.HK.

Exodus 20:13. Thou shalt not kill. HK.EW.LK.HK.

Genesis 9:6. Whoso sheddeth man's blood, by man shall his blood be shed. LK.HK.

Leviticus 24:7. And he that killeth any man shall surely be put to death. LK.HK.

Numbers 35:31. Moreover ye shall take no satisfaction for the life of a murderer, which is guilty of death: but he shall surely be put to death. LK.HK. LK.LK.

Revelations 21:8. But the fearful, and the unbelieving, and the abominable, and murderers, and whoremongers, and sorcerers, and idolaters, and all liars, shall have their part in the lake which burneth with fire and brimstone. HK.LK.

"All right, here goes," Pearl said. "'HK' and 'LK' are Herbert Kramer and Lorraine Kramer. 'PN' is Priscilla Nobles and 'EW' is Elton Washington. Herbert Kramer committed adultery by having sex with someone other than his wife, and he broke her heart. That's the first two sets of letters and numbers. He beat his 'servant' Priscilla Nobles and, I'm guessing, his wife Lorraine Kramer too. That's the third set, after Exodus 21:20. Both Kramers committed murder. That's the next four sets, Exodus 21:23-24 through the verse from Numbers. Herbert killed Elton Washington and Lorraine killed Herbert, 'a life for a life.' If Priscilla Nobles had killed him, her initials would be next to his in the 'Thou shalt not kill' verse. I think Lorraine was angry when she shot Kramer, and she was humiliated and feeling guilty when she decided to kill herself. She just didn't want to go on living. And that last verse, from Revelations, that's her thinking she and Herbert were both going to hell. I believe she meant for us to look all this up. It's her testimony and confession."

"Well, I'll be John Brown!" Emma Lou said again.

"Yeah, I think you've got it." Mr. Claude said. "What about you, Leon?"

"Yes, sir, that seems right to me," Leon said.

Pearl brushed away a tear.

"Makes me want to cry too," Hazel said.

"What bothers me," Pearl said, "is thinking about those two women going through all that without anyone knowing about it or being able to help them. Then even after Kramer was dead and everybody thought Priscilla did it, there still wasn't anyone trying to do much of anything for Lorraine. I kind of feel like all of us are a little bit to blame."

Emma Lou stepped over and put her arm around Pearl.

After no one else said anything more for a minute or two, Mr. Claude picked up a corner of the quilt and began to fold it. "Pearl, I need you to lock this up somewhere safe, and I need all of y'all to keep all this to yourselves. I mean it," he said, looking at Hazel. "It's important."

"Do you think this'll be enough to get Priscilla off?" Leon asked. "If we put it together with the knife Sadie Rose gave Elton and with what we think about the shotgun?"

Hazel and Grady wanted to know about the knife and shotgun, and Mr. Claude explained how he and Leon believed the blood smears and lack of handprints on the shotgun made it unlikely that Priscilla had been holding it before she passed out. How they believed Lorraine left it on the floor to make it look like Priscilla had dropped it there. And how they found Elton's knife among Kramer's things. "I don't know if it'll be enough for the sheriff and the prosecuting attorney to drop the charges against her," Mr. Claude said, "but I'm gon' take it to them, and if it's not, I'm pretty sure a good lawyer can use it to get her off when she goes to trial."

Over the next few days, Mr. Claude found out that an autopsy on Lorraine Kramer showed badly healed leg, arm, and rib fractures that must have occurred over a period of years, and even the coroner was willing to speculate that they resulted from beatings. Together he and Mr. Claude persuaded the district attorney—in light of the crazy quilt and what Mr. Claude told him about the shotgun and knife—to have Priscilla Nobles examined to see if she had a similar pattern of fractures. She had fewer and they seemed way less severe, but they were consistent with having been beaten. With all that and Priscilla's own story and her condition at the time of the murder, the authorities turned her loose.

Sadie Rose picked her up at the county jail. "Honey," she told Priscilla, "I'm gon' take you home with me, and you ain't gon' have to worry about nothing no more. I'm gon' take care of you till you get well, and I'm gon' keep seeing to your grandmomma and granddaddy like I been doing. And when you're ready, if you want me to, I'm gon' make a job for you over at the store."

Bobby Lee Kramer returned to Unionville to bury his mother, and shortly after he left, a "For Sale" sign went up at the entrance to Kramer Farm and ads for it appeared in newspapers in El Dorado, Camden, Little Rock, Ruston, Monroe, and Shreveport. Ed Bonneville and Roy Bill Gatewood continued to milk the cows. When they were not doing that, they were off looking for other work in case the new owner of the farm did not want to keep them on. They did not notice that the earthen dam at the deep end of the farm pond was breaking down and the water level was receding, or that anyone who looked closely could now see the top of a light-colored truck just below the surface.

Pearl ran stories about Lorraine Kramer's suicide and Priscilla's release and wrote an editorial piece bragging on Mr. Claude and Leon for their smart detecting. It looked like they would have to continue working together for a while longer because even though Jesse Culpepper was healing, he still was not in shape to come back to work.

Elmer Spurlock went through another round of rants at his church and with the Citizens' Council. He still had plenty of folks slapping him on the back for standing up for segregation, but he was not able to inspire any more cancellations at the *Unionville Times*.

Purvis MacDonald put up the remaining frames for the quilt show, and a week before it was to start, Emma Lou and Hazel, along with Almalee Jolly, hung all the entries they had to date, plus several of Lorraine Kramer's other quilts. Pearl had borrowed them when Bobby Lee was home. She did not want to put the crazy quilt in the show because she felt it would attract interest for the wrong reasons. Bobby Lee appreciated both gestures. Even with Lorraine's quilts, the display was still sparse, and Emma Lou felt so badly about it she was blaming herself. She worried that maybe the patterns she and Almalee came up with were not good enough to inspire people to make them up and enter the show.

Pearl knew the shortage of entries was a result of her editorials, not Emma Lou's patterns, and on Wednesday afternoon before the show was to open on Saturday, she seized on a solution that had been there all the time.

"I know where there're some quilts that would be perfect," she told Emma Lou and Almalee.

"We can't enter our own stuff, Pearl. That wouldn't be fair," Emma Lou said.

"I wasn't thinking of yours," Pearl said, grabbing her purse and heading for the front door.

"Where're you going?" Emma Lou called after her.

"To see Sadie Rose."

AUTHOR'S NOTE

Found in Pieces is a work of fiction. The state and national governmental and civil rights events and activities are real, but all real people and places are used fictitiously. Other names, characters, and events are products of the author's imagination, and any resemblance to actual events, places, or persons, living or dead, is entirely coincidental.

The *Unionville Times* never existed, but a good number of Southern editors underwent internal struggles about segregation like those experienced by the fictional editor in *Found in Pieces*, and they evolved their editorial policies in similar fashion, although generally over a longer period of time.

For historical background information about Southern newspapers and editors during the Civil Rights era, see especially: Gene Roberts and Hank Kilbanoff, *The Race Beat: The Press, the Civil Rights Struggle, and the Awakening of a Nation* (New York: Alfred A. Knopf, 2007); Ann Waldron, *Hodding Carter: The Reconstruction of a Racist* (Chapel Hill: Algonquin Books of Chapel Hill, 1993); and Jeffery B. Howell, *Hazel Bannon Smith: The Female Crusading Scalawag* (Jackson: University of Mississippi Press, 2017).

For historical background about the desegregation of Little Rock Central High School, see especially: Karen Anderson, *Race and Resistance at Central High School* (Princeton:

Princeton University Press, 2010); John A. Kirk, *Beyond Little Rock: The Origins and Legacies of the Central High Crisis* (Fayetteville: University of Arkansas Press, 2007); Elizabeth Jacoway, *Turn Thy Son Away: Little Rock, the Crisis That Shocked the Nation* (New York: Free Press, 2007); and Grif Stockley, *Ruled by Race: Black/White Relations in Arkansas from Slavery to the Present* (Fayetteville: University of Arkansas Press, 2009).

For additional helpful background see: David R. Goldfield, *Black, White, and Southern: Race Relations and Southern Culture, 1940 to the Present* (Baton Rouge: Louisiana State University Press, 1990); Neil R. McMillen, *The Citizens' Council: Organized Resistance to the Second Reconstruction, 1954-64* (Urbana: University of Illinois Press, 1994); Juan Williams, *Eyes on the Prize: America's Civil Rights Years, 1954-1965* (New York: Penguin Press, 1987); and Danielle L. McGuire, *At the Dark End of the Street: Black Women, Rape, and Resistance—a New History of the Civil Rights Movement from Rosa Parks to the Rise of Black Power* (New York: Random House, 2010).

I am indebted to many for invaluable assistance with *Found in Pieces*. Nancy Arn of the Barton Library provided important research help with Arkansas newspapers. Wayne Barrett, Ray Farris, Arnold Jones, John Ritchie, and Wanda Caldwell Woods—all of them citizens of southern Arkansas and northern Louisiana at one time or another—provided helpful background information in oral interviews. Friends and colleagues Juanita Battle, Richard Battle, Scott G. Eberle, Lisa Feinstein, Gigi Groulx, Allison McGrath, and Charles Lamar Phillips read all or portions of the manuscript in various drafts and provided invaluable feedback, as did Brady Andrew Adams. Shane Rhinewald advised and assisted with promotion and marketing preparation. Bruce Gore designed the cover and Amit Dey designed the interior. Kelly Johnson provided invaluable production assistance. I appreciate each of them.

My quilting and novel-reading spouse, Diana Murphy Adams, read and critiqued drafts and supported my efforts all along the way. Lastly, I am grateful to our children Brady Andrew Adams, Amy Kristina Hee Sook Adams, and Tong Tong Amanda Joy Adams who also provided encouragement, but more importantly, always reminded me of the need to understand and accept individual and cultural differences and demonstrate good will toward all. I am fortunate to love and be loved by them.

QUESTIONS FOR DISCUSSION

1. What obstacles did Pearl have to overcome to make a go of it as an owner, editor, and publisher of a newspaper in the 1950s?

2. Is it easier or more difficult for a woman to succeed in business today compared to 1958? Why? What has changed?

3. What events and other factors most influenced Pearl's evolving views about desegregation? Why? Which had the greatest influence? Why?

4. When a body was found in the town dump, who did you initially believe committed the murder? Why?

5. If you could change the end of the story, what would you have happen next for Pearl and in the town generally?

6. Are there any present-day parallels or any useful learnings in Mr. Claude's statements to Alan Poindexter and Neal O'Brien about why his recommendation for the deputy marshal's position was appropriate and about how he came to it? If so, what are they?

7. How does getting to know other people's values and beliefs and why they hold them contribute to understanding social, economic, or political issues? Do you think this occurred in *Found in Pieces* and, if so, in what ways?

8. In what ways has the news media, news coverage, and the practice of journalism in general evolved since the time when Pearl was publishing the *Unionville Times?* How do you regard those changes? Have they been positive or negative, or both to some degree? Why?

9. In what major ways have newspapers changed since the 1950s? Where do people today get the kinds of information that Pearl Goodbar provided in the *Unionville Times?*

10. How important to understanding national news is following and being knowledgeable about local news, and vice versa?

Earlier works by George Rollie Adams

South of Little Rock, a multi-award-winning novel

General William S. Harney: Prince of Dragoons, a biography

*Ordinary People and Everyday Life: Perspectives on the
New Social History*, a book of essays, edited with
James B. Gardner

Nashville: A Pictorial History, with Ralph Jerry Christian

The American Indian: Past and Present (first edition only),
a book of essays, edited with Roger L. Nichols

Awards for *South of Little Rock*

Winner, Next Generation Indie Book Award
for Regional Fiction

Winner, National Indie Excellence Award
for Regional Fiction

Bronze Medal, Independent Publishers Award
for Regional Fiction

Silver Medal, Readers' Favorite Award
for Social Issues Fiction

About the Author

GEORGE ROLLIE ADAMS is a native of southern Arkansas and a former teacher with graduate degrees in history and education. He is the author of *South of Little Rock*, which received four independent publishers' awards for regional and social issues fiction; author of *General William S. Harney: Prince of Dragoons*, a finalist for the Army Historical Foundation's Distinguished Book Award; coauthor of *Nashville: A Pictorial History*; and coeditor of *Ordinary People and Everyday Life,* a book of essays on social history. Adams has served as a writer, editor, and program director for the American Association for State and Local History and as director of the Louisiana State Museum in New Orleans. He is president and CEO emeritus of the Strong National Museum of Play, where he founded the *American Journal of Play* and led the establishment of the International Center for the History of Electronic Games.

See the author's website and blog at
www.georgerollieadamsbooks.com

Follow the author on Facebook at
www.facebook.com/georgerollieadamsauthor